The Wolf On

Terry Cloutier

Book 3 in the
**THE WOLF OF CORWICK CASTLE
SERIES**

Copyright © 2020 TERRY CLOUTIER

All rights reserved. No part of this book may be reproduced,
in whole or in part, without prior written permission
from the copyright holder.

Character List By Order Of Appearance

Lord Hadrack: The Lord of Corwick Castle
Lillia: Hadrack's granddaughter
Walice: Steward of Corwick Castle
Krinst: Villager
Hughe: Hadrack's eldest son
Taren: Hadrack's son
Kalidia: Hadrack's daughter
Camala: Hughe's wife
Lairn: Captain of the guards
Haral: Village halfwit
Frankin: Hadrack's grandson
Palina: Villager
Casia: Sabina's daughter
Jebido: Hadrack's friend
Baine: Hadrack's friend
Odiman: House Agent
Malo: House Agent
Tyris: Outlaw
Niko: Outlaw
Putt: Outlaw
Sim: Outlaw
Bastin: Lord Branton's son
Sabina: Tracker's daughter
Alvar: Gardener
Lord Branton: Lord of Springlight
Baylan: Cardian
Burel: Cardian leader
Rorian: Scholar
Thera: Rorian's wife
Kylan: Steward of Calban
Shana: Lady of Calban
Emand: Cordwainer
Laurea: Emand's wife

Son Partal: Priest
Topar: Son-In-Waiting
Son Michan: Priest
Bagen: Ruffian
Son Lawer: Overseer of the Complex
Nak: Tapeau
Old Barl: Villager
Ragna the Elder: One of the Nine
Ragna the Younger: One of the Nine
Wiflem: Soldier
Hervi Desh: One of the Nine
Prince Tyrale: Son of King Jorquin
Lord Corwick: The Lord of Corwick Castle
Son Oriel: Priest
Flidion: House Agent
Finol: Steward of Witbridge Manor
Daughter Eleva: Priestess
Jin: Daughter-In-Waiting
Margot: Ex-whore
Daughter Gernet: Priestess
Prince Tyden: Son of King Jorquin

Prologue

Despite my reluctance, I believe that I will have no choice but to take an innocent man's life today. I have taken many lives over the years, most of them with a sword in my hand and a curse upon my lips. But this particular man's life will not be taken by my weapons, but rather by a single word—should I choose to speak it. I have prayed all morning for some sign that my suspicions of innocence are correct. But so far, there has been nothing to indicate that the gods are even paying attention. The evidence against the accused is hugely damning, and I know that I will have little recourse without some help from Above, Below or Beyond, but to find him guilty.

For the last few years, I have allowed my eldest son, Hughe, to dispense castle justice in my name whenever the need arises. Which thankfully, has been rarely, as my interest in what typically tends to be trivial matters has waned as I've grown frailer. I prefer to stay in my chambers now, away from the daily hustle and bustle of castle life, where I console myself by writing about the past. Besides, I believe that Hughe should learn how to be fair and impartial now while a steady hand is still close by to advise him, rather than wait until that hand is gone and Corwick and its problems become his alone.

Today, however, will be far from trivial, and I know that my authority and experience will be dearly needed if we are to get to the bottom of this crime.

"Stop moving, my lord," my granddaughter admonished me as she struggled to pin a Unified Sun, Rock, and Star brooch on my crisp white tunic.

"I'm not moving, Lillia," I grunted moodily as I turned to look out the window of my bedchamber. Midday was fast approaching, I saw, which meant Walice would be knocking on my door at any moment.

Lillia stepped back with the brooch in her hand, looking at me in frustration. "Well, what do you call what you just did, then, if it's not moving?"

"I call it an old man stretching his aching neck," I said, waving her to continue.

I studied Lillia with her pretty face screwed up in concentration as she fought with the brooch. She was sixteen now, slender, and strong, with good teeth and long black hair just like her mother's and grandmother's. I felt a sudden pang of anxiety as I thought of my daughter and how I'd failed her, which inevitably led me further down the pathway of regrets to where Lillia's grandmother, Shana, always waited for me. I shook my head, willing away the thoughts of my dead wife and daughter as I focused back on the present.

"So, what do you think?" I asked as my granddaughter's hands tickled my white beard while she worked.

"About what, my lord?" Lillia replied distractedly. She studied the brooch critically as she turned her head to one side. "It's still crooked," she muttered as she tried again.

"About the boy," I said. "Do you think that he did it?"

Lillia stiffened and she paused to look up at me. "He's no boy, my lord."

"No," I agreed, "he's not. At least, not in body at any rate." I frowned. "But you didn't answer my question."

"I don't know what to think," Lillia said as she shifted her eyes away from mine.

I hadn't failed to notice the look of anger in those blue eyes before she'd looked away. "So, you think Haral did it?"

"I didn't say that."

"You didn't have to," I grunted.

"Her blood was on him," Lillia said tightly. "Everyone knows that." I winced as the pin on the brooch suddenly pierced my skin. Lillia's face creased instantly in concern. "I'm so sorry, my lord. Are you all right?"

I waved away the discomfort. "Frankin believes he's innocent," I continued.

Lillia snorted. "Frankin is just a boy. What does he know?"

"Your cousin may be only eight years old," I said. "But he's no fool and knows Haral better than anyone else in Corwick."

"And that's why Frankin's faith is biased," Lillia replied.

"And you have no bias?" I asked, raising an eyebrow. "You and the dead girl were friends, too."

Lillia tapped the brooch several times and then nodded in satisfaction. "There, all done, my lord. It looks perfect now."

I could tell by the stubborn look on Lillia's face that the subject of Haral's guilt or innocence was now over, at least in her mind. Lillia was a lot like Shana had been in that way. Once her mind was set on something, there was no changing it. The rape and murder of Lillia's friend, Krinst, was all anyone was talking about in Corwick, with some, like me, believing the halfwit, Haral, to be incapable of the crime. However, many more thought him guilty, and they were demanding that justice be served—the kind that involved swinging from a rope. I glanced out the window again, knowing that shortly I would have to decide one way or the other, which was the truth.

A knock sounded at the door as if on cue. "Enter," I barked a little too harshly.

The door swung open and my steward, Walice, stepped into the room. "Everything is in readiness, my lord."

"Where is my son?"

"Waiting for you in the great hall, my lord," Walice replied, his face expressionless.

I looked at him in irritation. "I told you I wished to speak with Hughe here in my chambers before the trial began."

The steward was a wiry man well past fifty years of age, with thick silvery hair and a pointed beard, which he had a habit of stroking with his right hand as he thought. "Yes, I realize that, my lord," Walice said with a curt nod. "I told him exactly that, but the commoners are quite worked up at the moment, so he felt it prudent to remain where he was."

I knew my people were incensed by the girl's murder, and rightly so, but I couldn't imagine that they would go so far as to raise arms against their lord. I indicated Wolf's Head, where the sword hung above the mantle. Walice obediently crossed the room and brought the weapon down before helping me strap it around my waist.

"Hughe thinks they would revolt?" I asked as Walice fussed with the sword.

"Certainly not," the steward said with a quick shake of his head. "At least, not against you, my lord. They love you. The two factions are at each others' throats like rabid dogs over this Haral business. Your son fears without his continued presence that a brawl may break out at any time, even within our walls."

"Factions?" I muttered as Walice removed my short sword, Boar's Tooth, from the wall and handed it to me.

"Those that believe Haral to be innocent, my lord, versus those convinced of his guilt. Both sides are becoming unruly and are hurling insults at each other as they await your ruling. Feelings are running hot over this tragedy."

I glanced at Lillia's face, unable to read her thoughts, though I was quite certain that I knew which faction she supported. "Hughe was right to stay, then," I grunted, impressed despite myself at the boy's good sense. I caught myself and snorted. Hughe was almost forty-five years old now and hadn't been a boy for many years. For some strange reason, I still thought of him as a senseless child, rather than a man.

Walice indicated my father's axe, a clear question. I nodded, accepting the heavy weapon and sliding it into the familiar sheath on my back. I always felt better with it close to me. "How do I look?" I asked.

"Like the great wolf of old, my lord," Walice said.

I limped forward and placed a hand on the steward's shoulder. "More like just an old wolf, I think you mean to say." Walice smiled politely as I drew my hand away. "Your father would be proud of you. You are every bit the steward that he was."

I thought of Finol, Walice's father. The old steward and I hadn't liked each other much, but we had respected one another greatly. So, it had been an easy choice for me to agree when Finol had begged me on his deathbed to take in his adopted son and let him train to become a steward like his father, and his father before him.

"He always spoke highly of you, my lord," Walice said, his mouth twitching slightly with amusement. "Though sometimes his stories of your exploits seemed more fanciful imagination than factual."

I laughed at that. "Trust me, Walice, when I say your father was many things, but fanciful was not one of them."

"Then all those stories he told me as a boy were true?" the steward asked, looking surprised.

I gestured to my table and the papers lying there. "I guess you'll just have to wait until my life's story is done to find that out."

Corwick Castle was not the largest castle in the Unified Kingdom of Ganderland, but even so, the great hall was bigger than most, and at the moment, it was crowded to overflowing with people. Most of those people were shouting and waving their arms in anger at the dais, where Hughe sat on the Lord's Chair, watching what was happening with hooded eyes. My other son, Taren, stood behind the Lord's Chair with his wife and my youngest daughter, Kalidia, who was holding her newborn son in her arms. Hughe's wife, Camala, was unwell and would not be attending.

Lairn, the captain of my guards, stood with six of my men to Hughe's right in a protective ring around the halfwit, Haral. People cursed the accused man and threw rotten vegetables at him or hurled them at Haral's supporters, who were tossing similar missiles right back. Haral, who was a big man with sloping shoulders and a slack face, seemed utterly confused by what was going on. His flat features continuously switched from bewilderment to fear and back again, while ducking any thrown object that got too close. I saw my grandson, Frankin, standing defiantly beside the bigger man holding his hand.

I frowned, wondering why the boy wasn't with his mother as Walice tried and failed to push his way through the mob.

"Out of the way!" the steward cried in frustration, shoving ineffectively at a hulking farmer from behind. "Make way for your lord, you filthy whoresons!"

The uproar inside the great hall was deafening. I knew everyone was focused on Haral and that none could hear the steward's shouted demands, so I impatiently drew my father's great axe and began to use the butt end to prod people out of our way. Eventually, the angry mob started to realize who it was that was in amongst them. I heard my name being passed from mouth to mouth through the crowd as the unwashed bodies started to move aside and then kneel as we passed.

By the time Walice, Lillia, and I reached the dais' base, the great hall had fallen mostly silent. My son stood and hurried to help me up the stairs, but I shook his hand off, knowing a show of strength before my people was needed right now. I limped up the steps, avoiding the shiny red entrails of a squashed tomato in my path, then I shuffled over to the Lord's Chair. I turned, glaring harshly at the kneeling villagers before finally I sat with my father's axe lying across my knees.

"I am ashamed of what I have seen here today," I said as Walice moved to stand to my left. Hughe, who was as big as me, though not quite as thick in the shoulders, stood off to my right side, while Lillia joined her aunt and uncle behind us. I leaned forward and scowled. "Do all of you make the rules in Corwick now?" I demanded.

"Forgive us, my lord," an older woman said from the front row. She paused to glare at Haral with naked hatred before focusing back on me. "None here meant any disrespect toward you, lord. We are just overcome with grief, is all."

"And who are you?" I asked. The woman's face looked familiar, but I couldn't place her.

"Palina, my lord." She lowered her eyes to the floor. I could see glistening tears sliding down her cheeks. "Krinst was my daughter."

"Ah," I said, remembering her now. "You have my deepest sympathies for your loss." I glanced at Haral, but he had become entranced by a fly that was circling lazily near the ceiling. The halfwit seemed oblivious to what was going on. I turned my gaze back to the grieving mother. "You have come here seeking justice for her murder, then?"

"Yes, my lord," Palina said.

"Then justice you shall have," I said grimly. I let my eyes rove over the crowded room. "But it will not be justice derived from a mindless mob bent on vengeance. We are not beasts here in Corwick, but civilized people with rules that must be followed. As your lord and master, I will listen to the evidence, and then I will rule fairly the way that I have always done." I lifted the axe and pointed it at the crowd. "Whatever my decision may be, you will accept it and move on with your lives. If you continue with the kind of foolishness that I just witnessed here today, then my justice will come for you next." I paused, letting that thought sink in, then I added, "Am I understood?"

Many heads began nodding.

"We bow to your wisdom in all things and trust in you to do what is right, my lord," Palina said softly.

"As you should," I grunted. I waved my hand. "Rise." Palina lowered her head in acknowledgment as the villagers began to stand, then she too stood with the help of a strapping lad who I assumed was her son. I flicked my eyes to Walice. "You may proceed, Steward."

Walice cleared his throat. "We are gathered before our great lord to determine the guilt or innocence of the man named Haral, born of Taster and Halena of Corwick." He turned to glance at the prisoner. "Let the accused step forward and plead his case."

Lairn grabbed the halfwit by the elbow, as one of my men placed the carved Judgement Stool near the edge of the dais facing me. I frowned at my grandson, who clung to Haral's hand stubbornly as Lairn led the two forward.

"Not the boy," I said gruffly. "The accused must be judged on his own."

Frankin looked as though he might protest, but I glared at him, letting him see the promise of punishment in my eyes, should he choose to defy me. My grandson hesitated at my look. I could see a flash of stubbornness cross his features, reminding me a great deal of myself at his age, before finally, common sense prevailed. He squeezed Haral's hand in solidarity and whispered something to him before moving away to join his mother, Kalidia, behind me.

"Sit," Lairn commanded, gesturing to the stool.

Haral blinked several times in confusion, then did as he was told, fidgeting on the hard oak as he stared at me in fascination. Drool slowly rolled down each side of his mouth, but the halfwit seemed unaware of it.

"Do you understand why you are here, Haral of Corwick?" Walice asked slowly. "What you are accused of doing?"

Haral glanced behind him at the villagers, then back at Walice and he shrugged, not saying anything. I studied the halfwit's eyes, searching for any signs of deceit or malice in them, but there was nothing but gentleness and confusion swimming within their depths. I knew as I looked at him that my suspicions of innocence were correct. Haral hadn't committed this crime.

Walice began to ask another question and I raised my hand, stalling him. The gods had not deigned to provide proof of the halfwit's innocence today, so I knew it was now left up to me.

"Do you know who I am, Haral?" I asked in a friendly voice.

Haral brushed his thick brown hair from his face and he nodded, his eyes fixed on me in fascination.

"Can you say my name?" I prodded.

"Lord," Haral said in a surprisingly high voice for such a big man.

"That's right," I said with a nod. "Very good. And where are we right now?"

"Castle," Haral said dutifully.

"Good. And the castle is where?"

Haral's face twisted in concentration, then he smiled. "Corwick," he said happily.

"That's correct," I replied with a smile. "We are in Corwick, and I am your lord. Do you understand?" Haral nodded eagerly. "So, when your lord asks you a question, what must you do?"

"Answer it?" Haral said, sounding unsure of himself.

"Yes," I agreed. "That's right. And when you answer your lord, what must you never, ever do?"

"Belch?" Haral asked innocently. Despite the tenseness in the room, laughter erupted at the halfwit's response. I could feel my own lips twitching upward in amusement as Haral looked around in surprise. I lifted my hand for quiet so that he could continue. "Mama told me to never belch or fart around a lord," Haral explained, looking down at his hands.

"Your mother was a wise woman," I said. "But I meant you must never, ever lie to your lord. Do you understand that?"

"Oh yes, lord," Haral said.

"Very well," I grunted, pleased with how things were going so far. I took a deep breath. "So, now I need you to answer some questions, Haral, and you must tell me the truth even if you don't want to. Will you do that for me?" Haral nodded, his face taking on a comical look of seriousness as he waited. "Do you know a young girl named Krinst?" I asked. The halfwit nodded again, staring at me with a blank expression. "Good," I said, encouraged by the lack of fear on Haral's face. "When did you see her last?"

"Yesterday," Haral replied immediately.

"Where did you see her?"

"In the meadow, lord," Haral said.

I glanced at Walice for confirmation. "She'd been picking blackberries near the stream," the steward said with a nod.

"Did you talk with Krinst, Haral?" I asked, focusing on the halfwit again.

Haral smiled and his face lit up. "She gave me some blackberries. I really like blackberries."

"What happened after you ate the blackberries?"

Haral looked confused. "Lord?"

"You ate some of Krinst's blackberries, then what did you do?"

Haral shrugged. "I don't know."

Protests immediately sounded, echoing angrily throughout the great hall. I looked up and glared at the crowd, silencing them with my eyes before turning back to Haral. I decided to try a different tact with him to see how he'd react. "I'm going to ask you a very important question now, Haral, and you must answer it honestly."

"Yes, lord," Haral said.

"Did you rape and kill Krinst after you ate the blackberries?"

Haral's mouth dropped open in shock at my words. I could see him struggling to say something, but nothing came out other than garbled, wet choking sounds.

"You must answer the question your lord has asked of you," Walice finally prodded from beside me.

Haral's mouth worked as he fought to speak. "Krinst is dead?" he finally managed to croak out.

"You know she is, you murderous bastard!" the dead girl's brother shouted in rage. He pointed at Haral as his mother sobbed into his shoulder. "Her maiden's blood was all over your filthy cock, you whoreson!"

"Silence!" Hughe cried as the two factions began shouting and throwing vegetables at one another again.

My son put his hand on his sword threateningly as he glared at the crowd. I decided to let him handle it as I collected my thoughts, waiting until relative calm eventually returned to the great hall.

"Yes, Haral," I finally said as tears began to slide down the halfwit's cheeks. "Krinst is dead. They found you half a mile from her body with your trousers around your ankles and blood on you. Do you remember that?" Haral suddenly looked scared and he dropped his eyes. "You have to answer me, Haral," I said, an edge to my voice. "Do you remember the blood?"

Haral sniffed and nodded reluctantly. "Yes, lord."

I sighed inwardly, starting to think that I'd been wrong about the halfwit after all. "Why was that girl's blood on you, Haral?" I demanded.

"I...I can't tell you, lord," Haral said, looking miserable.

"Because the bastard killed her, that's why!" the dead girl's brother shouted.

"Hughe," I grunted in annoyance, flicking my eyes to my son. I pointed at the angry boy with the head of my axe. "If that one says another word, take him outside and crack his head open." Hughe glowered at the boy as I focused back on the halfwit. "Why can't you tell me about the blood?" I asked, confused by Haral's reaction. Something wasn't right here.

Haral started to rock back and forth on the stool. "Because I promised I wouldn't say anything," he whispered. "It's a secret."

A secret? I thought in puzzlement. Was this some ploy, or was there more at play here than met the eye? I searched Haral's face again, looking for any signs of cunning or guile, but all I saw was heartbreak and misery. "So, you have a secret, do you?" I said, stroking my beard as I thought. "Can you tell me what it is?" Haral shook his head back and forth in response. "Why not?" I asked.

"Because I promised her I wouldn't," Haral said softly.

My eyebrows rose in surprise. "Krinst? You promised Krinst?" Haral shook his head again, not saying anything. I sighed in frustration, trying to understand. "You must tell me who you mean, Haral," I said, letting the halfwit see the resolve in my eyes. "The only chance you have to escape hanging is to tell me who you are talking about right now. Who did you promise not to tell?"

Haral opened his mouth, then he clamped it shut, looking frightened as he put his hands over his head and began muttering to himself. I decided I'd gone easy on the halfwit long enough. I was about to shout at him to answer me when I sensed movement from behind me. A tall, lithe woman had just stepped out from behind the curtains at the back of the dais. She dashed forward, shoving Walice heavily aside before I felt the cold, sharp blade of a knife press against my neck.

"He promised me, you bastard!" the woman hissed. Shouts of alarm arose as my men and my sons started to draw their weapons. "If even one person moves or pulls a sword, the old man dies!" the woman warned.

I held up my hand, stopping Hughe and the others. "Who are you?" I demanded.

"My name is Casia," the woman said. She chuckled at the blank look on my face. "No, Lord Hadrack, you don't know me."

Casia moved so that I could see her better. There was something vaguely familiar about this woman, I thought. Her nose was long and thin, with piercing green eyes set wide apart beneath high, elegant cheekbones. Her face looked worn and weathered from a lifetime out in the sun, with fine, web-like lines creasing the corners of her eyes. She was dressed in a man's tunic and tight trousers, and her hair, which was flaming red, was pinned up at the sides. Casia's hand holding the knife never wavered in the slightest at my throat.

"What do you want?" I asked as the hall fell silent with dread.

"Your death!" Casia spat back. "It's all I've ever wanted since I was a child."

I glanced at Haral, who was staring at Casia with obvious infatuation. I started to piece it all together. "You used the halfwit to get to me," I said, knowing that I was right. "You killed the girl and then smeared her blood on him, knowing that he wouldn't understand what was happening."

"I did," Casia agreed bluntly. She shrugged. "I heard you never leave your chambers anymore. I could have killed you there, but I wanted everyone in Corwick to see you die a coward's death. I knew your ego wouldn't let you leave something as important as a murder for your son to handle. All I had to do was wait."

"You killed an innocent girl and framed a simpleton just to kill me in public?" I said in outrage. "Why? I don't even know you."

"One stupid girl's life is a small price to pay to see the look on your face right now, you bastard," Casia replied with scorn in her voice. "You've committed far worse crimes than what I did and were rewarded for it. Now it's finally time for you to pay for those crimes."

"What are you talking about?" I asked as I felt hot blood trickling down my neck from the blade. "What crimes?"

Casia leaned close. "How about murder?"

"I've murdered no one," I said defiantly.

"Haven't you?" Casia said mockingly. "Since I was old enough to walk, all I heard from my mother was that any day now, the great Wolf of Corwick, the hero of the Pair War, would come riding back to whisk her away." I wrinkled my brow in puzzlement as Casia continued, "She used to stare out the window of our home for hours at a time, ignoring my father and me and everything else, just waiting and hoping that you would appear." Casia took a deep breath. "I hated you so much for that, hated how she made excuses for you and blamed herself for everything that happened. You broke my mother's heart, you bastard! But even that wasn't enough for you. No, you had to take her family from her as well."

Casia glanced at my sons and daughter and slowly shook her head. "You've led a fine life since then," she said bitterly. "Surrounded by your great castle, your luxuries, and a loving family, while my mother sat forgotten by her window, waiting for you to come back as she slowly withered away. She died last week, still looking out that same window, believing until the end that you'd come." Casia stroked the blade of the knife slowly along my neck. I felt it grate against the chain of my brother's Pair Stone that I still wore after all these years. "You might not have murdered my mother with your bare hands, Lord Hadrack," Casia whispered. "But what you did was far worse. You stole her life from her with cruelty and indifference. Taking it away a piece at a time, day after day and year after year, until nothing was left but an empty shell."

I could see tears threatening in Casia's eyes now, and I felt a sinking feeling in my chest. I suddenly knew who her mother was. "It doesn't have to end this way for you," I said softly. I glanced at the tense faces of my sons and men, knowing what was about to happen the moment she used the knife. "If you strike me down, they will kill you."

Casia shrugged. "I don't care. My parents are dead, and my husband and children died three years ago from the Yellow Death. I have nothing left to lose now." She smiled humorlessly. "I used to think the gods spared me from the plague so that I could take care of my mother, but now I know the truth." She pressed the knife tighter against my neck. I could feel my life's blood pulsing wetly against the cold steel. "It was to make you pay for what you did to her."

I wet my lips and stared at the girl's familiar features, seeing another face from long ago shimmering in their depths. "I remember your mother," I said. "Her name was Sabina. We were friends."

"Friends!" Casia snorted sarcastically. "Who are you trying to fool? You haven't given my mother a second thought for more than fifty years. I hope you think of her now and what you did as you burn at The Father's feet, you heartless bastard!"

I closed my eyes, picturing Sabina the first time that I'd seen her. She had been so young then, with her shimmering red hair and sparkling green eyes. So young and full of life and potential. I'd always regretted what had happened between the two of us on a mountaintop long ago, but, as the years had passed, I'd somehow managed to thrust it from my mind. Now, Sabina's daughter was here to thrust it back.

I knew Casia had every right to hate me, for what she had just accused me of doing was true. I had taken everything her mother had cherished, and I had destroyed it without the slightest feeling of remorse and then walked away. I realized the angry girl standing over me was my penance for what I'd done back then. I slowly relaxed in my chair, accepting her vengeance as my life coming full circle. I looked up, letting Casia see I was ready for, and unafraid of death as I waited for the slash of the knife that would finally release me from this world.

"I am truly sorry about your mother," I whispered. "I genuinely liked her."

"Then why did you do what you did?" Casia asked in a bitter voice.

"Because of a vow I made long ago," I said as my mind drifted backward in time.

1: Springlight

"This is madness!" Jebido grumbled. He leaned against a tree trunk, removed his right boot, and then winced as he stared down at his bloody foot. He cursed angrily—whether at his wound or the current situation we found ourselves in, I wasn't quite sure. "What are we supposed to do without siege engines?" Jebido demanded, his eyes flashing. "Knock politely on the gates and hope that they let us in?"

I grunted for an answer, silently agreeing with him. I sat down wearily on a stump and studied the steep road ahead of me that led up to a fortified town four hundred yards away. Dead men lay crumpled all along the road and around the town's walls. I wrinkled my nose as the wind picked up. The corpses were already beginning to stink as the day grew hotter. We'd been trying to take the town for the last three days and had lost almost half our force so far. The rest were camped along the edge of the sprawling forest that ringed the town, undoubtedly staring just as bitterly as I was at its imposing walls.

Jebido hopped awkwardly on one foot beside me as he tried to force the other back into his boot. I absently held his arm to steady him. "I swear, Hadrack, the man is deliberately trying to get us all killed."

Jebido was referring to Odiman, a House Agent whose command, unfortunately, we found ourselves to be under. Odiman was as unpleasant a man as I'd come across, except for maybe that bastard Carbet, I suppose. The stubborn House Agent was intent on breaking through the town's defenses as soon as possible, regardless of the cost to his men. Nothing could talk him out of it. The fact that we were ill-prepared for a siege of any kind didn't seem to concern him in the least. He just kept throwing us at the town's walls.

"Another day like this one," Baine said as he unhooked his bow and collapsed wearily to the ground, "and he'll succeed." He withdrew a knife from a sheath in his boot and began flipping it end over end aggressively. Baine had a habit of doing that when he was agitated.

"Why are we even here?" Jebido asked as he glared up at the town. "This place means nothing to either side. So why bother with it?"

I glanced through the trees behind us where Odiman and Malo had appeared, walking side by side in heated conversation. I shrugged my shoulders. "Obviously, it means something to someone," I said thoughtfully.

Malo had arrived in camp during our failed assault on the town that morning. We'd attempted to fashion a battering ram for the heavy gates the night before, but we had no carpenters or engineers along with us, and none of us had any idea how to build one. The result turned out to be an unwieldy, four-wheeled disaster with a sloping, uneven roof of green saplings that we'd struggled to push through the thick mud that lay at the base of the hill. The defenders had laughed and jeered at us when we wheeled the ram out into the open, and even though we'd splashed water on it first, they had managed to set the thing on fire before we even got halfway to the gates. Odiman had stubbornly insisted we press on with the attack anyway, so we'd rushed the town with shields and make-shift, twisted ladders in our arms. Our ill-fated and uncoordinated attack had been easily repulsed by a steady barrage of arrows coupled with hot sand and rocks that the defenders rained down on our heads from the walls.

The sting of the humiliation was still hanging over me as I closed my eyes, thinking about the events that had brought my men and me here. The war between the twin princes and Holy House — now referred to as the Pair War — had been raging since the death of King Jorquin a year ago. A year that had seen close to half the two hundred towns scattered along the unofficial border that separated Southern Ganderland from the North fall to the forces of either the Rock or the Sun. Jebido had told me he'd heard a rumor that one town had flown the Rock of Life and Blazing Sun banners twice each in a single week. Allegiances in this war, I thought glumly, seemed to be mainly decided in favor of whomever had the sharpest sword at their neck at any given moment.

I opened my eyes and looked up at the town as several of the more vocal defenders began taunting us from the walls, encouraging us to try again. The last rush against those walls had cost us close to a hundred men—men we could ill-afford to lose. The fresh corpses now lay entwined with the others from our previous attacks, while thick black smoke continued to rise from the remains of the ram. The ground leading up to the town was barren of foliage, muddy and rock-strewn, leaving anyone struggling to approach vulnerable to the town's formidable archers. A network of trenches crossed the road leading to the gates. We'd managed to fill in some of them to get the ram through, but the cost in lives for that wasted effort had been high.

The only cover around the entire hill was a narrow ridge of jagged granite on the western side. That ridge sloped from the top of the hill and ran down the length to disappear into a thick stand of oak and elm trees five hundred yards away. Odiman had initially tried sending men into the trees where the ridge began, hoping to use the formation as a bridge up to the town. However, the rock surface was so twisted and uneven that our forces had to pick their way through it at a crawl. The archers on the walls might not be as accomplished as Piths, but they were more than good enough to slaughter our men mercilessly.

After that, Odiman left the ridge strictly alone and stubbornly returned to his only other strategy—which was to rush the walls in force, hoping to overwhelm them eventually. I remember Lord Corwick had done the same thing at Gasterny, but unfortunately for us, the walls here were a hundred times stronger than Gasterny's had been and would not be so easily scaled.

The town was called Springlight for some reason that I couldn't fathom, and it was built in the shape of a six-sided hexagon, with a massive gate and bristling barbican facing me. Another entrance was set along the northern wall, with the road leading up to it dug up in a similar network of trenches as the southern route. The massive walls of stone were thick and thirty feet high, with bulky turrets placed at each of the six angles of the hexagon and on either side of the opposing gates. All the turrets flew a Rock of Life banner from their masts and Prince Tyrale's prancing golden lion. The pennants snapped harshly in the strong breeze that blew straight toward me, carrying with it the unmistakable smell of death and defeat. The remains of a small cluster of mud and straw huts that Odiman's men had razed on the first day of the siege smoked feebly along the base of the hill to the east. I could see charred and twisted bodies lying there as well.

"Maybe Malo brought a good lead for us this time," Jebido said, cutting into my thoughts. He shrugged. "The Mother knows you deserve it, Hadrack. Maybe that's why he summoned us here."

I nodded, not believing it. I could feel the familiar anger rising in my chest and I fought to squash it. Everything had been going so well last year—a year that seemed so long ago now. The woman I loved had just taken control of Calban Castle, and I'd managed to kill two more of the nine, Hape and Quant Ranes, leaving only five of the bastards left alive. I'd fully expected to get them all after that and finally get justice for Corwick, but less than a week after Lord Demay's death, King Jorquin had died and the war had erupted, changing everything.

Prince Tyden, who I now served as the rightful heir to the kingdom, had barely survived an assassination attempt by his brother the moment their father died. He'd escaped Gandertown more by luck than anything else and had retreated south with his forces to Halhaven. He'd also brought all the priestesses he could find with him, including the First Daughter as they fled ahead of the armies of the North. Within a matter of days, Daughter Gernet's vast information network collapsed as Prince Tyrale rooted out most of her supporters and executed them without the benefit of a trial. I'd tried to find the rest of the nine using the dated information we already had, but other than Hervi Desh—who somehow had risen to become one of Prince Tyrale's closest advisors—the others had simply vanished like spirits in the night.

Whether they were even now fighting in the armies of the North, or lay dead somewhere on a battlefield, I had no way of knowing.

"When has that bastard House Agent ever brought us anything but misery?" Baine grumbled from behind me.

"There's a first time for everything," Jebido said. He walked over to me and put his hand on my shoulder. "Just have faith, Hadrack. Maybe it's not going to be today, but sooner or later, The Mother is going to give you one of them. I guarantee it."

"Give me one?"

"Of course," Jebido said. "Think about it." He counted off on his fingers. "Calen, Searl Merk, and Quant Ranes all came to you. Not the other way around. I don't believe that was a coincidence."

"You think Mother Above sent them to Hadrack?" Baine asked, looking intrigued.

"Of course," Jebido said. "Isn't it obvious?"

"What about Hape?" I pointed out. "I found him, remember?"

"True," Jebido said thoughtfully. He wiggled a dirty finger in his ear, then looked at whatever he'd fished out before flicking it away. "But tell me this. Who was it that told you where he was?"

"Daughter Gernet," I replied.

"Who is an agent of?"

"Mother Above," Baine answered for me.

"Exactly," Jebido said, looking pleased with himself. He patted me on the shoulder. "So, my advice is to wait. The bastards will show up when She is ready, Hadrack. You'll see."

Jebido's words made sense. I could see the logic of what he was saying, but that didn't make me feel much better about it. I was twenty years old now, and it seemed to me as though all I'd been doing since I was a boy was waiting. First, while a prisoner in Father's Arse, then, as Einhard's sworn man, now oathbound to an unpredictable Daughter and moody House Agent. I bit my tongue, stopping myself from saying something sarcastic to Jebido. I knew my friend meant well in what he'd said. We were all tired and sick of this place, and taking my anger out on him would do nothing to improve our situation.

I saw Tyris approaching through the trees with some bread in his hands and I gestured toward him, glad to have something else to focus my attention. "Looks like our friend found something after all."

"About time, too," Baine grunted. "I could eat a boar, fur and all, right about now."

"No boar, I'm afraid," Tyris said as he held up a small, moldy loaf of bread. "This is all there was." He tore the bread into four pieces, handing them out.

"Where are the others?" I asked, pausing to pick a struggling weevil from my bread.

"Niko and Sim are sleeping," Tyris replied. "Putt is playing dice." I frowned at that. "Don't worry, my lord," the blond archer hurried to say. "I warned him about using crooked dice. He said he'd behave."

"He had better," I grumbled. Putt tended to cheat, and it had only been a month ago that he'd barely made it out of Laskerly alive after trying to swindle several of the locals there.

"Rumor has it that more supplies and reinforcements will be here the day after tomorrow, my lord," Tyris said.

"Two days!" Baine snorted as he chewed. He rolled his eyes. "The stupid bastards might as well just turn back now. The way things are going, we'll probably be dead long before they get here."

Tyris shrugged and sat down on the ground beside me with his long legs splayed out in front of him. "I'm just relaying what I overheard, lad. Don't blame me if you don't like the news."

I glanced at Baine, seeing anger flare up in his dark eyes. I shook my head at him in warning. My ordinarily cheerful friend had been unusually moody and on edge for weeks now. I'd seriously considered leaving him behind when we'd set out from Witbridge Manor a week ago, but Baine insisted that he be allowed to accompany us. I'd relented in the end, despite his obvious concern for his new wife, Flora, who was due to give birth soon and was having a rough pregnancy. I knew Baine's anxiety about Flora's health, as well as the realization that he would soon be a father, had a great deal to do with his unpredictable moodiness, so I tried to make allowances for it as much as possible. Besides, I couldn't imagine leaving Baine behind and not have both he and Jebido together by my side when there was fighting to be done.

I thought of Flora and the coming child. The one-time whore had been seriously injured last year during the attack on Calban, but she was young and had managed to pull through. Most of the credit for that was due to Haverty the apothecary's skill as a healer—that and Baine's undivided devotion to her. Thinking of Calban turned my thoughts to Shana. Both of us had reluctantly agreed that it would be safer to keep our distance from one another until the war was over. Calban was a strategic castle along the western coast, with access to land routes and sea lanes, making it ideal for launching offensives. But, it was also located in Northern Ganderland, far from our forces, which made it vulnerable to attack, should Prince Tyrale believe Shana's allegiance fell with the South. I shuddered at the thought of what the prince might do if he found out the truth.

Tyris tapped his boot against mine in warning, cutting off my thoughts as Malo approached, wearing a grim look on his face.

"Well, I guess we are about to find out what this is all about," I said as I stood and waited for him.

"You look well," Malo grunted, stopping in front of me. We locked arms briefly, then stepped back. I saw him glance at the blood crusting on my temple, where a well-thrown stone had partially careened off my helmet that morning. "I didn't expect you to join in the fighting, Hadrack."

I glanced at Odiman, who stood in the trees, glaring at us with his usual sour expression. "That bastard over there didn't give us much choice."

Malo scratched his shaggy beard. "My apologies for that. I'm afraid Odiman can be overzealous at times. Just the same, I want to thank you for coming. I wasn't sure if Gris would be able to find you and give you my message."

"It was a near thing," I said. "Finol told him where we'd be."

Malo nodded distractedly. He looked past me through the trees toward Springlight. "Formidable," he said almost to himself. "My information was that the town was weakly defended and would fall easily."

I turned and glanced behind me before focusing back on the House Agent. "Your informant is either woefully stupid or playing you for a fool."

"So it would seem," the House Agent muttered.

"So, what's this all about, Malo?" I asked. "Why do you need to capture this town so badly?"

Malo crossed his arms over his chest. "We don't need the town," he said. "We need what is inside of it."

I raised an eyebrow. "And what exactly might that be?"

Malo flicked his gaze over to my men, who were listening intently. "More of a who, actually," he said. The House Agent moved past me to the treeline and leaned against a towering oak where he could get a better view of the fortified town. "His name is Rorian." Malo glanced at me as I came to stand beside him. "He claims to be a scholar, but after what he did in Halhaven, it's safe to say that my doubts have been raised about that."

"What did he do?" Jebido asked.

The House Agent turned to look back, his expression angry. "He murdered several Agents and the Master Librarian of the Grand Holy House."

"Is he working for the North?" I asked.

"We believe so," Malo said with a weary nod. "He arrived in Halhaven a month ago, requesting to do research in the library there. His name was registered on the scholar scrolls, so the Master Librarian had no reason to suspect anything amiss." Malo ran his fingers through his thick hair as he talked. "Rorian spent almost every waking hour in the library up until two weeks ago, when, for some reason, he killed the Master Librarian along with several Agents who tried to stop him."

"Why would he do that?" I asked.

"We think the Master Librarian had grown suspicious of him," Malo said. "From what we've been able to piece together, Rorian was looking for something specific. We think he found it, and when the Master Librarian realized what it was, Rorian killed him."

"What was it?" Baine asked, clearly intrigued by the story.

Malo didn't answer him and remained focused on me instead. "Rorian managed to escape Halhaven, wounding two more Agents before getting away on horseback with some others waiting outside the walls for him. He's quite resourceful, this scholar, but luckily for us, Odiman's forces were close by at the time. We were able to cordon off the routes to the north, forcing him south." Malo pointed to Springlight. "Odiman chased the bastard here. I need to know what Rorian was doing in that library and what he found there."

I'd privately wondered why Odiman had divided his men up to surround the town, even going so far as to have watches patrolling all day and night. I knew we couldn't spare the men for it, but the House Agent had been insistent that no one get out under any circumstances. I'd assumed he was concerned that they would go for help, which had seemed unlikely to me. We were too far south for any substantial force of the North to be nearby. Now I knew he'd gone to those lengths to make sure that Rorian and his companions stayed where they were until either the town fell or Malo arrived.

"I can see why you would want this man after what he did," I said. "But that doesn't explain why we are here."

"I know we don't always agree on things, Hadrack," Malo replied after a moment. "But one thing that I do know about you and your men, especially after Calban, is that you can be trusted implicitly."

"Trusted to do what?" I asked in surprise.

"To say nothing about what we might find here," Malo said. "Both Daughter Gernet and I have our suspicions about what Rorian was after in the library, and if we are correct, then I'll need men by my side that I know I can depend on. The North has spies everywhere these days. We don't know who may be watching and listening."

"What about your fellow Agents?" I asked.

Malo made a face. "Telling them would be too risky. I've known Odiman most of my life and I trust him, but I can't be sure our order hasn't been infiltrated by now. Whatever we find in Springlight must stay a secret. That's why I asked for your help."

I thought about that, intrigued despite myself. "We'll help you in any way we can," I finally said. "But the only way you are going to find out what that man found is by getting over those walls over there, which isn't going to be an easy task."

"I agree," Malo said as he pursed his lips. "But either way, it has to be done. The sooner, the better."

I shook my head. "It's not that simple, Malo," I warned. "The town is too strong, and we are too weak. We're going to have to wait for more reinforcements before we can try again."

"And siege engines," Jebido added.

"And siege engines," I agreed. "If that doesn't work, then our only choice will be to starve them out."

"That could take months," Malo said in frustration.

"Yes, at the very least," I said.

Malo looked up at the branches over our heads and took a deep breath. "I can't wait that long, Hadrack," he finally said. "This is too important."

"Then I guess we better start digging a tunnel right now," Baine said sarcastically. "Because there is no way we are getting over those walls without those engines."

I nodded in agreement as I studied Springlight for any signs of weakness, knowing that it was pointless. I'd looked at the town from every angle possible over the last few days, but had seen nothing indicating an easy way inside. I'd even climbed the ridge to get a better vantage point before the archers on the walls had seen me and forced me to retreat to safety.

I paused as I thought of what Baine had said a moment ago, while he and Malo continued to bicker back and forth. My friend was being sarcastic about the tunnel, of course, but I thought back to Calban and the secret passageway that Lord Demay had constructed leading out onto the bay. Could it be? I wondered, knowing that it was unlikely, but feeling excitement rise in my chest anyway. I stooped and picked up my father's axe, then grabbed my shield.

"What is it?" Jebido asked me. "I know that look in your eye."

"Maybe nothing," I said with a grin. "Maybe everything." I glanced at Tyris. "Go get the others. The rest of you follow me."

I headed northwest through the forest, avoiding the open land around the town as I aimed for the ridge base while Malo, Jebido, and Baine followed behind me. The ground beneath the trees here was thick with blackberry vines covered in wicked barbs half an inch in length that could rip open a man's flesh in a heartbeat. Odiman's patrols had hacked their way through the wall of vines on the first day of the siege, creating a four-foot-wide trail, which I was careful to follow.

Six of Odiman's soldiers appeared walking toward me along the path as we drew nearer to the ridge. Most of the men were limping and were swathed in heavy bandages as they trudged wearily along, heading back toward where I knew a station for treating the wounded had been set up. Every experienced battlefield soldier had a basic knowledge of treating wounds, but we were lucky enough to have a barber surgeon along with us that was surprisingly competent. I knew the surgeon was doing a brisk business today, removing arrowheads, amputating limbs, and cauterizing wounds with hot oil, so the six wounded men would have a long wait ahead of them if they wished to see him.

The closest man to me was tall and wide, wearing a thick woolen cloak with the lower half of his face covered by a bloody bandage that he held pressed tightly to his wound. The other half of the man's face was marred by three long white scars across his left cheek. He greeted me and I nodded back as we passed each other.

Malo didn't even glance at the wounded men as he fell into step beside me. "Care to let me in on what we are doing out here?" he asked.

"All in due time," I said as a red squirrel scolded us from a perch high up in the branches.

"I'll say one thing about you, Hadrack," Malo muttered with a sigh. "Life is never boring around you."

I chuckled as we finally reached the ridge as Niko, Sim, Tyris, and Putt hurried to catch up. I studied the cracked and jagged rock formation that began as a single flat stone jutting out of the forest floor. The ridge quickly rose above me like a great beast bursting from the ground, then punched outward through the treeline toward the hill. The head lay in deep shadow from the intertwined network of branches above, while dark green moss grew in places along the stone, with thorny weeds and bushes bunched all around the base. Stunted trees stood here and there among the bushes, struggling to get roots down deep enough to find water that their bigger cousins might have missed.

"Do you remember that secret passageway in Calban?" I asked my companions once we were all together. Heads began to nod around me. "That castle is built on solid rock just like this here," I said, slapping the head of the ridge. "Yet they managed to chisel their way through it to the bay."

Malo looked at the formidable length of rock skeptically. "You think there is a tunnel leading to the town somewhere in all of that?"

I shrugged. "It's a possibility," I said. "What do we have to lose by checking?"

My companions all shifted their feet, glancing at each other with little enthusiasm on their faces. I felt momentary doubt take over me at their expressions.

Jebido ran his hand experimentally over the stone, pausing as several thin slivers broke from the surface with a wet-sounding crunch before sliding to the ground. "This thing isn't as solid as it looks," Jebido said thoughtfully as he ran his eyes over the ridge. "At least on top. Maybe you're on to something."

"And maybe we're just wasting our time," Baine said as he rolled his eyes.

"What else do we have to do right now?" I asked. "Everyone spread out. Look around the base for an entrance."

My men fanned out along both sides of the ridge. We began sliding our hands across the stone and using our feet to brush the shrubs and weeds aside. The eight of us went over every inch of the ridge on both sides right up to the treeline, pausing in our work only when one of Odiman's numerous patrols walked by making fun of us. Niko always had a witty response ready for the patrols, which we'd laugh at as the insults flew back and forth between them. Malo was the first to give up after more than an hour, followed by Putt, Tyris, and then the others, leaving me stubbornly continuing the search. Eventually, even I had to admit defeat and I joined them where they stood waiting for me at our starting point.

"It was a good thought, Hadrack," Malo said. "But we are no closer to getting into the town than we were. I'd better get back to Odiman and try to figure out what we are going to do."

The House Agent headed back along the path as Putt moved to the head of the ridge and started pulling himself up.

"Where are you going?" I demanded. I pointed toward the town. "They will skewer your arse before you get very far."

"I'm just going to take a quick peek, my lord," Putt grunted as he hauled himself over the edge. He stood, his body cast in flickering shadows as he turned to gaze back down at us. "I'll be right back."

Putt disappeared from view as Jebido removed his helmet and scratched his silver hair vigorously. "These infernal lice are driving me insane," he grumbled.

"Try bathing once in a while," Baine said with that familiar cheeky grin that I knew so well. "Either that or stand downwind from me."

Jebido chuckled, about to reply when Putt reappeared above us. "My lord," the outlaw said, sounding excited. "I found a hole that looks big enough for a man to pass through."

"So what, you red-faced bastard," Niko called up with a laugh. "That's just from years of rain and wind. There are probably hundreds of them up there like that."

"Not with a ladder leading down to the bottom, there isn't," Putt said.

2: Sabina

I had to hand it to Putt. I'd been up on the ridge myself and had been less than six feet away from what he'd just found, but I hadn't recognized the opening for what it was. To be fair, the entrance hadn't looked like much then, or even now for that matter. Besides, when I had been up top before, I had been more interested in studying the town to the east, not looking for hidden entrances.

The hole sat near the northern side of the ridge, surrounded on two sides by a weathered rock formation that rose far above our heads. The towering stone and tall trees of the forest worked together to cast deep shadows, making visibility in the area difficult. The entrance seemed like nothing more than a dark shadow among others, and it wasn't until you were right over the hole that it appeared to be more than that. Even then, it's doubtful anyone other than Putt would have noticed, as you had to stick your head inside and wait for your eyes to adjust to see the ladder where it lay in the darkness against the wall.

"How in the name of The Mother did you even think to look in here?" Jebido asked as he got down on all fours to peer inside. He grunted and twisted his body at an angle until he got his hand inside the hole, burying his arm up to the shoulder as he cautiously felt around.

Putt grinned and tapped his temple. "I'm always thinking. It just seemed to make sense that there might be something like this up here."

"Now I've heard everything," Niko said sarcastically. "Putt making sense." He lifted his hands palms to the sky. "Blessed Mother, I'm ready for you to take me now, because there is nothing left for me to see in this world."

"As if you're going to be meeting Her first," Putt muttered.

I grinned, secretly agreeing with the red-bearded outlaw as I nudged Jebido's backside with my foot. "So, what do you think?" I asked.

"It looks like there's a tunnel leading away from the ladder," Jebido said as he sat back on his haunches. He gestured to the dark opening. "But what is really interesting is it feels like there is a loose slab of stone set in grooves beneath the rim here."

"You mean like some kind of door?" I asked in surprise.

"Exactly," Jebido agreed.

"If that's true, then why is it open?"

"Good question."

"Maybe this is a trap, and they left it open on purpose," Putt suggested. "Hoping to draw us down there."

"I doubt it," Jebido said with a quick shake of his head. "Why risk it? They've done just fine slaughtering us from the safety of their walls." He glanced away to study the line of the ridge. "Whatever the reason is, we can't let an opportunity like this pass. If that tunnel does lead to the town, then my guess is it will follow a fairly straight path." Jebido pointed through the hanging tree branches toward Springlight. "Going by my eye, and assuming the tunnel slopes upward, then it should go through the wall right about where that granary sits."

I looked to the town, where I could see the still-smoldering wooden shingles of the granary roof Jebido was referring to. We'd tried using fire arrows to set the buildings ablaze more than once over the last few days, but our success had been moderate at best. Springlight must have an abundance of water, I guessed, not to mention enthusiastic and motivated inhabitants to help douse the flames. I was thankful now that the fire had failed, since if Jebido was correct about the granary, we would need the building to be intact to get through.

"All right," I said to my men, coming to a decision. "We're going down there. Sim, go back and tell Malo and Odiman what we found. Tell them we'll need a ram."

"For what?" Baine asked.

I stood over the entrance, looking down. "For what is waiting for us at the end of that tunnel," I said. It was a safe assumption that there would be a stout door blocking our access to the town. That, and undoubtedly guards as well.

"Not too big, though," Jebido warned. "We have to be able to get it through the hole."

"Why not just use these?" Sim asked, hefting his axe.

I shook my head. "Axes will take too long and make too much noise. I want to get through fast before they know what's happening."

Sim nodded and slid down the face of the ridge, disappearing through the trees. I unsheathed my father's axe. "I'll go first," I said, handing the axe and my shield to Jebido. "Wait for my signal, then the rest of you come down."

I sat on the cold stone near the hole, then dangled my feet over the edge of the rock until my searching boots found the top rung of the ladder. I grabbed each side of the rim with my hands and pushed myself upward, waiting as I let the ladder take my full weight. It seemed sturdy enough. I took a step down to the next rung, then the next before I paused as my shoulders grazed against each side of the entrance. I sucked in my breath, trying not to think about getting stuck. My armor screeched loudly, but by pressing down with my weight and continuing to hold my breath, I managed to slip through with only a few scratches across the metal for my trouble. I climbed down the last few rungs until my boots came in contact with the hard surface of the floor. Jebido dangled my father's axe down from above and I grasped it, then he squeezed my shield through with some difficulty and dropped it to me. I turned and blinked in the darkness. A narrow corridor led away from me.

"What do you see?" Jebido asked.

I glanced up at my friend's beak-like nose and shadowy features. "A face so hideous it would give even the bravest of men nightmares," I grunted.

"Very funny," Jebido muttered.

My eyes were starting to adjust to the gloom now, so I took several steps away from the ladder. I paused to look down as I stepped into a large puddle of stagnant water that rose to my ankles. I took several more steps with the sounds of my splashing feet echoed loudly off the walls. A faint beam of light cut through the darkness ahead, coming from a crack in the rock ceiling that was roughly the size of my fist at its widest point. I could see two similar holes letting in faint light about ten feet farther along the corridor. I was hopeful that there would be more like them along the way, as in my enthusiasm to get down the ladder, I'd neglected to bring a torch with me.

I turned and cupped my hands to my mouth. "All clear," I called out softly.

Jebido was the first man down the ladder, holding a flickering torch in his right hand. Leave it to my friend to always be practical, I thought. The torch's orange glow quickly lit up the corridor, revealing chiseled walls and a rounded ceiling that rose three feet above my head. A black, moss-like growth grew from the base of the walls, spreading upward toward the ceiling across the damp stone. The skeletal remains of a large rat lay crumbled in the corner to the right of the ladder.

Jebido caught his shield nimbly as Baine dropped it to him before climbing down himself, followed closely by the rest of my men.

"All right," I said in a low tone once we were all gathered together. "We go single file. Jebido will take the lead. No talking. This still might be a trap, but I want to know what we are dealing with before Malo gets here."

I drew Wolf's Head slowly, careful not to let the steel blade grate against my scabbard. Behind me, my men silently drew their weapons while Baine and Tyris nocked arrows to their bows. The corridor remained straight and narrow as we progressed, with a slight grade heading up just as Jebido had predicted. A jagged crack appeared in the ceiling every so often, letting in some light and a little fresh air, which had become stale as we moved deeper into the tunnel. I was having a tough time trying to ignore the relentless tickle at the back of my throat, and I could hear Putt coughing quietly into his hands.

We walked for another ten minutes or so as the corridor continued to climb upward until Jebido suddenly grunted in surprise. A thick, metal-studded door lay open and unprotected in front of us, with two men dressed in mail lying on the floor inside the corridor several feet from the door. Both men had their throats cut.

"Well, that explains why the entrance was left open," Jebido said grimly. "Somebody that didn't want to be in Springlight must have decided to get out."

"Rorian?" Baine asked.

Jebido shrugged. "That would be my guess."

"But why leave the tunnel open?" Niko asked.

"You probably can't close it from up top," I said. "It's too heavy and awkward. I'm guessing whoever killed these men had no choice but to leave it open."

"I thought Rorian and they were on the same side," Baine muttered as he gestured to the corpses.

"We don't even know for certain that it was Rorian," I said. "For all we know, this could be about something else entirely."

"Fine," Baine said with a shrug. "But how did whoever did this get past all of Odiman's patrols?"

I had been thinking the same thing as well. Malo told me Rorian was a resourceful man, so maybe it really had been him. Either way, whoever had killed the soldiers had gotten away by now. Or, more likely, were hiding close by in the forest waiting for an opportunity to do so.

I approached the dead men and knelt by the closest one, then ran the tip of my finger in the pooling blood. It was sticky, but hadn't crusted over yet, which meant the soldiers hadn't been dead for long. I wiped my finger off on the corpse's clothing, considering what to do next as I stood up. I knew if we went back now that there was a chance we would catch whoever had done this, but the bodies might be discovered in the meantime. If that happened, then the advantage of surprise would be lost to us. If Rorian was free somewhere above us, I knew Malo's interest in taking the town would end and he'd concentrate everything on finding the scholar. That didn't particularly bother me one way or the other, but if it wasn't Rorian who had escaped, then he was still inside, which meant now might be our only chance to get to him without a long siege. I knew we could break the door down later if the townspeople bolted it again, but if I were in their position and knew that the entrance had been compromised, I'd seal the door off permanently, rather than risk being overwhelmed.

"Putt, go back and tell Malo what we have found here and that we believe somebody got out," I ordered. "It might have been Rorian, or it might not have, I don't know for sure. That's up to him to decide. Tell him I'm going to secure the entrance before the townspeople get wind of what's happening. Just make sure that bastard Odiman sends me reinforcements."

"Yes, my lord," Putt said with a curt nod.

I approached the doorway and carefully peered around the wooden doorframe, prepared to duck back if I saw movement, but there was nothing except silence to greet me. A narrow corridor with bare walls of twisted planks lay in front of me with enough light coming in through the cracks between the boards to see. A closed, metal-studded doorway stood forty feet away at the opposite end of the corridor. Crude-looking murder holes spaced about three feet apart lined the planks on the right side of the passage. I studied them cautiously. Were there archers or men with pikes just waiting on the other side for some poor bastard to walk in there? I paused, listening for even the faintest sounds to indicate someone might be lying in wait, but I heard nothing at all.

Finally, I turned to Jebido. "I'll go in first," I said. "Wait until I get all the way across before you follow."

I stepped through the entrance, holding my shield at an angle to the murder holes, anticipating a sword or spear thrust at any moment. I slowly made my way down the corridor with my back pressed against the solidness of the wall behind me, pausing to listen after every few steps. All remained quiet, however, and I eventually reached the other side without incident. I approached the closed door and gave it a tentative nudge with my toe. I'd expected resistance and was surprised when there was none as the door swung inward with a creak that seemed loud to me in the stillness. I tensed when the door stopped abruptly. I waited for a count of three, listening, then pushed again, but I could tell something was blocking it from the other side. I took a chance and peered around the door. The body of a man lay on the floor, barring entry with his weight. I shoved harder, pushing the dead man aside, then stepped into a tiny room about six feet wide and maybe ten feet long.

The light streaming in from the corridor revealed a third doorway against the end wall. I moved forward. The handle on this door was made of cast iron and was strange looking, with a long narrow lever that twisted back and forth easily in my hand, though the door itself wouldn't open. It was more by accident than any cleverness on my part that I realized you had to pull while twisting the lever to the left until the door popped out of a skillfully-designed frame. After that, all I had to do was turn the lever to the right to slide the door open along well-greased rollers.

I could hear the others approaching along the corridor behind me as I stepped through the doorway into a large building. The interior had to be at least a hundred feet long, with a ceiling rising to a sharp peak forty feet or more above my head. Sunlight filtered through cracks along the walls and ceiling, revealing thick beams that ran down from the roof to join wider cantilever beams running horizontally along each wall. Crossbeams were attached to the cantilevers spanning the interior's width every ten feet, and these were secured on all sides to gigantic, roughly-shaped wooden columns. The columns separated the open space into individual stalls where barley, wheat, and oats were stacked in heavy burlap sacks. I could see rats scurrying around here and there, most looking well-fed as they studied me without fear. We were in the town granary, just as Jebido had predicted.

The building was eerily silent, but I could see blood puddling on the dirt floor not far from where I stood. A trail of that blood led toward one of the stalls, where I assumed we'd find another body or two. A double door sat at the far end of the granary, with several of the weathered planks missing on one of them, letting in additional light. The room smelled heavily of grains, mold, and dust, tickling my nose. I tilted my head sideways, listening, but other than the faint, pleasant sounds of a woman singing outside somewhere, there was nothing that seemed threatening to me. I took several more steps forward as the others came through the door behind me.

"So, now what?" Jebido asked me after he'd taken a quick look around.

"Baine," I said, pointing to a stall to my left. "Over there." I indicated the opposite stall on my right. "Tyris, you stand there and watch the door." I glanced at Jebido. "Now we wait for Odiman's men," I said.

Jebido dropped the torch to the ground and stamped it out. "That's good, Hadrack. For a moment there, I thought you might want to take the town with just the five of us."

I smiled, about to respond when Tyris hissed at us in warning. Someone had just stepped up to the double doors, blocking the light coming through from outside. I pushed Jebido and Niko toward Baine, while I scurried over to Tyris and dragged him down behind the piled grain sacks. I glanced across the granary to see Niko and Jebido crouching as we were, while Baine stood with his back against the rising column, his slim form hidden from the doors.

"And why do you wish to go in there?" I heard a feminine voice say from outside. "Why not just tell me what you need to say right here?"

"Because someone might overhear us, dear Sabina," a male voice replied in a lower, condescending tone.

"Who?" Sabina asked with a snort. "That inquisitive sparrow on the rooftop above us, perhaps?"

"Perhaps," the man agreed with a light chuckle. "They do tend to stick their beaks where they least belong."

I looked at Tyris and grimaced as someone fumbled with the door latch.

"What do we do?" the blond archer whispered as the double doors screeched outward on their hinges, flooding the entrance to the granary with sunlight.

I shrugged helplessly. What could we do? We would be seen if we tried to retreat now. I glanced behind me, thankful that the open doorway leading to the corridor was nearly invisible in the shadows at the back of the building. I took a cautious look over the grain. A handsome young man with a pointed black beard and a bright red velvet hat stood in the sunshine looking in. He lifted a hand to his eyes, blocking the glare of the sun that bounced off the dirt floor in front of him. A pretty girl with startling red hair that cascaded down to her hips stood beside him. She was wearing a light brown dress with a wide leather belt around her waist, while he was dressed in matching blue breeches and hose.

"Come, my dear," the young man said as he extended his arm to the girl. "Just like all adventures, this one begins with but a single step."

"I don't see much hope for adventure in there, Bastin," Sabina said, not moving. "Unless, of course, you mean for us to go ratting?"

Bastin chuckled. "Certainly not. I was being frivolous. Please, forgive me." He swept his free hand toward the interior of the granary. "Come inside for just a moment so that we might talk. I promise it will be worth your while."

I watched the girl as she thought it over, praying that she would refuse and they would leave, but after a moment, she smiled. "Very well. Since we have been cooped up for days by those horrible Sun worshipers, I suppose a little adventure of any sort would be welcome right about now. But only for a moment, I have to get back to my mother."

"Excellent," Bastin said as he ushered the girl inside. He closed the double doors behind them, then arm in arm, the two walked further into the granary.

I could see Baine peering at me with a question on his face as they drew closer. I shook my head. I had no wish to hurt either of these people if we didn't have to. I still had hope that they would leave quickly without ever knowing that we were there.

"Ah, this looks like an ideal spot," Bastin said as he paused two stalls away from where we were hidden. He seemed oblivious to the blood that stained the granary floor as he moved a sack of grain into the center aisle. He brushed it off dramatically and then bowed to the girl. "A throne fit for a queen, my lady."

Sabina smiled politely and sat, turning her profile toward me with her hands lying in her lap. "So," she said. "Now that I'm here, what's all this fuss about?"

Bastin knelt in front of her with one knee on the dirt floor. He took the girl's hands in his. "I have greatly enjoyed our time together, Sabina," he began. "When my father told me his long-time acquaintance was coming to Springlight seeking a cure for his ill wife, I must confess that I didn't give it much thought at the time." I could see the girl's face tighten at Bastin's words. "But," Bastin continued, not seeming to notice as he stroked her hands affectionately. "Had I known he would be bringing his charming daughter along with him, my attitude would have been decidedly different."

"Lord Branton's generosity knows no bounds," Sabina said, not sounding that enthused, I thought. She tried to draw her hands away, but Bastin refused to let her go.

"My father never forgets a friend," Bastin said. "Even a commoner such as your father."

"I'm grateful for the care your family is providing for my mother," Sabina responded.

I could tell by her body language that she was becoming uncomfortable with Bastin's attention. I glanced over at Baine, who rolled his eyes back at me.

"Ah," Bastin said, looking pleased. "That's good to hear. Gratitude puts things in the proper perspective for everyone involved. We live in trying times, I'm afraid, and it's good to have friends you can depend on. Wouldn't you agree?"

"Of course," Sabina said dutifully.

"It's unfortunate that your brother isn't here to be with your family during this time of duress."

"He had to stay behind to look after our house," Sabina replied.

"Yes," Bastin agreed thoughtfully. He rubbed a thumb lightly across the back of Sabina's hand. "I imagine he must be beside himself with worry for you and your mother."

"Undoubtedly," Sabina agreed. "But he knows that my father is here to watch over us. There is no man that I feel safer around."

"A fair point," Bastin conceded. "Your father is indeed a formidable man. I've heard it said that no one knows the Southlands better than he does, and that he could track a mouse through the densest forest if need be. Yet, even with all his skill, he cannot change the fact that your mother barely clings to life. Without the care that my family provides for her, your mother will likely die, regardless of your father's ability as a woodsman."

"I'm well aware of that," Sabina said, looking annoyed. "And I have already expressed my gratitude to your father."

"To my father, yes," Bastin said. "But not to me, and I am his heir." He drew Sabina's hand to his lips and kissed it, then stood, still holding her hand as he looked down at her. "Sometimes, there are better ways to show gratitude than mere words." His face abruptly turned hard and dangerous, the true man finally revealing itself. "I require a more robust sign that you actually feel the gratitude that you claim."

"I don't understand," Sabina said, though I could see by the growing apprehension on her face that she was beginning to.

"It's quite simple, my dear," Bastin replied. "You claim gratitude, but offer me nothing but empty words while feeding on the kindness of my family. What you seem to forget so brazenly is that your mother requires a physician's constant care, which logically means that care also requires constant money. Money that would have one day been mine when I inherit this town."

"Bastin," Sabina began to protest.

"Be quiet!" Bastin snapped. "I'm not finished." He looked to the ceiling far above his head. "Do you want your mother to die, Sabina?" he finally asked.

"Of course not!" Sabina said in a tightly controlled voice. I could see her cheeks turning the color of her hair in anger. I shifted where I crouched, prepared to leap forward if things got out of hand.

"Then, you have a simple choice to make," Bastin said with a cold smile as he gripped her hand tighter. I noticed the skin where he held her was turning purple from the pressure. "Do what I ask, and I promise that your mother will continue to get the care that she requires for as long as it takes. Refuse me, and I'll have your family removed from the manor house and sent to stay with the vermin who live on Beggar's Way."

"You can't do that!" Sabina said in outrage. "Your father would never allow it."

"My father is distracted with the assault on our walls, not to mention that bastard scholar we are protecting," Bastin said. He grinned. "He has left the running of the manor to me. So, believe me when I say I can, and I will have you removed unless you give me what I want."

Sabina glared up at Bastin bitterly. "And to think that I thought of you as a friend."

"That was your first mistake," Bastin said as he forced her hand between his legs.

"How dare you!" Sabina gasped in shock. She struck at Bastin with her free hand, but the young man easily grabbed her wrist.

"Now, let's not pretend that you have never done this before," Bastin said. "I imagine a common trollop like you must be well versed in the art of pleasuring a man."

I could see the madness of lust dominating the young nobleman's face and I growled low in my chest. I'd seen that same look in the reeve's eyes as he'd raped my sister. I stood up, not caring if I was seen now as I hefted Wolf's Head. I stalked toward the struggling pair. The girl continued to fight in the young man's grip, but Bastin just laughed and ground his hips into her hand even more. I was only two paces away when Bastin finally sensed my presence. His eyes widened in surprise when he saw me, and he opened his mouth to say something. I didn't give him the chance. I drew my sword back and rammed the hilt savagely into his open mouth. I heard several of Bastin's teeth snap with a sharp crack, and he screamed as he fell on his back, where he lay with both of his hands covering his shattered face.

I turned to the girl. "Are you all right?" I asked.

Sabina stood, looking bewildered as she pressed her hands to her chest. "Yes, I think so," she finally said. Her eyes were bright green, with small flecks of gold in them that seemed to glow. I felt myself becoming uncomfortable under her steady gaze. "Thank you," she added.

"Well, I can't say I blame you for that, Hadrack," Jebido said as he approached. He spit at Bastin's feet. "The problem with most noblemen is they don't usually spend much time worrying about the noble part."

Bastin groaned and sat up, looking dazed as he stared in disbelief at his blood-stained hands. Finally, he glared up at me, his eyes filled with hatred. "I don't know who you are, you bastard, but you are going to pay for this!"

"You're not the first man to tell me that," I said with a shrug. "Probably not the last, either."

"Who are you people?" Sabina asked as the rest of my men stood and joined us.

"Friends," I said vaguely. I glanced toward the corridor doorway. Where was Odiman?

I turned back to the girl just as Baine shouted to me in warning. I'd only taken my eyes off Bastin for a moment, but in that time, he'd managed to rise and draw his sword. Now he was swinging it at me with a look of rage twisting his bloodied face. I instinctively shoved Sabina with my right hand to get her out of harm's way as I lifted my shield. Sabina cried out in surprise and fell backward over the grain sack just as Bastin's sword clanged against my shield. I twisted sideways, absorbing the blow easily as I let the young lord's momentum carry him past me. For good measure, I gave him a hearty kick in the backside as he went past, sending him reeling toward Jebido. My friend stepped nimbly aside and stuck his leg out, sending Bastin sprawling into the dirt. The young lord lay in a cloud of dust for a moment, and then he pounded his fists on the floor in fury before he flipped over onto his back.

Jebido put the tip of his sword to the boy's throat. "I suggest you stay right there, lad," he growled as he looked over at me.

One flick of Jebido's wrist and the problem of Bastin would be over for good, but was it necessary? What Bastin had been about to do to Sabina warranted killing, that couldn't be disputed. But so had what the reeve had done to my sister all those years ago, and look how that had turned out. The death of Lord Corwick's brother—as deserved as it had been—had cost me everything that I had held dear as a boy. I was old enough now to understand that every decision a man makes has unforeseen consequences, even the smallest of them. I was reluctant to make the same mistake today that I'd made then. I glanced at Sabina as she rose and brushed off her dress, looking no worse for her fall. Perhaps the choice of whether Bastin should live or not wasn't mine to make.

"Do you want us to kill this bastard?" I asked the girl. I gestured toward Jebido. "Just say the word."

Sabina fixed her gaze on Bastin, studying him with cold eyes. Finally, she shook her head. "No, he's not worth it."

Bastin laughed at that, the sound harsh and strangled as he turned his head and spat, sending a broken tooth and blood spraying out from his shattered mouth. I shook my head at Jebido and he stepped back as Bastin fumbled for his fallen sword. He finally grasped it and used the weapon to help push himself to his feet, where he swayed almost drunkenly. Finally, Bastin lifted the sword and gestured with his other hand toward me. I glanced at Jebido, who just shrugged. I sighed. I'd never worked so hard at keeping someone alive.

"There's no need for this," I said, impressed despite myself at the boy's resolve. The young lord might be a raping bastard, but he was no coward.

"Oh, there is a need," Bastin grunted. He sniffed, dabbing at the blood running from his nose. "Now fight me, unless you are afraid."

I grinned back at him. I'd tried to be nice. I brought Wolf's Head up so fast that the young nobleman didn't have time to react as I struck at his sword, which flew from his grasp and landed five feet away. Bastin stared at me, his mouth hanging open in surprise, then he stubbornly limped over to the fallen weapon, groaning as he stooped to pick it up.

"Enough!" I snapped in irritation. "Or the next time I'll take your hand too."

Bastin straightened wearily, nodding to me in defeat. I could hear his ragged breathing as he pointed his sword unsteadily at Sabina. "Your mother is dead, bitch!" he rasped. Sabina's face turned pale as Bastin smiled at her, revealing a line of broken teeth and torn lips. He spat blood toward the girl, then turned to me and spread his arms. "I know when I'm overmatched. I yield."

I lowered my sword just as Bastin shouted something unintelligible and threw his weapon at me. I instinctively ducked as the sword spun wildly over my head and then clattered off one of the columns. Bastin was already running for the doors.

"Baine!" I grunted in annoyance. I pointed after the fleeing man. "Stop him, but don't kill the fool."

My friend nodded and nocked an arrow to his bow, barely pausing to aim before he loosed the shaft. Bastin cried out as the bolt pierced his upper thigh and he wobbled, almost falling, but somehow he managed to stay on his feet.

"Baine?" I grunted, glaring at him as Bastin limped painfully toward the doors. "Are you losing your touch?"

Baine grimaced and nocked another arrow. This time the shaft caught Bastin in the shoulder and he staggered and pitched forward. The young nobleman crashed heavily into the granary's double doors, bursting them open as he collapsed face down on the ground in a cloud of dust. A chicken that had been scratching at the dirt outside squawked in surprise and hopped into the air, flapping its wings in fright before landing clumsily and running away, clucking angrily.

Two soldiers standing across the street talking to a woman with a basket on her hip turned to stare in amazement at Bastin as he tried to push himself to his feet. The young nobleman saw the soldiers and called out to them as they ran toward the granary. One of the men knelt by Bastin's side, and I saw his face register his surprise when he saw the arrows. He leaned down as Bastin said something to him, then his head shot up in alarm. He peered into the granary, where we stood in the shadows while his companion shouted for help. A moment later, the watchtower bells began to ring.

"Damn," Jebido said, his face turning grim.

I glanced at the sober faces of my men. "It looks like things are about to get interesting."

3: The Granary

In less than the time that it takes to tell about it, the street outside the granary began to fill with soldiers. Baine and Tyris raised their bows to take down the two men who were half-dragging, half-carrying Bastin to safety, but I stopped them with a wave of my hand.

"Let them go," I said in resignation. "There will be blood spilled soon enough as it is." I turned to Sabina. "You had better hide somewhere until this is over."

"Why should I hide?" Sabina demanded, her eyes flashing. "I've done nothing wrong."

Jebido chuckled. "That's true enough, little lady. But that won't matter much if you are dead. Hadrack is right. If you try to walk out of here now, they will kill you."

Sabina lifted her chin in defiance and I sighed inwardly, beginning to regret my decision to let Bastin live. It seemed my fate was always to make the wrong choices and be saddled with stubborn women and stubborn horses.

"Don't be stupid," I said to Sabina harshly, trying to knock that stubbornness from her with cold fact. "After what just happened, do you think that bastard is going to welcome you with open arms? Trust me, a man like that won't forget that he didn't get what he wanted."

"He wouldn't dare do anything," Sabina said.

I could see a hint of uncertainty on her face despite her brave words. I glanced at Jebido, knowing he would have the words to convince her.

"Yes, he would," Jebido said, his face serious now. He gestured toward the street filling with soldiers. "Do any of those men out there answer directly to him?"

Sabina hesitated, then she nodded reluctantly. "Yes, I think so."

"Then trust me. The moment you walk out that door, you will get an arrow through your heart. There will be apologies for it later, of course. An accident in the heat of battle, they will say. But that won't do you much good, now will it?"

I could see Sabina thinking it over as the soldiers outside formed into a shield wall three ranks deep near the doors. I was surprised they hadn't rushed in, but assumed they had orders to wait in hopes the girl might come out.

"We better fall back to the tunnel while we still can," Jebido muttered as he ran his eyes over the granary. "There's too much space in here to handle them all at once."

"If we go back now, they will block the door and we'll never get through again," I said bitterly.

"At least we'll be alive," Niko muttered under his breath. I glanced at him crossly. "My lord," he added, coloring slightly.

Jebido and Niko were both right, of course. There were at least thirty men out there and probably more coming. I knew going back now would be the smart thing to do, even though it would probably mean losing the only way into the town. But a part of me was loath to give up an advantage like this one, as my gut told me Odiman just needed a little more time. Besides, I'd never been a man who liked to run. Horses and women weren't the only ones who could be stubborn, I thought with a shake of my head.

"This is what we are going to do," I said, coming to a decision. "While they wring their hands working up the courage to come in here, we'll build a wall of sacks on both sides of the columns near the back. That will force the bastards to come at us right down the middle. We should be able to hold them there until Odiman gets here."

Jebido looked at the grain sacks critically. "That's going to be bloody and nasty," he warned. "And I doubt we can last for long that way."

"We won't need to," I said as I took hold of a heavy sack of barley and began dragging it across the floor. I glanced at Jebido and grinned. "Besides, bloody and nasty has a certain appeal to it, don't you think?"

It took the five of us only a few minutes to move a fair amount of the grain sacks into the center aisle, where we stacked them against the existing bags on each side. Sabina stood in one of the stalls out of the way and watched us sullenly as we hurried to angle both walls toward where I intended to meet the enemy. I made sure to leave a gap between the two barriers large enough for only three men to stand side by side.

Bastin must have finally decided that Sabina wasn't coming out, for the soldiers began to advance toward the doors in a slow shuffle, walking shoulder to shoulder with their shields locked. I could hear many of them calling encouragement to each other and laughing, sounding very cocky and sure of themselves. I grinned, knowing that if all went well, that would quickly change.

I studied our defenses, and my grin slowly faltered. The improvised wall we'd built was four bags deep and just over my waist in height. Would it be enough? I wondered, starting to second guess myself. I would have liked the wall higher and wider, of course, but in truth, I hadn't expected we would be given as much time to prepare as we'd had. The wall would have to do. Now it would be left up to our blades and the skill of Baine and Tyris to hold them until Odiman arrived.

I motioned to the stalls behind me. "Baine, Tyris, one to each side," I said. "Wait for my signal and make every shaft count. Whatever happens, don't let any of those bastards flank us. Jebido, I want you on my left. Niko, you take my right." I took out my Pair Stone and kissed the smooth surface. "May The Mother watch over you all."

"You're Sun worshipers!" Sabina said, looking at me as if I were a horse turd that she'd just wiped off one of her shoes. "I knew there was something wrong about you."

"Sorry to disappoint you," I growled at her in annoyance. "I suggest you get your head down and stay put. Things are about to get bloody."

The enemy soldiers passed through the doors and were less than thirty paces away, advancing with a steady clomp, clomp of booted feet. Most carried square, steel-rimmed shields and wore long mail shirts covered by red surcoats with a roaring bear's emblem on their chests. They began taunting us and banging their weapons against their shields. I felt my pulse begin to quicken. There is no sound quite like the ring of a steel blade striking against a shield as men bent on your destruction bear down on you. It's both intimidating and intoxicating at the same time.

Most men fear the fury and madness of a shield wall. Some will soil themselves, heave up bile as they wait, or stand shaking as hot piss rolls down their boots. Jebido said to me once that a shield wall is as close to the horrors of The Father's inferno as a man can get in this world, but I have to say, I've never agreed with him about that. I have always rather enjoyed it.

I held Wolf's Head tighter, feeling the comfort of the leather grip in my hand as I fought the urge to hurl my body forward and take the fight to the enemy. I glanced sideways at Jebido, knowing that there was no man I would rather stand shoulder to shoulder with than him. We'd been through so much together, and as always, I was grateful that The Mother had put him and Baine in that wagon with me. Jebido grinned when he saw my eyes on him, clearly reading my thoughts as he pushed his helmet down firmly on his head. I smiled back and took a deep breath, certain that I could smell the hot blood coursing through the veins of the men advancing on us. In another moment, I knew that blood would be spilled in the dirt at our feet.

The soldiers finally reached a point roughly ten paces away from where we waited. I glanced at Baine and my friend nodded in understanding, his face dark with purpose as he stepped out from behind the column, his bow raised. Baine's bowstring thrummed, hurtling a spinning shaft into the right eye of a hulking brute of a man in the front row. The man sagged and dropped without a sound even as Baine nocked a second arrow and sent it flying after the first. I could hear Tyris' bow humming to my right as another man twisted and fell with a cry.

I waved Wolf's Head at the approaching men. "Come meet your deaths, you ugly turd suckers!" I screamed.

My challenge seemed to break the disciplined hold on the soldiers. They began to surge forward, cursing as they became entangled with one another as they quickly ran out of room. Some of the attackers along the edges tried to leap over our sack wall and outflank us, which I had been expecting. But, by leaving the shield wall's protection, it left them vulnerable to arrows, and Tyris and Baine quickly brought them down.

A short man with a crooked eye wearing a lopsided leather helmet reached me first. He bellowed, bashing his sword against my shield with fierce, single-minded determination over and over again. I stayed hunched over and let my shield absorb the blows, waiting, then I cracked Wolf's Head hard against his ankle when he paused to take a breath. The man screamed, automatically reaching for his injured foot as I swept the edge of my shield up into his face. He fell backward, spurting blood, only to be replaced by another man who hissed and spat curses at me. Jebido stabbed past my attacker's shield without hesitating, ripping through his mail. The soldier's curses turned into a whimper as he folded limply to his knees in front of me. I snarled down at him, then kicked him hard in the face, knocking the dying man back into the second rank behind him.

After that, it became a more cautious, strategic battle of cursing, sweating men crammed into a tight space, hacking and stabbing at each others' shields, waiting for that momentary opening that could seal a man's fate. I could smell the foul stink of sweat and fear all around me and the sweet, coppery odor of freshly spilled blood as it soaked into the dirt floor beneath my boots.

The soldiers had quickly given up trying to get over the sacks to get around us after seeing how deadly Tyris and Baine could be. Instead, they surged forward like a battering ram in a tight wedge formation, trying to push us back from our wall with their combined weight. We were holding them for the time being, but I was tiring quickly, as were my men. Niko suddenly dropped to one knee beside me with a surprised sounding grunt. I thought we'd lost him, but then he forced himself to his feet and returned to the fight. I noticed a wet gash along his left side, but there wasn't time to worry about it as an ugly bastard with missing teeth and dented armor arrogantly pushed himself to the front of the wedge.

He pointed a war hammer at me. "Enough!" he shouted. "You and me right now to settle this."

The man was big and stupid looking, so I grinned mockingly at him and nodded my acceptance. We had just gained some time and some much-needed rest for my men. My opponent smashed his shield against his chest, working up his courage, then he ran toward me, swinging for my head. The move was quick and powerful, but unimaginative and precisely what I'd expected. I automatically lifted my shield to counter him as I started to cut Wolf's Head toward his midriff. I saw the ugly soldier's face light up in triumph, and I realized with a sinking feeling that I had just made a mistake. He wasn't as stupid as I had thought.

The soldier broke off his attack and whirled with breathtaking speed, ramming his shield viciously into the armpit of my upraised arm as he kicked out at my exposed shin. I winced as the steel reinforced rim bit deep into my flesh, feeling the entire length of my arm go numb as I tried to twist my leg out of the way. I managed to dodge most of the force of the kick, though there was still enough strength left in it to stagger me. I had to lower Wolf's Head to maintain my balance, and with a dead shield arm, I couldn't block the killing blow that I knew was coming. I did the only thing that I could think of and I lunged forward under his downward swing, catching the bastard in the face with the crest of my helmet. I felt the soldier's nose collapse beneath my metal helm and he squealed, falling back as he pawed at his face. I planted both my feet firmly in the dirt and swept Wolf's Head up, cutting the man's jugular as blood sprayed over me in a wide arc before he fell.

"Come on!" I screamed, as the rest of the soldiers hesitated and unconsciously backed away from me. My face and armor were drenched in blood and I could feel the madness of battle on me. I would have charged all of them right then and there if Jebido hadn't physically held me back. "Is that the best you can do?" I shouted. I shrugged Jebido off and spit on the man I'd just killed. Then I laughed in contempt. "Are you men, or are you babes still suckling at your mothers' withered tits?"

Bodies lay strewn all around our make-shift wall, helping in their own way to add to it as Lord Branton's soldiers stood watching us in silence. There were no shouts of confidence or laughter coming from them now, only the sounds of ragged breathing whistling through their teeth. I laughed again as the soldier who had inherited the point of the wedge slowly shifted away to face Niko instead of me, dropping his eyes as another reluctantly took his place.

"You!" I said, pointing to the new man with my sword. I could see that he was more boy than man despite his size and mail, with barely enough whiskers on his chin to call it a beard. I had known women with more hair on their chins. The boy stared at me over his shield with wide, frightened eyes. I could see that he was visibly shaking. "The pain will be horrible," I promised him in a deep growl. "Whatever you have heard, I promise you the pain will be a hundred times worse than that. I'll make sure of it."

The boy shuddered as the soldiers around him began to bang their shields unenthusiastically, working up the courage to advance. I saw the boy turn his shield just a fraction, opening himself up. I smiled grimly, knowing what was about to happen. Tyris' bow instantly thrummed from my right and an arrow appeared in the boy's neck just below his left ear. He gagged, his eyes widening in surprise as he clawed at the shaft before he fell face down on top of the bodies at his feet. Then the others charged.

"We can do this!" I shouted as the three of us braced for the impact. "These whoresons are one scratch away from running!"

Jebido, Niko, and I stood shoulder to shoulder in the gap with our shields overlapping as the wedge crashed into us full force. It was agony for me to keep my shield arm up, but I just ground my teeth and absorbed the pain. To lower it now meant certain death for all of us. My shield was vibrating on my arm as hungry weapons searched for a way past it while my boots began to slip on the vomit, blood, and shit-caked floor. I cursed as the three of us were slowly being pushed backward and I leaned forward, bent almost double as I dug my boots in, trying to gain traction. I could hear Jebido and Niko grunting in effort on each side of me as they fought to hold on. I knew in another moment the enemy would be inside our make-shift walls—when that happened, it would be over.

"Hadrack!" Jebido gasped with his sweat-covered face bare inches away from mine. "We've got company!"

I took a quick peek over the heads of our adversaries and I groaned. More men were running into the granary. There is only so far stubbornness and bravado can take you in this world, I realized. It was time for us to retreat. I opened my mouth to order us back to the tunnel just as I heard the clatter of armor and weapons coming from behind me. I took a glance over my shoulder and grinned in triumph as Odiman and his men appeared through the gloom.

"It's about time!" Niko grunted between clenched teeth as he blindly stabbed over his shield. An answering blade came back, probing for vulnerable flesh. "No you don't, you bastard," Niko said as he chopped the sword away.

"I hear you washerwomen need some help!" Odiman shouted. He waved to his men and pointed at the soldiers. "Kill the bastards! Kill them all!"

Odiman dashed forward and leaped onto our wall, balancing himself on the sacks of grain as he hacked down at the pressing bodies. More men continued to pour through the hidden doorway, swarming over the bags on either side of us as Lord Branton's soldiers began to fall back in disarray.

"Enough," I said as Niko started to follow. I put my hand on his shoulder and glanced at Jebido. "Take a moment, you two. Let Odiman handle this. You've earned it."

Niko lowered his sword and shield with a weary nod. "Oh sure," he said. "The bastard shows up now just when we were getting the upper hand." He winced as he gingerly probed at his wound. "I'm sure he'll take all the glory afterward, too."

"He can have it," I replied. "The sooner we take this town and find Rorian, the sooner we can go home. That's all I care about."

Jebido sheathed his sword and leaned over with his hands on his hips, breathing heavily. He looked up at me after a moment. "A shield wall is a young man's game, Hadrack. Please remember that the next time you ask me to stand with you."

"Nonsense!" I said. "You were as fearsome as I've ever seen you."

Jebido snorted, waving a hand at me as I turned to watch the battle unfolding along the granary aisle. Lord Branton's soldiers had fallen back initially from surprise, but now they had regrouped and were pressing Odiman and his men, giving as good as they were getting. More reinforcements were joining them from the street, but more of our men were also coming from the tunnel. I could see men wielding pitchforks and hoes in amongst the enemy soldiers now, and I knew that some of the townsfolk had joined in the fight as well. The battle for Springlight would be won or lost right here, I thought grimly.

"My lord," Niko said, nodding toward the tunnel door. "Putt and Sim are here."

I turned. "What news of Malo?" I asked as my men joined us.

"Beating the bushes for Rorian like a man who has just lost his last Jorq," Putt said. "So far, there's no sign of him or anyone else."

I whistled for Baine and Tyris to join us, then frowned as I saw Sabina's pale face peek out from behind a sack of grain in one of the stalls. I'd actually forgotten about her. I debated going to talk to her just as sudden shouts rose from behind me. Three of Odiman's men were pushing their way out of the hidden doorway as they stumbled weakly into the granary. The men collapsed to the floor on their hands and knees, coughing and gagging, while behind them, I could see thick black smoke pouring out from the top of the door.

I felt a jolt of fear surge through me as long fingers of crackling fire poked through the smoke, licking hungrily at the wooden doorframe. I could hear screaming coming from deeper inside the corridor just as the building's back wall suddenly shuddered, shaking the floor beneath my feet. The roof of the passage caved in with a boom, cutting off the screams and sending dust and debris hurtling our way. Putt cursed loudly in surprise as a chunk of wood struck his helmet with a clang. I shouted for my men to fall back as fire erupted from the entrance in a hungry ball, enveloping the soldiers kneeling there before sweeping upward along the planks. I winced at the screams coming from the burning men as the entire back wall erupted in flames that surged impossibly fast toward the ceiling.

"We have to move!" I shouted, using my shield to ward off the heat. "Everyone out now!"

The granary was quickly filling with smoke, but both sides battling near the doors seemed utterly oblivious to the danger as the flames rapidly reached the crossbeams and started to creep toward the support columns. I knew we didn't have much time before the granary came crashing down on all our heads.

I hurried over to Sabina and grabbed her hand, dragging her after me as I focused on the sunlight coming in through the doors. Thick black smoke was rolling along the ceiling and then curling downward menacingly like the fingers of hungry spirits. I could see Odiman cursing and fighting within a confusing swirl of shields and swords ahead of me. I shouted to him in warning, but my words were lost in the noise of the battle.

I finally gave up on the House Agent and ran for the right wall of the granary, where I could see a small gap had opened up in the ranks of fighting men. I glanced over my shoulder to see Jebido five steps behind Sabina and me before we were enveloped in a thick blanket of smoke. The light was gone instantly, with nothing left to guide us through the darkness but terrified screams and the sounds of the roaring flames. I clutched Sabina's hand tightly, shuffling forward like a blind man and swinging my shield in front of me as I searched for a way out. My eyes were burning as if a thousand tiny knives were being thrust into them all at once, and finally, unable to take it anymore, I forced my eyelids closed. I'd have to trust in my other senses to get us through.

I made it another few feet before my lungs started to feel as though they were about to explode inside my chest. I began to cough uncontrollably, and I could hear Sabina coughing hoarsely beside me. I gripped her hand tighter, determined not to let her go just as my shield banged into someone in front of me. I sensed whoever it was swing at me and I raised my shield without thinking, feeling the other man's weapon clang against the metal rim. I dropped to my knees, pulling Sabina down as well, surprised that there wasn't as much smoke near the floor. I lowered myself down onto my stomach, dragging Sabina along with me. The air was still foul here, but preferable to higher up. I desperately drew air into my tortured lungs as my attacker continued to swing his sword wildly above me. I couldn't see anything but his boots, but I could see the smoke swirling above my head with every swing as he searched for me in panic. I waited until his boots had turned away from me, then I drew Wolf's Head and stabbed upward. The man screamed and I felt him shudder on my blade, then he fell heavily to the floor less than two feet away from me. I hadn't had time to worry whether I was fighting friend or foe, and I was greatly relieved to see that the dead man wore Lord Branton's bear emblem on his chest.

 I turned to Sabina, who was trembling uncontrollably with her body pressed tightly against mine. "Are you all right?" I managed to say hoarsely out of my ravaged throat. She looked up at me and nodded weakly. I heard Jebido calling out my name from somewhere within the dense smoke. "Here!" I croaked. I cleared my throat and spat, then tried again. "Jebido, over here! Get down! The air is better near the floor!" I waited for Jebido and the others to crawl to us and I tapped each one on the helmet as I counted. Everyone had survived. They were covered in soot, with the odd burn here and there, but other than that, seemed intact. I coughed and swept smoke from my face, realizing even at floor level that it was getting harder to see and breathe now. I pointed ahead into the wall of smoke. "I think the doors are that way somewhere. Stay low and follow me."

 I started to crawl forward, having to make my way over twisted, bloody bodies that lay scattered on the floor. I winced as I touched a dead man's mail-covered arm, feeling the searing heat of the metal burning my flesh. I could hear men screaming in panic around me, and twice someone stepped on me and then hurried away. The smoke was thick and the heat intense as I pressed my face into the cooler dirt, fighting to breathe while I pulled Sabina along behind me.

Finally, my helmet banged into a solid obstruction in front of me and I paused, gasping as I looked up. Above me, the smoke wall chose that moment to part for just a moment and I felt my heart sink. We had reached the granary doors, but they were closed! I could hear men pounding with their weapons on the doors and I ground my teeth in frustration. The townspeople had barricaded the doors, I realized, willing to sacrifice their own men in a bid to save the town.

In truth, I can't say I blamed them for it, from a strategic point of view. Killing a few of their men to destroy both the invaders and the tunnel made sound tactical sense. Had I been them, I probably would have done the same thing too.

"Damn!" Jebido said as he crawled up beside Sabina and me and took in the situation. "Now what?"

I didn't have time to reply as a terrible screeching sound came from above us. "Cover your heads!" I shouted in warning.

I lifted my shield to protect Sabina, groaning at the pain in my shoulder as a charred, burning hunk of wood as long as my arm collided against the shield and then bounced off. Smaller burning pieces fell all around and on top of us, with another large chunk careening off my helmet, stunning me. A great gaping hole had been ripped open in the ceiling above us, with massive gouts of flames instantly shooting upward, feeding on the fresh air from outside. The smoke around me seemed to be drawn upward as well, and I could make out objects again.

I pulled Sabina to her feet just as a crossbeam attached to a column at the back of the granary broke away and crashed to the floor. The column wobbled as a portion of the roof above it collapsed, then slowly tipped over, burning fiercely as it dropped to the ground. Sabina clung on to me desperately as the floor beneath our feet shuddered, while dust and debris swept down the length of the granary, mixing with the smoke and clogging my already overwhelmed senses. I could hear a strange ringing in my ears, amplified by the terrified howls of the men around me trying to break down the doors. I shook my head, trying to clear the ringing sound as I stooped down to help a stunned-looking Jebido to his feet.

"Are you all right?" I asked, afraid to let him go.

Jebido's cracked and soot-covered lips stretched obscenely in an attempt at a smile. "Still with you, Hadrack," he rasped. The bridge of his nose was scraped raw and burnt red at the hooked tip. He glanced at the barricaded doors. "What do we do now?"

I hesitated as my men all stared at me in expectation. I didn't have the heart to tell them that I had no idea, and instead, I looked around at the burning walls that boxed us in. Whatever I decided, I knew it would have to be soon before the fire ate through the main supports and the building collapsed on top of us. Soldiers from both sides were using their swords, axes, and war-hammers to pound at the doors, but I could see through the cracks that the townspeople had nailed thick planks over them. I knew that it was futile.

Another column fell behind us, rippling fire along its length before slamming into the next column in line. The fallen pillar shattered into six or seven charred pieces from the impact as the one still standing wobbled unsteadily. Several of the crossbeams attached to the standing column broke off and fell, leaving only one still clinging on stubbornly. I knew that pillar wouldn't stay upright for long and I suddenly had an idea.

"There!" I cried, pointing at the column.

Baine wiped the sweat from his eyes and looked behind us. "There what, Hadrack?" he asked.

"You'll see!" I shouted. "Follow me!"

I started to head back the way we'd come and Jebido grabbed my arm, stopping me. "Are you insane!? We'll die if we go back there."

"We'll die if we stay here too!" I hollered back in his ear. I looked him in the eye. "Trust me!"

Then I turned and started to run, using my shield to deflect the heat as I dodged around the pockets of enraged flames that reached out for me. I didn't bother to look back over my shoulder to see if the others were coming. I knew they would be. I reached the weakened column and tore at my singed cloak, winding strips of the cloth around my hands. Then I positioned myself on the side of the massive pillar facing away from the burning outer wall and started to push.

"I swear, boy!" I heard Jebido grunt as he joined me and put his shoulder to the pillar. "If this works, I'm going to give you the biggest, wettest kiss of your life!"

"Don't threaten me or I'll stop!" I promised, hissing the words out from between my teeth as I dug my shoulder into the wood and pushed.

There was only enough space for four men to work effectively, so Sabina, Baine, Niko, and Tyris stood behind Putt, Sim, Jebido, and me and pushed against our backs. We heaved, gasping as burning planks fell all around us, but though the crossbeam wobbled and the column swayed back and forth slightly, it wouldn't fall.

"Do I have to save your asses for a second time today?" I heard someone holler from behind me.

I glanced over my shoulder as Odiman appeared through the swirling smoke with more men running behind him. I saw some of the men were wearing red surcoats, but I barely gave it a second thought. Everyone inside the granary had one common goal now, survival, and there were no enemies here anymore. The entire left side of Odiman's face was burnt away, leaving only raw, melted skin hanging along his jawline where once a magnificent beard had been. He grinned at me painfully and pushed Sabina out of the way, then snapped at the men, forming them quickly into ranks of four. Odiman and Sabina joined the last rank as each man put his hands on the man's back in front of him.

"We're ready, Hadrack!" Odiman shouted.

"All right!" I called. I pointed up at the crossbeam keeping the column in place. "Keep your eyes on that! If it falls on you, it'll crush you!" I pressed my shoulder against the wood again. "Heave!" I shouted. We leaned forward as one solid unit, and I could feel my boots immediately starting to slide on the ashes that blanketed the floor like black snow. Putt turned one of his feet sideways behind me and jammed it against the back of my heels, helping to support me. I could hear voices crying out, many of them pleading with The Mother or The Father for help, but the First Pair weren't listening, and the crossbeam held fast. "Hold!" I finally shouted in defeat, lifting my hand.

I took in great gulps of foul air, knowing everyone needed a short rest before we tried again. A section of the roof gave out near the sealed entrance and I turned in dismay, expecting the granary to collapse along with it, but somehow the building held. I could hear horrible screams of agony rising over the roar of the flames and I knew that unless we wanted to join those poor souls, the pillar had to fall now.

Jebido pressed his lips to my ear. "We need to rock it, Hadrack," he said. I looked at him in confusion. "Back and forth," Jebido explained, using his hand to show me. "If we get some friction up there, it might break the crossbeam free."

"Friction?" I looked up at the burning wood and leaned close to him. "But it's already on fire, Jebido! How much friction does it need?"

Jebido just shrugged helplessly at me and we put our shoulders to the column again. "All right!" I called out over my shoulder. "Give me everything you have this time! Then hold for a count of three, then push again. Do that until I say stop! Now heave!" We leaned into the wood again and I could feel the column slowly shifting forward. We pushed and then eased up, and pushed and eased up again, then did it a third time. "Enough!" I finally cried, looking up.

Was there a wider gap between the crossbeam and the pillar now than before? I could see orange and blue flames dancing weakly all along the crossbeam's length, but though the wood was stained black and smoking, it seemed to be resisting the fire somehow. Just our luck that we had to get the only beam in the entire building that wouldn't burn, I thought with a curse. A large section of the roof around the column suddenly shifted and then caved in, dropping burning planks and shingles on our heads. I heard men screaming from behind me and I felt something smack hard against my shoulder. I staggered and dropped to one knee.

"I've got you," Jebido said, helping me to my feet.

I nodded my thanks to him and looked up. A fresh, jagged hole in the ceiling had appeared, revealing clear blue sky above us with black smoke venting out of it in a huge plume. I realized the pillar was free from its upper moorings now except for the stubborn grip of our crossbeam. I glared upward. I'd never hated anything as much as that ugly piece of wood.

"Your day is done, you bastard!" I promised with a grunt. I glanced behind me at the men's darkened, haunted faces, pausing as my eyes met Sabina's. She looked small and frail, and very frightened, I thought, but there was also fierce determination on her face as well. I gave her a brief smile of encouragement, then I turned and braced my shoulder against the wood again. This time, I told myself, this time, it goes down. "Ready?" I called. I heard the creak of armor as men took up positions behind me and I felt Putt's strong hands once again on my back. "Don't stop, no matter what!" I cried as I threw myself forward. I could feel the column shifting in protest on its base beneath our combined weight and my heart leaped. "More!" I screamed. "Give me more! Keep pushing!"

Something cracked loudly above us. I looked up as the crossbeam pulled away from the column until finally, only a small, decorative wooden arch the builders had used to secure it to the pillar was left holding on. I could see the arch vibrating under the strain, and then, finally, it snapped in half. The end of the crossbeam was at least three feet wide, and now that it was free, it dropped straight down so fast that I didn't have time to react. I felt the rush of air as the beam whistled past my face, then it crashed into the dirt, tearing a deep gash into the floor before finally snapping in two. Behind me, I could hear the men cheering hoarsely.

"Keep pushing, you whoresons!" I snarled. "We're not done yet!"

I jammed my shoulder against the pillar, feeling the mass resisting us as it teetered back and forth on the wooden base. Jebido was gasping for air beside me as I blinked away hot tears brought on from the smoke and acrid stench rising off the charred wood an inch from my face. I shook my head, trying to clear my vision, then looked up as the column groaned like a wounded animal. For one heart-stopping moment, I was positive that it was going to fall on us as the column seemed to hang suspended at an angle, with the fate of all our lives hanging in the balance as well. I looked away and closed my eyes, praying to The Mother to help us. Finally, I felt the pillar slowly settle back onto the base before it started to tip steeply the other way.

"Let's put this bitch down!" I screamed, knowing that if it rocked back again, we were finished. "Give me everything you have if you want to live!"

I could feel the column still resisting, almost as though toying with us, then we seemed to reach a critical point in its balance and a sharp snap sounded from the base. The pillar sagged, the fight finally gone as it slowly toppled toward the raging inferno that covered the far wall. I held my breath as the falling pillar hit the support beam on the wall, hoping the weight and momentum would be enough to break through. If it wasn't, we were all dead.

The support beam wasn't as stubborn as the crossbeam had been, however, and the pillar smashed past easily, then cut through the burning planking like a hot knife slicing through sheep lard. The column finally came to rest with a loud boom on top of the piled sacks as dust, grain, and debris flew into the air. A jagged, six-foot gap appeared in the sheet of flames as the wall disintegrated, letting in bright, beautiful sunshine that pierced the heavy swirling smoke. Men began cheering all around me as they scrambled to get over the grain sacks and escape. I pushed Jebido ahead of me toward the opening as Sabina and Odiman appeared through the smoke.

"Malo was right about you," Odiman said out of the side of his ravaged mouth as he and I helped Sabina down through the gap in the wall.

"How so," I grunted, not caring in the least.

"He said you're a pig-headed bastard with a mean streak," Odiman said as he paused to look at me. "He also said there's no man he would rather have by his side in a fight."

Odiman grinned lopsided at me, then he turned and leaped to the ground. I jumped down right after him, landing heavily and falling to one knee.

"You beautiful bastard!" Jebido cried as he dragged me to my feet and drew me away from the burning building. Finally, when we were a safe distance from the heat and flames, he hugged me to his chest. "We did it!"

"I swear, Jebido," I growled in his ear, swaying with exhaustion. "If you try to kiss me, I'll put you on your ass."

4: The Wolf and The Stag

I remember the summer that I turned six years old being hot and dry. There had been no rain for several months that year, leaving most of Corwick's crops wilting limply in the fields. We were known as the Kingdom of the Flins then, as that had been several years before the Ganders conquered us and we became Southern Ganderland. I recall my parents speaking together in whispers after chores each night, worried about something called taxes and the lord's wrath, should the crops fail. I was too young to understand their fears, of course, and my memories of that time have mostly faded, though I do believe rain came midway through the season, salvaging some of the yield.

One clear memory I do have of that hot summer is Bloomwood, the sprawling forest that lay to the north of Corwick. Bloomwood was designated a Royal Forest, but that didn't stop poachers from hunting there, even though the penalty for it was hanging if the foresters caught them. For some reason that he'd never explained, my father was allowed to hunt in the forest as much as he wanted. A fact that seemed entirely natural to me at the time. At six, I considered my father to be the most important man in the world, and I couldn't imagine anyone telling him that he couldn't do something.

That summer, with work in the cracked and parched fields all but a waste of time, my father decided to take me and my older brother, Lallo, to Bloomwood to search for the legendary red deer stag known as The Big Hart. This was to be my first hunt, and I remember being so excited that I barely slept the night before. My mother had been horrified at the idea, of course, as all mothers would be, but my father had assured her I would be safe with him and Lallo to watch over me. The stag we were after was said to be twice as big as usual, with a moss-covered rack as long and as tall as a man. Some claimed that The Big Hart had lived in the wilds of Bloomwood for more than a hundred years or more. I don't know if that part of the story is true or not, but I do know that on our second morning, a frightening lightning storm appeared that set the forest ablaze for miles around. My father had us retreat to the rock-strewn highlands to the east, where there were few trees and sparse grass, so we were relatively safe there from the raging flames.

The world burned all around us that morning, as a hot wind blowing from the south helped to stoke the fire's fury. By midday, the sky was so dark with black smoke that it could easily have been mistaken for the middle of a moonless night, if not for the eerie glow given off by the blaze. I can still hear the birds' shrill calls as they flapped away in panic by the thousands and see all manner of wildlife fleeing for their lives. At one point, a large silver wolf and a giant red stag appeared, running side by side along a boiling stream with the flames nipping at their haunches. The wolf and stag disappeared quickly from our view within the smoke, and we never did know what became of them. Did the three of us actually see The Big Hart that day? I have always liked to think that we had.

I was still young and naive enough back then to ask my father why the wolf hadn't just killed and eaten the stag. He'd chuckled and told me that even the worst of enemies would set aside their differences to escape a common foe. They will do this, he'd said, simply because their survival instinct outweighs everything else—even hunger. But, once the danger has passed, the wolf, still being a wolf, will very quickly revert to its true self and will try to kill the deer. While the stag, being a stag, will do the only thing that it can and try to flee.

That lesson from long ago weighed on me heavily as I let my gaze rove over the blackened, coughing survivors who had escaped the granary. Most lay sprawled out on a well-manicured lawn, with a few standing or sitting hunched over with their helmets off, hacking up black slime. Not long ago, these very same men had been deadly enemies, but, just like the wolf and the stag from years ago, they had set aside their hostility and worked together in a desperate bid to survive. I wondered how long that spirit of cooperation and camaraderie would continue to last and, for that matter, who would be the wolf and who the stag when it finally ended?

    A low wall of cut stone partially blocked my view of the street, but I could hear shouts coming from there and see townspeople working frantically to douse the roofs and walls of the surrounding buildings with buckets of water. I looked up at the scorched outer wall high above me where it joined the granary, but the ramparts were free of guards. It appeared that our escape had gone unnoticed, at least for the time being. Burning the granary and losing their seed stock along with it must have been a tough choice for the townspeople to make, I knew. Not to mention the danger of losing other buildings or even the entire town itself if things got out of control. So far, the gamble seemed to be working, as the fire appeared to be contained to just the granary alone.

    The lush grass of the lawn I stood on followed the low stone wall, finally giving way to a cobblestone pathway fifty feet to the north of me that led to a Holy House built of smooth limestone. The steeply pitched roof of the Holy House was sheathed in heavy, dark red clay tiles, so I guessed with that and its thick walls, the House was probably as impervious to fire as any building could be. That probably explained why no townspeople were working there, which I was grateful for, as we would have been in plain sight of them if they had been.

    I glanced down at Sabina, who lay on her back five feet away from me, staring up at the sky as she fought to draw air into her lungs. Her dress was torn at the shoulder and most of the hem at her ankles had burnt away, revealing soot-encrusted legs. I noticed her scorched leather sandals were barely clinging to her red and peeling feet. My men lay beside Sabina, while Odiman stood near his men, his ravaged face raised to the sky with his eyes closed. A cool breeze was blowing over us, a relief after the searing heat from moments before. I could see the wind toying with the few long strands of beard left clinging to Odiman's chin that the flames had spared.

Combined, the House Agent and I had twelve men between us that had made it out alive. Not even enough to man a full set of oars, I thought grimly, let alone enough to conquer an entire town. I turned sharply as something inside the granary behind me collapsed, then, with a groan of resignation, the building slowly caved in upon itself, sending flames and sparks shooting skyward.

Jebido and I watched the final death throes of the granary together in silence. "We have to move, Hadrack," he finally said as the last column wobbled and then fell. The joy of cheating death from a moment ago was gone from his features now, replaced by a grim seriousness.

"I know," I grunted back. I'd been thinking the same thing.

One townsman and seven soldiers had survived the flames with us. I saw several of them staring at Jebido and me with tired, wary eyes. The townsman was lying on his side and looked to be sleeping or unconscious, while a soldier with a badly singed beard sat beside him, repeatedly coughing into his hand. The soldier hacked and spat, then wiped his hand on his trousers as he glanced briefly over his shoulder at the short wall behind him. I didn't fail to notice that he casually loosened his sword in its scabbard when he turned back. The wolf and the stag will always revert to kind, I thought.

"Any ideas?" I asked.

Jebido nodded. A flap of oozing skin hung off the tip of his nose, but he seemed unaware of it. "We go for one of the gates while we still have surprise on our side."

"That's what I was thinking, too," I said, having come to the same conclusion. If we could get control of one of the gates, the remainder of Odiman's forces outside might notice. But first we had to deal with the enemy right here. I knew one side or the other would eventually become the wolf, and I was determined that it would be us. "This has to be fast," I grunted.

"Yes," Jebido agreed. "And quiet."

I crooked a finger at Baine and Tyris, who still lay on the grass recovering. "We are going to try for the gates," I whispered as they joined us. I frowned at Baine. "Where is your bow?"

"Burned right off my back," Baine said unhappily. His face was blackened with soot and a four-inch cut on his cheek was seeping dark blood. He turned to show me the back of his leather armor, which had been seared clean through. I could see charred, puckered skin running in a line across his back through the tear. "The quiver too."

I glanced at Tyris. "Yours?"

"Still usable, my lord," Tyris answered. The archer's eyes were ringed in black circles like a raccoon.

"Good," I said. I glanced at Baine. "Do you still have those knives of yours," I asked, "or did they burn too?"

The last I'd checked, Baine had at least five knives hidden away on his body somewhere.

My friend slowly grinned. "I have them."

I gestured toward the soldiers. "We'll follow your lead, then."

"Give me whatever gold you have," Baine said.

I frowned. "Why?"

"We need a distraction."

I nodded and, careful to keep it hidden from the town's soldiers, I removed my money bag and slipped it into Baine's hand.

"That's it?"

"You are the one who wanted to stop at that inn," I said in annoyance. "Remember?"

"A fair point," Baine responded, having the grace to at least look slightly embarrassed.

He turned and began walking toward the enemy, jingling the moneybag loudly to get their attention. I saw several of Lord Branton's men lift their heads curiously as Jebido and I casually shifted to their right, pretending to be watching the remnants of the burning granary. Odiman frowned at us, then his scalded face hardened in understanding as he realized what we were doing. He began to circle to the left.

"Gentlemen," Baine said, pausing in the center of the sitting men. He indicated me. "My lord and master is a very wealthy man. He has asked me to reward you for your courage in helping him to escape." Baine held the moneybag up and jingled it again. "This is but a small token of his gratitude. There will be plenty more to follow."

Two of the soldiers stood eagerly, and one even put out a blackened, shaking hand. Baine smiled kindly at the man, repeating his promise of more to follow as he opened the moneybag. He started to move forward, then stopped just out of reach of the soldier's open palm as he turned the moneybag upside down. The coins inside slid out, gleaming in the sunlight as they twirled downward end over end to land in the grass. Both soldiers gasped and immediately fell to their knees, searching for the gold, while the rest of their companions held back in indecision. I glanced at the man with the singed beard, who was looking directly at me and ignoring the fallen money completely. Suspicion lay heavily on his face as he put his hand on the hilt of his sword and started to get to his feet.

No fool this one, I thought just as a knife appeared in each of Baine's hands. I'd seen Baine work with knives before, and I knew what was about to happen. I drew Wolf's Head just as Baine dropped to one knee and threw both weapons at once in opposite directions. One knife caught the man with the singed beard in the throat just as he reached his feet. The other sank to the hilt in the eye of a soldier holding up a coin in triumph. Both men sagged limply and collapsed as Tyris' bow sounded from behind me. A soldier sitting near me screamed as an arrow lodged in his bicep and he began to thrash about in agony. I was on the man in three quick strides, cursing under my breath as he continued to wail like a child who has just been flogged.

"Be quiet," I growled as I landed my full weight on his chest, cutting off his cries.

I'd taken an arrow during battle before, and I have to say, I was a little embarrassed by the man's antics. It doesn't hurt that much. The wounded man looked up at me, shaking his head in pain and terror as he tried to gain enough breath to say something. I didn't give him a chance as I quickly sliced the blade of my sword across his neck, silencing him for good. Jebido was already past me, swinging his sword wildly at a man with his hands up to protect himself. I saw another soldier twist and fall as Baine threw a third knife.

I stood, glowering as I stalked toward a soldier with a severely burned face sitting on the ground in apparent shock. He started to backpedal away from me with one hand while tugging awkwardly at his sword with the other. I hooked my toe under his knee and drew him across the grass to me, then lashed out with my foot, flattening his nose. The soldier collapsed on his back, then tried to push himself weakly away from me with his legs. I twirled Wolf's Head in my hand and stabbed downward through his mail and into his chest as he gagged, choking on his own blood before he died.

I pulled my sword free and stood up, ready for more, then slowly relaxed. All the soldiers were down, and Odiman was striding toward the unconscious townsman with his blade dripping blood. I started to protest, but Odiman either didn't hear me or didn't care. He slammed his sword savagely into the man's back.

"You should have talked to me first before you tried this," Odiman grunted angrily as he tore his sword free from the corpse.

"There wasn't time!" I snapped, annoyed by the man's tone.

We held eyes for a moment, then I looked away, watching Baine retrieving his knives. Now was not the time for a power struggle if we wanted to survive. Baine carefully cleaned his weapons on the grass, while Tyris worked at wiggling his arrows free from the bodies. I glanced again to the street. The attack had gone better than I could have hoped for, and no alarms had sounded as far as I could tell. Our movements had been vicious and quick and had taken only moments. The speed and savagery had even surprised the rest of our men, who were just now getting to their feet, most still looking dazed from the fire and confused by the sudden turn of events.

I glanced at Odiman. "We have to get to one of the gates," I said.

"I'm aware of that," Odiman said sarcastically.

"What about your men out there?" Jebido asked. "Will they come to our aid, or sit on their hands without you to lead them?"

Odiman paused for a heartbeat. His face was blistered red and black, with clear mucus running from the sores. Even the man's eyebrows were gone, I noted, making his already ravaged face seem even more hideous. "They will come," the surly House Agent finally said with a growl. "Malo will see to that."

"Malo is chasing after Rorian," I pointed out. "He might be miles away by now."

Odiman sighed and I could see the anger slowly fading from his eyes. "Then we'll have to kill every one of the bastards ourselves," he said with a grunt. I was surprised to see a faint smile crease his blackened lips. "How do you want to handle this, Hadrack?" he asked.

I took a moment to collect my thoughts. I was sure Odiman was testing me and I was determined to make the right choice. But what was it? I had no idea what could be waiting for us once we reached the streets of the town. Should we march along in a shield wall, or try to bull our way through? A shield wall would be safer if they had archers, but it would also be slower and allow time for the enemy to prepare. I knew men were going to die no matter which choice I made, so I decided that at least with a quick rush, there was a chance some of us might survive.

"I say we go hard and fast," I answered decisively.

Odiman nodded in approval. "A fine choice."

"Which way do we go?" Baine asked, glancing from me to Odiman. "North or south?"

"The southern gate," Odiman said immediately. There was no sign of the anger in him now, only cold, hard reason. I found my opinion of the House Agent going up a notch as he pointed to the north. "The trenches along the northern road are still open. My men can get to us sooner using the southern route."

"There will be an awful lot of the bastards on the walls and gates by the time we get there," Jebido warned.

I smiled wearily at him. "There always are."

Baine nudged me with his elbow. "Hadrack, where is the girl?"

I glanced to where I'd last seen Sabina lying on the grass, but she wasn't there now. I spun around, searching for her. Then I cursed when I saw the top of her red hair moving fast along the other side of the short wall. "Sabina!" I called out. "Wait!"

Sabina turned and looked back at me. Our eyes met briefly over the wall, and then she started to run.

"Damn," Jebido grunted. "So much for catching them by surprise."

"The wolf and the stag," I growled in disgust. I guess I shouldn't have been surprised that Sabina would betray us the first chance she got. But for some reason that I can't explain, I'd started to think of her as being on our side.

"What?" Jebido said.

"Nothing," I muttered. I looked at Odiman. "We have to go now before she alerts them."

Odiman glared around at his men and mine. "If someone falls, you leave them behind. All that matters is taking the gate." He pointed at Tyris. "You stay in the middle and keep your head down. We are going to need your bow again before this day is through."

Odiman and I took the lead while my men and his bunched together in a pack around Tyris behind us. I saw Baine clutching one of the fallen soldier's swords uncomfortably, and he grinned weakly at me. I knew my friend would have given just about anything to have a bow in his hands right about now. We swept around the low stone wall and rushed out onto the street. Feminine screams sounded almost immediately at the sight of us as men, women, and children with slopping buckets of water scurried to get out of our way. Sabina clearly hadn't warned them about us yet. I wondered why not.

Two soldiers in full mail standing together in the street stared at us in amazement as we bore down on them. They seemed unsure of what to do, but Tyris' bow hummed twice in rapid succession before they could decide. Both men fell twisting to the ground, and then we waited as the blond archer broke ranks to retrieve the arrows he'd shot. I ground my teeth in frustration at the delay, but I knew every arrow in Tyris' depleted quiver would be needed now.

The dirt street was wide and straight, cutting through the middle of the town, with narrow cross-streets appearing every fifty paces. Tall houses lined both sides for as far as I could see, most pressed tightly together, helping to block our view of the outer walls and gates. Odiman and I led our men at a fast trot, expecting an attack at any moment. We traveled three blocks without seeing anyone, which surprised me, but as we reached the fourth block, a lone soldier appeared coming out of a three-story building. The man cried out in surprise at the sight of us and started to draw his sword, though what he expected to do against so many armed men, I'll never know. Sim was the closest man to him and he lashed out with his axe, catching the soldier solidly in the stomach. The man screamed and fell backward into the building, disappearing except for one boot that hung over the threshold of the door. Suddenly, the watchtower bells began to clang urgently from the south, followed immediately by answering bells from the north and west. Either Sabina had finally warned them that we were coming, or someone else had.

We made it several more blocks without running into anyone other than a blind man taking a piss in the street, until finally, the houses gave way to a market square. I slowed, then halted, suppressing a curse. There were no fishmongers, vintners, nor butchers selling their wares in the market today, but instead, a densely packed mob of townsfolk stood waiting for us, blocking the exit to the south. There had to be at least fifty of them, I guessed. I could see most held axes, clubs, pitchforks, hoes, or just about anything else imaginable that might kill a man.

A tall, thin man with torn trousers and long black hair tied back stepped forward from the crowd. He had the air of leadership about him as he pointed a club at us. "You have gone far enough," he said. "Drop your weapons."

I heard movement from behind me and I glanced back. More townsmen were coming up the street behind us. Odiman whistled a quick command and the back rank of our men automatically turned to face the new threat.

"Get your rabble out of our way!" Odiman growled, pointing his sword at the thin man. "Or our boots will be walking over your twitching corpses as we pass."

Most of the townsmen seemed agitated and nervous as they clutched their makeshift weapons. I knew that they had a right to be. None wore armor and, other than one skinny fellow holding a rusted sword with a broken tip, had no real weapons to speak of. They did have the numbers on us, however, but we wore mail or leather armor, had shields, and were armed with swords, axes, and a bow. But, more importantly than just that, we were all warriors—men who were well experienced in the art of dealing out death and destruction. I could see that most of those blocking our way were shopkeepers, potters, clothiers, clerks, and, from the looks of one old fellow missing all his teeth near the back, cobblers.

"Where are the soldiers?" I heard Jebido mutter from behind me.

I had been wondering the same thing myself. I glanced at the force milling in the street behind us again, but saw no armor or weapons there either. Why send inexperienced townsmen against an armored foe, when they could have easily sent solders in their place? I thought of Lord Corwick and how he'd used men bound to him by fealty to take Gasterny. The heartless lord had cared nothing for the lives of those men. Was Lord Branton a similar breed of man willing to sacrifice these people just to wear us down first?

The difference here from Gasterny, though, I realized, was these men were not poor farmers dependant upon a lord's generosity to survive. Many of these men had businesses and wealth of their own, so they should have been less willing to sacrifice their lives. That's what soldiers were paid to do. I knew there had to be another explanation.

"This is your last warning," the thin man threatened. "Drop your weapons, or we will kill the lot of you."

Odiman took a step forward. "Go ahead and try," he said with a sneer that twisted his already hideous face even more. "But bear in mind, you stinking farmer, that my blade will be coming for you first." He glanced at a short man in the front row dressed in fine clothing that tried and failed to hide a ponderous belly. "And you will be next, little one. Fat men tend to squeal like pigs when you poke them with a sword."

The small man's face lost its color and he inadvertently took a step backward from the angry House Agent.

"Wait," I said. It had suddenly dawned on me what might be going on here. I moved to stand beside Odiman. "My name is Hadrack," I said to the thin man. "Who are you?"

"Alvar," he replied suspiciously.

Alvar was wearing heavy boots, dirt-encrusted trousers, and a soiled tunic. His hands and fingernails were stained with rich black earth, and I could see heavy calluses on the tips of his fingers and his palms. Odiman had called Alvar a farmer, but I'd known farmers most of my life. Something told me that this man was not one of them. Many towns and castles employed gardeners that understood herbs and plants, with their most important task being to keep the walls clear of ivy and other such things that could be used to scale them. I suspected he was one of these.

"You are the town's gardener, then?" I asked. Alvar grunted in surprise before he slowly nodded. "I thought as much," I said. "An important position to be sure." Beside me, I could feel Odiman becoming impatient. I hurried on, "Do you hear those bells?" I asked, pointing vaguely over the man's shoulder.

"I hear them," Alvar said grimly. "Those are for you."

I grinned. "Are you certain?"

"Hadrack," Odiman said, turning to me in exasperation. "What is this all about? We're wasting time talking to these fools."

I ignored him. "Where are the soldiers, Alvar?" I asked.

The gardener tried to keep his face neutral, but I'd just seen a brief flicker in his eyes. I realized my hunch was correct.

"We don't need them to crush the likes of you," Alvar said, trying to bluster.

"That could be why the soldiers aren't here," I said agreeably. I smiled and took another step forward. "But I think the truth is many of them died in that granary back there, and now the rest can't leave the walls, because those bells aren't really for us."

Odiman glanced at me in surprise. "Malo?" he asked.

"I think so," I said. "He must believe Rorian is still inside the town."

"Rorian?" the gardener said with a frown. "What does that scholar have to do with anything?"

"He's why we are here, you halfwit!" Odiman shouted. "Do you really think we give a priest's withered ball-sack about this cursed place?"

I could hear the townsmen muttering among themselves uncertainly. These men weren't fighters, and I knew all they wanted was to live their lives and be left alone. I decided to offer them that, along with a healthy dose of fear to wash it all down.

"Our men are going to be coming over those walls anytime now," I said. "You know, and we know that there aren't enough soldiers left to stop them." I shook my head sadly. "These are savage, brutal men who have spent the last few days being slaughtered and humiliated by you people. What do you think those men will do once they take the town?" No one answered me, but I could see frightened glances being exchanged. "They are going to burn this place to the ground," I said harshly. I pointed at Odiman. "Men, just like this, are going to come over those walls hungry for blood. They are going to kill every last one of you in ways that you can't even imagine." I paused, letting that thought sink in. "And when they are done with you, they will use and enslave your women and slaughter your children." I snorted and shook my head. "And for what? To protect some murderous scholar that cares nothing for any of you?"

"Lord Branton granted him sanctuary," Alvar said. "We have no choice in the matter."

I could see the gleam of worry in his eyes now. "Do you think those men out there will care?" I asked. "Even if they fail today by some miracle, more are on the way here." I glanced meaningfully at the townsmen. "A thousand more, with siege engines as well that will smash your walls to pieces. Think of what your lives will be like as burning pitch, stones the size of carts, and diseased animal carcasses are rained down on your heads. Is that what you want?"

"What choice is there for us?" Avar asked bitterly. "We must obey our lord."

"Why?" I said bluntly.

Alvar blinked at me, looking startled. "Why?" he repeated in confusion.

"Exactly," I said. "Why must you obey him? Lord Branton will likely not be lord of this town after today. My guess is the man will be lucky to salvage his life, let alone his property. Springlight and all your fates will soon be in the hands of Prince Tyden, the true heir to the throne. If you are smart, you will recognize that and bend a knee to him now before it's too late." I leaned forward, giving them my best wolfish grin. "Our prince can be a most kind and generous ruler," I said. "But he can also be cruel and unforgiving to those he believes has wronged him. You might consider that before you choose your next move."

The townspeople were all gaping at me in astonishment. Even Odiman was looking at me with an expression of wonder on his savaged face.

"You want us to betray our lord?" Alvar asked in disbelief. "Renounce The Father and Prince Tyrale in favor of the Sun and the heretic prince?"

"Yes," I said firmly. "Though I suggest you don't use that term again to describe the True King." I swept a hand behind me. "Join us, and I swear that your lives and the town will be spared."

"I don't...I don't know," Alvar said uncertainly. He turned to the fat man and several others as they conferred, while behind me, I could hear the townspeople there engaged in heated exchanges as they debated my offer. Finally, Alvar turned back to us. "Do you swear that what you say will hold true?"

"Bend your knee and pledge to serve the True King, and you have my word that no harm will come to any of you or this place," I said.

Odiman cleared his throat beside me. I could see just a hint of amusement twisting his peeled lips. "I am a House Agent," he added. "As such, I have the authority to act in the name of both the House and the True King. Kneel and say your words, and you have both of our solemn vows that no harm will come to you or your town."

The townspeople hesitated for a moment longer, then one by one, they slowly knelt.

5: The Pursuit

As it turned out, Lord Branton was a mean-spirited, arrogant man in his fifties that I disliked from the very moment that I set eyes on him. Even after we'd taken the town with the help of Alvar and the others, he had acted as though it were he who was still in charge and not us. The man never stopped barking orders, and his sharp tongue continuously spat vitriol and hatred in all directions like the cornered rat he was. I had expected a more gracious lord by what Sabina had said about him, but now I understood where his son, Bastin, had gotten his arrogance and spitefulness.

It was a great relief when Odiman and Malo finally lost patience with them both and banished the bastards from our walls, not letting them take any of their possessions along with them. Not even their clothing. Townspeople lined the ramparts facing south, laughing and jeering at the lord and his son as they were prodded naked through the gates and out onto the road. The House Agents had allowed the pair to use a partially lame, wretched-looking old mule with enough food stacked across its bowed back to last for several days. Niko had joked that he'd never seen three uglier asses in all his life as man, boy, and beast trudged down the hill together in dejection. Lord Branton loudly berated his wounded and limping son the entire time, and we could hear his shrill voice echoing through the surrounding forest long after they were finally lost from view.

Malo's search for Rorian in the forest had proved fruitless in the end, and though he'd sent out patrols with trackers in all directions, no evidence was found that the man had gotten out through the tunnel. The only conclusion left was that for some reason, he had changed his mind and returned, and was even now hiding inside the town. An exhaustive search began as Odiman's men—with the townspeople's help—went from building to building looking for the scholar. But, after turning up nothing except a basement full of chained whores, and a corpse that had been rotting for several days, even the stubborn House Agent had to eventually admit failure.

"This entire thing has turned out to be a complete waste of time," Jebido said in disgust once the search had ended.

My men and I were waiting in the market square, standing around a stone fountain filled with surprisingly clear water as Malo and Odiman talked nearby. Odiman's face was swathed in bandages, but as far as I could tell, the House Agent seemed oblivious to any pain. A weathered statue of the First Pair holding hands stood in the center of the fountain, with a thin stream cascading down from somewhere in between their clasped hands. I'd seen the same pose before depicted in a mural painted across the Holy House ceiling in Corwick when I was a boy.

I sat on the edge of the fountain and shrugged. "At least we are alive," I said to Jebido. "I wouldn't have laid odds on that happening this morning."

"I've been wondering something," Jebido said, looking down at me. "How did you know the bells were for Malo and not us?"

"I didn't," I replied with a tired grin. "Not until I said it, anyway."

I yawned and took off my helmet as I dipped my hand into the cool water behind me, cupping some and rubbing it over my face and the back of my burned neck. My palm came back covered in dried blood and pasted soot. I took several more handfuls of water and scrubbed the best that I could, then swirled my soiled hand in the fountain, staining the water red and black. I felt overwhelmingly exhausted and I closed my eyes, enjoying the warmth of the sun on my face. A shadow broke the rays warming me and I cracked an eye open to see Malo standing over me. I sighed at the look on his face.

"They didn't find him," the House Agent said bitterly.

"I know," I grunted. "You're in my light," I added. Malo shifted sideways, looking at me in annoyance. "So, what do we do now?" I asked, not caring. I just wanted to sit where I was, listen to the water running and not move.

"I'm sending out patrols across the Southlands," Malo answered. "We must have missed Rorian in the forest somehow. It's the only explanation." The House Agent took a deep breath. "Maybe we will get lucky and one of those patrols will catch the bastard." He didn't sound overly optimistic to me. "For now, you and your men can go home. If I need you, I will send for you."

I nodded, not minding that answer at all. It would be good to return to Witbridge Manor after the last few days. I glanced at Baine, who was joking with Niko and Tyris. Flora might have had the baby by now and I knew my friend would be happy at the news that we were leaving.

"Someone could be hiding him in town," Jebido said, looking thoughtful. Alvar and the other town leaders were talking twenty yards away and Jebido gestured toward them. "Maybe letting them help with the search wasn't such a good idea. I'd trust that gardener over there, but that fat fellow and some of the others look like they would sell their own mother for a taste of gold."

Malo glanced at the townsmen. "You think one of them would take that chance?"

Jebido pursed his lips and shrugged. "Maybe. Who knows what motivates a man's heart?" He sat down beside me and looked up at the House Agent. "If I were you, Malo, I'd search again, but this time have only our men do it and be a little more ruthless. If Rorian is still here, he won't be expecting a second search."

"That's not necessarily a bad idea," Malo said. He stroked his beard and peered up at the sun. "There is still plenty of daylight left." I could see hope returning in his eyes as he looked at me. "Hadrack, I want you to organize this. Take as many men as you need."

I glanced sideways at Jebido in irritation. "Thanks a lot," I grumbled. Jebido made an apologetic face as I turned back to Malo. "You know it's going to be a waste of time, don't you? Somebody got out of that tunnel, regardless of what your trackers say. It had to have been Rorian."

"If there is any chance that he's still here, then I have to try," Malo said stubbornly.

I stood up wearily, straightening my stiff back. I knew arguing with Malo any further would be pointless. "Fine, if that's what you want. But I'm leaving with my men if we don't find him this time."

"Agreed," Malo said.

I put my helmet on. "So, what's this scholar look like, anyway?"

"Alvar told me he's tall and built like an ox," Malo said. He brushed his fingers along his cheek. "The bastard has three white scars right about here." I could feel the blood in my veins turn cold at his words. "What's wrong?" the House Agent asked at the look on my face.

I groaned out loud, picturing the wounded men that we'd seen on the way to the ridge earlier that day. It all seemed so long ago now, as if it had been weeks, rather than hours.

"Rorian's not here," I said, feeling an admiration for the man despite myself. The scholar must have had steel flowing in his veins to walk past us like he had. I'd suspected nothing amiss, and he had even greeted me like an old friend as we passed each other. I quickly told Malo and Jebido what I knew. I could see the dismay in the House Agent's eyes turning to anger as I talked.

"Those damn trackers swore to me that there were no signs," Malo said, his voice shaking with fury.

"Perhaps you need better trackers," Jebido said sarcastically.

I stared at my friend, thinking of Sabina and what Bastin had mentioned about her father's ability to track even a mouse through a forest. I hadn't sought out Sabina after we had captured Springlight, because, in truth, I was still angry at her for betraying us after we'd saved her life. She hadn't shown herself since the town had fallen either, and I had been more than happy to just forget about her. Up until now, that is.

"I think I know someone that can help us," I said.

"He's not here!" Sabina whispered angrily, glaring at me with her arms crossed over her chest.

The girl had changed out of her burnt clothing into a long white dress with flared sleeves and bright yellow accents along the hem. She'd also taken the time to wash herself, though the red, inflamed skin on her cheeks still retained some of the black soot from the fire.

"Where could he have gone?" I asked, not believing her.

We were in Lord Branton's manor house in one of the upper bed-chambers. An older woman lay in a large, four-poster canopy bed behind us, while a silver-haired man knelt beside her. I watched him open a vein in her arm with a lancet and place a bowl underneath to catch the weak stream of blood. Some of the blood dribbled messily onto the bedclothes, but the man didn't seem to notice.

"Keep your voice down!" Sabina hissed. She glanced behind her at the bed before facing me. "You're lucky that I agreed to see you at all," she added in a low tone.

"As if you had any choice," Malo growled at her. He grabbed her arm aggressively, giving it a firm shake. I could see the urgency in his eyes. "Now stop playing games. Tell us where your father is!"

"I'm telling you the truth!" Sabina snapped back, jerking her arm free. "He's gone." She moved to an elegant mirrored mahogany cabinet that stood along one wall and picked up a sheet of parchment. She gave Malo a cold look, then turned to me. "Can you read?" I nodded, not saying anything. "Good, then read this and maybe you will understand."

I took the parchment, curious despite my anger at the girl. My reading and writing had improved in the last year, but I still had some trouble now and again. What was written in this short letter, however, was relatively simple to understand. I finished reading, my anger lessening as I turned to the House Agent. "She's telling us the truth, Malo. Her father really is gone."

"Where?" Malo grunted at me in disbelief.

I sighed, thinking of the men Rorian had been with that morning in the forest. "He went with Rorian through the tunnel," I answered. Malo just gaped at me in surprise as I continued, "Rorian offered him fifty Jorqs to guide him to the coast."

"What?" Malo said, looking incredulous. He turned on Sabina aggressively. "What kind of father would abandon his family during a siege?"

"He didn't abandon us!" Sabina snapped in irritation. "He believed your forces were too weak to take the town. He must have decided to take the risk."

"Why?" I asked. "Why would he go, especially with his wife being so sick?"

"He knew we couldn't depend on Lord Branton for much longer," Sabina said. She glanced at the silver-haired man kneeling by her mother. "Physicians cost money. Money that we don't have."

"So, he just up and left," Malo said in disgust. He began to pace angrily. "Do you really expect us to believe that your father didn't tell you?"

Sabina glared at the House Agent. "I wasn't here. How could he?" Sabina turned to me, her eyes flashing. "Why do you want to see him, anyway? He's done nothing wrong."

I sighed in frustration. "Our trackers can't pick up Rorian's trail. We were hoping your father could help us with that. That's all."

Sabina's face slowly relaxed and she chuckled contemptuously. "Of course they can't," she said. "My father is with him, which means your men aren't nearly good enough."

I glanced at Malo, trying to find something positive in all this. "Well, at least we know they are heading for the coast. Now we know where to look."

Malo rolled his eyes. "Do you have any idea how big the coast is?" I looked at him dumbly as he pointed at the letter in my hand. "And for that matter, does it even mention which coast this man is referring to?"

I shook my head, feeling like a fool. "No, it doesn't."

Malo dropped his hand to his side in resignation. "That's what I thought. Rorian has several hours head start on us, Hadrack, and he could be heading west, east, or even north for all we know. We'll never find him now."

I could see by the look on Sabina's face that she was debating whether or not to say something. "What is it?" I prodded her.

"I can help find this man for you," Sabina said, looking torn as she looked at her mother again. "But if I do, you have to promise to pay for my mother's care, and let my father go when you catch them."

"How can you help us?" I asked.

"Because she knows exactly where they are going," Malo said. He glared at Sabina. "I knew you were lying."

"I'm not lying," Sabina said. "I have no idea where they are heading, just like I told you." She lifted her chin proudly. "My father taught me all that he knows about woodcraft, so if there is anyone other than my brother who can track them, it's me."

Malo paused, clearly weighing his options, until finally, he nodded in decision. "Very well. You have my word that if you help us find Rorian, no harm will come to your father."

"And my mother?" Sabina demanded. She gestured behind her. "What about her?"

"We will pay for her care," Malo promised. "Not only that, but I know just the man who might be able to cure her."

In less than an hour, we were riding along the trail that led to the ridge west of Springlight. Three packhorses with enough provisions to last for five days trailed behind us, with the lead packhorse tied to the back of Sim's saddle. It felt good to be united with Angry once again, though I could tell by the baleful glare the big stallion had given me when I'd saddled him that the feeling was mostly one-sided. I couldn't blame the horse, I suppose. After all, he'd just spent the last few days lolling and grazing in relative luxury in a lush clearing half a mile to the south.

We came to the spot where I had seen Rorian earlier that day and halted our horses as Sabina dismounted, telling us to remain where we were. The same red squirrel from hours before—or perhaps an exuberant cousin—scolded us loudly from the trees above our heads. Angry stamped his feet and gnawed at the bit while we waited, making it clear to me that he was far from happy that his relaxation time was over. Sabina walked twenty feet away from us, then lowered herself to the ground with her head held at an angle a few inches off the trampled pathway. She was dressed in high-topped, brown leather boots, tight black hose, and a long white tunic underneath a leather vest. She had a bleached, bone-handled knife at her waist, and her red hair was parted in the middle and braided down her back.

Sabina finally started to move forward in an awkward, crab-like motion, pausing every foot or so, her face set in concentration. Eventually, she stood up and returned to her starting point, staring at the worn ground critically with her hands on her hips. She began to use her feet to measure distances, muttering to herself, and I could see by the look on Malo's face that he was becoming increasingly impatient. I shifted in my saddle uncomfortably as we waited, trying to ease the pressure on my tailbone as I caught Baine's eye. My friend was riding a feisty three-year-old brown mare and he shrugged at me, looking both bored and resentful at the same time. Baine had not reacted well when he'd learned that we would be going after Rorian instead of going home as we had thought.

"All right," Sabina finally said. She lithely pulled herself up onto her horse and swung it around. "We can go now. They went south."

"I could have told you that," Malo grumbled, looking annoyed. "It doesn't take any skill to figure that out. We already knew they were heading that way. You just wasted precious time coming out here for nothing."

Sabina's eyes flashed in anger. "Is that so?" she snapped. "Then, I suppose you also figured out what each man was wearing on his feet?" Malo looked at her blankly. "No?" she said mockingly. "How about their weight and ages, or that one of them has one leg shorter than the other?" Again, Malo said nothing. Sabina snorted. "Well, can you at least tell me how many men there are?"

"Six," I replied, knowing Malo hadn't even looked at the men who had passed us that morning. I remembered five others with Rorian, though I could only recall the scholar's scarred face.

"At least someone is paying attention," Sabina said with a sniff. She pointed down as she kept her gaze on the House Agent. "Do you have any idea just how many different tracks there are on this path?" Malo glowered back at her, starting to look uncomfortable. I have to admit that I was enjoying watching him squirm under the girl's relentless gaze. "The only thing we know for sure is this spot was the last place they were seen. That's why we are here. Now that I can recognize their footprints, I'll be able to follow them wherever they go."

"So why didn't the other trackers find them if they can be followed that easily?" Baine asked.

"Who said it was easy?" Sabina replied curtly. "Besides, I'd bet your trackers didn't even look here. That's why my father had those men pose as wounded soldiers. He knew no one would be looking for them in plain sight."

"Very well," Malo said, looking slightly mollified. "What do you suggest we do now?"

"Now we go back to the horses in the clearing," Sabina answered, kicking her mount into motion. She glanced at the House Agent over her shoulder. "Because I guarantee you, there will be six of them missing."

Sabina was right, of course. Six horses were missing, with one of them being Odiman's mount, a dappled stallion with a patch on his forehead. The horses were kept in a large, kidney-shaped clearing of rich grass that cut through the forest a half-mile south of Springlight. Malo stood a foot from the treeline, interrogating four crestfallen-looking boys whose jobs it had been to care for and protect the horses. The House Agent kept pacing back and forth in anger as the boys stared at the ground while he shouted at them.

"Poor bastards," Putt said in sympathy.

"Maybe if they had done their jobs and stopped Rorian, we'd be heading home right now," Baine said a little too gruffly.

Niko snorted. "Boys with crooked bows and dull knives against six armed men?" He looked at Baine in amazement. "If they had, they would be dead and Rorian would still be gone."

"Besides," Tyris cut in as he leaned on his bow. "You can't blame them. How could they have even known who Rorian was?"

"They couldn't have," I grunted. I motioned toward the House Agent. "Malo knows that. He just needs to vent some anger at someone. Those four make a fine target."

I looked away and shielded my eyes from the sun that was slowly heading toward the treeline. Soon it would be too dark to pick up the trail unless we got moving. I watched Sabina as she continued to methodically cover the clearing in a slow walk, working from the center and making her way outward in swooping circles. Several of the horses were following her curiously inside the rope barrier that kept them confined.

I thought back to how Baine and I had followed Carbet and the other Cardians' pointed boots through the woods near Gasterny, eventually leading us to Shana. Neither Baine nor I were skilled woodsmen by any means, but that trail had been an easy thing to follow compared to what Sabina was dealing with now. How she could find the tracks she was looking for in all the overlapping footprints and hoofmarks scattered across the clearing was beyond my ability to understand.

Sabina crouched down near the clearing's eastern side, then looked to the trees and stood, disappearing beneath the outreaching branches. I tensed, wondering if I should go after her just as she reappeared and headed toward us. Malo had finally finished berating the four boys, and he came to stand beside me.

"I've found the trail," Sabina said. She pointed behind her. "They headed east through the trees by that big aspen."

"Good," Malo grunted, searching the forest with his eyes. "At least now we know which coast they are heading for." Sabina shook her head in disagreement. "What?" Malo growled.

"My father is a cautious man," Sabina said. "Knowing him, that trail heading east is just to throw off any pursuit. I'm going back there on foot now to confirm that. I just wanted to let you know. I suggest the rest of you mount up and follow me, but don't get too close until I find which direction they turned."

Once again, Sabina was soon to be proven right. Our quarry had headed east through the trees in a straight line for about fifty yards, just as she'd said. They hadn't worried about the stolen mounts' tracks at all, and I could easily make them out even from Angry's back. The trail meandered through the forest until it reached a shallow, slow-moving stream, where it abruptly ended. The rest of us waited on the fern-covered banks of the stream as Sabina stepped into water that barely covered the top of her boots. Small pebbles lined the stream's bed and were deposited at least six inches above the waterline on both banks. We'd had little rain recently, which explained the sluggish water flow, but I could easily picture this same stream gushing wildly from spring runoff or after a heavy rainfall.

"The girl is good," Jebido said beside me, looking impressed as he braced himself on his pommel.

Sabina had initially gone up and down the twisting stream until she'd seen what she wanted. Now she squatted thirty feet away from us near the far bank, silently studying the colorful stones on the shore. Finally, after long minutes, she grabbed a single pebble and held it up. I heard her grunt in satisfaction before replacing the stone.

"They went north," Sabina said, gesturing ahead of her. "Bring the horses, but stay behind me."

Malo glanced my way, looking worried. If they reached the northern border, I knew they would be hard to catch. The House Agent kicked his horse into motion, splashing through the stream as the rest of us followed. We traveled slowly, staying well back as Sabina moved forward in a sweeping pattern through the trees. The light was starting to dim as we progressed, but I noticed that the trail was gradually shifting westward. Finally, we reached a dense thicket of blackberry bushes bunched around a massive oak tree. Sabina paused, carefully moving aside the thorny shoots as she peered inside. She stood that way for a long time, then glanced to the west with a slight smile playing on her lips.

"Well?" Malo demanded. "What now?"

Sabina turned, ignoring the House Agent as she crooked a finger at me. Malo frowned and I shrugged at him, then dismounted and approached the girl.

"See there?" Sabina said, holding aside a branch thick with black and red berries.

I looked inside, but all I saw were more berries. "What am I looking for?"

"The shoot at the top there," Sabina said. "Look how it is completely free of ripe berries." She let the branch go, then carefully pulled aside another. "Same thing here."

"So?" I said. "Birds and animals eat berries all the time."

Sabina let the shoot fall back into place. "That's true," she agreed. "But birds won't fight their way through the thorns when there are plenty of berries to pick from in front." She grinned. "As for animals and insects, they nibble away here and there. Rarely if ever, do they take the entire berry, let alone all of them in the same spot."

"Your father?" I asked.

"Without question," Sabina said. "They're not heading east or north." She pointed to the west. "They are heading that way."

We followed the trail for the rest of that day until the fading light forced us to make camp, and the next morning we were back on it the moment the sun rose. By the time we were twenty miles from Springlight, our quarry had mostly given up covering their trail, which meant we were able to move much faster. I was sure we would catch up to Rorian after that, but as each hour drifted into the next, our quarry somehow managed to stay ahead of us.

On the third day of the pursuit, the trail suddenly broke off into three sets of twos just as we reached the overgrown banks of a dried-out riverbed that headed north. One set of tracks broke off to the east, one to the north, following the riverbed, while the other turned west. Sabina crouched down beside her horse at the break-off point and absently ran her hands along one of the hoofprints. She looked up, examining the land as the breeze toyed with her long braid.

"My father knows someone is following them," she finally said. "They split up here to confuse us."

Malo's face turned dark at the news. "How could he know that?" he asked, looking at her suspiciously.

Sabina shrugged. "Probably a gut feeling. He gets them sometimes."

"So, what do we do?" I asked before the House Agent could comment.

Sabina stood and dusted off her hose. She pointed along the riverbed. "The man with the short leg and the one that spits phlegm went north. The one who squirts bloody shit ten times a day went east with the skinny one."

"Which means your father and Rorian went west," Malo said, looking in that direction. "And that's the way we go."

Sabina shook her head firmly and motioned to the riverbed. "No, we go north."

"What?" Malo snapped. His horse fidgeted beneath him and it took a moment for him to calm the animal. "I'm not letting Rorian get away again."

"He won't," Sabina said confidently as she swung back into the saddle. "My father is going to cover his trail so well now that even I won't be able to follow it." She looked to the riverbed again. "But those two fools out there couldn't hide their trail in a rainstorm." She glanced meaningfully at the rest of us. "Catch them, and I'm sure with the right persuasion, they will gladly tell you where Rorian and my father are heading."

And she was right. They did.

6: The Cove

The hidden cove—called Mouth-On-The-Sea—was almost a half-mile long, with magnificent, sun-bleached limestone cliffs overlooking it that rose at least three hundred feet. A crescent-shaped shale beach stretched out far below me, where I lay peering over the cliff's edge. I shaded my eyes against the setting sun, just able to make out the forms of three boats beached at the far northern end of the cove. Several roaring bonfires burned higher up on the beach, flickering wildly in the wind. I could see the faint silhouettes of men as they moved around on the ships and shore. It appeared to me as though they were preparing to set sail, and I knew we didn't have much time left if we wanted to catch Rorian.

The wind whistled in my ears and flapped at my cloak as great-beaked seabirds screamed and cawed above me, filling the sky. I could hear the sound of the surf even above the calls of the birds as the water broke along the shoreline, rattling the millions of tiny shale that blanketed the beach. A long, thin ridge of limestone joined the cliff where I lay and curled around the southern end of the cove, cutting off the beach as it jutted out to the west at least two hundred yards into the sea. The ridge dipped down at the end almost to the waterline, then swept around to the north before it flared upward dramatically to form two impressive arches of jagged rock. An enormous hole had been worn within each archway, courtesy of thousands of years of tidewater wearing away at the limestone.

Thousands of gannets packed the top of the ridge and the arches. Each bird looked identical to the next with their light-brown heads, white bodies and black wing-tips. The seabirds appeared fat and ungainly at first glance as they flapped their wings and jostled for space on the arches. But I realized that awkwardness was just an illusion, broken the moment they sprang into the air and dove bill first into the water with blinding speed and grace.

"Mother's Eyes," Jebido said from beside me, following my gaze. "Some believe it is a doorway to the world Above." Beneath me, the sea surged madly around and through the twin openings as the waves slapped against the stone, sending white foam spraying upward toward the gannets lining the ridge. "Legend has it that if you can swim through the right eye," Jebido continued, "then make it back through the left, all your sins will be absolved and you will be transported directly to The Mother's side."

"Really?" I said in surprise, trying to imagine swimming in those treacherous waters. "Has anyone ever made it?"

Jebido grinned. "Only corpses so far."

"Maybe it's just a big rock where fools go to die," Baine grunted from my other side, looking unimpressed. "Did either of you two stop to consider that?"

I glanced at Baine's sour face and sensed Jebido shrugging beside me. Baine's mood had grown blacker over the days as we made our way westward, but there was little that I could say to help. I knew my friend desperately wanted to return to Flora, but I needed his bow and experience with me right now, so he was just going to have to deal with his anger on his own. I turned as I felt a hand tap my shoulder.

"Sim found a way down, my lord," Putt said, crouching low behind me.

Jebido, Baine, and I withdrew from the edge of the cliff, careful not to break the skyline. The men below hadn't posted guards as far as I could tell. Most likely secure in the knowledge that they were safe from attack where they were. But, like Jebido was always telling me, it was better to be overly cautious and stay alive, than be careless and find yourself dead.

We retreated to the remnants of an ancient stone fortress that sat fifty yards away from the edge of the clifftop. The fort had been built long before the First Pair's birth, back when frightful beasts and godless bands of savages were all that roamed the land. There were many such relics spread across both Southern and Northern

Ganderland, though no one seemed to know for sure who had built them.

Crumbling limestone foundations covered in moss and lichen rose behind the fortress where once a small town must have stood. Twisted vines, long swaying grasses, and thick bushes covered in prickly thorns grew wildly throughout the ruins. Sabina was grooming her horse near the fort's decaying northern wall, while the rest of my men waited near the western gates' skeletal remains.

"You found a way down?" I asked Sim as we approached.

Sim nodded, but I could see worry lying heavily on his face. "Yes, my lord. There is only one. A steep, narrow gulley with landings and stairs chiseled into the stone in places. It's a tough descent, but leads all the way to the beach."

"That's good news," I said. "So why do you look like you just found a goat turd floating in your beer?"

Sim grimaced and swept the ground with his boot, clearing a section of scrub-brush as the rest of my men joined us.

The big outlaw crouched and dug his finger into the dirt, drawing a curved line. "This is where Rorian's boats are, my lord," he said, making a mark at the northern tip of the curve. He made a similar mark at the opposite end. "And we are here." He made a third mark close to the boats. "The top of the gully begins here. But unfortunately, it cuts down the face of the cliff at an angle, heading back to the south."

I frowned, understanding now why Sim had looked so worried. "So, how far away from them will we be once we reach the bottom?"

Sim stood up and shrugged. "Perhaps a hundred, maybe a hundred and fifty yards."

I sighed, trying to imagine crossing that distance in our heavy armor over an unstable, shale-covered beach that would be shifting and rolling beneath our boots the entire way. The enemy outnumbered us greatly as it was, and with what awaited, I knew we would be out of breath before we got halfway to the boats. If they had archers with them, we wouldn't even make it that far.

"Can we get the horses down there?"

"Not a chance," Sim said with a shake of his head.

I nodded, not surprised. "All right then, any suggestions?" I asked, looking around at my men.

"Why not wait until they are sleeping?" Niko suggested.

I grimaced. "Because it looks to me like they're getting ready to leave."

"At this time of day?" Putt said in surprise.

"So it would appear," I replied. I glanced at Malo. "What do you think?"

"We have no choice here," Malo grunted. His flat face looked anxious beneath his hood as his cloak rippled in the wind. "If they set sail now, we'll never catch Rorian. We have to attack."

"And if they have archers?" I asked. "You know as well as I do what will happen then."

"There is no other way, Hadrack," Malo growled, his eyes flashing.

"There might be," Sabina said as she came to stand beside me. "What about walking right up to them?"

Niko started to snicker and I gave him an annoyed look, silencing him. "All ideas are listened to no matter what," I said reproachfully. "You know that as well as anyone. The only reason we are here at all is because of Sabina, so give her the respect she deserves."

Niko looked properly chastised as he mumbled an apology to Sabina.

I could see a glint of gratitude in the girl's green eyes as she took a deep breath. "The way I see it, the only way you can catch them by surprise is if I go down there first to distract them."

"What?" I grunted in disbelief.

Sabina held her hand up before I could say anything else. "Just listen to me, Hadrack. My idea will work. My father will make sure that nothing happens to me."

"You don't know that he is even down there," I protested.

There had been no sign of the horses the two men had ridden on to get here. I knew they couldn't have taken them down to the beach, so where were they? Part of me suspected Sabina's father had already collected his money and had ridden away with the horses.

"He's here somewhere," Sabina said stubbornly. "I would know it if he wasn't."

I realized there was little to gain in arguing that point by the set look on her face. "Even if your father is still here," I said, trying to dissuade her another way. "What makes you think that he can, or even will help us?"

"You don't know my father," Sabina responded.

"That's true enough," I said, giving her that. "So, let's just say we all agree and you go down there alone, then what?"

"Once it's dark enough, I'll start an argument with my father," Sabina said. "I'll make sure I'm near the boats and cry and shout a lot. Everyone should be focused on me, which means their backs will be turned away from you."

"That's not a bad plan," Jebido said thoughtfully. "If we stick to the base of the cliff, they might not see us until we are right on top of them."

"It's too risky," I said with a shake of my head. It was a good plan. Better than anything else we'd come up with so far. But even so, I was reluctant to put the girl in danger. Sabina seemed confident that her father would be able to protect her, but from everything I had seen and heard about Rorian, I wasn't so sure.

"Is it any riskier than marching across that beach?" Sabina challenged me.

She had a valid point, I knew, which galled me to no end. "Why do this at all?" I asked to change the subject. "You led us to Rorian just like you promised you would. You don't have to take this chance."

"Because I don't trust him," Sabina said, stabbing a finger at Malo. "And the only way to make sure he keeps his word is to catch that man down there. That's why!"

I'd told Sabina about Haverty while we traveled and I knew she had set all her hopes on the strange apothecary. I still felt bad about possibly giving her false hope, but I also knew that if anyone could cure her mother, it was Haverty.

"Well," Malo said dryly after a moment. "I'd say your feelings on that are pretty clear. "He glanced at me. "We're running out of time and this idea is the best chance we have. I say we do it, but she doesn't go alone. You and I will go with her."

I saw coldness rise in Sabina's eyes at his words. She shook her head. "Not you," she said. "I'm willing to take Hadrack and Jebido along, but nobody else."

The House Agent's features turned hard and I put a hand on his arm before he could say anything else. "It's probably better this way, Malo," I said. "Jebido and I can handle this. We'll need you to lead the assault anyway." Malo looked as if he might protest, and then he seemed to change his mind. He nodded curtly and walked stiffly away as the rest of my men followed him. I turned to Sabina, who was staring at the House Agent's back with disdain. "He's not a bad sort once you get to know him," I said. "He's just focused on his task."

"He's an ass!" Sabina spat under her breath.

I grinned. "We'll compromise, then, and just say Malo is a very focused ass."

Sabina's face softened and she studied me thoughtfully. "You're not like the rest of them, are you?"

"I'm not?" I responded, surprised by her sudden mood shift. "How so?"

Sabina shrugged and half-smiled. "I don't know what it is." She put a hand on my arm and stared up at me. "There is something different about you."

I glanced away for a moment, suddenly embarrassed by the look on Sabina's face. I'd seen that look in the eyes of women before, and I wasn't sure how to react to it coming from her. The light on the clifftop was fading fast now, the backdrop of pink and orange-streaked sky to the west broken only by the girl's slim silhouette. The wind whistled around us, riffling our clothing as the flared end of Sabina's thickly-braided hair twisted and flopped against her back. We were only a foot apart and I felt a sudden, almost overwhelming desire to pull this fiery, red-haired girl to my chest and kiss her. I could tell Sabina sensed it as well. She leaned forward and closed her eyes just as I angrily squashed the feeling. There was only one woman for me, and her name was Shana.

"We better get moving," I said gruffly, turning away. I saw sudden hurt twist Sabina's features, but I kept going, heading for Jebido. "Are you ready?" I growled at him.

Jebido looked up sharply, surprised by my tone. I saw his eyes flick over my shoulder to Sabina. He frowned. "Is everything all right?"

"Fine," I said, trying to take the edge from my voice. I didn't want to have to explain to my friend what I'd been thinking a moment ago. I didn't want to have to explain it to myself, either, for that matter. I glanced at the colorful sunset, knowing the beach below us would still be bathed in weak sunlight, though it wouldn't last for much longer. "We have to go before we lose the light," I said, motioning him to follow me.

Sim led us to the path that he'd found, which turned out to be even steeper at the onset than the big outlaw had suggested. I gingerly made my way into the darkened gully, and once I had a firm foothold, I turned to help Sabina down as Jebido guided her from behind. Sabina seemed more aloof toward me now, or perhaps it was just my imagination. Either way, I knew I needed to thrust what had happened between us from my mind and focus on the job at hand. Malo and the others waited at the rim, watching us as we slowly picked our way downward.

The gully floor started to level out after about twenty feet, though there were so many jagged rock formations in our path that it was necessary to cling to the northern wall to squeeze past them. It had been almost chilly earlier on the clifftop with the strong winds, but inside the gulley, it was surprisingly hot and stifling as the rock around us released trapped heat. I could feel the sweat dripping from beneath my helmet and I shook my head, trying to whisk the moisture away from my eyes.

The chasm began to widen just as we came to a flat landing cut into the stone, with a flight of cracked steps leading away that curved dramatically southward. I followed the stairs until we reached a dark, rounded entrance cut through solid rock that could only have been made by men. I glanced behind me at Sabina, who was sweating just as much as I was. She deliberately refused to meet my eyes, staring at her feet. I turned away with a shrug and stepped inside as pitch darkness descended on me. I focused on the window of weak light that I could see at the other end as I carefully began moving forward. I could hear small pieces of rock crackling under my boots—the sounds amplified even more as Sabina and Jebido cautiously entered the opening behind me. Finally, I reached the other side and stepped out onto a landing, where another set of crudely-cut stairs awaited.

I paused and glanced over my shoulder into the dark, gaping hole. "Everyone all right?" I asked in a low tone.

"Fine," Sabina's voice rose tightly out of the darkness.

"Good here," Jebido called from behind her.

I waited for them to join me before we carefully made our way down the uneven stairs, which eventually led to a deep, rounded trench. The walls rose impossibly high on both sides of us, with shadowy ledges jutting out that I had to duck under as the gully floor began to slope downward dramatically. Bracken grew in thick patches on and around the ridges and I used their long stalks to steady me with one hand while I helped Sabina with the other. We eventually made it to ground level and I paused to give us all a chance to catch our breath.

We were standing in a natural crevice that opened out onto the beach, and I could see the tiny stones covering it glistening in an almost hypnotic red and pink glow. The surf pounded relentlessly against the shale along the shoreline, scattering it effortlessly with each powerful surge as the sharp smell of salt, fish, and vegetation swept over me. I took my helmet off and wiped at my forehead, letting the breeze coming off the water cool me.

"That was the easy part," I said as I replaced my helmet. I glanced at Sabina. "There is still time to change your mind about this."

"Let's just get on with it," Sabina said sharply. She crossed her arms over her chest. "The sooner we do this, the sooner it's over and I can get back to my mother."

"All right, have it your way," I grunted in irritation. Jebido was looking at Sabina and me with a puzzled look on his face, and I did my best to ignore him. "Sabina will take the lead just like we discussed," I said. "Jebido and I will follow." I was about to put my hand on Sabina's arm, then saw the warning in her eyes and changed my mind. "Just remember what I told you, Sabina," I said instead. "If something goes wrong, run back here as fast as you can and wait for Malo. Do you hear me?"

"Nothing will go wrong," Sabina said, refusing to look at me. She pressed her lips tightly together as two circles of color burned hotly on her cheeks.

I sighed and shook my head, knowing the tentative friendship that we'd been forging over the last few days appeared to be over. I took a moment to draw out my Pair Stone, kissing it first before saying a prayer aloud to The Mother. I didn't fail to notice the black look Sabina gave me, and I'm ashamed to admit that I took a little pleasure from her obvious annoyance. I glanced at Jebido when I finished praying and he nodded that he was ready.

"Let's do this," I said, tucking the Pair Stone safely beneath my armor.

A rounded outcrop that protruded out from the face of the cliff hid us from the northern part of the beach, helping to shield us from the full force of the wind coming off the sea. Sabina took a deep breath, then stepped around me onto the beach as powerful gusts whipped at her clothing. The setting sun was halfway below the horizon now, but the glare was right in my line of sight, partially blinding me as we followed the girl. I lifted a hand to block the light as sea-spray carried on the wind quickly soaked my cloak and armor. Jebido was doing the same thing beside me, though Sabina seemed immune to the sun, wind, and spray. She walked toward the camp with her chin held high, appearing confident and at ease. Somehow she'd let her hair loose from the braid and the long wet strands danced and whirled madly around her head.

The shale that blanketed the beach reached all the way to the base of the cliff, and the colorful stones clattered and grated musically with each step we took. My boots were sinking almost to my ankles as we slogged along and it quickly started to feel like I was trying to fight my way through waist-high water with a horse balanced on my back. Jebido was already panting beside me and I could hear my own breath rattling in my chest almost as loudly. Attacking head-on would have been a disaster, I now knew.

We continued walking for another thirty feet before finally, a shout of discovery arose from the north. I squinted at the shadowy figures as they moved toward us, trying to see past the sun's glare and the relentless spray. The men opposite finally halted and stood bunched together near the wind-whipped fires. I could hear their whistles and cat-calls as they got a good look at Sabina. She had been right again, I realized. Sabina was the perfect distraction.

"Hadrack!" Jebido hissed over the wind beside me. "There is only one boat left!"

I looked to the beach in alarm. Two deep grooves along the shoreline near the remaining boat were all that remained to show that other ships had been there. The surf was already busily at work, filling the grooves in with each surge.

"Well, well," a man called to us, grinning as he took two steps forward. He was tall and thin, with a clean-shaven face and red, inflamed sores along both sides of his jawline. "This isn't what we were expecting at all."

I reached for my sword even as I felt a growl of hatred rise in my chest. All the men facing us were dressed in mail, wore red capes that snapped around their shoulders, and had long, black pointed boots on their feet.

The soldiers on the beach were Cardians.

7: Cardians

Jebido told me once that all Cardians were just turds with legs who would sell their own mothers to make a profit. I remember I had chuckled at that description of them, not fully understanding my friend's antagonism at the time. I had only met three Cardians back when he'd said that, and two of them had died without ever uttering a single word. Which, come to think of it, is the way I prefer Cardians. I hadn't believed at first that the entire race could be as vile as that bastard Carbet had been, but after having met enough of them over the last few years, I knew now that they were.

I felt Jebido's strong hand cover mine, holding me back. "Not yet," he grunted under his breath. "Patience."

The sun was rapidly sinking below the horizon of the sea now, leaving a fading pinkish-red sky in its wake that stained the water the color of blood. I slowly loosened my grip on Wolf's Head. Jebido was right, of course. Rushing forward and getting us all killed would accomplish nothing. I counted sixteen Cardians, most of whom had begun to spread out in a line facing us. They were ignoring Jebido and me, focusing on Sabina with a mixture of wonder and lust on their weathered faces. Thankfully, none were holding the dreaded longbows that I remembered from Gasterny.

Sabina had told me earlier that her father was tall and wide, with the same hair color as hers, along with a bushy red beard. I quickly scanned the men's faces opposing us, but Sabina's father didn't appear to be among them. I'd been right all along, I knew. The tracker had ridden away from this place with his money and the horses. Rorian wasn't on the beach either, I saw, not that I was expecting him to be. Our luck just didn't seem to run that way.

I took a moment to study the remaining boat. The Cardians had driven it far up onto the shore with the bulky hull buried deep in the shale and oozing muck. The vessel was different from other boats that I had seen before, all of which had been sleek and long, with rounded hulls and sides built low to the water. This ship was ungainly-looking, with a broad, flat belly and impossibly high sides that curved upward at the stem and stern. A thick oak deck dominated the stern, with a similar, smaller platform built along the bow. A lower deck joined the two together, where a single mast with a furled sail stood at the center. The ship didn't look as though it had been designed for beaching to me, and I guessed the Cardians were stranded here until the tide floated them free.

A heavily-bearded man stood by the bow of the ship, leaning his arms on the gunwale as he cut slices from an apple and popped them into his mouth. He regarded us with cold, unfriendly eyes as he ate. I noticed a thick rope ladder hanging over the side of the bow near where the Cardian stood, dropping at least fifteen feet to the beach below. A single lantern, swinging wildly in the wind, hung from a hook at the boat's stern.

I wasn't sure how much Malo and the others could see from where they waited at the base of the cliff, despite the lantern and the bonfires blazing along the beach. Would they be able to tell that two of the ships were gone from that far away? We'd agreed that Malo would wait until darkness had entirely fallen before leading the men across the shale. But now that Sabina's father was gone, the distraction we had planned wouldn't work. We needed a new strategy. I was desperately trying to come up with one just as Sabina took the initiative.

"Where is my father?" the girl demanded in an aggressive tone.

"Your father?" the tall Cardian grunted in surprise. He studied the darkening beach behind us before focusing back on Sabina. "And who might that be?"

"I'm right here!" a squat, wide-shouldered Cardian shouted from the line of men. He spread his arms toward Sabina, then made puckering sounds through his lips. "Come and give your old papa a big wet kiss."

The other Cardians laughed and one of them called out, "Who are you trying to fool, Baylan? No woman would spread her legs for you, even for all the gold in Cardia."

"A bald-faced lie, you bastard!" Baylan spit back. "I've bedded my fair share. Just ask anyone!"

The man on the ship cupped a hand around his lips. "Sheep don't count!"

Laughter rang out again as Baylan turned, casting a baleful glance behind him.

"My father was the man who guided Rorian here, you fools!" Sabina said harshly, cutting through their merriment.

"The tracker is your father?" the tall Cardian asked, clearly caught off-guard as his grin faded.

"Yes," Sabina said. "Now tell me where he is."

The Cardian studied her thoughtfully. "I see the resemblance now," he said grudgingly. He pointed to the north, where a dark mass of limestone cliffs cut off our view of the sea. "He just passed around those rocks out there." His grin returned. "If you can swim fast, little lady, then maybe you can catch him."

Sabina pressed her lips together in anger. "You're lying," she said. "I know my father. He wouldn't have gotten on any ship."

The Cardian shrugged. "Believe whatever you want. It means nothing to me."

Sabina looked to the empty sea as surging waves topped with foaming crests rolled across its murky surface. The wind had picked up even more since we'd reached the shore, turning the waters mean and angry. I could see dismay and indecision on the girl's face at the news her father had left on the ships. It was a surprise to me too, but regardless, the problem of the Cardians remained. I knew I had to do something now before they became any more suspicious of us.

"I'm Alwin of Witbridge," I said, introducing myself.

"What of it?" the Cardian grunted back in disinterest.

"Your name?" I asked, trying to keep my voice even.

The Cardian frowned. "Burel," he replied coldly as he studied me.

"Burel," I repeated with a weary nod. I took my helmet off and rubbed my hair vigorously. "Well, Burel, we have a problem. My companion and I were told to bring the girl here because she has important information for Rorian." I glanced at the sea and frowned. "They were supposed to wait for us."

"He never mentioned that to me," Burel said, looking unimpressed. "What kind of information?" he added.

"Something for his ears alone," I replied. I tried to keep my face blank, afraid the Cardian would see the distaste I felt for him there. "All I can say is it involves gold." Burel perked up at that, as did his men, just like I knew they would. Cardians were so predictable.

I could see an equal amount of suspicion and greed fighting for dominance in Burel's dark eyes. "Tell me what you know," the Cardian finally said, "and if I think it's worthwhile, I'll pass it on to Rorian."

"I can't do that," I said with a firm shake of my head. I glanced at the boat as the stern rolled and pitched on the waves. The tide was rising quickly, I saw, and I needed these men to turn their backs on the cliffs soon before the ship was free. The eight of us were outnumbered, but I knew my men would be more than a match for the Cardians. I just needed to get them across the beach first. "Take us to Rorian on your ship," I said, hoping to draw the Cardians toward the water, "and I promise he will reward you once he hears what we have to say."

"A Gander's promise is like a fart in the wind," Burel grunted. "Gone before you even know it was there. Besides, our orders are to stay right where we are."

"Then tell us where Rorian is heading and we will find another way," I said.

Burel just blinked at me, saying nothing. Finally, he nodded to himself. "I think you're lying. There is no gold."

I raised my hands in exasperation. "What would we have to gain by lying about it?" I asked.

"I don't know," Burel said. "But something's not right about you, and I'm going to find out what it is." He put his hand on the hilt of his sword. "Tell me what you are really doing here, or I'll poke holes in the girl until she squeals the truth."

I'd had just about enough of the bastard and I stepped in front of him. I was taller than Burel, which meant that he had to look up at me. I could tell he wasn't used to that and didn't like it at all. "You couldn't slit the throat of a drunken old cripple snoring in his bed," I growled down into his face.

Most Cardians, I'd come to learn, were cowards at heart, preferring overwhelming odds rather than equal terms. I was reasonably sure that Burel would be no different, but there is only so much a man can take. If I could goad him into fighting me, I figured I could toy with the man long enough for the others to approach unseen. The gamble was that Burel might have no honor at all and just ignore my insults, setting his men on Jebido and me instead.

"Be careful, Gander," Burel warned, his eyes flashing with anger.

I could tell the man was close—he just needed an extra push. "You are one ugly bastard," I said with a snort, my hand on my sword. "It's a wonder you are even allowed to walk around without a sack over that face."

Burel cursed and began to draw his sword just as Sabina surprised me by stepping between us, putting a hand on each of our chests.

"Enough of this nonsense!" she snapped. "My father is getting farther away by the minute while you two engage in a pissing match." She poked a finger against Burel's breastplate. "Who do you think it was that helped Rorian escape from Springlight?" she demanded. Burel's eyebrows rose. "That's right," Sabina said. "Of course I know about that, because it was my father and me who got him out of there." She waved a hand at Jebido, then motioned to me. "And these two helped us, so stop being an ass and accept that we are all on Rorian's side here."

Burel paused, looking taken aback. Sabina brushed past him without another word, hurrying across the shale toward the boat.

"Hey!" Burel shouted after her. "Get back here!"

The other Cardians stood shifting from one foot to another, muttering uncertainly, but none moved to stop Sabina. Burel started after her, cursing, his face black with anger as Jebido and I followed closely behind. Sabina reached the water's edge, which had risen dramatically and was beginning to curl around the grounded ship's bow. She waded into the surf, then paused by the rope ladder as she glared up at the Cardian leaning on the railing.

"Don't just stand there, you witless oaf, help me aboard!" she ordered.

The heavily-bearded man stared down at her in astonishment, a slice of apple halfway to his lips.

"Where do you think you are going!?" Burel yelled as he reached the shoreline.

The tall Cardian stomped into the water, clutching at Sabina's shoulder, but she slipped nimbly away from his grasp just as a wave crashed against her legs. She stumbled awkwardly and then fell to her knees as a second, larger crest washed over her. I started forward to help, then paused as Jebido laid a hand on my arm. I looked at him, but all my friend did was shake his head imperceptibly and hold me back. I watched in growing alarm as Sabina struggled to stand up, spitting out a mouthful of seawater even as the tide swept over her again. She pitched forward from the force of the wave, disappearing beneath the water, then resurfaced, swinging her arms wildly as the surging tide dragged her farther from the shore.

Burel stood with his arms folded over his chest, watching dispassionately, while the rest of the Cardians ran to the waterline. They began to laugh and point as Sabina floundered helplessly. I looked at Jebido. My friend had a slight smile on his face and it dawned on me what was really going on. Sabina had given us our distraction after all.

I glanced over my shoulder at the wall of darkness beyond the fires. Had Malo made it across the beach by now? Would he see this as the opportunity that it was? I pointed at the back of a short Cardian dancing with excitement along the shoreline, then I waited. I didn't hear the hiss of the arrow over the noise of the surf, the wind, and Sabina's convincing cries of distress, but the dancing man suddenly arched his back, then tumbled forward into the water. I grinned. Tyris or Baine had understood what I'd wanted. The Cardian next to the fallen man bent over and tugged at his companion in surprise, then he grunted, reaching for a quivering shaft sticking from his neck as he fell. A clatter of boots on shale sounded behind me as my men swept around the bonfires. That's all the incentive I needed, and I drew Wolf's Head.

"Kill the bastards!" I screamed as I rushed forward. "Kill them!"

It took a moment for the Cardians to realize what was happening to their rear before they turned, pulling desperately at their weapons. Burel whirled in the knee-deep water, his ugly face dropping in astonishment as my men attacked. Before the tall Cardian could even take a step, two arrows thudded simultaneously into his chest, flinging him backward. Burel landed in the water with his arms spread wide as the sea eagerly snatched at his body, dragging it away.

I caught a fleeting glimpse of Sabina's stark white face as she clung to the boat's hull near the stern, then I reached the line of Cardians bracing along the shore. I snarled, finally letting the pent-up rage inside me free. A quick backslash with Wolf's Head and the first man to attack me with a clumsy swing fell writhing at my feet. I barely glanced at him as I pressed onward. More Cardians were converging on me, screaming their hatred. I lifted my shield, blocking a powerful sword thrust from my left that rang loudly off the shield's metal boss. Then I ducked and whirled as a second Cardian attacked from my right. That man's blade swept past my head harmlessly as I shoved him off-balance with my shoulder. I dropped to my knees, gutting the man to my left. He squealed as I twisted my blade savagely in his flesh and yanked it free even as I threw my shield into the face of the off-balance Cardian, knocking him flat on his back. I bounded toward him as he lifted his sword, cursing at me. I kicked the weapon from his hand contemptuously, then plunged Wolf's Head into his chest.

Weapons clashed all along the beach as men screamed and died. The sounds of the battle seemed oddly muted as the wind howled and the surf roared. I pulled my sword free from the corpse, then straightened, suddenly free of adversaries. Tyris and Baine stood in front of the bonfires, their dark silhouettes framed by the flames as they shot coolly and calmly at the Cardians. Malo, Putt, Niko, and Jebido fought together in a shield wall as they forced a dark mass of

Cardians toward the water. Sim fought alone twenty paces farther down the beach, swinging an axe wildly at two Cardians retreating into the sea in panic beneath the big man's furious onslaught.

I heard Baine shout something, the words lost to me on the wind, and Sim stepped back just as one of his opponents sagged with an arrow in his chest. Sim roared as the man fell, throwing himself at the remaining Cardian. He smashed against that man's upraised shield with a vicious blow of his axe and I saw the blade lodge firmly in the thick wood. The big outlaw wrenched at the weapon, then let it go as he flung himself on top of the Cardian. Both men disappeared beneath the waves just as I heard a faint scream coming from the direction of the ship.

I whirled to see the apple-eating Cardian hanging far over the gunwale of the boat with a long fish gaff in his left hand. He'd just used it to snag Sabina beneath the armpit and was dragging her slowly upward against the hull as she thrashed wildly in its hooked grip. I cursed and leaped over the body of the man I had just killed, racing toward the water. The Cardian had Sabina high enough now that he could wrap his free hand in her wet hair. He tossed the gaff aside, then grabbed her with both hands while Sabina beat ineffectually up at him with her fists. I could hear the man laughing as Sabina bucked and twisted in his grasp. I ran for the prow of the boat, but the Cardian had had the foresight to pull up the rope ladder. I tried leaping for the railing, but my searching fingers didn't even come close. I cursed and glanced at Sabina again. I knew I only had moments before the bastard got her over the side. I grunted in frustration, then plunged into the sea.

I could feel the surprisingly cold current swirling around me as I pressed forward, tugging at my legs with every step. I glanced behind me at the beach, hoping Baine or Tyris would notice what was happening, but all I could see from my vantage point were unidentifiable shadows locked in combat. I realized I should have called for the archers help right away and cursed myself for reacting without thinking. Now there wasn't time to go back to alert them. I also knew that with the wind and surf, it was unlikely Baine or Tyris would hear me if I shouted out to them from where I was. I had to assume that I was on my own.

I moved deeper into the water, clutching Wolf's Head in my right hand, and wiping my eyes with the other as each successive wave splashed spray into my face. The floor began to slope dramatically beneath my feet, and after two more steps, I was up to my shoulders in seawater, coughing up salty brine and stumbling over uneven rocks. I was surprised at how quickly the water had deepened and deathly afraid it would be over my head at any moment. I glanced up at the Cardian, whose face was set in fierce concentration as he struggled to lift Sabina. He seemed completely unaware of me making my way toward them in the water. I thought about trying to throw Wolf's Head at the man, then discarded the idea. My balance on the slippery rocks was precarious at best. I might hit Sabina by accident.

The Cardian had reached an impasse, I saw, unwilling to let her go, but also unable to get her fully over the gunwale. I could hear his agonized groans of effort as he fought to maintain his balance on the deck and hold onto the girl at the same time. I had to get Sabina away from the bastard before he got her over the side. Once he had her, the Cardian would have a hostage that he could use as leverage against us.

I took several more cautious steps and finally stopped beneath the struggling girl. I reached up with my left hand, trying to latch onto her as the cold seawater rose over my mouth and splashed into my eyes. Finally, I managed to grasp one of her kicking feet and I yanked on it just as a powerful wave rocked the stern of the boat and swept around the hull. This one was three times the size of any other that I'd had to deal with so far. I turned my face away and spread my legs, bracing myself for the impact that I knew was coming. I felt the Cardian above me tugging harder on Sabina as we fought over her, and I heard her agonized howl of pain just as the wave crashed into me. I staggered from the force of it as my right boot slipped on the slime-covered rocks. I lost my grip on Sabina's foot and fell just as rushing seawater swept over my head, filling my mouth. Then the current took hold of me.

I twirled head over ass, feeling myself being drawn farther out to sea. I fought against it, helpless as a cork in a waterfall before suddenly the flow of the tide reversed. It swept me backward almost contemptuously to where I had been moments before, then released me. I immediately sank downward like a stone, battered, and stunned as I found myself dropping to the bottom of the seabed. I flailed my arms until I got my legs under me and fought to stand until finally, I broke the surface. I lifted my face to the sky and sucked in air greedily as I twisted my neck to look up at the boat. The Cardian had managed to pull Sabina halfway over the railing now. He had one balled fist still entwined in her hair and his other hand wrapped around the back of her neck as he pushed down, while she clutched madly at the gunwale.

I looked up at the hull, but there was nothing to grab for a handhold. I cursed in frustration. I only had moments left before he had her, and desperate, I reached as high as I could and stabbed Wolf's Head deep into the side of the oak planking. I unsheathed my father's axe and held it in my right hand while I grabbed the hilt of my sword with my left hand. Then I waited.

The Cardian was cursing over and over again, tugging at Sabina. Finally, he lost patience and pounded her several times across the back with his fist. I saw the girl sag weakly under the blows, then the Cardian leaned far over the gunwale and grabbed her legs to flip her over the side. My opportunity had come. I flexed my knees, squatting in the water as far as possible while still gripping the sword hilt. Then I thrust upward with my legs and pulled on the sword at the same time. The Cardian's eyes widened in fear as I burst out of the water and swung the axe one-handed, catching him with a meaty thunk on the side of his head. I heard his neck snap with a satisfying crunch and saw blood spray outward as he fell backward out of sight, then I dropped back into the sea.

Sabina flailed her arms and legs above me as she lost her balance and tumbled after me, splashing awkwardly into the water five feet away. I struggled to my feet and sheathed my axe as I fought my way through the waves, then grabbed her arm and drew her to me.

I lifted her slight form into my arms and carried her toward the shore as I coughed and hacked up seawater.

We reached shallower water and I lowered Sabina to her feet as I peered anxiously into her face. "Are you all right?"

Sabina looked up at the boat and shuddered, then pressed herself against me. "You saved my life," I heard her mumble. "Again."

"He wasn't going to kill you," I said with a weary smile as I held her. "He just needed a hostage." I didn't bother to add that once the bastard had gotten away, he probably would have slit her throat and thrown her body into the sea. I didn't see the point. Instead, I tried to urge her toward the shore, but she resisted, shaking her head. "But we need to get you warm," I protested.

"Just a moment longer," Sabina said. She looked up at me with pleading eyes. "Please, Hadrack."

I sighed in discomfort as I shifted my gaze to the shore. The battle was over now, I saw, and my men were combing the beach with torches from the bonfires as they called out my name. I realized we must be nearly invisible with our bodies pressed together and the dark bulk of the ship behind us.

"We're over here!" I shouted.

"Hadrack?" Jebido hollered back. "Is that you?"

"Yes. Sabina and I are fine."

Jebido moved to the water's edge, lifting his torch. "What are you two doing out there?"

"It's a long story," I said. "The Cardians?"

"All dead but one," Jebido replied. "Malo is talking with the bastard right now."

I grimaced, remembering the talk the House Agent had with the two men we'd caught up with several days ago. They had eventually told us Rorian was heading for the cove after some none-too-gentle prodding from Malo and his short sword.

"Everyone all right?" I asked. I tried to guide Sabina toward the shore again, but she just held me tighter and shook her head stubbornly. I thought about pushing her away, but I wasn't willing to chance her anger a second time after what had happened on the clifftop. This slight girl, I'd learned, did not react well to rejection.

"Fine," Jebido answered. "Sim and Putt are banged up a bit, but nothing too serious."

I nodded, relieved as I lifted Sabina's chin. She had a bruise on her forehead and her scalp showed blood where a chunk of hair was missing. I noticed her face was deathly pale and her lips were turning blue as she shivered in my arms.

"We need to get you out of the water," I said, this time a little more forcefully. Sabina turned reluctantly as I put an arm around her waist, supporting her as we headed for the shore. "You were very brave," I told her. Sabina smiled wearily and put her head on my shoulder. I'd never met anyone, I realized, who could be so strong-minded one moment, and then utterly vulnerable the next. "Pretending to drown was a brilliant idea," I added. "What made you think of it?"

"It wasn't my idea," Sabina said as we reached the shore. She smiled gratefully at Jebido as he helped her out of the water. "It was the seas." She saw the confused look on my face. "That first wave actually caught me completely by surprise. I didn't have much of a plan after getting to the ship, so I just decided to go along with it and see what happened."

I grinned, shaking my head as Malo strode stiffly toward us.

"We need to talk," the House Agent said gruffly. He motioned for me to follow him as he headed up the beach.

I sighed, shrugging at Baine and Jebido as I trailed after him. Malo stopped between the bonfires with his arms crossed over his chest. The driftwood the Cardians had used to make the fires cracked, popped, and sizzled as I halted in front of him. I put out my hands, warming them over the flames.

"So?" I finally asked. "What is it now?"

"The Cardians were waiting for the men who escaped from Springlight with Rorian," Malo said. "After that, they were heading back to Cardia. That's why they stayed behind."

"Ah," I said with a shrug. "I thought they needed the tide to free the ship."

"That too, I suppose," Malo agreed, looking distracted.

I could see something in the House Agent's eyes. A wariness I had only seen before when he was about to give me bad news.

"But that's not what you called me over here to tell me, is it?" I said.

Malo shook his head. "No, it isn't. I know where Rorian is heading now." He paused. "But you are not going to like it."

I felt my face tighten. "Tell me," I growled.

"Hadrack, they are going to Calban."

I stared at Malo in disbelief. What possible reason could the scholar have to go to Calban? I thought of Shana and I shook my head. There had to be some mistake. Shana hated Cardians more than I did after what they had done. I knew that she would never allow them back within her walls.

"The man wasn't lying," Malo said. "Just in case that's what you are thinking. I don't like it any more than you do, but trust me, Rorian is sailing for Calban."

"But it doesn't make any sense," I said. "Why would he go there of all places?"

"I don't know," Malo muttered. "The Cardian died before he could tell me." He flicked his eyes to the hulking boat behind me. "But if we hurry, we can catch the bastard before he even gets near the place."

8: Sea-Dragon

The Cardian ship was called *Sea-Dragon*, which I have to say, was a fitting name for her. She had appeared ugly and ungainly while trapped on the beach. But, once the tide lifted the boat from her bonds and we guided her into deeper waters, *Sea-Dragon* cut through the rolling waves with an effortlessness that belied my first impressions. I thought of the gannets that I'd observed back at the cove, seeing a marked similarity between the plump seabirds and the hulking ship. Both appeared awkward and clumsy-looking at first glance. But put them in their element, and they miraculously transformed into something graceful and powerful.

Fortunately for us, Putt had been the son of a fisherman before he'd fled his father's beatings, so he had a rudimentary knowledge of sailing. Since no one else had the slightest idea how to sail *Sea-Dragon* properly, Putt was duly elected captain by process of elimination. I found it rather comical to watch the red-haired outlaw as he strutted back and forth on the stern deck, puffing out his chest and barking orders. As it turned out, Baine had a deft hand on the rudder, so he was nominated pilot, while the rest of us became deckhands beneath Putt's disapproving eyes.

Sea-Dragon had a single, large square sail, which had a surprising amount of ropes and lines attached to it that all had to work in unison to function correctly. None of us had ever heard of a halyard, buntline, or clewline before, but we slowly learned under Putt's scornful tutelage. At one point, our new captain and Tyris came close to blows and I'd been forced to step in before knives were drawn. I pulled Putt aside after that and reminded him rather forcefully that he served at my pleasure, not the other way around. Putt had been more respectful once I'd had my say, though he still tended to speak a little too harshly when someone didn't understand what he wanted.

The ship had been designed to be either a warship or a trading vessel, depending upon the need. Putt told me she was called a cog, a new breed of boats that was becoming more popular. The fore and aft platforms—called castles—were protected by thick walls where archers could rake arrows down on smaller vessels. She had a long and roomy hold that smelled of rat shit, mold, and piss, and her lower deck had enough space to carry perhaps as many as ten horses. Since we couldn't bring our mounts down the cliff to the ship, I left Sim behind with instructions to guide the horses back to Halhaven, where he was to inform Daughter Gernet of the turn of events and then wait to hear from us. Malo and I had agreed we would worry about how we'd get back to Halhaven later once we dealt with Rorian.

I'd ordered Sabina to go with Sim as well, but the girl had her own ideas about that. Her father was out there somewhere and she was going after him, and no amount of arguing from me or anyone else would change her mind. I'd briefly considered leaving her behind anyway, but after everything she had done for us, I realized she deserved to come along. If it were my father on that Cardian boat, nothing would stop me from following him either.

We had been sailing beneath a moonless sky for more than three hours, and the sea ahead was almost as black as my mood. I stood alone on the forecastle with my legs braced against the wind as it tore at my hair and clothing. A small patch of churning water lit by a lantern hanging from the bowsprit was all I could see as I scanned the darkened skyline. It had taken a lot of time for us to figure out how to get *Sea-Dragon* out to sea and running beneath the wind, despite Putt's knowledge and instructions. Time that had allowed our quarry to get even farther ahead. I knew we wouldn't be able to catch up to them tonight, yet a part of me hoped that I was wrong. I was unusually tense and irritable and I needed to vent my frustration out on something. I couldn't think of anything better than giving Wolf's Head some Cardian blood to taste.

I turned as a noise sounded behind me, groaning as Jebido climbed up the wooden ladder to the platform. My friend's silver hair snapped wildly around his head as he shuffled unsteadily toward me, fighting against the pitch of the ship. I nodded to him in greeting, trying to keep the annoyance I felt at having my solitude broken from showing on my face.

"I think Putt is enjoying his new position in life a little too much," Jebido said as he came to stand beside me.

"I've already spoken to him about it," I replied, trying to keep the irritation from my voice.

"Uh-huh," Jebido muttered, looking unconvinced. "That you did. But the man has a thick skull, Hadrack. It might take a few more words, this time with a little more meat on them to get through to him."

"I'll take care of it when I go back down," I grunted. "If Putt gets on your nerves before then, you can always toss him overboard."

Jebido smiled wistfully. "Don't tempt me." *Sea-Dragon* crested a large wave and her deck rolled beneath our feet as Jebido clutched awkwardly at the gunwale. He looked nervously over the side of the hull. "Are you sure it's a good idea to sail at night?"

I flicked my eyes at him, surprised by the slight quiver in his voice. "Why wouldn't it be?" I asked.

Jebido grimaced. "What if we hit a rock or something?"

"Then we sink," I said with a disinterested shrug. "If that's The Mother's plan for us, then so be it. I'm tired of worrying about things that I can't control."

I hadn't been able to keep the edge from my voice this time and Jebido pursed his lips thoughtfully while he studied me. I turned back to the sea to escape his probing gaze.

"Is everything all right, Hadrack?" Jebido asked.

"Why wouldn't it be?"

"I don't know," Jebido said. "You seem upset."

I took a deep breath, staring down into the water. Jebido was my friend and a man that I had looked up to my entire life. I'd never held anything back from him before, but I couldn't tell him how conflicted I felt right now. We were racing across a darkened sea— chasing after a man that had been nothing but bad news since I'd had the misfortune to hear his name. That man was sailing directly toward the woman I loved for reasons that I couldn't even imagine, while we followed after him with a girl that I barely knew, yet couldn't stop myself from thinking about. I'd tried all night to picture Shana's face the last time I'd seen her, but every time I did, Sabina's pale features and green eyes would appear instead. I knew it was ridiculous, but I couldn't help but feel that I was betraying Shana somehow with my thoughts.

"It's the girl that's bothering you, isn't it?" Jebido said.

I sighed and turned to face him. Jebido had an uncanny way of getting right to the heart of the matter. It was quite frustrating, actually. I decided before this went any further, that I would try to throw him off the scent. "Yes," I replied. "I can't wrap my head around why Rorian is heading for Calban. I'm worried about Shana."

Jebido nodded in agreement. "I know, so am I." He frowned. "But that's not the girl I'm talking about, and you know it." I looked down at the deck as Jebido put his hand on my shoulder. "Want some friendly advice, lad?" he asked. I didn't answer, knowing that it wouldn't matter one way or the other what I said. I was getting Jebido's advice whether I wanted it or not. "You are a young man, Hadrack, with a lot of life ahead of you."

"How is that advice?" I grunted.

Jebido shrugged. "I'm just trying to say that you shouldn't beat yourself up for enjoying being around a pretty girl. There are very few things in life that can give a man pleasure. Pretty women are one of them, so why not enjoy yourself?" He looked to where Sabina sat on one of the benches below us. "The Mother knows if I were twenty years younger, I'd be sniffing around her too."

"I'm not sniffing around her!" I protested, perhaps a little too loudly.

"Maybe not," Jebido said with a wink. "But trust me, that girl sure is sniffing around you." He sighed and shook his head. "You have been through a lot already, Hadrack, but you're still naïve about things sometimes."

"Honor isn't naïve," I muttered as I turned away from him and leaned on the railing.

"Honor?" Jebido repeated in mock surprise. "Who said anything about that? I've never met a man with more honor than you. All I'm saying is you and Sabina are both young right now. But I have a little secret for you. Despite what you believe, that won't last forever. My advice is to take advantage of that youth while you still can. No one would blame or judge you for having a little fun."

I didn't reply. Instead, I stared moodily out at the water as I thought about what Jebido had just said. I was shocked by my friend's surprising views on my problem. I knew he cared deeply for Shana and his almost callous words seemed very out of character. I glanced over at him. "So, you are telling me I should just go and rut with Sabina and not worry about the consequences?" I shook my head in disgust. "You sound like a Pith."

"Fine, let's try to come at this another way," Jebido said, ignoring my jibe. "What did you and Lady Shana talk about the last time you were together?"

"What?" I asked, caught off-guard. Jebido just stared at me, waiting. "I don't know," I finally said. "That was months ago."

"And yet," Jebido said with a chuckle, "I'd wager she could recite everything you spoke about word for word. Women are like that."

I sighed. "Do you have a point, Jebido?" I asked. "Because if you don't get to it soon, I'm the one who will be jumping overboard."

"The point, Hadrack," Jebido said, clapping me on the back soundly. "Is during all the time the two of you spent together, did you ever promise her you would be celibate?"

I gaped at him, astounded that he could even ask such a thing. "What kind of question is that?" I demanded.

"The kind that requires an answer."

I hesitated. It had never even occurred to me to make such a promise. Why would it? A part of my brain—the part that I'd been fighting all night—gleefully latched onto Jebido's words, using it to justify what I had been thinking about Sabina.

"That's what I thought," Jebido said at the look on my face. "So, why the guilt then? You have done nothing wrong, and even if you choose to lay with Sabina, you're not married or even betrothed to Lady Shana. So, where is the problem?" I took a deep breath, not answering. Jebido turned me toward the ladder. "Go sleep on it. I'm sure you will see things clearer in the morning. I'll take the rest of the watch."

I hesitated. If I stayed where I was, I knew Jebido would just keep talking about this all night long.

"I'll go," I finally said. "But make sure you come and get me in a few hours."

"I'll do that," Jebido agreed.

Even though our talk had accomplished nothing useful in my opinion, my black mood had lifted somewhat. I paused halfway down the ladder and glanced back at Jebido, who was gingerly rubbing the scabbed-over burn that dominated the tip of his nose.

"Picking at that thing won't make it any smaller," I said with a wry grin.

Jebido snatched his hand away from his nose guiltily and grimaced at me. "Very funny."

Jebido didn't awaken me like I'd asked, and it wasn't until the first rays of sunlight started to sneak over the gunwale and tickle my face that I finally awoke. I stared up at the sky—which was already a bright blue and clear of cloud cover. I could hear the harsh calls of seabirds as they circled high above the ship as I slowly sat up and scratched at my scalp. Niko was sleeping soundly on his side near me, snoring softly with an empty bottle tucked into his chest. I had no idea where he'd gotten the wine, but I knew I would have to put a stop to it right away. Niko was a good-natured, likable fellow, but put enough drink in him and he would turn black and dangerous in the blink of an eye.

I could see Malo and Putt moving around up on the sterncastle, while Baine stood with his back to me near the rudder, staring down into the sea. I glanced at the bow, where Jebido and Sabina stood together on the forecastle talking. I felt a moment of anxiety, afraid my friend might be telling her of our conversation the previous night. I heard Sabina's musical laughter as it drifted down to me and I relaxed, realizing Jebido would never break that confidence.

I stood and pissed into the sea, enjoying the warmth of the sunlight on my face as I relieved myself. The eastern skies were still showing a hint of pink, which promised a beautiful day ahead. Niko muttered something unintelligible in his sleep behind me and I glanced down at him. The young outlaw scratched at his scraggly beard, releasing the empty bottle, which rattled noisily away across the deck. He grumbled fitfully, then turned onto his back and opened his eyes, blinking up at me.

"Morning," I said cheerfully.

I felt surprisingly well-rested and as if a weight had been lifted from my shoulders. The whispers of desire that had plagued me since I'd met Sabina had finally been silenced, banished somehow during my sleep. I looked up at Jebido and said a silent word of gratitude toward him. It had felt like my friend was pushing me toward Sabina last night. But, by pointing me in that direction so obviously, he'd actually turned me away from it. Which I suspected had been his intent all along. From now on, I resolved, I would keep Sabina at arms length. We would still be friends, of course, but nothing more than that.

"Good morning, my lord," Niko said as he sat up. He yawned and stretched his arms, then blinked up at the sky. "Not much of a wind," he muttered.

I glanced up at the slack sail in surprise. I hadn't noticed, but Niko was right. We were barely moving at all.

"My lord!" I heard from above. I shielded my eyes and craned my neck to see Tyris balancing on a small wooden platform near the top of the mast. He held onto the tip of the pole with one hand and pointed to the north. "I see sails ahead!" He held up a pair of fingers. "Two of them!"

I stared in the direction the blond archer had pointed, but saw nothing other than rolling waves and blue sky. I headed for the sterncastle at a run, climbing the ladder two rungs at a time. Malo was waiting for me when I reached the top.

"Is it them?" I asked eagerly.

"It's them," the House Agent confirmed with a growl. I leaned against the railing and peered north, just able to make out what looked like two shimmering masts on the horizon. Malo glanced up at the limp sail, then the sky. "Not that it's going to do us much good without the wind at our backs."

"How long have we been sitting like this?" I asked.

"Since before dawn," Malo replied sourly. He gestured to Putt with a thumb. "This one says the wind will return eventually, which is an easy prediction to make. He just won't commit to when. It could be in an hour, two hours, or two days for all we know."

"Soon," Putt said confidently. He sniffed the air and looked at me. "I can smell it, my lord."

"You said that a while ago," Malo grunted.

"And I'm still not wrong," Putt insisted. "It's coming any time now. You'll see."

Putt had *Sea-Dragon* running about a mile off the coast. The red-haired outlaw had wisely kept us close enough to keep land in sight, but far enough out that we were safe from running aground on any hidden reefs or shoals that might be lurking closer in. I studied the unfamiliar coastline made up of craggy cliffs, dense forests, and sloping hills of rock and grass.

"Where are we?" I asked.

Putt shrugged. "Near as I can figure, about three days from Calban, my lord."

"Three days with a good wind behind us, you mean," I muttered.

"True," Putt agreed. He gestured ahead. "The only good news is, if we're not moving, then neither are they."

"Maybe," I grunted, not convinced as I focused on our quarry.

I thought back to the grooves that I'd seen on the beach where the Cardians had landed beside *Sea-Dragon*. Those ruts had been much shallower than the one *Sea-Dragon* had made. I suspected they had been left behind by the sleeker and smaller Cardian longboats that I was more familiar with, rather than by cogs. If that was the case, then I knew those ships had banks of oars, which meant our quarry would be able to keep going, even without the wind. I leaned my back against the railing and explained my worries to Malo and Putt.

"If that's true, then we will never catch them," Malo said when I finished.

The House Agent flexed his hands open and closed impotently, looking frustrated as he stared north. I knew how he felt. Every moment that we sat stranded where we were increased Rorian's lead on us and brought him that much closer to Calban. I felt a lurch in my stomach when I thought about what that might mean. I doubted the Cardians had forgotten the humiliation of being run out of Calban a year ago. I also knew that they would gladly take revenge on Shana and her people if they had the chance. I wasn't sure how they expected to get into the castle, considering Shana's hostility toward them. But one thing I had learned about the scholar so far was that it would be a mistake to underestimate him.

A long, frustrating hour went by, followed by another, while we waited helplessly for Putt's promised wind that would not come. Malo and I took to pacing past each other across the deck in mutual impatience. Every so often, the House Agent would pause in his strides to glare at Putt accusingly. The red-haired outlaw could do nothing but shrug and look away, which did little to mollify Malo.

Finally, at midday, with most of the crew dozing in the shade against the sidewalls along the lower deck, the limp sail began to flutter lazily as a faint breeze sniffed at it curiously. I braced my hands on the railing, praying to The Mother to not let it falter as I felt the gentle caress of the wind across the back of my neck. The sky had been clear all day, but now I could see a wall of white clouds rolling toward us far to the south, with small puffs of advance scouts moving quickly ahead of them. The sail suddenly snapped loudly like the crack of a whip and then began to fill as the wind strengthened. My men rose and cheered as *Sea-Dragon* finally came to life beneath our feet. I cheered right along with them.

"I told you so, my lord! I told you so!" Putt cried out over and over again as he danced a jig beside me.

The red-haired outlaw finally gained control of himself and he began barking orders with renewed vigor like a man who had just escaped the gallows. I glanced at Malo, who actually allowed a momentary smile to crack through his usually dour features, thinking perhaps that Putt just may have. My men ran to obey Putt's commands, while Baine dashed for the rudder. I glanced to the north, but the masts we'd seen there earlier had long since disappeared. Would we see them again before Calban? I wondered, feeling that familiar thud of dread in my stomach.

Putt set Malo and me to tinkering with the sail, pulling out every trick that he could remember from his youth to gain us more speed. He ordered Niko and Tyris to go down to the hold and throw some of the heavier cargo overboard. Poor Niko had tears rolling down his cheeks as he and the blond archer tipped several barrels full of wine over the gunwale.

Sea-Dragon began to move even faster once we had lightened her, running with the wind as she rejoiced in her sudden freedom. We were all in a jubilant mood—though Niko still pouted somewhat—as we lined the fore and stern castles, studying the skyline in anticipation. Finally, after more than an hour, Tyris cried out the words we'd all been hoping to hear.

"I see the bastards!" the blond archer shouted from above. He pounded his fist against the mast in excitement. "We're gaining on them! By The Mother, we're gaining!"

And so we were.

Minute by minute, the masts of Rorian's ships grew larger, until finally we could make out the misty forms of the vessels themselves. I nodded as we drew ever closer, my guess confirmed. The Cardians had longboats.

The coast to our right—what Putt referred to as starboard—was jagged and rocky, with knife-like ridges of rock dotting the waters that could easily tear the hull from a ship. I was doubly glad Putt had kept us so far from the shoreline, though surprised to see that Rorian was running his boats much closer to land than we were. I assumed his pilots knew the waters here as well as whatever dangers might lurk beneath them.

"They are using the oars and the sails in tandem, my lord," Putt said, pointing to the rhythmic flashes of light near the water where the sun glinted off the Cardian blades. "They have seen our sails and are trying to outrun us." He glanced at me. "Though how they know we're not fellow Cardians is a mystery to me."

"Burel was supposed to head back to Cardia from the cove," I said. "Rorian knows that." I stared ahead at the fleeing ships, picturing the scar-faced man looking back at us. The scholar was resilient, cautious, and smart, I thought with grudging respect. "He must have figured out something is wrong."

"That explains it, then," Putt said. "But what they are doing shows the bastards are desperate."

"How so?" I asked.

"We're faster than they are, my lord, and they know that. They are trying to draw us closer to the coast, hoping with our bigger hull that we'll get holed." Putt grinned yellow teeth at me. "Luckily, I'm not stupid enough to do that." Putt's grin faded. "What exactly is the plan once we catch up to them, by the way?"

"Get us close enough to board one of them," I said, "and our swords will take care of the rest. Once we've taken one, we can chase down the other." Putt had begun making a clucking sound of disapproval between his teeth before I had even finished talking. "What?" I asked in annoyance.

"Well, my lord," Putt said, hesitating as he glanced at me sideways. "No disrespect to you, but you are not a seaman. You don't understand what you are asking. Boarding a ship on an open sea is risky, even for an experienced crew, which we clearly are not. Baine only has a few hours on the rudder, while those Cardians out there have probably been piloting ships since they were boys. Not to mention those longboats are far lighter and more maneuverable than we are."

"You could pilot us," I suggested. "That would free up Baine's bow."

Putt shook his head. "I can't be the hands and the eyes, my lord. The sail will need adjusting constantly. I can't pilot and worry about what the rest of you are doing at the same time. Besides, I've never actually steered a ship before. Of the two of us, I'd say Baine has the steadier hand."

I sighed. "So, are you telling me that it can't be done?"

"No, my lord," Putt said. "It can be done, we just have to be smart about it." He glanced at me appraisingly. "Suppose we manage to board one of them. Then what happens?"

"Then we kill the bastards," I said immediately.

"Maybe," Putt said doubtfully. "But we are few and they are many."

"They're Cardians," I said contemptuously. "Each of us is easily worth ten of them."

"Normally, I'd agree with you on that, my lord," Putt said. He gestured to the water. "But out here, we won't have surprise on our side, nor solid ground beneath our feet. We are talking about a narrow deck that will be rocking and bucking beneath us like an enthusiastic whore. Anything can happen in that situation. The Cardians may be inferior warriors, my lord, but they are the ones familiar with this kind of fighting, not us. That second ship won't sit idly by, either. The moment they see us trying to board the first one, they will come to their aid."

I frowned as I studied the fleeing ships, picturing the scenario Putt was laying out for me. I realized the red-haired outlaw was right. It wasn't going to work. "So, what do you suggest we do?" I finally asked.

Putt smiled. "We lessen the odds, my lord." He stroked the railing affectionately. "The prow on this beauty has a thick, reinforced apron around it—ideal for ramming. I suggest we sink one of the Cardian ships first. If we hit them amidships just right, we'll smash right through their thin hull. Then we can try to board the second one. Or sink it too if you prefer."

I looked at the wooden prow of the ship that jutted out at an angle ahead of us. I had my doubts about what Putt was suggesting. "Are you sure that will even work?"

"Don't worry, my lord," Putt said. "*Sea-Dragon* is clinker-built, which means the planks of her hull are strong and overlap, like this." He held his hands up, one over the other. "This ship is a beast, my lord. She'll get the job done as sure as I'm standing here. I swear it."

"But you just told me Baine is too inexperienced to attempt to board them," I pointed out. "What makes you think he can manage something like this, but not the other?"

"We will lull them to sleep first," Putt explained. He held up his hands again, this time side by side. "We stay a length or two ahead of the lead ship off their port side bow, like this, and pace them. Then, when we've got favorable sea and wind, we cut hard to starboard." Putt smashed one hand against the other with a resounding smack. "They won't be expecting that and won't have time to evade us."

"What happens if the second ship decides to ram us?" I asked. "Won't we be vulnerable in that situation?"

"They can try," Putt said dismissively. "But after seeing the first ship go down the way I know it will, I think they'll choose to avoid us and try to flee instead."

I took a deep breath, considering Putt's words carefully. I played the scene out in my mind, knowing many things had to go right for this to work. "What if the Cardians decide they don't want to be paced?" I asked.

Putt shrugged. "What can they do? We're bigger and faster than they are."

If I were Rorian in that situation, what would I do? I wondered, knowing even as I thought it what the answer was. "What is to stop them from coming after us and trying to board us instead?" I asked, unable to hide a smile at the welcome thought of action.

Putt chuckled. "Let them. Those longboats of theirs sit low in the water. The bastards will have to climb our walls with ropes if they want to get to us." The red-haired outlaw's eyes gleamed. "There is nothing easier than skewering a man coming up a rope, my lord."

I put my hand on Putt's shoulder and squeezed in thanks. "It's a good plan, Putt. I'll talk to Malo and see what he thinks."

Malo had climbed the mast earlier to get a better look at the Cardian ships. I could see him starting to pick his way back down to the lower deck and I decided to wait where I was for him. Putt was right about one thing. Boarding one of those longboats would be difficult with the few men I had, especially if we had to fight both crews at once. Defending *Sea-Dragon* would be difficult as well if it came to that, but at least we would have control of the battleground and room to maneuver. But if the Cardians chose not to attack us and allowed us to pace them, we might still get damaged in the coming collision. Enough damage, perhaps, that it might prevent us from going after the second ship. Each option had its risks, I knew, but I'd never been in a battle yet where risk wasn't involved. I didn't expect I ever would.

The House Agent climbed back up to the platform and I filled him in on what Putt and I had discussed. I had expected instant hostility to the idea of sinking one of the Cardian ships, but Malo seemed surprisingly receptive as I talked.

"I don't agree with Putt very often," Malo said when I finished. "But this time, I think he's right."

"Rorian might die if we pick the wrong ship," I warned.

"We'll have to make sure of that first," Malo said. "If Putt can get us close enough, do you think you can identify him?"

I thought of the big man with the scarred face I had seen in the woods near Springlight. "I'll recognize him," I promised.

"Then I think we know what we have to do," Malo said.

I sent Putt to inform the others of our plans, then took out my weathered whetstone as I leaned against the railing. I began to sharpen Wolf's Head with an even, steady stroke as I waited for us to catch up to the Cardians. I could feel the weapon almost tingle in my hands in anticipation as the stone rang against the steel. Every few minutes, I glanced to the north, watching as we slowly gained on the fleeing ships.

Sabina climbed up to the sterncastle while I worked, and she came to stand beside me. We hadn't said much to each other since I'd awoken that morning. I nodded to her in greeting, preparing myself as she glared at me in a way that had, unfortunately, become very familiar lately. It was always a toss-up which girl would appear—the angry one, or the happy one. I knew by her look which one this was and why as I kept my focus on the whetstone.

"Jebido just told me that you are thinking about sinking one of the ships," Sabina said. I could hear the disbelief and anger in her voice. "Is that true?"

"Yes," I confirmed as the whetstone rang down the sword edge like a musical instrument. I blew on the weapon's blade, then thumbed it carefully. "Not sharp enough," I said absently as I started again.

"That's it?" Sabina demanded. She pointed ahead of us. "Have you forgotten that my father is on board one of those ships?"

I hesitated in mid-stroke and looked at her, then resumed my work. "I have not," I said in a steady tone. "You don't have to worry. We're not going to sink Rorian's ship. Your father will be fine."

"What if he isn't with Rorian?" Sabina demanded.

I looked at her blankly. I hadn't considered that possibility, I realized. "He will be," I said, trying to sound confident.

"How can you be sure of that?" Sabina asked.

I held Wolf's Head out and peered down the blade, then reversed it to study the opposite side. Satisfied, I sheathed the sword as I faced the girl.

"I can't," I admitted.

"Then promise me if you see him on the other ship, you won't sink it," Sabina said. She put her hand on my arm and searched my eyes with hers. "Promise me you will find another way."

"I'm sorry," I said, looking away guiltily. "I wish I could, but I can't promise that. I hope your father is with Rorian, but if not, then you have to realize there are bigger things at stake here than just one man's life."

"Maybe to you!" Sabina snapped. "You and your precious Shana!" I could see tears threatening in her eyes now. "But what about me? My father means everything to me!"

"I'm sorry," I said as I put my hand on her shoulder.

Sabina pulled away from me. "Sorry!?" she spat. She shook her head. "I don't think you are at all. To think that I—" She hesitated, looking at me searchingly as tears began to flow. "Forget about it!" she sobbed as she brushed past me and hurried down the ladder. I could hear her crying as she reached the lower deck and collapsed against the sidewall.

"A mystery, that one," Malo said gravely as he came to stand beside me. He peered down at the sobbing girl with an expressionless face. "Hard as an oak board on one side, and soft as a feathered pillow on the other."

"Maybe we should—"

"No, Hadrack," Malo said with a shake of his head. "The choice is the right one. Despite what you probably think, I'm not without sympathy for the girl. But we didn't force her father to go with the Cardians, and we can't let his presence influence how we approach things. If he's with Rorian, then he stands a chance to live. If not, then regrettably, he will die."

"Uh, my lord," Putt said from behind me in a strange tone. "We may have a problem."

The red-haired outlaw was staring south and I turned to follow his gaze. The horizon behind us had transformed, now black and angry-looking, and I could hear distant thunder starting to rumble from somewhere within its threatening mass. The wind began to pick up, becoming colder as the sea started to slap soundly against *Sea-Dragon's* hull with increasing strength. I noticed even the air I breathed had slowly changed, tasting coppery now, like blood. I felt a thud of dread in my chest as the brewing storm expanded before my eyes with alarming speed. Malo and I shared a look, and I knew the House Agent was thinking the same thing that I was. Not again! The bastard wasn't going to get away again!

"Will it miss us?" I asked Putt hopefully. The outlaw didn't answer, but I could see the worry on his face as the wind tugged at his red beard. I took his continued silence to mean no. "Can we outrun it or get around it, then?"

Putt shook his head and he gestured to the dark, sinister clouds that covered the skies. "There is nowhere for us to run, my lord. If we try to get closer to land, we will be dashed on the rocks. We have to try and weather the storm out here and hope for the best."

"How long do we have?" Malo asked, his face grim.

"Minutes," Putt answered bluntly. He glanced at us, the beginnings of fear in his eyes now. "Storms move fast on the water, and this one looks nasty." The outlaw leaned over the railing as the ship began to buck and kick like an unbroken horse beneath us. He cupped his hands around his mouth. "Baine!" he shouted down.

"What do I do?" I heard Baine call out, sounding panicked. "The rudder feels like it's going to come off in my hands!"

"Tie yourself to the railing and hold onto that rudder!" Putt shouted back. "Run *Sea-Dragon* with the wind. Whatever you do, don't let her swing her beams to the waves!" He turned urgently to Malo and me. "Get the others and reef that sail!" I stared at him stupidly as Putt made an impatient face. "Roll the sail halfway, my lord, like I taught you. If that storm gets here and the sail is full, it will push our nose into the sea and we'll capsize."

Malo and I raced for the ladder as I shouted for Tyris, Niko, and Jebido to join us. We made it to the lower deck and headed for the mast just as huge raindrops started to fall. The drops were hesitant at first, but then the skies broke open with a crash and it became an instant deluge, pounding against my head and shoulders.

Niko shouted something at me as we converged on the mast, but I couldn't hear him over the howling wind and rain. I pointed upward and motioned to him what was needed just as the boat suddenly lurched sideways. I lost my footing and collided awkwardly against the young outlaw and we both fell, rolling end over end until we crashed heavily into the sidewall. I lay still for a moment, stunned, then struggled to my feet, fighting to keep my balance as *Sea-Dragon's* deck creaked loudly in protest beneath me. A massive wave rose above the ship, hanging there for a moment, then it surged over the gunwale toward me. I staggered beneath its force, spitting seawater as the wave buried Niko's still form beneath a solid wall of water.

I shook my head, blinking away the salt that burned my eyes. A small casket bounced and spun crazily past me before the wind snatched at it and drew it over the side. I grabbed Niko and half-carried, half-dragged his still form toward the center of the ship. I paused and checked to make sure he was still alive, relieved when I felt a weak pulse. I knew Malo and the others needed my help and I looked around in desperation, afraid Niko would get swept overboard if I left him where he was. I saw the hatch to the cargo hold was open, so I lowered the young outlaw's limp body down inside where he'd be safe. It was the best that I could do for him.

Sea-Dragon bellowed like a wounded animal as she thrashed and rolled, battling gamely to remain afloat. I stood up, fighting to keep my balance just as the top spar on the mast disintegrated before my eyes. The wind howled in triumph, snatching at the shattered sections of wood as it whisked them away. Then the storm went to work on the rigging, tangling the halyard hopelessly and worrying away at the sail until a massive rip appeared. I started to shout a warning—though I can't imagine what anyone could have done anyway—just as the entire right side of the sail tore off and flapped away.

Sea-Dragon instantly began to wallow in the water and her stern started to give way, slowly turning her nose toward the waves. Putt had warned Baine about letting that very thing happen and I knew he would need my help. I headed for the stern but managed only two steps before the ship shuddered as though it had been struck. The deck began to tilt sharply beneath me and I staggered, holding on as the portside bow started to list dangerously close to the waterline. I closed my eyes, waiting for that first bite of cold sea that would signal the end.

Sea-Dragon groaned and trembled as the wind and waves buffeted her, but her builders had made her stout, and somehow she resisted, until finally, miraculously, she slowly leveled out again. I opened my eyes, surprised to be alive as I pressed onward through the blinding rain. Then I stopped in dismay. The rudder was gone—snapped off—and only a frayed rope flapping madly in the wind remained behind to show where it had been.

Baine was gone too.

9: Stranded

    The storm continued to rage, but I barely even noticed it now. It seemed impossible that Baine could be dead, yet I knew without a doubt in my mind that he was. No man could survive those waters for long. I felt my knees go numb with weakness as the realization struck me that I would never see him again. I should have come to Baine's aid sooner, I thought guiltily. He would still be alive if I had. I'd failed my friend when he needed me the most, and I knew that no matter how long I lived, I would never be able to forgive myself.
    I'm not ashamed to admit that I wept then as the ship stubbornly fought the rolling waves. I could feel the gale both pushing and tugging at me at the same time, as though trying to tempt me to let go of the railing so that I might share in Baine's fate. The chances were good that *Sea-Dragon* would be swamped by one of those waves soon anyway, I knew, so either way, I was fairly sure that the storm would get its wish in due course. Finally, I spat down into the sea that had taken Baine from me. If this storm wanted me, I resolved, then by The Mother, it would have to come and take me kicking and screaming.
    I turned away, struggling back along the deck to take shelter in the enclosure beneath the sterncastle. There were no walls to protect me here, just eight stout oak beams to hold up the decking above my head. Even so, the open space still managed to provide some relief from the wind, spray, and rain. I hugged a post and stared out at the roiling sea as the storm shrieked in fury as it sought me out, clearly irked that its prey had escaped—at least for the moment. The severed rope that Baine had used danced and twisted wildly along the railing in front of me, openly mocking my sorrow.
    Putt and Malo eventually appeared, looking for me. They stopped by my side, silently taking in the missing rudder and frayed

rope. I could see the dismay on their dripping faces when they realized what had happened, but neither one said anything. I imagine the look on my face discouraged that. Both men shared a glance, and then they turned away without a word, though Putt paused momentarily to put his hand on my shoulder in commiseration. I watched them head back the way they had come, fighting against the whipping wind and rolling deck. I knew there was no reason to stay where I was any longer and that my help might be needed elsewhere, but truthfully, I just wanted to be alone. This place was as good as any other on the ship for that. Besides, we had half a sail and no rudder. *Sea-Dragon* and everyone on board her were entirely at the mercy of The Mother and The Father now. I knew there was nothing any of us could do to change that.

"Hadrack?"

I shielded my eyes from the spray coming off the gunwale, watching as Jebido struggled unsteadily across the deck toward me. I held out a hand to him as he approached, drawing him to me as a wave washed over the deck, soaking us both and almost knocking my friend from his feet. Jebido put his hand on my shoulder to steady himself as he grabbed onto the same beam as me.

"Is it true?" Jebido asked as he hugged the post tightly. His face looked deathly white, but I could tell by his expression that he already knew the answer to his question. He just needed to hear it from me.

I dropped my eyes and nodded. "I came too late," I managed to say, hearing the bitterness in my voice.

"It's not your fault, lad," Jebido said. I could see the sorrow in his eyes as he looked to the sea. "Baine is with Mother Above now, Hadrack. There is nothing more that we can do for him. But now I need you to come back with me. We lost the other half of the sail, and Malo wants us all to take refuge in the hold until this blows over."

"Why?" I asked. "If we are to die out here, then I want to greet death with a curse on my lips, not spend my last moments cowering in some rat-infested hold. I'll stay where I am."

"Don't be a fool, Hadrack!" Jebido shouted at me over the wind. He tugged at my arm. "Listen to me, you stubborn bastard! I've already lost one son today, and I'll be damned if I lose the other! You either come back with me right now, or I swear I'll pick your giant ass up and carry you there myself!"

I sighed and looked out to sea again. I knew Jebido wasn't just making an idle threat. He would do everything in his power to make me go back with him—even if it meant carrying me. I felt suddenly weary; the fight gone from me, and I turned to him. "Fine, Jebido," I said. "You win. I doubt you could have carried me more than five feet anyway."

"Maybe not," Jebido said, looking hugely relieved. "But I would have damn well tried."

I took one final, regretful glance at the sea, then followed Jebido out into the storm. We clung to each other as the ship lurched, working our way cautiously along the slippery deck to the closed hatch. I let Jebido descend into the ship's belly first, then I followed, locking the hatch firmly behind me as the wind above tore at it, trying to pry it back open. A single lantern lit the interior of the hold weakly, swinging from the rafters as I climbed down the ladder. The hold was roomier now that most of the cargo was gone, though the stink of rat shit and piss remained. Someone had also been sick recently, I noted, adding to the stench.

My men were braced along both walls, sitting on the floor and hanging onto whatever they could as the ship rocked and shuddered as it courageously fought the storm. The atmosphere inside the hold felt charged with a mixture of fear, apprehension, and grief. It seemed I wasn't the only one who had been affected by Baine's death. Niko had recovered, I was happy to see, with only a bruised temple to show for his ordeal. He greeted me, thanking me profusely for what I'd done for him as I lowered myself down beside him. Sabina sat opposite me, propped up between Tyris and Sim. I could tell the girl was trying to catch my eye, but I had no interest in her pity right now, so I pretended not to notice.

The ship's hull started to creak alarmingly behind my head, and I had a vision of the wooden planks suddenly bursting open, pouring tons of cold, merciless seawater on us. I quickly thrust that thought away as Malo staggered to his feet and rushed to the opposite end of the hold, where he began gagging and retching over one of the few remaining crates that had escaped being thrown overboard. I felt my stomach churn at the sounds of the House Agent being sick and I closed my eyes, trying to ignore the seesawing motion of the ship.

An hour passed as we waited for death to come for us. Then another, but despite the fury of the storm raging over our heads, *Sea-Dragon* somehow managed to remain afloat through it all. Eventually, the sounds from outside began to lessen, and the ship's rocking slowly started to diminish. Was it over? I wondered. No one said anything as we listened hopefully, not wanting to give voice to the thought that maybe we would live and tempt the gods into changing that. Finally, unable to take the silence any longer, I stood up on shaky legs and headed toward the ladder. Malo watched me wordlessly, his face pasty white as I climbed and lifted the hatch a crack to peer outside. The rain was still falling heavily, I saw, but coming down straighter now as the wind had tapered off somewhat.

"It looks like it might be weakening," I said to the others. "I'll go take a look."

I flipped open the hatch and climbed onto the deck, then moved to the gunwale. I saw nothing behind or to the sides but grey, unfriendly skies hiding behind sheets of rain, with giant, menacing waves rolling bellow them. Then I peered ahead as *Sea-Dragon* crested a wave and her bottom flattened out. I cursed at what I saw. A black mass of rock stood directly in our path, jutting up from the sea like a clenched fist less than two hundred yards away. I knew without a doubt that I was looking at the death of us all. The gods weren't done with us yet, it would seem. I could see more rocks poking out from the water like the spine of a giant reptile to the reef's right, with open sea to the left.

I was helpless to do anything but clutch the gunwale and pray as a giant wave arose, sweeping against our starboard bow, causing the entire ship to shudder. White foam and spray shot up and over the gunwale, falling onto the deck with a sharp slap as *Sea-Dragon* slowly began to turn from the force of the wave, offering it her stern. The ship straightened out, rocking back and forth as she gamely rode the swell like the stubborn beast that she was as I hung on for my life. We reached the crest of the enormous wave and I stared down in awe, fascinated despite myself by the power of the sea as we slowly tipped, then plunged into the waiting trough below. I could hear a strange howling sound ringing out and it took me a moment to realize that the noise was coming from me. The ship's nose cut into the frothing sea like a sword blade, burying her bow and forecastle deep into the rolling tide. I didn't think *Sea-Dragon* would be able to come back from all that weight, but somehow she muscled through, shuddering as she slowly rose, shaking seawater from her decks like a wet dog.

    I wiped the spray from my face, peering ahead anxiously. Where was the reef? The force of the wave had knocked us off our path, I finally saw with relief, putting the rocky barrier thirty feet away from our starboard bow. Would it be far enough? I held my breath, envisioning knife-like, rocky protrusions hiding below the surface just waiting to eviscerate the hull, but nothing happened as we hurtled past. I caught a fleeting glimpse of another ship hung up on the jagged reef, twisted and broken on its teeth. Men were struggling weakly in the water and I saw a sudden flash of red in their midst. I grimaced. Cardians! A man lifted a hand in desperation when he saw me, shouting for help. I just stared down at him dispassionately as *Sea-Dragon* quickly left him behind. Even if I could have, I wouldn't have lifted a finger to help him. I watched as the Cardian's head disappeared beneath the waves, wondering absently if it had been Rorian, not really caring one way or the other.

    The sheeting rain began to lessen as the sea propelled the ship forward, slapping me now with big, cold droplets that had me shivering in no time. Within minutes, the wind began to weaken even more, smoothing out the waves, though the skies above remained grey and threatening. Niko cautiously poked his head up from the hold and looked around. He saw me standing by the gunwale, my hands still clutching it, my fingers aching from holding on so tightly.

"Is it finally over, my lord?" he asked shakily.

"I think so," I said, aware of the shake in my own voice. I carefully released the gunwale and moved to help the young outlaw up. "Is everyone all right down there?"

"A few bumps and bruises," Niko said. His face saddened. "I'm sorry about Baine, my lord. Malo told us not to say anything, but—"

"Then don't," I said gruffly, cutting him off. I didn't want to talk about Baine. Not yet. Maybe never. Instead, I glanced up at the ravaged mast with its dangling rigging and torn bits of sail. The platform was still intact, at least. "Get up top and let me know what you see."

"Yes, my lord," Niko said.

The young outlaw scaled the mast as Putt appeared from the hold, followed by Tyris and a very ill-looking Malo. Jebido was next, and he turned and helped Sabina up onto the deck.

"Damn," Putt muttered as he stared around at the battered ship. The red-haired outlaw had come to love *Sea-Dragon*, and I could tell he was dismayed at the beating that she'd taken.

"Anything?" I called up to Niko.

"Nothing, my lord. But it's hazy and hard to see more than fifty yards."

"Stay up there and let me know the moment you see land," I ordered. The wind was lessening by the moment, now less than a tenth of what it had been at the height of the storm. I glanced at Putt, who was still talking to himself as he surveyed the ship. "What do we do now, Captain?"

"Do, my lord?" Putt said, looking thoroughly shaken. "There's nothing we can do. We have no rudder or sails."

"Then find a way!" I snapped, irritated by Putt's willingness to give up. "One of the Cardian ships has sunk, but the other might have survived," I said tightly, "and I'll be damned if I'm going sit here helpless while they keep going."

Putt stared at me blankly.

"Hadrack—" Jebido began, reaching out to me.

"Don't!" I said, slapping his hand away. "Whatever it is, I don't want to hear it."

I stalked off angrily, heading for the stern, where I drew my sword and lopped off the offending rope hanging there. I glared at it, then threw the rope as far as I could into the sea. I stood, bracing my hands on the railing as I stared down at the wake left behind from *Sea-Dragon's* passage. The ship's momentum had already begun to ease, I realized. Soon we would be at a standstill, stranded in the middle of nowhere and helpless to do anything to change that. It was beyond maddening.

"My lord?" Putt said tentatively from behind me. I turned. The outlaw was holding a red cape in his hands. He held it up. "There might be a way to reach land using these."

I frowned. "Tell me," I growled.

"There are several crates of these in the hold," Putt explained. He looked apologetic. "The Cardians probably had a spare sail down there too, but we couldn't find it."

"Which means it ended up over the side," I said as I leaned against the gunwale and crossed my arms. "Which you recommended we do."

"Yes, my lord," Putt said, coloring.

I gestured to the cape. "So, you're suggesting we make a sail using those, is that right?"

Putt grimaced. "Yes, and no, my lord." He fidgeted under my glare. "We found several sewing needles, but not enough yarn to make a full sail, so I suggest we make many smaller ones." I took an impatient breath as Putt hurried to explain. "We can tie them together at the corners, my lord, then attach them to the rigging. There will be gaps, of course, but it should work."

I took the cape and fingered the material. "Is this silk?" I asked, surprised by the elegance and softness.

"Afrenian silk, my lord," Putt said. "Nobody weaves it better." He grinned, looking a little more confident now. "What we have on this ship is probably worth a fortune."

"Won't the wind just shred them?"

"Probably," Putt said. "But I'm hoping they can last long enough to get us to land. We can replace any that rip." The red-bearded outlaw shrugged. "It will be slow going to be sure, but it's our only chance, my lord."

I rubbed my finger along the silk thoughtfully. "Suppose it does work, what good will it do us without a rudder?"

"Ah," Putt said. "Now, that part is fairly easy. My father was a drunken, womanizing bastard, my lord, but even so, the man could sail. Our rudder hit a shoal once and snapped off, much like what probably happened to us. I was terrified, certain we would die out at sea, but my father just cursed me for being a witless fool and explained how we would use a drift anchor to steer us home."

I perked up. "That sounds promising," I said. "How does it work?"

"We need something heavy," Putt said. "I imagine one of the crates the capes were stored in will do nicely. We'll fill the crate with whatever we can find, then tie two ropes to it and drag it behind the ship." He grinned. "We attach one rope to the starboard stern, the other to the portside. Shorten the rope on one side, and the ship will turn the other way. It's rather simple, actually."

I stared at Putt in surprise. "That's it?"

"That's it, my lord," Putt said. He shrugged. "It's not perfect, of course, but given the alternatives—"

"We'll do it," I said, cutting him off. "The sooner, the better."

I looked up. The sun was struggling to break through the heavy clouds now, even as it slid westward across the sky as dusk approached. Small pockets of rain persisted here and there, slapping us with raindrops intermittently. A giant plume of water suddenly rose from the sea off the starboard bow, twisting and turning thirty feet away from me. I stared at it in fascination, realizing it was a waterspout as it pranced almost daintily across the surface. I could feel the wind rifling my wet hair as the waterspout closed the distance between us. It paused, hovering less than ten feet from *Sea-Dragon's* hull, spiraling around and around, then slowly unraveled and fell, returning itself to the sea.

"A good omen, my lord," Putt said as Jebido and a queasy-looking Malo joined us. "The Mother is letting us know that She is watching over us."

"Let's hope so," I grunted, not convinced as I filled the others in on Putt's plan.

Malo looked dubious when I was through. "It won't work," he said bluntly.

"It will," Putt replied stubbornly. "As long as we tie the capes securely and the wind stays down, it will work."

"Do you have a better plan, Malo?" I asked.

The House Agent just looked at me sourly with puffy, bloodshot eyes.

"Won't the tide eventually just push us toward land?" Jebido asked Putt. He looked east. "We can't be that far out."

The outlaw grimaced. "The sea is a fickle mistress. She's as likely to send us farther out to sea as not. If I was betting my life on it, and I am, then I'd not wait around to see which direction she decides to send us."

It took us the rest of that day and the better part of the night to prepare the Cardian capes and Putt's improvised rudder. There was little wind to speak of when we finished and I decided it was pointless to try to fumble our way in the darkness trying to install the sail. Besides, I could see the exhaustion in the others' eyes.

"I'll take the first watch," I said. "Niko, I'll come and wake you in three hours."

"Yes, my lord," the young outlaw said.

I climbed the ladder to the sterncastle and stared out to sea, feeling a deep sadness take over me. Are you happy where you are, Baine? I wondered as the now calm waves lapped lazily against *Sea-Dragon's* hull. Are you safe and content, with plenty to eat and endless women to pleasure you? I thought sadly of Flora and Baine's coming child, not relishing having to tell her of his death once we returned to Witbridge Manor. If we returned, I thought moodily. A half-moon winked down at me as I looked up at the star-filled sky, wishing I could see Baine's face and hear his laugh just one more time.

"Is the World Above everything we expect, my friend?" I whispered to the sky.

"Hadrack?"

I turned, surprised as Sabina hesitated on the ladder. She stared at me, her head and shoulders all that was visible above the deck.

"Oh," she said, looking relieved. "I thought you were alone, but then I heard voices."

"Just me talking to myself," I said as I helped her up the ladder.

We stood facing each other, both suddenly silent.

"I couldn't sleep," Sabina finally said. She moved to the railing and I followed her, both of us leaning on it as we stared down at the water. "I'm sorry about Baine," she said. I didn't respond, though I felt my body tense. "I know how much he meant to you. Jebido told me everything the three of you went through in that horrible mine." She shook her head. "It's a remarkable story."

I sighed. Sabina was just trying to help, I knew. Getting angry at her seemed pointless. I felt myself start to relax. "I don't know what I will do without him," I admitted, saying it as much to myself as to her.

"You'll do what you have always done," Sabina replied. "You will survive and grow stronger."

I glanced at her. "What exactly has that old goat been telling you?"

Sabina smiled wistfully. "He loves you so much," she said. "He would do anything for you and Baine."

I swallowed, feeling a knot twist in my stomach. "Jebido talks too much," I said gruffly. "I think his mind might be going."

"We both know that's not true," Sabina said. She put her warm hand over mine. It felt good and I left it there, enjoying her touch. "You know, sometimes it feels like I have known you all my life, Hadrack."

I grunted at that, not sure how to respond.

"I remember the first day that I met you," Sabina continued. "You seemed so brash and arrogant. I remember wondering why your men followed you so willingly."

"They follow me because they swore an oath and I pay them," I said. "There is no mystery to it."

Sabina looked unconvinced. "I think there is a lot more to it than that. Besides, you don't pay Malo. The man's an ass, but he's also a House Agent, with all the prestige that entails. Yet he listens and obeys you too.

I snorted, genuinely amused at the idea. "Malo doesn't obey me," I said. "He has his own agenda. He's fine with letting me lead as long as it aligns with his interests. In the end, Malo answers only to the Daughters."

"Maybe," Sabina said doubtfully. "But I can tell he respects your opinion, and maybe even fears you a little."

I chuckled. "Malo isn't afraid of anything."

"He's afraid of Rorian," Sabina noted.

"That's different," I said. "Malo's only afraid of what the man might have taken from Halhaven. It's not the same thing."

I'd told Malo and the others about the Cardian ship that I had seen smashed against the reef but had kept it from Sabina. Perhaps that was wrong of me, but I saw no reason to worry her about it now. If the sea had taken Rorian and her father, then we'd find that out sooner or later.

"And what did he take?" Sabina asked. "Nobody has bothered to tell me."

"That's because we don't know," I said. "Not even Malo can say for certain."

Sabina looked skeptical. "Do you trust him?"

"Malo?" I asked, looking at her in surprise.

"Yes. He told you he doesn't know what Rorian took, but if that's true, why go to such lengths to catch him then?"

I knew Sabina had a point. I'd had the same thoughts on more than one occasion. "It doesn't matter," I said, sharper than I had intended. "This will all be over soon. Then my men and I can return home and you can return to your mother." I could see the sudden concern on Sabina's face at the mention of her mother. "Don't worry," I said, softening my tone. "Haverty will have arrived in Springlight by now. She's in good hands."

Sabina hugged her arms to her chest. "I hope so," she said. "It's been so difficult this past year for our family. First, my mother fell ill, and then my brother was injured in the war." She glanced at me, tears threatening in her eyes. "I have never been apart from them like this before, either."

"Your brother was a soldier?" I asked, knowing he had to have fought for the North.

Sabina nodded. "He and my father both." She lowered her eyes and stared at the deck. "My brother lost his arm at Dunnedin."

I grimaced. Dunnedin skirted the unofficial border between the North and South and had been the site of the first clash between the forces of the Rock and the Sun last year. One of many such to come. The battle had lasted two days and had ended in a draw, but not before more than three thousand men had lost their lives. I hadn't been involved, but had heard it had been a savage, bloody affair.

"My father hung up his sword to care for Mother when she fell ill," Sabina continued. "And all we had to live on was my brother's army wage and whatever money I could make washing clothing." Her face fell. "You can't fight without a sword arm. If you don't fight, you don't get paid."

"How did you manage?" I asked.

Sabina shrugged. "My father was given some money as a parting gift from his lord. Enough to feed us for a few months, but not enough to pay for the care my mother needed."

"So your father went to Lord Branton for aid," I said, understanding now.

"Out of desperation," Sabina admitted. "We had nowhere else to turn. My father knows something about Lord Branton. Something bad. I don't know what it is, but it guaranteed his help. At least for a while." Her eyes turned bitter. "Until you people showed up and changed everything."

I said nothing to that, thinking how the whims of the gods governed all our lives. I'd watched a puppet show in Halhaven last year and I envisioned all of us dancing and pirouetting like those puppets had as the First Pair worked our strings. Did we have any control at all, or were we simply mindless dolls put here for their amusement? I thrust the image away, uncomfortable with the idea.

"So, when Rorian offered to hire him as a guide—" I started to say.

"My father jumped at the chance," Sabina finished for me.

We stood together in silence for a time, then Sabina took a deep breath. "I think I can sleep now." She leaned forward and kissed me gently on the cheek. "Despite everything that has happened, I'm glad I met you, Hadrack."

Sabina walked away after that, her boots clacking loudly across the decking before she disappeared down the ladder. I stood by the railing after she was gone, watching the hypnotic motion of the sea as my mind sifted through a jumble of disjointed thoughts. Baine was dead—think about something else. Shana was in danger—think about something else. Sabina's eyes staring through me the way that they did—think about something else. The remaining nine still breathing after all these years. The thoughts went around and around until finally I couldn't take it any longer and I climbed down to the hold to wake Niko. Sabina lay curled up against one wall and I chose a spot far from her. My last thoughts were of two sets of eyes. One sparkling blue, the other shimmering green, with me trapped between them.

Then I slept.

10: Landfall

The next morning began crisp and bright, with a moderate breeze blowing from the southwest.

"Perfect!" Putt exclaimed as he blew heartily on his hands. He and I stood on the sterncastle as the sun slowly rose above the horizon, turning the sky around it a cheerful pink and orange. Thin tendrils of white mist lifted lazily off the water below me, dancing like tiny wraiths as Putt pointed east. "Somewhere that way lies Ganderland, my lord." He grinned at me. "My gut tells me we will be on dry land by midday."

"That probably means we're doomed," Niko said sarcastically, his voice echoing just loud enough for us to hear as he and Tyris carefully unraveled our makeshift sail across the lower deck.

I watched them work, wondering if all the labor and preparation from the night before would prove to have been nothing but a waste of time. I prayed it wouldn't, for we had no other options if Putt's plan failed.

Eighty bright red capes made up our sail, each of which had initially been lined with either fox or wolf fur at the collar. We'd painstakingly removed the fur and then laid out the capes end to end and side by side to form a square. Each cape was roughly four feet wide by five long, though by the time we had finished tying them together, they were considerably smaller.

The knotting had been a slow and frustrating process, carried out by Sabina, Jebido, Tyris, and me, while Malo and Putt worked on the drift anchor's design. Putt taught us a tying method that he called a hook-knot, which I found impossible to do and thoroughly confusing. The knots were designed to be used on ropes, not slick cloth like the capes. I found that no matter how hard I tried, my fingers were just too big and clumsy for such delicate work. Sabina and Tyris, on the other hand, caught on fast and seemed to have no trouble with it at all. Eventually, we worked out a system where Jebido and I kept the capes aligned, while the girl and archer tied them together.

I heard a loud splash behind me and I moved to the back railing. Malo and Jebido were peering down into the water below me as the weighted-down crate they had just thrown overboard bobbed up and down on the swells. The improvised anchor slowly began to sink, finally disappearing below the surface as frothing bubbles gurgled noisily in its wake. Two ropes attached to a pin in the center of the crate led back to the ship. These were nailed firmly to either side of the stern. The lines played out as the drift anchor dropped, then reached their limit at the same time and snapped taught with a twang. *Sea-Dragon* instantly shuddered as her nose lifted and she started to wobble in place like a fish on a hook. I glanced over at Putt, frowning.

"Nothing to worry about, my lord," Putt said with an easy grin. "They're just getting acquainted, is all."

I nodded. "Now what?"

Putt headed for the ladder. "Now, we get the extra yards and attach that sail."

The Cardians, like Putt's father, were bastards through and through, yet just like him, they were also good sailors. A good sailor, Putt had told me, was also a cautious sailor. The Cardians had stored a replacement mast and several yards along the gunwales in case of emergencies. I was very grateful that they'd had the foresight, though I wished they had thought of a rudder as well. The yards were long and made of solid oak, thick in the middle and tapering at each end. We folded the top of our tied capes over one yard, and then Putt used nails and a thin slat of wood to secure the sail to the yard. For extra measure, we wound lengths of rope around everything as well.

Next, we did the same thing at the bottom using the second yard. Once we'd attached the sail at both ends, we rolled the bottom yard along the deck until the two oak beams met, then lashed them together. After that, we hoisted the entire thing up to the mast and reattached the top spar. Then, with Niko, Tyris, and me balancing on top of the new beam, we started to lower the bottom pole down with ropes while Malo and Jebido steadied the sail with clewlines that we had rigged along each side.

"Easy there!" Putt shouted as Niko slipped, dropping his side of the sail faster than the other. "Are you trying to tear it, you clumsy bastard!?"

Niko glared darkly at Putt, but the young outlaw said nothing as Tyris and I worked to catch up to him.

"Right," Putt finally said, nodding in satisfaction as we eventually evened out the sail. He glanced at Malo and Jebido. "Get ready on those lines. Once the wind gets a real taste, those ropes are going to jump in your hands."

We were about halfway through unwinding the sail when the wind finally found it and the capes began to flutter reluctantly. We carefully lowered the sail down the rest of the way as Malo and Jebido braced themselves on the deck in preparation, but nothing happened. I frowned in disappointment. Some of the capes were flapping weakly, or just hanging limp, while others bulged out suddenly, straining at the knots before collapsing again.

"The wind is getting through the gaps!" I shouted down to the deck in frustration. "It's not going to work."

"Patience, my lord," Putt called up confidently. "We just need a stronger breeze."

Despite his words of assurance, I could see the concern on Putt's face as he bit his lower lip in worry. I was sure I'd just heard him mutter a prayer under his breath as well. We waited in silence, staring at the bright red capes as though our lives depended on it— which of course, they did.

I balanced myself on the top spar and clutched at the rigging as I studied our make-shift sail for long minutes, hoping for any signs of life. Finally, a powerful gust of wind arrived, rifling my hair and whipping at my clothing. The Cardian capes began to billow out, snapping and twisting as though alive as the wind filled them one by one. I held my breath. Would they stay like that this time, and would the hook-knots work even if they did?

The gusts coming off the sea strengthened by the moment as the capes began to thrash wildly against their bonds, yet hold they did as *Sea-Dragon* slowly started to move forward. I turned, laughing as twin sprays began to shoot up from around the bow, growing stronger as we picked up speed. Below me, the others cheered and pounded each other heartily on the backs.

I pointed down at the red-haired outlaw in triumph. "You did it, Putt!"

"No, my lord," Putt said, looking weak with relief. "We did it."

The wind continued to blow steadily for us, and though Putt's improvised rudder was far from perfect, we were eventually able to turn the ship eastward and keep it heading mostly on course. *Sea-Dragon* tended to drift on us and the anchor needed constant adjustments, but compared to the alternatives, there were no complaints from anyone.

I ordered Tyris up the mast to watch for land, while Malo and I worked the drift anchor and Jebido and Niko controlled the sails. Putt did what ship captain's do, which was remain on the sterncastle and bark orders while Sabina brought us some tepid water and hard biscuits that she'd found in the hold.

Several hours passed as we crept slowly across the sea, until finally, Tyris cupped a hand around his mouth. "Land ho!"

I climbed the sterncastle ladder eagerly at the welcome words, greeted by the view of a faint, hazy landmass far off on the horizon.

"Ganderland," Putt said wistfully. He took a deep breath. "It will be good to be home, my lord."

I nodded, thinking the same thing. Then I felt a blackness descend upon me. Returning to Witbridge Manor was all that I had thought about for days. Yet now, without Baine by my side, my eagerness to see her stone walls again had waned.

"We'll go home only when I know the Cardians are dead and all is well at Calban," I growled.

"Of course, my lord," Putt said, looking embarrassed. "I wouldn't want it any other way."

The coast of Ganderland grew as we bore down on it, filling the horizon to the north and the south. Finally, as the sound of surf breaking against rocks began to reach our ears, Putt had Jebido and Niko swing the sails while Malo and I hauled on the starboard rope, dragging in the drift anchor. We slowly began to turn, until eventually we were running along the coast as close as we dared. The shoreline before us revealed nothing but thick woodlands and staggering cliffs that plunged directly into the sea. Hard, hostile, and completely inaccessible. We'd have to wait to make landfall.

"Stand ready, my lord," Putt said as he peered down at us. "No deviation now. Keep her straight as an arrow. We can't afford to wander off our line."

I nodded up to him in understanding. The drift anchor still tended to stray to the left, which hadn't been much of a problem earlier when we were happy just to be heading in an easterly direction. But now, any slight change in our course might send *Sea-Dragon* toward the coast where a shoal or hidden reef could be waiting. An hour went by with little change as tall, bristling cliffs, stony ridges, and inhospitable forestlands rolled along our starboard bow in an endless line. Keeping the ship sailing straight and true was exhausting work, and my hands were burnt raw from the rasp of the rope as we fought to keep our course.

"A lagoon, my lord!" the red-haired outlaw finally cried in excitement as he appeared over the railing above us. "As pretty and inviting as a virgin on her wedding night, she is. Wait for my signal, then send us hard to starboard." I opened my mouth to respond, but Putt was already gone. "Niko!" I heard him roar. Wake up, you lazy bastard! On my command, you pull on that line like it's your pathetic cock! You hear me?"

"I hear you, oh wise and great Captain," Niko's voice echoed back. "But I warn you, this rope is a lot smaller than I'm used to dealing with!"

"I very much doubt that!" Putt shouted out with a laugh. "Now pull, boy, pull!" Putt suddenly appeared above us again. "All right now, my lord. Bring her in hard and fast."

"Will do, Captain," I responded with a grin as Malo and I started to draw in the rope.

The drift anchor slowly rose to the surface as we labored, fighting us like the giant wolf herrings that Putt had told me he'd fished for as a boy. *Sea-Dragon* hesitated in indecision, rocking on the waves before she reluctantly started to come about. I clung to the rope as it bucked in my grip and glanced up at the sterncastle, but the red-haired outlaw was looking ahead with one hand up, telling us to wait.

Finally, he pointed at me. "Now, my lord. Let it go now!"

Malo and I released the rope as it hissed wetly against the gunwale on the way back to the sea. I leaned out, looking past the support beams of the sterncastle to the bow. Low, overhanging cliffs of dark stone covered in moss and dancing reed grass rose on each side of a half-moon shaped gap that lay directly in front of us. A thin wall of sand and rock stretched like a crooked finger in front of the lagoon, leaving barely enough space for *Sea-Dragon* to pass between it and the imposing wall on the portside. My breath caught in my throat. If Putt had miscalculated even a little, we would end up on the cliff face or with our hull sliced open by the reef. Green water and sunbaked white sand shimmered on the other side of the barrier, with thick, impenetrable shrubs and tall trees surrounding the beach like an entrenched army.

"To port, my lord!" Putt cried, his eyes wide as he looked down at us. "To port now, or we're on the rocks!"

Malo and I scrambled for the rope, dragging it in as the ship stubbornly fought the change in direction. I glanced up for further instructions, but Putt was gone.

"Putt!" I shouted. I cursed when no answer came back. "Can you hold it here?" I asked Malo.

The House Agent nodded. I leaned out over the gunwale to see what was happening, then ducked back just in time as *Sea-Dragon's* hull scraped along the cliff, tearing away a gap in the sidewall. Small chunks of granite pelted the deck like hail.

"We're through, lads!" I heard Putt's cry from above. "Brace yourselves. We're heading for the beach!"

Malo and I ran for the protection of the overhang as small and large stones clattered loudly against the decking. I staggered as a rock the size of my fist caromed off my shin and hobbled the last few steps as *Sea-Dragon* shuddered beneath me. The lagoon was shallow and still, and the ship's keel dug into the soft loam beneath the water, reducing our momentum as we headed toward the beach. We finally reached the shore, barely crawling along as *Sea-Dragon* slid to a shuddering stop with the tip of her bow just kissing the white sand. We'd made it!

"Are you all right?" I asked Malo as I flexed my leg.

The House Agent didn't respond. He was looking past my shoulder, his face hard and dangerous. I turned. A battered-looking ship lay drawn up on the beach in a small inlet behind the cliff. The mast was missing, but I recognized it, nonetheless. It was the Cardian longboat. Men in red capes worked with axes near the treeline, chopping at a tree they had felled to make a new mast. The Cardians paused in what they were doing to stare at *Sea-Dragon* in amazement. Then, at a barked command that carried to us over the still water, they grabbed their shields that lined the longboat's hull and began to run toward us.

"To arms!" I shouted.

I drew Wolf's Head and swung my legs over the lower deck's gunwale, then dropped six feet into the knee-high water. Malo landed beside me with a splash and we waded toward the beach together. I heard more splashes coming from behind me, but didn't bother to look. I knew Jebido and the others were coming. I counted seven Cardians bearing down on us, with more jumping over the side of the longboat. Two figures had stayed behind, I noted. One of them was Rorian, I realized with mixed emotions, while the other was a woman.

"Malo," I grunted as we reached the beach. I gestured toward Rorian with my sword.

Malo's eyes narrowed when he saw the scholar. "I was hoping the sea hadn't claimed that bastard," he growled. The House Agent gestured toward the charging Cardians. "We'll kill these first. After that, we can have a long-overdue chat with our friend."

I nodded, eager for some action after being cooped up on *Sea-Dragon* for so long. Jebido, Putt, and Niko joined us on the sand, but only Jebido had the foresight to bring a shield with him. I shook my head, not surprised. Jebido never disappointed.

"This is going to be an awfully lonely shield wall," Jebido said dryly as he glanced around at the rest of us.

I looked behind me to the ship, where Tyris waited on the forecastle with his bow. The nearest Cardian was twenty paces away, sprinting across the sand. I could hear his grunts of effort and see spit-bubbles frothing at the corners of his mouth as he raced to reach us first. Be careful what you wish for, I thought as I gripped Wolf's Head tighter, waiting for the right moment. Finally, I saw it and I grinned.

"You know what the problem with shields are, Jebido?" I asked out of the side of my mouth.

"What would that be?" Jebido muttered, one eyebrow arched.

"Sometimes, the damn things just get in the way," I said.

Then I charged.

The approaching Cardian screamed a challenge when he saw me coming. He was big and ugly, and held his shield out in front of him awkwardly as he ran. He shifted his sword, balancing it on top of his shield like a spear as he bore down on me. I could tell by the set look on his face that he was intent on ramming right into me like that. I rushed straight for him, heedless of the danger as my opponent's face broke out into a wide grin. I knew he thought he had an easy kill on his hands.

I waited until less than three feet separated us, then, just as he cried out in triumph, I dove feet first and slid along the hot sand, hurtling beneath his outstretched shield and sword. I plunged upward with Wolf's Head into his vulnerable belly as he passed over me, then twisted and rolled away before coming to my feet. The man fell, whimpering as the second Cardian in line hesitated, coming to a shuddering stop three paces from me. He stared at me stupidly, shocked by what I'd done. I didn't wait for the man to regain his senses. I just hacked him down with a vicious backhand, then swung at the man coming up behind him, who dodged my off-balance swing with surprising speed. This new Cardian was tall and thin, with beady eyes and a long tongue that protruded from his mouth obscenely. He didn't have a shield either, but seemed more than comfortable with that fact as he came after me without hesitation.

"You bastard! You bastard! You bastard!" the thin man hissed around his flopping tongue as he swung powerful, two-handed strokes at me.

I took a step back under his furious onslaught. Despite the bizarrely flickering tongue—which I found both repellant and hugely distracting—the Cardian was good. I was faster than most men, but so was he, and I was hard-pressed to keep his blade from getting through my guard.

Jebido had drilled into me over the years to watch for patterns in a man's fighting, and as Malo and my men swept past me to engage the remaining Cardians, I began to see my opponent's pattern. Tongue straight out—defensive. Tongue flicks left—attack high and right. Tongue flicks right—attack low and left.

I smiled, knowing I had him.

"What are you grinning at, you ugly turd?" the Cardian demanded as we circled each other warily.

"I was thinking that it's a shame you never studied under my good friend Jebido, is all," I said. "That is going to cost you your life."

The thin Cardian snorted as our blades scraped against one another, probing for a weakness. "I've never been beaten, Ganderman."

"Until now," I growled.

I hurled myself forward, striking hard and fast. First high. Then low. Then high again as I forced the Cardian back across the sand. The thin man grunted loudly with each parry, while his tongue remained pointed at me the entire time like a sullen child's. I paused and stepped back, giving him a breather and a chance to take the offensive. The Cardian hesitated, blinking at me in surprise as the ever-present tongue retreated into its hole in confusion. Then, after a heartbeat, his tongue popped back out through his lips again like a giant, slime-covered, purple worm. I waited, biding my time until it slowly curled to the left. He was going high and right, just as I'd hoped.

I attacked recklessly, deliberately missing a clumsy swipe with Wolf's Head and paying no heed to the Cardian's blade as he brought it up into a striking position. I saw the man's eyes light up as he saw me suddenly vulnerable, then he swung down at my unprotected head.

But now I was inside his guard.

I clamped my left hand around his right wrist, halting his strike. The Cardian automatically grabbed my right wrist with his left hand so I couldn't plunge Wolf's Head into his unprotected side. Which was what I had expected he'd do. I grinned at him. My opponent might be as fast as me, but he wasn't nearly as strong. I held his sword arm effortlessly, then slowly turned Wolf's Head toward him as the Cardian fought desperately to stop me. I could see fear in his eyes now as his tongue darted in and out of his mouth wildly. The tip of my sword swung upright until it was mere inches from the Cardian's soft throat. His arm shook as he fought to hold me back, and I could see the realization of defeat rising in his eyes.

"Mercy," the Cardian pleaded in a whisper.

"Not today," I grunted. Then I thrust upward.

The Cardian's eyes rolled up in his head and he shivered in my grip as though cold. Warm, thick blood gushed from his neck, soaking my blade and drenching my hand. I let the man fall as I pressed onward, joining Malo and the others as we forced the enemy back toward the inlet where the longboat lay. Dead men in red capes lay scattered along the shoreline as the weak tide lapped lazily at their corpses. I could hear Tyris' bow thrumming from his vantage point behind me as men twisted and fell beneath the blond archer's skill.

I noticed Rorian amongst the swirling mass of men now, having finally joined in on the fighting. The scholar was exchanging wild sword thrusts with Jebido as they battled across the sand. I headed at a run in their direction. A Cardian appeared before me, snarling with rage as he tried to cut me down. I twisted sideways to avoid his overhead slash, then grabbed him by the neck and pulled him down as I smashed my knee into his face. The man sagged and crumpled to the ground as I kept going, until finally I stood shoulder to shoulder with Jebido, facing the scholar. Rorian frowned at my approach and he paused, taking two steps back, watching us both warily.

Jebido glanced sideways at me. "What took you so long?" he asked. My friend was breathing heavily and looked winded.

"I was busy," I grunted. "This one's mine, Jebido."

"You'll get no argument from me," Jebido said. He offered me his shield. "You are going to need this, Hadrack. The man can fight."

I brushed away the shield.

"Best take it, boy," Rorian growled. "I don't want people saying I had any kind of an advantage after I kill you."

"Then toss your shield aside if you are so concerned about what others think," I replied in challenge.

Rorian looked thoughtful for a moment, then he shrugged. "Upon reflection, I think I'll just kill you now and worry about my reputation after the fact."

"I thought you might," I grunted. A Cardian behind the scholar twisted with a cry and dropped with an arrow in his belly. I looked around as more of the bastards continued to fall. I grinned at the scholar. "You seem to be running out of men."

"So it would appear," Rorian said, looking surprisingly unconcerned.

He took a step forward and I retreated, our blade tips touching. I continued to back up, moving away from the others battling around us so that I'd have more room to maneuver. I glanced sideways at Malo, who had just skewered a man with his short sword. The House Agent looked alarmed when he realized who my opponent was.

"Hadrack?" Malo called out to me uncertainly. "We need him alive."

I thought of all the misery the man before me had caused, culminating in Baine's death. I couldn't kill him, I knew, but I could exact some revenge for what he'd done. Revenge in the form of blood. Malo said something else to me, but I closed my ears to his words. I gestured to the Rorian with my free hand. "Let's dance," I whispered.

Rorian smiled calmly in acknowledgment, though his eyes remained cold and calculating. He pulled his shield tight against his side and turned, presenting me with a smaller target. Then he advanced, probing at my defenses with quick, almost careless strokes of his weapon. I could see the ropey muscles in his arms flexing and rolling with each effortless swing that he took. Rorian might or might not be an actual scholar, I realized, but as I watched his smooth, practiced movements, I knew that my opponent was a formidable warrior. Perhaps I shouldn't have been so hasty in rejecting Jebido's shield, I thought as I parried a powerful stroke.

The sounds of battle were slowly fading as I gave more ground to Rorian. I took a moment to glance around. Most of the Cardians were down, with three still alive and kneeling in the hot sand with their hands on their heads. Niko and Putt stood over them, holding swords to their throats. I flicked my eyes to the woman on the longboat. Even from where I stood, I could see the tension on her face as she watched. Who was she? I wondered. I shook that thought away. I needed to focus on only one thing right now, I told myself, flicking my eyes back to the scholar. Study the bastard and look for his weakness. I shifted my grip on Wolf's Head to both hands, then moved across the sand on the balls of my feet while forcing the scholar to turn and face toward the sun.

Rorian looked amused. "That won't save you," he said.

He opened his mouth to say more, then surprised me by launching himself forward in a blur. The scholar's blade came for me, all business now as it sought out my throat and a quick end to the fight. The muscles in my arms moved by instinct, bringing up my guard and blocking his weapon as steel rang against steel. Rorian pressed forward on his sword, using his shield arm as well as he tried to unbalance me. I braced my legs in the sand and pushed back, with neither of us able to gain an advantage. I could see the mockery in the other man's eyes as we glared at each other over the rim of his shield.

The bastard thinks he's toying with me, I realized, feeling rage rise in me. Rorian laughed and finally broke the stalemate, skipping backward nimbly. But not before a parting shot from Wolf's Head clanged with power off of his shield. The scholar grinned, flexing his shield arm grudgingly as we circled.

"You've got real strength there, boy," Rorian said, looking impressed. "But you lack discipline. It's almost a shame to kill you."

"I wish I could say the same thing," I growled.

I could feel the white-hot battle rage inside me begging for release, and I knew if this went on much longer, I would have to let it loose. Once that happened, I wouldn't be able to stop myself from bashing past Rorian's shield and killing him. I glanced at Malo, who was watching us intently with his arms crossed over his chest. The House Agent must have recognized the look in my eyes, for he frowned and shook his head at me. A clear message.

I cursed under my breath in frustration as I focused back on Rorian, who twirled his sword effortlessly in his hand as he waited. I needed to disarm the man somehow without killing him, but that was easier said than done when someone as skilled as Rorian didn't have any qualms about killing me. I needed to find another way.

"Maybe we can come to some kind of arrangement," I said as the scholar and I weaved back and forth, searching for an opening.

"Such as?" Rorian asked in an even tone.

"Such as, we let you live and you give us what we want," I suggested.

Rorian chuckled. "And what is it, exactly, that you want from me?"

"Whatever you stole from Halhaven," I replied.

"Ah," the scholar said knowingly. "I assumed that's what this was all about."

He took a half-hearted swing at me, which I easily blocked. Maybe I was getting through to him after all, I thought, feeling encouraged. "Look around you, Rorian," I said. "You're finished. Most of your men are dead, and you are going to die here along with them unless we make a deal."

Rorian chuckled. I was hugely impressed by his lack of fear. "I'll grant you this wasn't exactly my plan," he said. "But that's the way life goes sometimes."

"Then maybe it's time to change your plans," I said. Rorian nudged at my sword with his, but I could tell that he was listening. "All you have to do is give us what you took from Halhaven. We are going to get it, anyway, so why not make things easy on everybody and just hand it over?"

"And if I do?"

"Then you and the girl can go free," I promised.

I saw the scholar's gaze flick to the longboat and the woman standing there. His expression changed for just a moment when he saw her. I hesitated, following his eyes. I'd seen something just now in those eyes. Something deep and unyielding that had flared for a single heartbeat. Then it suddenly dawned on me what it had been. Love.

"Regrettably, I cannot accept your terms," Rorian finally said, his face turning hard again. "There is a certain amount of honor at stake here. I'm sure you understand."

I nodded, disappointed, but not surprised. I knew what I had to do now to end this.

"Malo," I said, keeping my eyes on Rorian. "The woman on the boat." I saw Rorian tense as I glanced sideways at the House Agent. "I want you to go over there and kill her."

Malo gaped at me in surprise. "What?"

"You heard me," I growled. I pointed at the scholar. "If this bastard doesn't throw down his sword right now, kill her and toss her bloody head at his feet."

"You wouldn't dare," Rorian said tightly, looking uncertain for the first time now.

"Keep that sword in your hand any longer, and you will find out what I'll do," I replied, my voice hard and filled with menace.

Rorian stared at me searchingly, and then he tossed his weapon onto the sand at my feet.

11: The Codex

I wouldn't have let Malo go through with it, of course. I have been called many things in my life, but a butcher of women is not one of them. I've always liked to believe Malo wouldn't have done my bidding anyway, but nothing was ever a certainty with that man. The look I'd seen in Rorian's eyes had lasted only a moment, but it had been enough for me to see deep into his soul. Women can either be a source of strength for a man, or a source of weakness— sometimes even both. It was clear to me that whoever the woman was, she was Rorian's weakness.

"You chose wisely," I said as I hooked my toe under the scholar's sword and flicked it across the sand.

Rorian began to shake his head, his hands on his hips. "You wouldn't have done it," he said regretfully. "I saw it on your face just now."

I grinned back at him. "Of course not. I don't make war on women."

Rorian surprised me by returning the grin as he smoothed his beard. "A shrewd move. I'm impressed. I let your reputation cloud my judgment, which is a mistake I don't usually make."

"Reputation?" I said. "You know me?"

"Who in this world hasn't heard of the Outlaw of Corwick by now?" Rorian answered.

I glanced over my shoulder at Tyris, who was striding toward us along the beach, his bow slung over his shoulder. Sabina hurried behind him, her face a jumble of emotions as she tried to keep up. I gestured to the stricken longboat as the archer reached us. "Tyris, fetch the lady from the ship and bring her to me."

"Yes, my lord," Tyris said.

"Who is she?" I asked as I focused back on Rorian.

"My wife," the scholar replied. "Thera."

That explained the look then, I thought. Sabina stopped beside me, her hands on her hips as she glared at Rorian.

"Where is he?" she demanded. I had forgotten about her father during all the excitement.

"Who?" Rorian asked.

"The man who led you to the coast," I said. "This is his daughter."

Rorian's eyebrows rose. "You are Sabina?"

"That's right," Sabina said, looking surprised. "Now, where is he?"

"I imagine on his way back to your mother," Rorian said. "I understand the poor woman is ill." He glanced at me. "The Cardians were intent on killing him once we reached the cove. The only way I could convince them not to was by telling them that I still needed his skills."

"So, that's why he got on the ship with you," I said, understanding now.

"Yes," Rorian nodded. "He was furious, of course, but he didn't have much choice in the matter." The scholar turned to Sabina. "I cut your father's bonds so that he could escape once we beached for repairs. I haven't seen him since." He frowned. "I know he wouldn't have left if he'd known you were here."

"Why would you help him?" Sabina asked suspiciously.

"Because I gave him my word that he would be safe," Rorian said, "and I keep my promises."

Sabina thought about that for a moment, and then she turned to me. "I have to go after him."

"And do what?" I asked. I looked at Rorian. "How long has he been gone?"

Rorian shrugged. "Three hours or so. You'll never pick up his trail now."

"I won't need to," Sabina said, sounding determined. "I know where he's going." She turned, then paused to glance over her shoulder at me. "I need some of the supplies from the ship."

"Take whatever you want," I said, knowing by the set look on her face that there would be no talking her out of leaving. "I'm sure the Cardians have plenty that we can use."

"Thank you, Hadrack," Sabina replied gratefully. She hesitated and I saw her mouth open as if to say more. Then she looked down at the sand before turning away without another word, heading back along the beach.

"Where is it?" Malo demanded, coming to take Sabina's place beside me as he glowered at Rorian.

"Where is what?" the scholar asked.

"The codex, you murderous bastard," Malo growled. "I know that's why you were in Halhaven."

I glanced at Malo in surprise. Codex? Tyris arrived with Thera before Rorian could respond. The two embraced warmly and I could see relief in the woman's eyes as she held her husband. Rorian finally broke the embrace and he motioned to Malo. "This is the House Agent that has been hounding us so stubbornly, my dear." Thera's hair was an odd shade of brown, looking almost coppery in the harsh sunlight. She wore a long-sleeved blue dress that was cinched at the waist by a tablet-woven belt of coarse wool. A string of simple beads hung around her neck. The scholar's wife was young and slender, with a thin face that was all sharp bones and harsh angles. She stared coldly at Malo. "And this fellow with the strange grey eyes," Rorian continued, turning to me, "is the famous Outlaw of Corwick."

Thera gave me the same cold look, though I did warrant a slight nod of acknowledgment, at least.

"Give me the codex," Malo said tightly, barely glancing at the woman. He thrust his face aggressively forward, pausing an inch away from Rorian's nose with his hand on his sword.

Rorian shrugged, looking unfazed. "I can't give that which I do not have, House Agent."

"You're lying!" Malo hissed.

"You have my word," Rorian insisted.

"Which is worth about as much as a month-old mouse turd," Malo spat. He took a step back, still fingering his sword. "I know you went to Halhaven in search of the codex, so don't try to deny it."

"That's not why I went," Rorian stated emphatically. "I was looking for something else."

"Something worth killing for?"

Rorian grimaced. "Taking the Master Librarian's life was never my intent, House Agent. His death was unfortunate."

"Sure it was," Malo said between clenched teeth. He took a deep breath. I could see the struggle he was undergoing as he tried to contain his anger. "What did you find in Halhaven then, if it wasn't the codex?"

"Knowledge," Rorian simply said. His eyes started to twinkle. "Expensive knowledge for those who will pay."

Malo pursed his lips. "So, you know where it is, then?" The scholar hesitated and Malo's grip tightened on his sword. "Tell me what you know right now, or I swear I'll do to your wife what Hadrack wouldn't."

Rorian looked unimpressed. "While I don't doubt you are capable of murder, House Agent." He motioned to me. "I don't believe this one will allow that to happen."

"Hadrack isn't in charge here," Malo growled. "I am. Now start talking."

Rorian turned to me, a challenge in his eyes. I hated the bastard for all the trouble he had caused, but the man was right, and he knew it. I'd managed to bluff him once, but the scholar had the measure of me now.

"I'll tell you what you want to know on two conditions," Rorian said, satisfied that he and I had an understanding. "First." He pointed at Malo. "You guarantee my wife and I safe passage back to Afrenia."

"You're Afrenian?" I said, surprised. "We thought you were a Cardian."

Rorian chuckled, and even Thera's down-turned mouth twitched slightly in amusement. "Thankfully, no," the scholar said. "That would be too depressing to contemplate."

"And the other condition?" Malo asked warily.

"You match what the Cardians were going to pay me to find the codex. Do that, and I'll tell you where it is."

Malo sighed, not looking surprised. "How much?" he asked.

"Five hundred Cardian gold coins," Rorian said without blinking an eye. He smiled. "Jorqs will do just as well, if you prefer."

"That's outrageous!" I heard Niko gasp.

I turned. The young outlaw had inched closer to hear us better and his sword was now a foot away from the captive Cardians' throats. "Niko!" I roared. "Pay attention to your task, or you'll be on your knees next to those bastards!"

Niko blanched at the rebuke and hurried back to his post. "Yes, my lord," he said, his face turning a dark crimson.

"So, do we have an agreement?" Rorian asked Malo.

"Wait here," Malo grunted. He turned away, motioning me to follow.

I could tell by the way Malo held his shoulders that he was expecting an argument from me. If he tried to hurt the girl, I vowed, he would get one.

"Rorian's right," I said the moment we were out of earshot. "I won't let you do it."

"We can't trust him," Malo said as if he hadn't heard me. He studied the scholar over my shoulder as we talked. "His wife is the only leverage we have. We don't have to kill her, just bloody her up a little. The bastard will talk once the screaming starts."

"No," I said firmly, crossing my arms over my chest. "I've seen you work with that short sword of yours, Malo. I won't let you do that to a woman."

"You swore an oath to serve Daughter Gernet's interests, Hadrack. Getting that information is part of that oath."

"I didn't swear to torture women," I responded hotly.

Malo snorted in frustration. "If we give him what he wants, how do we know he won't just send us out on a fool's errand and then keep his deal with the Cardians?"

"We don't," I said, shaking my head stubbornly. "But it's the only way that I'm willing to do this."

Malo's eyes flashed with anger. "I didn't think you were this weak, Hadrack," he said bitterly.

I shrugged, not caring what he thought. "Call it whatever you want."

Malo took a deep breath, then brushed past me to stop in front of the scholar again. "Very well," he said. "I agree to your terms. Safe passage back to Afrenia and payment of five hundred Jorqs once we have the codex."

Rorian smirked and shook his head. "No, House Agent. The payment of five hundred Jorqs will happen before we leave for Afrenia, or I don't talk."

Malo glared at the scholar, locking eyes, until finally he grunted and looked away. "So be it."

Rorian put out his hand. "I want your word, House Agent."

"You have it, you bastard," Malo growled. They locked forearms and shook. Two strong men who clearly didn't like each other. "Now, tell me what I want to know."

"The Halas Codex is hidden in a cave somewhere near the Complex," Rorian replied.

I frowned in confusion. What was the man talking about? The Halas Codex had already been found several years ago, hidden inside a book in the Complex monastery. That codex and its one legible page was the reason the kingdom and Holy House were embroiled in a civil war right now.

"Hold on," I said, lifting a hand. "Are we talking about the same codex that I think we're talking about?"

"Yes, and no," Malo answered.

I looked at him in disgust. "The last time I heard about that damn codex, Malo, it started a war."

"And this one can end it," the House Agent grunted roughly in reply.

"What if the codex doesn't say what you want, House Agent?" Rorian asked mockingly. "Will ending the war be just as important then?"

"Can someone please tell me what is going on here?" I said, getting angry now.

"There is a second Halas Codex," Malo explained. He took a deep breath. "An exact duplicate of the original found in the monastery."

"What? How?" I said, stunned.

The implications of what I'd just heard were staggering. A complete, legible copy of the Halas Codex would lay to rest any doubt about which god was the more powerful. Which, in turn, meant the war would conceivably end. My heart lurched in my chest as I realized that my oath to Daughter Gernet would end as well. For the first time in my life, I would be beholden to nobody, free to fulfill the vow that I had made to my family. It was an intoxicating thought.

"Five months ago," Malo continued, "a scribe working in the Complex discovered a short notation left behind by a man named Waldin. That message was written over four hundred years ago, claiming that Waldin had made a copy of a remarkable codex that he'd discovered. A codex that he swore had been written by the First Son and Daughter, Ardena and Dilestra."

"The Halas Codex," I breathed in wonder.

"It can only be," Malo agreed.

"Who was this Waldin fellow?" I asked.

Malo shrugged. "No one seems to know. It hardly matters. What matters is what he did with that copy of the codex. The North control access to the Complex, but we have people there who got word to us about what has been happening. The Sons and Tyrale's people are hunting everywhere for the codex, but so far, nothing has been found."

"And it won't be," Rorian said, looking amused. "Not where they are looking, anyway. The North knows nothing about the cave, nor do your spies."

"And what are you, then, if not a spy?" Malo asked crossly.

"Just a man doing the job he was hired to do."

"By Cardians?" Malo spat back in disgust.

Rorian shrugged. "Their gold is just as good as yours."

"What do Cardians want with the codex?" I asked as Malo's face turned mean.

"What do Cardians always want?" Rorian replied with a snort. "Money, of course." He smiled. "Not that I can blame them, I suppose. I'm not above the lure of riches myself, after all." Rorian's eyes gleamed. "Just think of how much the twin princes would pay for such a prize. If the words inside that codex name The Father, then the Daughters will have no choice but to surrender power to the Sons and endorse Prince Tyrale. The same the other way if it turns out The Mother is named. Either way, the Cardians are giddy at the prospect of finding the duplicate and selling it to the highest bidder."

"So, they hired you to find it for them," I said. "Why you?"

Rorian grinned modestly. "Let's just say that I have unusual talents. I've worked with the Cardians before. They know they can trust me to get the job done."

"Yet here you stand, telling us everything for gold," Malo said, not hiding the contempt in his voice. "So much for trust."

"Not just for gold," Rorian said as he glanced at his wife meaningfully. "If that's all this was about, I would never tell you."

"Why go to Halhaven and not Mount Halas directly if you suspected the codex was there?" I asked.

"Getting into the Complex would have been difficult, if not impossible at the time," Rorian said. "I had a way in, but I had to wait for the right moment. I decided that while I waited, I would try to come at the problem of where the codex might be in a different way. That different way led me to Halhaven."

"A different way, how?" Malo asked.

"By finding out who Waldin was," I answered for the scholar, knowing that I was right.

"Correct," Rorian said, looking impressed. "I thought that if I could learn more about him, then maybe I could figure out why he made a copy of the codex and what he did with it. I began my research in Gandertown, but after several weeks of sifting through old records, I learned that most of the archives from Waldin's time had been moved to Halhaven's library after the Border War."

"And when you found what you wanted in Halhaven, you murdered the Master Librarian and two House Agents," Malo said bitterly.

"Yes," Rorian admitted. "But I meant what I said earlier, I didn't want to kill anyone. I was only in Halhaven for research, nothing else." The scholar sighed, looking genuinely upset. "The old man just wouldn't keep his nose out of my affairs. One day he saw my notations and realized what I had found. I couldn't chance him telling anyone, so I was left with little choice. I tried to kill him quietly, but he was surprisingly spry for a man of his age. Your fellow House Agents heard the commotion and I was forced to flee. The rest, you know."

"But why were you going to Calban, then?" I asked. "That part makes no sense to me. Lady Shana is no friend of Cardians."

"I'd heard that," Rorian agreed. "But in this case, it wouldn't have mattered. She would have had to let us in."

"Why?" I asked suspiciously.

"We were going for the Pilgrimage," Rorian answered.

I stared at him, understanding now as I started to put things into place. The Pilgrimage happened once a year as Pilgrims arrived in either Calban on the west coast or Taskerbery Castle on the east. From there, they made the long trek on foot—called The Walk—to Mount Halas. Shana had told me about The Walk once, but I had been preoccupied with her naked back as I'd kissed it and had barely listened. The Pilgrimage dated back more than a thousand years, and no one who wished to take The Walk was ever denied, not even Cardians.

I could only imagine what Shana's reaction would have been, had Rorian and the Cardians actually reached Calban. I knew she would have had no choice but to let them in, much as it galled her. A thousand years of tradition and etiquette could not be easily ignored over what some would call petty grievances. The forces of the Rock would have to let the Pilgrims into the Complex as well. A perfect cover for Rorian to go after the codex. I glanced at the scholar's wife, understanding her place in this now as well. All Pilgrims had to make The Walk in pairs—one man and one woman.

Rorian saw my eyes on Thera. "You must forgive my wife for not speaking, gentlemen. I assure you, it has nothing to do with rudeness. You see, she was ten years old when her father cut her tongue from her in a drunken rage." Rorian put his arm around his wife and held her affectionately. "She killed him later that night with the knife he used as he lay in a stupor on the floor. The bastard may have taken her tongue, but he couldn't take her spirit."

"You planned on posing as Pilgrims to gain access to the mountain and find the cave, then?" Malo said, having come to the same conclusion as me.

"Yes," Rorian agreed.

"Where is it?" I asked.

Rorian shrugged. "That's the real question. I found a letter from Waldin that mentions the cave is four miles from the Complex. He didn't say in which direction. All I know is he described looking out from the entrance at giant mushrooms."

Malo and I shared a look. Giant mushrooms? I shook my head, knowing they would be long gone by now.

"Why do you think the codex is in that cave?" Malo asked.

"Because Waldin wrote in that letter about a treasure inside worth more than all the jewels and gold in the kingdom," Rorian said. "What else could he have meant?"

"And that's all you have to go on?" I asked, feeling let down somewhat. "How do we know Waldin wasn't talking about something other than the codex? Or for that matter, that the same man even wrote this letter that you found? Waldin is a fairly common name, you know."

"It is the same man," Rorian insisted, looking confident. "Trust me."

"Who was the letter to?" Malo asked.

"A woman," Rorian replied. "Her name was Verica. I believe she might have been a Daughter-In-Waiting, but I'm not certain. I wasn't able to find out anything else about her in my research."

Malo played with his beard as he thought about what we'd learned. "We can't chance the codex falling into Prince Tyrale's hands or the Cardians," he finally said. "We have to get up that mountain and find the cave, whatever the cost."

"How are we going to do that?" I asked. "The North will have the mountain sealed."

Malo gestured to Rorian. "We'll go in as Pilgrims, just like he was going to do."

"That's going to be a problem, House Agent," Rorian said. "Because of the war, every Pilgrim had to make their intentions known months in advance. You need a special pass issued by the Complex overseer himself to get up the mountain now. We were supposed to meet a man named Juliax during The Walk who would have them. Show up without those passes, and I imagine you will just be killed outright."

Malo cursed softly under his breath. "This Juliax person, is he a Cardian?"

"I don't know. I have never met him."

"Then how will you know him to get the passes?" I asked.

"He's going to find us," Rorian replied. "He has our descriptions."

Malo frowned. "Well, that is going to be a problem," he admitted.

"One last thing, House Agent," Rorian said. "By my calculations, the Pilgrimage is set to begin in three days. Once The Walk leaves Calban, it will be too late to join. Whatever you plan to do, you had better do it soon. You are running out of time."

"I'll go," I said. I lifted a hand before Malo could respond. "Rorian said that he and Juliax have never met," I pointed out.

"So?" Malo said. "Juliax knows what he looks like."

I gestured to Rorian. "Describe him."

Malo frowned as he looked the scholar up and down. "A big man," he said. "Strong, with hard eyes and a scarred face."

I grinned as Malo turned to me in sudden understanding. "That could describe me perfectly, don't you think?" I asked.

"You forget one thing, Hadrack," Malo said. "The Pilgrimage has to be walked by a man and a woman together." He glanced at Rorian's wife. "I doubt this one will agree to help us somehow."

My grin slowly faded as I turned my eyes on Thera. She was cold-looking, but not unattractive, with a slight body and that strange, coppery hair. I realized there was someone else who could pass for her. I turned, glancing back to *Sea-Dragon*.

Sabina.

12: Calban

I was worried that Sabina might have already left by the time I returned to *Sea-Dragon*, but I found her sitting on a crate in the hold with several biscuits clutched in her hands. She looked up as I climbed down the ladder. Her face, I was surprised to see, was wet with tears.

"Sabina?" I said softly. "I thought you would be gone by now."

Sabina sniffed and wiped at her eyes with the back of her hand. "So did I," she whispered.

"What's wrong?" I asked.

Sabina shrugged helplessly. "I don't know. I suddenly had this feeling that leaving would be a terrible mistake. I've been sitting here trying to convince myself to go."

"A terrible mistake, how?" I asked.

Sabina stared at me for a moment with red-rimmed eyes before she looked away. "You really don't know, do you?"

I crouched in front of her. "Sabina, listen to me. Malo and I have a problem. We need your help."

"Of course you do," Sabina said as she blinked away tears. She laughed bitterly. "That's all I'm good for."

I hesitated, not sure what to say to that. I have always felt awkward and foolish around a crying woman, afraid to open my mouth and only make things worse. This time was no different, but I knew every moment wasted lessened our chances of getting to Calban in time for the Pilgrimage. Whatever problem Sabina had right now could be dealt with later, I reasoned. First, I had to get her to agree to help us.

I took the biscuits from her and set them aside, then took her hands in mine. "Sabina, there is a second copy of the Halas Codex," I said bluntly.

Sabina sat up in surprise. "Another codex?"

"Yes. That's why Rorian went to Halhaven. That's what all of this has been about. He found out where the second codex is hidden, but now we need your help to get it."

Sabina blinked at me through her tears, her face twisted in confusion. "What do you need me for?"

I shifted position to ease the pain in my thigh where I had taken a Pith arrow years ago, and then told her everything. Sabina listened carefully, her tears disappearing while I talked.

"So, if we find the codex, will it end the war?" she finally asked when I was finished.

"I think so," I said with a shrug. "At least, I hope so. Whichever of the twins gains the support of both sides of the House will have a huge advantage. Probably enough that the other one will have little choice but to concede their claim to the throne."

"What if it's the North?" Sabina asked, watching me closely. "Can you live with that?"

"Yes," I said, not hesitating. And it was the truth. The Mother would always be first in my heart, but if The Father should be named, and because of it, the war ended, then yes, I could live with that fact.

"Then I will help you," Sabina said as she stood. She smiled, no signs of tears or sadness on her face now. "I was right to stay."

"What about your father?" I asked.

"He would be the first one to say if my help can somehow end this horrible war, then I must do it," Sabina said firmly. "So that is what I am going to do."

I put my hands on her shoulders in gratitude, resisting the urge to hug her. "Thank you," I said.

"I agreed to help you," Sabina said, staring at me with an odd look. "But I want something from you first." I raised an eyebrow as she put her arms around my neck. She looked up at me. "Kiss me, Hadrack. Kiss me just this once, and after that, I'll do whatever you need me to."

I hesitated in surprise. I had promised myself that Sabina and I would always just be friends and nothing more, but for the sake of a kingdom embroiled in a vicious war, one kiss seemed a small price to pay. I nodded my agreement, thrusting my uneasiness and guilt aside as I leaned down and pressed my lips to hers. I closed my eyes, imagining I was kissing Shana, confident that she would forgive this small betrayal for the greater good.

I don't know how long we stayed that way, but eventually I heard someone clear their throat behind me. I turned to see that Jebido had come down the ladder, where he stood at the base, watching us. I broke away from Sabina and moved back guiltily.

"Sabina has agreed to help us," I said gruffly.

Jebido looked from me to her, his face expressionless. "So it would seem," he said dryly.

Malo and I decided we would take the time to replace *Sea-Dragon's* rudder and sail, rather than use the smaller boat to travel to Calban. The mast on the longboat would have taken almost as long to replace, anyway, so either way, we were going to lose valuable time. I didn't relish going back out to sea again, but I reasoned if I had to, I would rather have *Sea-Dragon's* stout deck beneath my feet if we ran into another storm.

The three captured Cardians, while as sour of mood and personality as all their race, were none-the-less experienced seamen. Putt found heavy shackles and chains in the longboat and he bound the three together, then set them to work fashioning a new rudder and repairing the damage from the storm. The rest of us removed our make-shift sail and replaced it with the hemp sail from the longboat. It was smaller than the original, but it would have to do. We also found a spare sail in the longboat's stores, which we took along with all the food supplies and five barrels of fresh water.

Once we were ready to leave, everyone except for Putt and the women—who remained on *Sea-Dragon*—pushed the longboat out into the lagoon. We tied heavy ropes to *Sea-Dragon's* stern, then using the oars, towed the larger vessel off the beach and past the finger-like reef guarding the entrance until we were safely away from the rocks. Transferring from the smaller longboat up onto the cog was trickier than I had anticipated, especially with three reluctant and cursing Cardians chained together. In the end, we managed it reasonably well, though Niko did slip and fall into the water and needed quick rescuing before being crushed between the hulls. After that, it was a simple matter to unfurl *Sea-Dragon's* new sail and let the wind take her.

I stood alone on the sterncastle and watched the empty Cardian longboat grow fainter in the distance as it wallowed on the tide behind us. The sleek ship was barely noticeable when finally, the sea tossed it up against the barrier guarding the lagoon, crushing the hull into fragments on the sharp rocks.

"Fate is a strange bedfellow, wouldn't you agree?"

I turned to see Rorian standing behind me with his legs braced on the deck as he moved easily with the ship's rhythm. I frowned and turned away. I had no wish to even look at the man, let alone speak to him.

Rorian either didn't recognize my mood or just didn't care as he came to lean on the railing beside me. "I have to admit that you are not exactly what I envisioned you to be."

"And what is that?" I grunted as I stared out to sea. I had a momentary urge to grab the scholar by the neck and ass and toss him overboard.

"A brute," Rorian said. "A thoughtless, bloodthirsty brute of low intelligence and even lower morals."

"Sorry to disappoint you."

"Oh, I'm far from being disappointed," Rorian said with a shrug. "If anything, I am intrigued by you. I'm rather glad now that I didn't kill you back there."

I turned to face him. "You wouldn't have," I said, holding his eyes. "Malo and the codex are the only reason you are alive right now. If it had been up to me—"

"If it had been up to you, you would have taken that famous sword of yours and bashed past my shield, then gutted me," Rorian said, interrupting. "I understand you believe that is the way it would have gone." He grinned. "Perhaps if you had gotten lucky, it might have. But I doubt it."

"You are an arrogant bastard," I growled. "I'll give you that."

"Not arrogant," Rorian said. "Just aware of what I can and cannot do."

"Then maybe we will get another chance to find out what you can do," I said, fingering Wolf's Head.

"Maybe we will," Rorian replied evenly. He glanced at Malo, who stood below on the lower deck watching us. "But not today."

"No, not today," I agreed as I let my hand drop to my side. Malo had made a deal with the scholar and honor demanded that it be adhered to, much as it galled me.

Rorian chuckled. "You wear your thoughts on your face like a fine cloak, Hadrack of Corwick," he said. "Easily seen by all but the most casual observer."

"Is there anything else?" I asked impatiently, turning back to the sea. "If not, then leave me be."

I sensed, rather than saw Rorian bow. "Of course. Forgive the intrusion."

For the next two days, *Sea-Dragon* skimmed across the Western Ocean, propelled by favorable winds and calm seas. We released one of the Cardians from the group, a thin, quiet man with bad teeth and even worse breath, who claimed that he was an experienced pilot. The man's name was Yanak, and we shackled him to the rudder and posted a guard to keep watch over him. Seeing him standing there reminded me of Baine, and eventually, I just stopped going to the stern altogether so that I wouldn't have to look at the bastard. The other two Cardians worked in tandem from sunup to sundown, repairing the ship and scrubbing the decks and hold.

On the third morning after we left the lagoon, Niko called down from the mast platform, "Calban, my lord! I see it!"

And so he had.

I ran to the gunwale and stared at the castle that appeared as a dark mass on the horizon, growing larger by the moment. Her giant spires were still heavily shrouded in mist, and her walls shimmered from the heat and distance as though they were dancing. Yet there could be no question where we were—the island castle of Calban.

I felt my fingers gripping the gunwale tightly, eager to see Shana after so long apart. Putt began to unfurl the Cardian banner above the sterncastle as I'd instructed him to the moment we saw Calban. The red pennant, with its screaming raven and outstretched claws, snapped loudly in the wind over my head as it unfurled.

"How long?" Malo asked Putt.

"An hour," the red-haired outlaw replied after taking a thoughtful glance at the castle. "Perhaps less if the winds increase."

I took a deep breath. An hour, then we will know. Had we made it in time, or had Baine's death been for nothing? I thought of Shana, knowing how busy she must be preparing for the Pilgrimage. I smiled, picturing the determined look on her face that I knew would be there as she organized the castle and made sure that all was in readiness. The master of Calban, as host, was responsible for the care, safety, and outfitting of the Pilgrims. A daunting, expensive task, considering Shana had told me last year that there had been well over four hundred Pilgrims that had made The Walk.

"You're thinking about her, aren't you?" Sabina said as she came to stand beside me. She shielded her eyes and peered at the castle, her face set in a stony, unreadable mask.

"I was just thinking how difficult it must be, having to organize such a complicated thing as a Pilgrimage," I said. "Feeding hundreds of Pilgrims for days must be a considerable challenge."

Sabina sniffed, looking unimpressed. "The Lady of Calban has a steward and countless underlings at her command for that," she said. "Besides, I imagine she is too busy scolding her chambermaids for the slightest mistake to give it much thought."

I glanced sideways at Sabina in annoyance. "You don't even know her, yet you have already judged her. How is that fair?"

"I never said that it was," Sabina responded tightly.

"Hadrack?"

I turned, having to suppress a chuckle as Jebido strode toward me. He was dressed in Cardian clothing, with a bright red cape around his shoulders and highly-polished, pointed boots on his feet.

Jebido glowered at me as he saw my lips twitch in amusement. "Malo wants to see you," he said. I opened my mouth to comment on his clothing just as Jebido held up a hand. "Not one word, Hadrack, or I swear by The Mother, you will regret it."

"I was just going to say that I would be right there," I said innocently.

Jebido studied my face suspiciously, then he turned away, his pointed boots beating against the deck with every step.

"I know you and Jebido have a long history," Sabina said disapprovingly, "but he should show you more respect."

I looked at her in surprise. "Who says that he doesn't?"

"It's just not right," Sabina said, not answering me. "People are laughing at you behind your back. If you are to be a lord, you must act the part."

I frowned. "Who is laughing?"

"Everyone."

I shook my head and chuckled. "No one is laughing at me, Sabina, but even if they were, what of it? Jebido is like a father to me, and I have his respect where it counts." I pointed to my head and then my heart. "Here and here."

I found Malo, Jebido, and Rorian in deep conversation on the sterncastle.

"Rorian says we are to dock at the northern gate," Malo said as I joined them. "Then we have to wait until an official comes to inspect us."

I frowned. "What's the purpose of that?" I asked Rorian.

The scholar shrugged as he headed for the ladder. "Just being cautious, I imagine."

"What do we do with the Cardians?" Jebido asked as Rorian reached the lower deck and strode toward the forecastle where his wife waited for him. "Those bastards could ruin everything if they open their mouths."

"We don't need them anymore," Malo grunted. "I say we slit their throats and toss them overboard."

I glanced down to the lower deck, where the two Cardians shackled together were working on their hands and knees, scrubbing the decking. The thick oak planking was already as clean as it would ever be, but the task kept them out of trouble. Malo was right, of course, the Cardians were a liability. But killing them outright, though the wiser choice, seemed wrong to me.

I glanced at Rorian, where he now stood on the forecastle with his wife. She was making strange motions with her hands, which was her way of communicating, Rorian had told me. The scholar laughed when she finished, then he responded with the same hand movements. Rorian was not the person I had expected, and I'd felt my hatred of him slowly fading as the trip progressed. I tore my eyes away from the couple, angry at myself. Rorian was to blame for Baine's death. I needed to remember that.

"What do you say, Hadrack?" Malo asked, cutting into my thoughts.

I could see the House Agent examining me, his face already clouding in anticipation of an argument. I felt a coldness come over me as I thought about Baine. Sometimes leadership meant making hard choices. I pointed to the shackled Cardians. "Toss those two overboard. If they can work together to make it to shore, then they have earned the right to live." I headed for the ladder. "I'll talk to the other one."

Niko was leaning against the gunwale dozing in the sunlight with his arms crossed when I reached the stern. The young outlaw heard me approaching and he pushed himself to his feet guiltily.

"My lord," Niko said, looking as though he expected an angry reprimand.

I stopped in front of Yanak with my legs spread and drew Wolf's Head as the Cardian's face blanched. I gestured over my shoulder. "In another minute or two, your countrymen are going for a swim." Yanak's throat started to quiver with fear. "I've decided that since you have done such a fine job of piloting us here, that I'll let you live." I pursed my lips as I studied him. "You do want to live, don't you?" Yanak's head bobbed up and down repeatedly, and his hands began to shake on the rudder. "Then you will guide us safely into Calban, where a man will board the ship. You won't speak to him. You won't even look at him. Is that clear?"

"Very clear, lord," he said, lowering his eyes.

I heard a commotion behind me as Malo, Jebido, and Tyris forced the Cardians over the gunwale. The two men begged and sobbed, the chains attached to their shackles rattling as they pleaded, but their words fell on deaf ears. Malo finally lost patience and he used his sword to prod at one of them, causing him to lose his balance. The man fell with a cry, echoed by his companion as he was dragged down into the sea as well. The Cardians bobbed up and down on the swell as they swept past us, their cries for mercy quickly fading as *Sea-Dragon* rapidly left them behind.

I glanced once more at Yanak. "Remember," I warned. "Not a word, or your fate will be ten times worse than theirs."

The thin Cardian, for all his faults, was a superb pilot, and he brought us into Calban with a skillful touch that I could only envy. I studied the dock as we slid into our berth, noticing that it had been expanded since the last time I had been there. I thought of the day we had rescued Shana from her husband's cruel execution. It all seemed so long ago now. We had almost made our escape from this very spot, only to be thwarted at the last moment by Cardians. It seemed whenever there was evil afoot, Cardians could always be relied upon to be knee-deep in it somehow.

Tyris and Niko threw lines ashore to several sun-bronzed men dressed in thin tunics, wool trousers, and wearing flimsy, reed-woven sandals on their feet. Within moments, both our stern and bow were lashed tightly to thick iron rings embedded into the piers along the dock. I glanced up the incline to the castle, awed as always by Calban's sheer size and grandeur. The northern gate that I remembered so well was hidden from my view by an outcrop of rock. A procession of soldiers had just appeared around that rock, and they marched toward us, dressed in matching blue surcoats with Lady Shana's white dove emblem on the front.

A short man with a neatly trimmed white beard and balding pate walked in front of the soldiers holding a long walking stick. I felt a smile of recognition break out on my face. It was Kylan, the accomplished Steward of Calban. I hadn't expected the steward to be the one to meet us. Had I known it would be him, I wouldn't have seen the need to have the Cardians thrown overboard. Kylan's face was etched in seriousness as he drew closer, and he regarded our ship and its raven banner with obvious distaste. I was certain I could detect a note of anger in his movements as he halted on the faded planking of the dock less than ten feet from our hull. I'd taken the precaution to don a hooded cloak, afraid some of the residents in Calban would recognize me. I stood on the sterncastle and waited as Tyris, dressed in Cardian finery, leaned against the gunwale below me.

"A pleasant day to you, good sir," Tyris said to the steward with a nod.

I silently cursed the archer. You are supposed to be a Cardian, you fool, I thought with a snort. You're being too polite.

Kylan frowned suspiciously as he squinted up at Tyris. "You are too late," the steward said. "The Pilgrimage has already begun. Lady Shana requests that you leave her lands immediately. You may try again in a year, The Mother and Father willing."

Tyris glanced up at me uncertainly.

"Has The Walk begun already, then?" I rumbled from beneath my hood.

Kylan shielded his eyes and craned his neck upward to see me. "It has," he confirmed.

I put a hand to my ear. "Yet, the drums do not roll, old man," I said, "nor do the trumpets blare." I lowered my hand. "Either you are mistaken, willfully stupid, or simply just don't like Cardians, eh?"

I could see Kylan coloring as he glared up at me. "The Walk begins momentarily. There is no time to inspect your ship before it starts."

"Then delay The Walk while you inspect us," I said dismissively. I needed to get Kylan aboard without any of the soldiers accompanying him suspecting that anything was amiss. I motioned to Niko and Jebido, who began to maneuver a gangplank into position.

"I cannot," Kylan said. "I do not have that power. Return in a year. That is the best that I can offer you."

"What of your Lady, then?" I asked, amused by the look of pure loathing on Kylan's face as he glared at me. "Can she not delay it?"

Kylan looked uncertain for a moment, then he sniffed and stood straighter, composing himself. "She can," he affirmed, "but as her steward, the discretion to ask her for that delay falls upon me." He turned to leave. "I see no reason to ask, so you must go."

"What would it take to make the lamb understand my need?" I asked softly. Kylan hesitated, looking back at me uncertainly. "Perhaps if you were to tell her it was a wolf who asked?" I carefully lifted my hood, giving Kylan a partial view of my face. The short steward's eyes widened in surprise. "Please," I said, gesturing to the gangplank. "Send a runner to the Lady and ask for a delay, then come aboard. I have much I want to discuss with you."

It took a moment or two for Kylan to regain his senses before he snapped a quick command to one of the soldiers and hurried up the gangplank. I climbed down to meet him, drawing the steward beneath the sterncastle away from prying eyes before we embraced.

"Hadrack?" Kylan said, still looking surprised as we drew apart. Malo, Jebido, and the others came to stand around us. The steward's eyebrows rose. "You are all here," he said in wonder. He turned back to me. "What is the meaning of this? What is wrong?"

"How long can Lady Shana delay the start of the Pilgrimage?" I asked, ignoring his questions.

Kylan frowned as he thought. "Not long, I imagine. Perhaps an hour, no more than that."

"It will have to do," I said, wishing we had more time.

"But what is this about?"

I quickly filled the steward in on what was going on. His mouth dropped open at the news of a second codex and he stared in fascination at Rorian and Thera as I explained their role in the Pilgrimage.

"So, you want to take their place?" Kylan said, motioning to the scholar and his wife. He glanced at Sabina. "Just you and this girl here against the might of the North and the power of the Sons?"

"Well, when you put it that way, it sounds daunting," I said. "But yes, that's our plan."

Kylan shook his head. "I don't know, Hadrack. If anyone else told me they wanted to try something like this, I would call them insane."

"Yet, you will help us?" I asked.

Kylan snorted. "Of course I will help you. But we must hurry. The Pilgrims are already on the beach. Lady Shana will delay them at my behest, but I expect she won't be happy about it."

"She will be when she sees why you asked," Jebido said, indicating me with a grin on his face.

"Yes," Kylan said, sounding distracted. "This Juliax that you spoke of, do you have any idea who he might be?"

"No," Malo said. "All we know is he will contact Hadrack somewhere along The Walk."

"Which means he could be anyone," Kylan said. "He could be a Pilgrim, a retainer, or even one of the hangers-on that follow The Walk. He could even be one of our men for all we know."

"Which means we have to be doubly careful," I said. "I can't let anyone inside Calban recognize me."

Kylan rubbed his beard as he thought. "Keep the cloak and hood on when we enter the castle. We have several hundred Pilgrims this year, with seven lords, two dukes, and even one minor prince from some island kingdom that I have never heard of, so it won't be that unusual. Once you enter the Preparing Rooms, however, that will be different."

"Different how?" I asked.

"Your clothing, armor, and weapons will be taken from you," Kylan explained. "You will be given a simple tunic to wear and nothing else. Any special status you had going into that room will not exist when you come out." Kylan grimaced. "At least in theory, at any rate."

"Does that go for both of us?" I asked, glancing at Sabina.

"Yes," Kylan said. "I suppose you should be grateful. In the beginning, Pilgrims made the journey to the mountains naked."

"What about us?" Malo asked. Like the others, the House Agent was dressed in Cardian clothing, although he seemed less uncomfortable in them than my men did.

"All retainers are welcome to accompany the Pilgrims along The Walk, but they must never come near them or speak with them during the day. Only at night once camp has been set."

"What about the Pilgrims?" I asked. "Can they talk amongst themselves?"

"Certainly," Kylan said.

Malo and I shared a look. "So, either Juliax is a Pilgrim and will contact us during the day," I said.

"Or you won't hear from him until the evening," Malo finished for me.

Kylan shrugged. "So it would seem." He frowned as he glanced at Malo. "Some of your faces are known inside Calban as well, so I suggest Hadrack and the girl come inside alone with me. I will send someone to collect the rest of you and take you to the beach after they have reached the Preparing Rooms. That way, none will suspect you are together. Once you are on The Walk itself, it won't matter."

"Good," I agreed. "Can you arrange it so I can see Shana?" I asked. I saw Sabina's face cloud over at my words.

"I will see what I can do," Kylan said as he ushered us toward the gangplank. "I can't promise you anything. We are quickly running out of time, but I will try."

Kylan's soldiers formed a ring around Sabina and me, and with the short steward leading us, we marched up the steep incline toward Calban. The northern gates were open and waiting for us, but the castle itself seemed almost deserted. I realized everyone must be waiting on the southern beach by now, preparing to send off the Pilgrims. Kylan led us through the upper bailey and thick barbican down to the middle bailey, where he stopped in front of a squat stone building with two soldiers standing outside the doors.

"We can go no further," Kylan said. He gestured to the set of heavy doors. "Inside, you will find all that you need. When you are ready, you will exit from the back of the building, where two girls will escort you from the castle." Kylan looked at me in warning. "Remember, once you step through those second doors, you must not speak. To do so before you enter the cordon of The Walk will mean instant rejection."

"I understand," I said as I squeezed Sabina's hand in reassurance.

A soldier ran toward us and he whispered something into Kylan's ear. The steward nodded and motioned the man away as he turned to me. "The Lady has delayed The Walk as requested. She is on her way, but will have very little time to talk. You must be quick with your words."

"Is she going to speak with both of us?" Sabina demanded, a little too forcefully, I thought.

Kylan regarded her in surprise before he glanced at me appraisingly. "No, child. You and Hadrack will be taken to separate rooms. The Lady will meet with Hadrack alone."

"That's not fair," Sabina said, starting to pout. She glared at me. "I thought we were in this together. Why am I being left out?"

"We are in this together," I said gruffly. "But what is to be said between Shana and me is for us alone." I indicated the doors as the soldiers to either side opened them. "Let's get on with this."

The room inside was empty of furnishings, though surprisingly large and cool, with a wizened old man and old woman waiting for us. The man and woman were the same height and looked almost identical. They both repeatedly bowed, showing dark gums as they grinned toothlessly.

"An honor, Pilgrims," the man said. "A great honor."

"An honor," the woman repeated. "A great honor."

"You will come this way, yes?" the man said to me, indicating a closed door to his right.

"You will come this way, yes?" the woman said to Sabina, indicating a closed door to her left.

I leaned close to Sabina. "I'll see you soon," I whispered. "There's nothing to worry about."

Sabina gave me a dark look as the old woman led her away. I turned and followed the old man toward the door on the right. He paused at the entrance, gesturing me inside as he swung the door open.

"Are you Juliax?" I asked softly as I stepped past him through the entrance.

The old man just looked at me blankly as he shut the door firmly behind us. I hadn't really expected him to be Juliax, but I figured it needed to be asked just the same. The room was about twenty feet long by ten feet deep, with a narrow door on the back wall set to one side of an empty, soot-covered fireplace. A small desk sitting in the center of the room was the only furnishing. A leather-bound ledger lay open on the desk and the old man went to it, perching himself on a stool. He picked up a quill and dipped it in ink.

"Your name, Pilgrim?"

I hesitated, almost saying the wrong name. "Rorian," I answered. "Rorian of Afrenia."

The old man grunted in acknowledgment as he wrote in the ledger. When he finished, he pointed the feathered end of the quill at me.

"Please remove your weapons and clothing, Pilgrim. I will log your possessions in this book. Once you return from the Pilgrimage, they will be returned to you."

I nodded, having been warned by Kylan that this would happen. I removed my sword, which was just a battered old blade that I'd taken from one of the Cardians. I had no intention of leaving Wolf's Head or my father's axe behind in this place and had left them in the care of Malo. The old man took a long white tunic, thick belt, and a pair of heavy leather sandals from a drawer. He placed them on the desktop as I disrobed. Once naked, I reached for the tunic, but the old man stopped me. He stood, holding a container filled with white powder as he advanced on me.

"What's that for?" I asked suspiciously.

"The skin of the gods," the old man said. "Stand still," he added, muttering under his breath in a strange sing-song voice as he flicked powder on me with his hand.

I closed my eyes, wrinkling my nose at the lavender smell, then jumped as I felt the old man's hands on me, rubbing the powder into my skin.

"The Mother and The Father had skin the color of newly-fallen snow," the old man explained, grinning his blackened gums at me. "You have been in the sun your entire life. To start this sacred journey, they must see you as you were meant to be." He frowned. "Where is your pass?" I opened my mouth, unsure what to say just as the old man waved his hand in the air. "Never mind. My place is not to question." He began to mutter to himself as he worked the powder into my skin. Finally, when he finished, he stepped back and surveyed his handiwork. "You have the look and muscles of a god, Pilgrim," he said in admiration. "What I wouldn't give to be young again and look like you." He grinned and winked at me. "I'd bed every pretty woman I could find, and even some of the ugly ones."

The old man's grin faded as a sudden knock sounded at the back door. "What's this, then?" he grunted, looking annoyed as he headed for the door. He swung it open and gasped in surprise. "My Lady," he said, bowing repeatedly. "An honor, Lady. An honor."

"I understand you have a late arrival here with you, Larret," Shana said. "I wish to speak with him."

The Lady of Calban stepped into the room dressed in a shimmering cloak of red and green that fell to her ankles. Her long black hair had painstakingly been plated with golden twine, and it hung like a thick, elegant rope down one side of her chest, almost reaching her waist. Our eyes met across the room and her lips twitched in amusement when she took in my white-powdered nakedness.

"Rorian of Afrenia, my lady," Larret said, glancing between us uncomfortably. He frowned and indicated the tunic on the desk. "Please clothe yourself, Pilgrim." He turned to Shana. "My apologies for the unseemliness, my lady."

"I've seen naked men before, Larret," Shana said with laughter in her voice. "Though rarely have they been this handsome."

I moved to the desk and grabbed the heavy tunic, dropping it over my head. The wool felt scratchy and uncomfortable.

"Please, leave us, Larret," Shana said. "I wish to speak with the Pilgrim alone."

Larret looked as though he might protest, then he silently crossed the room, exiting through the main door.

"I wasn't sure if you would be able to come," I said as I cinched the belt around my waist. I took Shana's hands in mine. "I'm glad you did."

"Kylan told me what's happening," Shana said. I could see worry in her blue eyes now. "If they catch you—"

I put a finger to Shana's lips. "They won't," I said. "I'll find the codex and end this war, I promise." I had asked to see Shana despite how busy I knew she was for one specific reason. I lifted her chin, marveling once again at her staggering, almost mystical beauty. I took a deep breath, willing myself to say the words. "And when the war is over, there won't be a need for us to hide anymore." I looked at her, letting her see in my eyes what I felt in my heart. "I'm a simple man, Shana, good with a sword and quick to anger. That's about all. I have land and title right now that aren't mine. When the war ends, I will be left with exactly what I had when it started, which is nothing. You are one of the highborn, with the blood of kings in you, and I am a wanted man and the son of a peasant. I have little to offer you but devotion and love. Yet, even so, will you consider becoming my wife?"

Shana blinked at me in surprise. "Of course I will," she said without hesitation. I could see tears welling in her eyes. "Being your wife is all that I have ever wanted since I met you, Hadrack."

I grinned in relief. "Then, that is what we will do," I said, feeling my heart soar. "The moment the war is over, we will marry." I drew Shana to me and kissed her deeply, stopping only when Larret knocked loudly on the door behind me.

"My lady," the old man called through the thick wood, sounding anxious. "The Pilgrims grow restless beneath the hot sun and the music has begun. You must hurry."

"You have to go now," Shana said softly as we held each other. We drew apart reluctantly and I moved to the back door.

"Hadrack," Shana called as I reached for the door handle. I stopped and turned. She was playing nervously with her fingers. "Please be careful, husband-to-be."

I grinned back at her. "When am I not, wife-to-be?"

13: The Walk

Sabina was waiting for me when I got outside, dressed in a belted, bulky tunic similar to my own and somehow managing to look impatient and annoyed at the same time. I'd exited the building into a small alcove hemmed in by the towering castle walls that stood less than ten feet back from the door. An alley led off to my right, and I could hear the sounds of cheerful music and excited voices coming from the shore's direction. Two young girls, both about ten years old, stood beside Sabina, each holding a single, bright yellow flower in their hands.

I was glad Sabina and I weren't allowed to talk to each other at the moment, as I could tell by her dour expression that she wasn't happy about how long I had taken inside with Shana. I could only imagine what her reaction would be, should she learn that the Lady of the castle and I were to be wed. Sabina's face and arms were powdered as mine were and it clung to her hair like a white veil. I frowned as I felt the small clumps of whiteness in my own hair, wondering how Juliax could identify us looking the way that we did.

"The skin of the gods will wear off in a day or so, Pilgrim," the closest girl to me said, reading my thoughts. "It is tradition that you begin The Walk in this fashion."

I nodded to her in relief. The girl had shiny black hair that fell to her shoulders, and she wore a brown, long-sleeved dress with a high collar. Stitching's of ducks adorned the hem and the sleeves of the dress. I thought she looked vaguely like Betania, who had been murdered by that sniveling coward, Carbet. I smiled warmly at the black-haired girl as she handed me her yellow flower. Her companion wore a similar dress, though hers was white without any stitching. She gave her flower to Sabina.

"These flowers represent all life within the First Pairs' domain," the girl that looked like Betania said in a practiced tone as she and her companion held hands. "Born from seed, they pushed their way out of the darkness and into the light, struggling to prosper and grow strong before blossoming into the glory that you see before you."

"But, as with all things," the second girl chimed in, "the day will come when these flowers will wither and die, returning once more to the earth-womb from whence they came."

"But not to be forgotten," the first girl said solemnly.

"No, never forgotten," the second girl agreed.

"So too shall you both grow strong and prosper in this world," the black-haired girl said.

"To bloom just like the flowers," the second girl added, "as you reach for the sun and Mother Above, while the roots of your feet remain planted firmly in the soils of Father Below. A true balance of love and harmony that all beings must learn before moving on to the next realm."

"Until finally, many years from now," the first girl continued, "you will wither and die like these same flowers, returning to the Mother's womb from whence you came."

"But not to be forgotten," the second girl said.

"No, never forgotten," the first one agreed.

The two girls bowed their heads, falling silent, both with tears in their eyes. Sabina and I waited, unsure of what we should do, until finally, the girls looked up.

"Please, Pilgrim," the black-haired girl said to me. "Hold the stem of the flower in your right hand between your thumb and finger."

I did so clumsily, trying not to crush it accidentally.

"Please, Pilgrim," the second girl said to Sabina. "Hold the stem of the flower in your left hand between your thumb and finger."

Sabina did as she was asked.

"Now," the black-haired girl said, her eyes shining. "We must hurry. Join hands and follow us."

The two turned together, striking off down the narrow corridor between the castle walls and the building. I held out my hand and Sabina took it, her small fingers lost in mine.

"Are you all right?" I whispered in her ear as we followed after the girls.

Sabina barely nodded, not looking at me. The girls disappeared around the corner of the building as we hurried to catch up. People were milling about near the keep and they began to shout and wave brightly-colored strips of cloth over their heads when they saw us.

"Bless you, Pilgrim!" an older woman cried as she ran to embrace me. There were tears in her eyes as she kissed me heartily on both cheeks. Her breath smelled strongly of onions, I noticed absently. "Bless you for your courage to take The Walk during these terrible times." She clutched at my arm desperately as I started to pull away, staring up at me with film-covered eyes. I noticed her lips were frosted from the powder on my cheeks. "Please, my son disappeared at Pond's Drop. I've heard no word from him since. Please, Pilgrim, will you ask the First Pair how he fares when you reach Oasis? His name is Kreech."

Oasis was a sacred place in the heart of Mount Halas itself, where the First Pair had lived during their time in this world. It was there that a Pilgrim's prayers had the best chance of being heard. I patted the woman's shoulder to let her know that I would do what I could for her. More people were reaching out to me now, and I could feel their touch on my skin, hair, and tunic. They were reaching out to Sabina in much the same way. The hands upon us were gentle, though, almost reverent, and finally, soldiers appeared to move the people back.

We hurried on through the barbican and down the incline into the lower bailey, then out the front gates. The music was deafening now that we were outside the castle as the notes echoed off the stone walls behind us. Our guides continued along the rock-chiseled road, heading for the long wooden bridge that led to the southern shore. Sabina and I hesitated, startled by the hundreds of pairs of eyes that had turned to focus on us.

Hordes of people stood along the sand-covered beach, with musicians of every stripe perched on an extended wooden platform playing their instruments. I could see drummers, pipers, fiddlers, harp, and lute players swaying and dancing with the chaotic rhythm. Ropes attached to posts that had been pounded into the sand cordoned off a pathway down the beach, holding the people back from a long line of Pilgrims that were dressed identical to us. The Pilgrims stood in rows of two—a man and a woman per row. I could see the line stretching to the horizon. I whistled, impressed.

"Pilgrims!" the black-haired girl hissed anxiously. "You must hurry! The speeches have already ended. If you are not inside The Walk when the music stops, they won't accept you!"

I felt a sudden thud of dread in my chest and I dragged Sabina after me as we sprinted toward the bridge. I could hear the crowd urging us on as our sandals slapped against the rough planking. I glanced toward the platform where the musicians were dancing in a frenzy as they banged their drums, blew on their horns and flutes, and plucked at their stringed instruments.

Don't you stop yet, you bastards, I thought as we reached the halfway point of the bridge. We caught up to and passed our guides as they hurriedly stepped aside to let us go around them. The black-haired girl and I exchanged a quick, worried look, and then we left them behind. We must have made quite the sight, Sabina and me, running hand in hand as we were, covered in white powder with our tunics flapping in the wind and each of us holding a dainty flower in the air.

We were three-quarters of the way across the bridge when the music reached an ear-splitting crescendo, with the deep, rhythmic beat of the drums dominating. People along both sides of The Walk began falling to their knees, one hand held to the sky, one hand plunged into the sand as they swayed and contorted in religious fervor. Some of the Pilgrims inside The Walk knelt as well, losing themselves to the moment, as one by one, the instruments began to go silent. I ground my teeth as we ran, terrified that we weren't going to make it in time.

"Faster!" I gasped at Sabina, taking a chance that none could hear me over the music and cheering.

"I can't go any faster!" came back the breathless reply.

I cursed, then in one quick motion, I flung Sabina over my shoulder, not losing a step or my grip on my precious flower as I kept running. The people on the beach began to cheer louder, caught up in the drama as I raced with my burden for the end of the bridge. I could see out of the corner of my eye that only half a dozen drummers at the front of the platform were still playing now. A short woman with enormously fat legs and wearing a ridiculous, plumed hat sat near them plucking on a harp, while a thin man with bulging cheeks stood behind her blowing on an ox horn. That was all.

I reached the end of the bridge, gasping for air and tasting blood where I'd bitten into my lip. I looked ahead. I had perhaps a hundred yards to go through thick sand to reach the ropes. Eager hands pushed me onward as I ran, even as the woman with the harp and the man with the ox horn stopped playing, leaving only a single drummer left, who sat alone, striking a lonely beat on his drum. That man was squat and round, with rosy cheeks and hair shorn close to his scalp. I glanced at The Walk, where the rest of the Pilgrims had turned to watch. Seventy-five yards to go.

The squat drummer finally stood up and grimaced regretfully at me, striking the stretched calfskin over his drum one last time. Fifty yards to go and I felt my lungs burning in my chest, certain that my legs were about to give out beneath me. I felt horrible defeat rising in me just as I saw Malo jump onto the platform. The House Agent stood out in his bright Cardian garb even among the musicians. He ran to the squat man and ripped the drumsticks from his hands and then struck the surface of the drum with one of them. Malo glared at me fiercely, nodding for me to continue as he hit the drum again, and again, over, and over in a steady rhythm.

I felt relief wash over me as I half-staggered, half-ran to The Walk barrier while people of every shape and size cheered me on, slapping my back and rifling my powdered hair good-naturedly. I heard Sabina yelp in outrage as some of the bolder men pinched and squeezed her bottom as we passed.

I set Sabina down by the ropes and grabbed her hand, relieved to see that my flower was still intact, though a petal was missing and the stem was lilting to one side. I lifted the flower to the crowd in triumph and motioned with my eyes that Sabina should do likewise. We stood there for a moment, basking in victory as Malo beat his drum and the crowd whistled and cheered.

Finally, I lifted the rope over our heads, and together, Sabina and I entered The Walk.

Two days later, the euphoria, pomp, and pageantry of The Walk was long gone. Replaced instead with the grim reality of what we were up against. We marched from the moment the sun came up, until long after it went down and darkness fell, with no rest or letup. At night, we slept on the ground, huddled together in our meager tunics against the chills. Each Pilgrim was allowed a small hunk of bread and a little water at midday, but that was all. I was told this was necessary to cleanse our bodies of weakness and impurity before we reached Mount Halas. I considered the idea utter nonsense, of course, though many of my fellow Pilgrims seemed quite content, even happy with the arrangement.

I believe myself to be as pious as the next man, but, even so, I couldn't understand what difference it made to the First Pair whether my back hurt or not, or that my stomach grumbled unhappily. I wisely kept those thoughts to myself, however. Juliax hadn't contacted us yet, and Sabina and I had decided to keep our heads down and our eyes open until such time that he did.

"How long until we reach the mountain?" Sabina asked.

I glanced over the heads of the line of Pilgrims in front of me. We were picking our way through a rock-strewn valley, with thick forestlands rising to either side. I could see the many ridges of the Father's Spine mountains far in the distance, dominated by the majestic, white-tipped peak of Mount Halas. As far as I could tell, the towering mountain seemed no nearer today than it had yesterday.

"Another week at this pace, I think," I said, taking a guess.

Sabina sighed unhappily. "I don't think my sandals can make another hour, let alone a week."

"Mine too," I replied in agreement.

A bald man walking ahead of us turned at our words, smiling in a friendly fashion. His name was Emand, a cordwainer, which he had explained to me was a maker of new shoes. I couldn't even imagine what it must be like to own a pair of new shoes. His wife walked beside him, tall and thin as a broom handle, with the dour personality to match.

"The Watchers will replace them, my good man," Emand said jovially. "You need only ask." He was short, plump, and always smiling—the exact opposite of his wife. Emand gestured behind us to the seven covered wagons that trailed the line of walkers. "Your tunics as well, should that be needed."

I turned to look back. The Watchers were here to care for the Pilgrims, and it was they who gave us our meager food and water each day. I snorted as I studied the wagons rolling slowly along. So far, I would say our caretakers were not living up to their name. Grizzled-looking soldiers rode attentively to either side of the ox-pulled wagons, keeping wary eyes on the hills above us. The threat of bandits was real, I knew, though the soldiers seemed more concerned about an attack from the forces of the Sun than anything else. I thought those concerns groundless, however, as The Walk was sacred to both sides. More soldiers rode to either side of the procession, and even more rode ahead of us. Malo and my men rode somewhere far to the wagons' rear with the other retainers of the wealthier Pilgrims.

I'd had an opportunity to talk to Malo on our first night and he told me that my men were being well-fed and were in good spirits. It seemed we Pilgrims were meant to wither on the vines of the First Pairs' love, yet our caretakers and guards could eat and drink as much as they wanted.

Malo spoke with Shana before The Walk left Calban, and she agreed to send a messenger to Daughter Gernet, requesting the five hundred Jorqs to pay the scholar. Once Rorian had his gold, Shana would then send him and his wife home on *Sea-Dragon*, after which the big cog would return to the island castle. I had come to feel possessive of the ship and was reluctant to part with it, so I had requested it be held in my name. I had no idea what I would do with a vessel like *Sea-Dragon,* but neither Malo nor Shana had any issues with me laying claim to her.

"Where was it you said you were from again, Rorian?" Emand asked me.

"Afrenia."

"Ah, that's right, a wonderful place. I get my best leather from there." Emand tapped his chest. "I'm from Hillsfort. Have you heard of it?" I nodded, trying to keep the distaste from my face. I remembered Hillsfort and that murderous bastard Hape all too well. The shoemaker gestured to his wife. "And Laurea, here, is originally from Cardia." He chuckled. "I must tell you how we met. It is an interesting story."

Sabina and I glanced at each other at the mention of Cardia. Was this a test? I wondered. Could this pleasant little man be Juliax?

I felt Laurea's cold eyes take me in from head to toe, but all she did was sniff slightly in disinterest, then look away. I remember long ago wondering if the Cardian women were as unpleasant as their men. If Laurea was any indication, then I had my answer. Emand continued to prattle on about how he and his wife met. He claimed that it had been love at first sight, which I had a hard time imagining. I listened with one ear, making the appropriate noises of interest when I thought they were required. Finally, we reached the head of the valley and the plump shoemaker was forced to conserve his breath as the grade began to slope upward dramatically.

"I'll finish the story later," Emand promised me between wheezing gasps.

"I look forward to it," I said, forcing a smile.

We marched across northern Ganderland as another long day passed, with the tip of Mount Halas always beckoning us onward. The mountain shimmered like a white jewel above us, looking close enough to reach out and touch, yet forever out of our grasp. We were passing through a pleasant forest of beech and fir trees on the morning of the fourth day when a commotion arose ahead. The entire line of Pilgrims slowed uncertainly and then came to a stop. We were expected to maintain five feet between each row of Pilgrims at all times as we marched, and the procession had stretched out in a rambling line through the trees almost half a mile long. I watched curiously as several soldiers kicked their horses forward to investigate.

"What's going on?" I asked Emand, unable to see more than ten rows ahead as a bend in the trail cut off my view.

"I'm not sure," the cordwainer muttered. His eyebrows rose as one of the horsemen came racing back around the bend, only to turn around again once he had reached our rear, leading one of the wagons.

"Move aside, Pilgrims!" the soldier cried urgently, motioning us out of the way as he thundered past.

Sabina and I stepped dutifully into the trees as the wagon bounced and jostled after him, then we cautiously moved back onto the path. We stood and waited, unsure of what to do as we slapped at hungry insects for almost half an hour, until finally, the line began to move again.

I could hear choked sounds of weeping echoing through the trees ahead, growing louder as we drew closer. We came around the bend to find a man lying prone along the path, his eyes open wide and looking surprised by death. A Watcher stood above the body with his hands on his hips, while a woman knelt on the ground, holding the dead man's hands to her chest. The grieving woman glanced at us as we walked by, and I quickly shifted my gaze away from the look of anguish in her eyes. I felt Sabina's hand clutching for mine and I took it, squeezing as we trudged onward.

By the eighth day of The Walk, we had lost a dozen Pilgrims, five of whom had died, while the others had just given up, too exhausted to go on. My feet were bleeding, blistered and raw, and I was already on my third pair of sandals. We were told The Walk would reach the garrison at the base of Mount Halas the following night, which was welcome news to all. I was beginning to feel more and more anxious with each step, however, as our contact still hadn't appeared.

"What do we do if Juliax doesn't show up?" Sabina asked, clearly thinking the same thing that I was. She glanced ahead at Emand and his wife. The two were gamely marching on, though both appeared near the end of their limits. Sabina lowered her voice even more. "You told me Rorian said if we reach the mountain without those passes, they will kill us."

"He didn't know that for certain," I said just as softly, trying to allay her fears. "It was just a guess. Don't worry, Juliax will get us the passes. You'll see."

Each Pilgrim wore a thin chain around their neck with a small medallion attached to it with a number stamped into the metal. These were the passes that we needed. Emand had a sharp eye, and he'd asked me where ours were on the first day. I'd had to do some quick thinking to come up with a reasonable explanation for why we didn't have them. I told the cordwainer that I was concerned that one of us might lose our passes on the trek and that our retainers carried them for safekeeping. The shoemaker's eyebrows had risen at that and I'd seen respect in his eyes. If you had retainers on The Walk, then logically, it followed that you must be important.

"But what if he doesn't get them to us?" Sabina asked, looking unconvinced. "Then what?"

I shrugged. "Then we come up with a different plan."

The next day began hot and humid, with a dense fog shrouding the forestland we traveled through. Two more Pilgrims had died the night before, both from the same pair. The two had been life-long partners, married for fifty-three years, and had been found lying huddled together in each others' arms. We buried the couple along the road in the fog and one of the Watchers said a few words over their graves before we solemnly moved on. Juliax still hadn't contacted us and I was beginning to think that Sabina's fears were about to come true. Malo and I had talked the night before, and we agreed that we needed to continue being patient, though I could detect a note of worry in the House Agent's eyes as well.

The fog finally lifted around midday, just as we entered the Father's Spine mountain range. A narrow dirt road that Emand told us had been built almost six-hundred years ago wound its way around the base of one of the smaller mountains at the head of the range. We marched past giant, tilted slabs of granite that lined the slope like sentries as the road eventually straightened out, cutting through a field of dancing yellow flowers. I realized that the flowers were identical to the ones we had been given at the start of The Walk. Mount Halas finally rose before us as we left the field behind—the mountain standing almost twice as high as the others.

"Not long now," Emand said with a tired smile as he glanced over his shoulder. "We should reach First Step by nightfall."

First Step, I'd learned, was a garrison that sat at the base of Mount Halas. There was only one trail up to the mountain top that was accessible, and First Step guarded it. It was there, I knew, we would have to produce our passes.

The afternoon wore on, with the sun beating down mercilessly, determined not to go easy on us as The Walk slowly came to a close. We eventually left the field of flowers behind, following the road as it led us through deep rocky canyons and thick forests. We came to a gleaming, peaceful lake ringed by giant spruce trees, and, in a moment of rare generosity, the Watchers let us stop along the shore to quench our thirst.

Some of the less modest Pilgrims—myself included—stripped off our sweat-stained tunics and jumped into the cold water, laughing like children as we splashed at each other. Sabina declined to join us, but I could feel her eyes on me as I swam and wrestled with some of the other younger men. The water was invigorating, lifting my spirits, and I could feel its soothing touch washing away all of my doubts.

My good mood lasted for several more hours, right up until the sun began to sink in the west and I got my first view of First Step's walls. The garrison sat high on a slope at the base of the mountain, built with the end walls on each side curved like wings to meet the imposing rock face behind it. Red streaming Rock of Life banners snapped from the turrets, with here and there Prince Tyrale's golden lion joining them. I was surprised to see the Blazing Sun banner was also flying from one of the turrets. Tall iron braziers burned along both sides of the road leading to the garrison, beckoning us onward as dusk fell and horns signaled our welcome from the walls. The gates slowly opened and soldiers appeared, marching forward to form lines on either side of the road. Two men on horseback came through the gates next. They paused and waited as the lead Pilgrims far ahead of us stumbled toward them.

"The one on the right," I said, pointing to the mounted men. "Is that a Son?"

Sabina looked ahead, squinting. "I think so. The little bald fellow beside him looks like a Son-In-Waiting, too."

"That's what I thought as well," I said.

There were no Daughters in evidence that I could see, not that I had expected there to be. I watched as the riders dismounted, moving forward as the first couple arrived. The Pilgrims held hands as they slowly knelt before the Son, who placed his spread fingers on each of their heads. I imagine he was saying something flowery and elegant, but we were still too far away to hear anything but mumbling. The kneeling Pilgrims finally stood and removed their passes from around their heads before dutifully handing them over to the Son-In-Waiting. The bald apprentice called out the numbers on the medallions in a loud, sing-song voice that echoed dramatically off the mountain face. A man stood on the parapet above the gate, holding a thick ledger. He glanced down at it quickly before calling out two names in confirmation. The Son spread his hands in the air at the names, said a few words, then motioned that the Pilgrims could enter the garrison behind him.

"Hadrack?" Sabina said. "What are we going to do?"

I looked at her as the next pair of Pilgrims stepped forward. "I have no idea," I replied honestly.

The long line of Pilgrims moved ahead surprisingly quickly, the Son, apprentice, and the man with the ledger falling into a practiced rhythm that wasted little time. Before we knew it, only Emand and his wife, and another pair ahead of them were left to pass through the gates. The Son motioned the next couple forward and they knelt before him as he placed his hands on their heads. Sabina and I were holding hands as we waited and I could feel the cold sweat of fear coating her palm. The garrison soldiers and our escorts remained lined up along both sides of the road, watching in eery silence. I examined each man's face in desperation, hoping that one of them might reveal himself to be Juliax, but no one moved or even bothered to look at us.

"You had best summon your retainers soon, Rorian," Emand said as the man with the ledger called out several names. The cordwainer winked at me. "It would be a shame to survive the hardships of The Walk, only to lose your lives now before the adventure truly begins."

The Son began beckoning Emand and Laurea forward. "Juliax?" I blurted out at the little man.

"What?" Emand asked, pausing to look back at me.

"Are you Juliax!?" I hissed at him.

The shoemaker gave me a perplexed look, jumping in surprise as his wife snapped something urgently into his ear. Emand shrugged at me as the two moved away.

"We have to run!" Sabina said under her breath as we reluctantly took several steps closer. I could feel her trembling in my grip. "It's our only chance."

"Run where?" I grunted out of the side of my mouth. I turned, searching the faces around us again as the man on the walls began calling out Emand and his wife's name. No one moved and I knew we were out of time. Juliax wasn't coming. "All right," I finally whispered, tightening my hold on Sabina's hand. "We'll make toward the Son like we are expected to. Kneel and wait for my signal, then break for their horses. Hopefully, we can catch them by surprise and ride out of here."

"My lord!"

I turned to see Putt and Malo pushing their way through the line of soldiers. Malo was waving two medallions dangling from chains over his head. A tall soldier cursed a challenge as the House Agent shouldered him aside, but Malo ignored him as he sprinted toward us.

"You found Juliax!" I said in relief.

"Not exactly," the House Agent responded. He handed Sabina and me a medallion as I looked at him quizzically. "There isn't time for a long explanation, so I'll be brief. Remember the first Pilgrim who died in the forest?" Both Sabina and I nodded together. "That, unfortunately, was our mysterious Juliax."

"Ah," I said, understanding now. I held up the medallion. "How did you get these, then? Did the woman paired with Juliax give them to you?"

Malo shook his head. "No, she returned home after his death." The House Agent grimaced. "I imagine when they buried the bastard, they didn't notice the extra passes hanging around his neck."

I blinked in surprise, realizing something was wrong as I looked at the medallion I held. "What did you do, Malo?" I growled suspiciously. "You couldn't have had enough time to go back and get them. So, whose are these?"

"You're right," Malo agreed. "There wasn't time. They belong to the old couple who died last night."

"But how—" Sabina began to say.

"Putt and Niko dug the bodies up after everyone left this morning," Malo cut in impatiently. He turned to me. "I wanted to make sure that if Juliax didn't appear, then at least we had another option."

I cursed under my breath. "But they are going to call out the wrong names, Malo!" I hissed. "Don't you see the problem here? Some of the other Pilgrims already know us as Rorian and Thera. What are they going to do when they hear us called by different names?"

"I didn't say that it was a perfect solution," Malo said crossly. "I was hoping it wouldn't be necessary to use them. But unless you want to try kneeling before that Son without any passes at all, then I'd say it's this or nothing."

"Pilgrims," the Son called, smiling as he motioned us forward. "Come, come, my children. You are the final pair. Come to me and be recognized so that we can all go inside and celebrate. I'm tired of standing on these aching feet while my stomach pines for its supper."

"This better work," I grumbled unhappily at Malo.

"It will," the House Agent assured me. "Just stay calm and keep a level head, and you will be fine."

Sabina and I started to walk toward the waiting Son and apprentice. The priest wasn't tall, coming to my shoulders at best, but he was broad in the shoulders and had a solid build that was beginning to thicken noticeably beneath his black robes.

"Kneel, my children," the Son said as we approached.

The Son's voice was smooth and soothing, and his eyes shone with a tired kindness as we knelt by his sandaled feet. I noticed that his toenails were long, curled, and dirty. The priest put his hand firmly on my head and I could feel the steely warmth of his fingers where they pressed against my scalp.

"In all things, there is a first and a last," the Son said. "It has been a privilege for me to grant so many deserving Pilgrims access through these hallowed gates this year." He smiled down at us sadly. "You two shall be the last to gain entry in these troublesome times full of confusion and misunderstanding. Perhaps that is as it should be, for never have I seen a finer pair kneeling before me than I see right now. There is nothing but kindness and goodness coming from you both, and it warms my heart to see it. You exude qualities that The Mother and The Father place within all of us, though sadly, many choose to ignore them. War and bloodshed have ravaged our great kingdom this past year, yet the determination, perseverance, and comradeship needed to complete The Walk by each pair lends hope to us all that soon our people can be whole again."

I closed my eyes, barely listening as the priest continued talking for several long minutes, until finally he asked us to stand. I rose, helping Sabina to her feet. The Son gestured to the bald apprentice, who I guessed was no more than ten or eleven years old.

"Please present your passes, my children," the Son said, sounding tired now.

Sabina and I obeyed silently, and then we waited as the apprentice called out the numbers. A moment later, the shouted response that I had been dreading came from the garrison walls.

"Parm and Chesle of Bent Springs!"

I winced and held my breath, waiting for the expected outcry at the unfamiliar names, but none came.

The Son smiled as he swept his hand toward the garrison. "Welcome to First Step, my children."

14: First Step

Once Sabina and I passed through the gates of First Step, everything we had known so far about The Walk changed. Children brought us flowers the moment we entered, giggling shyly as they handed us wreaths of yellow petals that they insisted be worn on our heads like crowns. Spitted calves, fallow deer, and wild boars twisted slowly on spits hung over roaring bonfires in the center of the courtyard. Pilgrims danced and twirled around the flames to the sounds of cheerful violas, fiddles, and tambourines. My stomach rumbled greedily as the wind carried the smell of the cooking meat our way.

"Welcome, fellow Pilgrim!" a man cried, stumbling up to me. His hair and beard were long and dirty, and he held a bottle in one hand as he wobbled unsteadily. He was dressed in a sweat-stained tunic similar to mine, though he also wore a fine pair of leather trousers and thick leather boots that I could only stare at in envy. A crown of flowers identical to the ones Sabina and I wore sat perched upon his head. The man waved the bottle toward the crowded courtyard. "Welcome to paradise, friend!"

"Yes, thank you," I muttered as I looked around.

Long tables lit by torches and covered in luxurious, colorful cloth, stood in front of the Holy House, attended by smiling Sons-In-Waiting. All manner of fowl, meats, fish, fruits, and vegetables lay piled high on the tables in a dizzying array of riches. Pilgrims were milling about in front of the food, talking, eating, and laughing. I felt my mouth watering uncontrollably. I glanced at Sabina, seeing an answering gleam of hunger reflected in her eyes. The drunken Pilgrim almost fell as I started to move forward and I had to grab him by his foul-smelling armpits to hold him up.

"Bless me, that was close," the man giggled, breathing a waft of heady wine into my face. He grinned lopsidedly as he tapped my arm in thanks. "You came the Calban route, yes?" I nodded distractedly, my eyes returning to the feast as the man took a long drink from the bottle. "I knew it," he said. He burped loudly and pounded a finger into my chest. "Count yourself lucky. The eastern route was many times worse."

Sabina began making her way toward the tables and I set off after her as my companion followed, clutching annoyingly at my sleeve.

"Seven Pilgrims lost their lives on the way here," I grunted over my shoulder, trying to shake off his hand. "That doesn't seem lucky to me."

"Bah!" the drunkard snorted, waving the bottle at me dismissively. "That's nothing." He took another pull of wine as we reached the first table. "We lost thirty-two."

I glanced at him in surprise as I grabbed a thick slice of roasted duck sitting on a wooden block. The outer skin of the duck was burnt crispy black, just the way I liked it. I shoved the meat into my mouth, moaning in pleasure at the taste.

The drunkard plucked at my sleeve again. "Did you hear what I said, Pilgrim? Thirty-two!"

"I heard you," I said as I chewed.

Grease ran down both sides of my mouth as I ate, dripping off my beard. I swallowed the last of the duck, then wiped my beard with the back of my hand. I selected a blood-red slab of veal next as my stomach gurgled greedily. Sabina stood on the other side of the table from me, gnawing heartily on the leg of a hare. She grinned around a mouthful of meat at me and I grinned back. I took the bottle from the drunkard's unfeeling hand and drained the last of it, then threw it aside as I resumed eating.

"We would have fared much better," the Pilgrim continued, seeming not to have noticed that I'd taken his wine, "had that bastard outlaw not attacked us."

I paused with dripping veal halfway to my lips. "Outlaw?"

"Yes," the drunkard said. "The Outlaw of Corwick. That turd of a cockroach attacked us on the fifth day out. The Lord of Evensmire is taking the Pilgrimage this year, and he brought twenty of his retainers along." The man attempted a clumsy wink. "Not to mention a sizable donation to Oasis that whoreson of an outlaw must have learned about."

I frowned in puzzlement. "Did you see him?"

The Pilgrim nodded, staring down at his empty hand in confusion. "I did." He looked around, blinking stupidly, then signaled a peasant walking by. "More wine!" He turned back to me. "Big and fearsome looking, he was, with a great blond beard hanging down to his waist." The drunkard shuddered. "They say he's rolled a fingerbone in that beard of his for every man that he has killed."

I shook my head, chuckling at the thought as I ate. An imposter using my name and the fear associated with it, I realized. "That would be an awful lot of bones if the rumors are true," I pointed out. "He would have to have a beard down to his ankles." The Pilgrim looked at me strangely, clearly wondering if I was teasing him or not. "So, what happened?" I asked as I crammed a wedge of sweet southern pear into my mouth.

"The bastards waited until The Walk had passed, then they attacked the guards and retainers behind us. Everything was confusion and swirling dust, and no one knew what was happening. The Watchers tried to flee when they realized who was attacking, but they had only one way to go, which was our way. We were traveling along a narrow valley at the time and didn't see the wagons coming until they were on top of us. More than a hundred Pilgrims were injured, with twenty-eight killed." He glared at me fiercely. "Twenty-eight innocent souls that the Outlaw of Corwick murdered. I know the True King has already put a heavy price on that bastard's head, but someday, The Father willing, I hope to be there to see him pay for those twenty-eight lives. No man deserves to burn more than he does."

"Perhaps someday he will," I said softly.

The drunkard muttered something that I didn't hear, then he ambled off, leaving me to eat in peace. I turned back to the table, accepting a bowl of steaming lamb stew from a heavy-set Son-In-Waiting. Sabina was engaged in conversation with a woman I didn't recognize, so I turned away, blowing on the food. I froze as Emand the cordwainer stood before me, regarding me with hard eyes. Gone was the cheerful, pleasant man that I'd walked The Walk with, replaced now by a man filled with anger and suspicion.

"Give me one good reason why I shouldn't say something, Rorian, or whatever your name is," Emand said crossly. "I'm giving you the courtesy to explain yourself now only because of the bond we developed during The Walk."

I paused for a moment, rolling lie after lie over in my head, then I set the bowl down. The lies wouldn't work, I knew, so all that was left to me was to tell him the truth.

"Because if you tell anyone what you know, then the one chance that I have to stop the war will be gone."

Emand blinked in surprise, looking uncertain. Then his face hardened again. He crossed his arms over his chest. "Tell me."

I put my arm around the plump man's shoulders and drew him away from the table. "I'm sorry I had to lie to you about our names, Emand," I said. "I don't know who to trust here."

"Your name isn't really Rorian?"

I shook my head. "No."

"It's Parm, then?"

"Not that either," I said. "My name is Alwin. Alwin of Witbridge. Sabina and I—"

"Sabina?"

"The girl you know as Thera," I said. "Rorian and his wife were supposed to join The Walk, but we replaced them."

"But why did they call you Parm, then?" Emand asked, looking confused.

"Because someone was supposed to meet Rorian to give him passes into First Gate, but that man never made it. We had to use other passes at the last moment. That's why different names were called."

"Is that why you called me Juliax earlier?" Emand asked. "Was that the man you were supposed to get the passes from?"

"Yes. I thought you might have been Juliax because of your wife."

"My wife?"

"The passes for Rorian and Thera were obtained by Cardians. Since you said your wife came from there, it seemed possible to me that you might be Juliax."

"Well, I'm obviously not," Emand said with a snort. "I'm just a simple cordwainer, just like I told you."

I nodded absently. "I know that now. I apologize."

Emand and I paused near one of the bonfires, just out of earshot of an old peasant turning a wild boar on a spit. A second peasant dipped a tin mug tied to a stick into a barrel of water, then poured the contents onto the meat as the boar skin sizzled and steamed.

"You said that if I told what I know about you, then you wouldn't be able to stop the war," Emand said. "What did you mean by that?"

I glanced away. Sabina was making her way toward us, a look of concern on her face. I turned back to Emand and told him about the second codex and why Sabina and I were here. The cordwainer listened attentively, the anger and suspicion leaving his eyes as I talked. Sabina joined us halfway through my explanation, and between us, we finished the story.

"A second codex," Emand breathed in wonder. "I can't believe it."

"Believe it," I said firmly. "Emand, you can't tell anyone about this. Not even your wife."

"But, I've never kept anything from her," Emand said, looking crestfallen. He glanced at Sabina. "You understand, don't you?"

Sabina put her hand on the little cordwainer's arm. "I do, I truly do." She indicated me. "But Had—"

"Alwin," I cut in sharply.

Sabina swallowed, reddening as she glanced at me apologetically. "Alwin is right. We are taking a huge risk by telling you."

"It's not as though you had a choice," Emand pointed out.

"I could have lied to you," I replied. "I didn't do that because both Sabina and I trust you." I put my hand on the cordwainer's shoulder. "You are a good man, Emand of Hillsfort, and that's why I felt you should know the truth."

"But what if Laurea asks me why people are calling you by different names?"

I shrugged. "Just tell her there was a mistake when the names were called out. We were so tired that we just went along with it to get inside."

Emand frowned and rubbed his chin. "I don't know, Alwin. That seems a little weak."

"It would be better if you go back to calling me Rorian."

The cordwainer sighed in resignation. "Very well, Rorian, but you don't know my wife. Laurea has a way of getting the truth out of me."

"Not this time," I said, letting Emand see a glint of warning in my eyes. "Give me your word that you won't tell her." I stepped forward until I was towering over the little shoemaker. "I consider you a friend, Emand, but what I told you was said in confidence. If you tell anyone, including your wife, I will consider it a betrayal of our friendship." I stepped even closer. "I do not react well to betrayal."

Emand swallowed. "I understand, Rorian. I won't say anything. You have my word."

We were scheduled to set off up the mountain early the next morning, but even so, the festivities went on well into the night. A tent had been provided for every Pilgrim pair, and once we'd eaten our fill, Sabina and I slipped away to find ours. Malo and my men were waiting outside the tent when we located it, having been banned from joining in on the feast. None of the other retainers or soldiers had been allowed to eat, either, which seemed fitting to me, considering how well they had all eaten these last few days compared to us Pilgrims.

Our tent turned out to be quite spacious, with luxurious furs lining the floor from one end to the other. Subdued flames fluttered from within a squat iron brazier that sat in the middle of the tent, lighting the interior. I could see clean clothing for both Sabina and me stacked neatly in piles in one corner, with two pairs of supple leather boots sitting next to them. Fresh fruit in brightly colored clay bowls and three bottles of wine sat on a small table near the clothes. Niko headed directly for the wine, a grin of happiness crossing his features.

"Not yet," I said gruffly, snapping my fingers and pointing to the furs. "Sit." I grabbed an apple from one of the bowls and tossed it to him. "This will have to do for now."

Niko dropped to the floor as he stared at the apple in his hand with distaste. The rest of my men sat as well.

"I understand you had a problem with that cordwainer," Malo said from where he stood by the entrance. "Is everything all right?"

"I hope so," I replied. "I had to tell him about the codex."

"What!?" Malo exploded. "Why would you do that?"

"Because he heard us referred to by the wrong names, Malo," I said in exasperation. "Just like I warned you might happen. I had to tell him the truth. Nothing else would have convinced him to stay quiet."

"What about his wife?" Sabina asked, chewing on her lower lip. "He still might tell her, despite what he promised."

"He might," I agreed with a sigh. "If he does, then it's a good bet we will all be dead before morning."

Silence filled the tent at that unwelcome thought, until finally, Malo sighed in resignation. "Very well. There's no point in worrying about events we have no control over. Hadrack, I suggest you and Sabina try to get some sleep. Tomorrow is going to be a long day for you both." He turned. "Tyris, Putt, I want you two to stand watch outside the tent. If you see any soldiers coming this way, get everybody out of here as fast as you can."

Both Tyris and Putt looked to me for confirmation and I nodded my agreement.

"And supposing these soldiers do come," Putt said. "Where do we run? The gates are sealed."

"We will worry about that when and if the time comes," Malo grunted. "Jebido and Niko can relieve you in four hours."

"Where are you going?" I asked Malo as he headed back outside.

"To see if I can fix this little problem with your names before it gets any worse," the House Agent responded over his shoulder.

Sabina picked up a brown cotton dress from the stack of clothing on the floor and held it up to herself. It seemed a little small to my eye, but the garment was sturdy-looking, at least. It would be a vast improvement over the dirty, baggy tunic she currently wore. Sabina glanced at me with a question in her eyes.

"On your feet," I said gruffly to my men, understanding what she wanted.

I led everyone outside to give Sabina some privacy while she dressed. The music was playing just as gayly as before, with drunken Pilgrims staggering here and there amongst the tents. I signaled for Putt to take up a position in front of the entrance to our tent. Tyris would guard the back.

"I have a bad feeling about all this, Hadrack," Jebido muttered as we waited outside.

A Pilgrim tent similar to ours stood twenty feet away from us. I could hear musical feminine laughter coming from inside, followed by a man groaning loudly. Firelight from the brazier reflected two distinct shadows entwined on the floor, leaving little doubt about what they were doing in there.

"When is the last time you had a good feeling?" I asked Jebido with a smile on my lips. "You are the most pessimistic man that I know."

"It's not pessimism," Jebido said with a snort. "It's caution. There is a difference." He pointed to his silver hair. "I've gotten to this age because I'm cautious. It's something you might consider trying once in a while. You just might live longer if you do."

"I've done all right so far," I said. "Besides, who wants to get old, anyway?"

"Old like me, you mean?" Jebido asked, his eyes narrowing.

I glanced at my friend and grinned. "Something like that."

Sabina called us back before Jebido could respond, and I heard both he and Niko whistle loudly as they passed through the entrance ahead of me. I stepped inside and then stopped in surprise. Sabina had cleaned herself somehow and had let her hair down and combed it as well. The dress I thought would be too small for her had a plunging neckline and fit perfectly, accenting her firm breasts and slim build. Sabina leaned forward and whispered something in Jebido's ear. My friend's eyes widened as he listened, then he opened his mouth to say something just as Sabina took his hand, staring at him as a silent message passed between them.

Finally, Jebido turned away and grabbed Niko by the arm. "Come, lad, we'll be sleeping outside tonight," he said.

"But what about the wine?" Niko demanded in dismay as Jebido herded him through the entrance.

"I'll find you some damn wine somewhere else. Now get moving."

"Finally, we're alone," Sabina said once they were gone. She had taken off her worn sandals, I noticed, and glided soundlessly over the furs toward me. "I'm tired of fighting this thing between us, Hadrack. We both know where this is going, so let's just accept it."

"Sabina," I said, feeling uncomfortable as she stopped in front of me. "I don't know what you think is going on between us, but it has to stop."

"Can you honestly say that you don't desire me?" Sabina asked coyly. She put her hands on my chest and stared up at me, our faces inches apart. I stood spellbound, unable to tear my eyes away from her. "We have cheated death too many times since we met, Hadrack. Soldiers could come for us tonight and we might never have another chance like this. I don't want to die without having been with you at least once. That's all I am asking. Just one night."

"Sabina," I managed to say. I stared at a spot over her shoulder. "You know how much I care for you."

"Yes, I do," Sabina said. "But I also know you desire me as well, Hadrack of Corwick. Admit it. I can see it every time you look at me." She glanced down at my tunic in triumph. "And the proof of that desire grows right before my eyes."

I could feel my face coloring, angry at my body for the betrayal. I put my hands around Sabina's wrists and gently pushed her away from me. "This can't happen, Sabina. I'm committed to Shana."

"Ha!" Sabina snorted. She glanced down again. "That part of you doesn't seem to agree."

"We are to be wed," I blurted out.

"What?" Sabina snapped, recoiling as though I had slapped her. "What did you just say?"

"Lady Shana and I are to be married," I said hurriedly. "That's why I needed to talk to her alone. To ask for her hand in marriage." Sabina took two steps backward, her face registering her shock. "I'm sorry," I said gently. "I love Shana. I have from the moment that I met her."

"Married," Sabina said in a low tone, more to herself than to me.

"Yes, but you and I will always be friends."

I took a step forward and Sabina put her hands up to stop me. "Don't touch me!" She pointed at the exit. "Get out of here, Hadrack! Get out right now!"

I hesitated, trying to think of something to say, even though I knew there could be no words that would help. I took a deep breath, then spun on my heel.

"Well, that didn't go so well," Jebido said when I stepped outside.

I closed my eyes and shook my head. "You heard?"

Jebido chuckled. "The wrinkled and deaf old Sons on top of Mount Halas probably heard that commotion." He sighed. "I can't say I'm surprised by it, though."

"What am I going to do?"

Jebido shrugged. "There isn't much you can do. You have to be true to yourself, Hadrack, or else you wouldn't be the man that I know you to be."

"I hurt her, Jebido," I said bitterly, glancing back at the tent. "You should have seen the look in her eyes."

"Life is about pain and hurt, as well as love," Jebido said. "She will get past it. She's a sweet child, just a little young for all this."

"But what if she decides not to keep helping us?"

"Then you will just have to find another way up that damn mountain," Jebido said firmly.

"There is no other way," I said as Jebido guided me away from the tent.

My friend slapped me on the back and grinned. "Now who is the one being the pessimist? There is always another way."

15: Topar

The next morning began cold and dreary, with rain that fell in sheets and drenched everything it touched. My men and I had risen before daybreak, shivering and miserable, unable to sleep on the muddy ground. We stood pressed together near our tent, talking as we huddled against the rain while we waited. No soldiers had come for Sabina and me during the night, and other than a fight three tents down that had left a Pilgrim sightless in one eye, the evening had been mostly uneventful. Malo still hadn't reappeared as people began to stir, and I finally decided to send Niko off to find him.

"You're going to have to go in there sooner or later," Jebido said, motioning to the tent. He shook his head vigorously, sending water droplets spraying in all directions.

"I know," I muttered, glancing at the closed flap.

"She's had all night to get over it, my lord," Putt offered with a shrug. "I'm sure she has come to her senses by now."

"Have you met her?" I said with a snort. "She is not the type to just get over things."

"What if she decides not to continue with this, my lord?" Tyris asked. "Then what do we do?"

I took a deep breath, blinking the rain away. "Hopefully, it won't come to that." I wiped my eyes on my wet tunic. "We will have the answer soon enough, either way." I squared my shoulders, then headed for the entrance. I pushed the flap aside and stuck my head inside. "Sabina? May I come in?"

I heard a sound that might have been a grunt of permission and I stepped inside. The brazier fire was reduced to glowing coals now, giving off barely enough light to see.

"Hadrack, you're drenched!"

Sabina stood off to one side of the entrance. She still wore the dress from the night before, though an open cloak was draped over her shoulders now. She had replaced her worn sandals for the heavy boots as well. Sabina's voice had sounded pleasant and free of anger to me, and her face appeared calm, almost peaceful. I studied her cautiously, feeling a glimmer of hope that perhaps all was forgiven.

"It's raining quite heavily outside," I said tentatively. I brushed at my tunic, trying to wick some of the water away. "I'm sorry to say that it won't be an enjoyable climb today."

Sabina laughed cheerfully. "I hardly think a little rain will be enough to stop us now that we are so close."

I frowned, confused by her manner. "Sabina, is everything all right?"

"Of course, silly," Sabina said. "Why wouldn't it be?" She pointed to the clothing that had been set aside for me. "You should get out of that wet thing and get dressed."

I could feel cold water running down my back as I stared at her. "You're not mad?"

"About what, Hadrack?"

"About what I told you last night. About my getting married."

Sabina waved a hand casually in dismissal. "Of course not. I have no say in what you choose to do. You are a grown man, after all. Lady Shana is a wonderful choice from all that I have heard about her. I'm sure you and she will be quite happy together. I was just tired from the journey and took it out on you. I apologize." She moved to the entrance and raised her hood, glancing back at me. "I'll just step outside so that you can dress in private."

Then she was gone.

I watched the canvas flick back and forth behind her. What had just happened? I wondered. I shook my head, forever mystified by women as I peeled off my soaked tunic and tossed it aside. I dressed quickly, relishing the feel of the dry trousers and boots. The tent flap opened behind me and Malo pushed his way inside as I pulled a thick woolen shirt over my head.

"There you are," I said. "Where have you been all this time?"

"Waiting to see that priest from last night's ceremony, Son Partal."

"All night?"

"Yes," Malo replied. "There was already a crowd of people waiting to speak with him in the morning. I wanted to make sure I got to him early."

"And did you see him?"

"I did," Malo confirmed. "I explained there was a mistake in the book and that you are really Rorian and Thera of Afrenia."

"And he believed you?"

"Eventually," Malo said. "It took some convincing. He made me swear on The Father's name that I spoke true."

"Lying to a Son is a sin and will get you burned, Malo," I grunted as I drew the heavy cloak left for me around my shoulders. I sighed in contentment at the warmth.

"One more sin will hardly matter now," Malo said with a shrug. "Son Partal had the Names Ledger corrected, so you are officially Rorian and Thera again. You shouldn't encounter any more problems."

"That's one less thing to worry about, then," I said.

Malo withdrew the leather sheath holding his short sword. He handed it to me. "Pilgrims aren't allowed weapons, so be sure you hide this well. Hopefully, it won't be needed."

"Thank you," I said gratefully. I took off my cloak and hung the sword around my neck by the leather thong, settling it into the small of my back. I would have preferred Wolf's Head or my father's axe, of course, but it still felt good knowing that the sword was there.

The House Agent held out his hand as I put my cloak back on. "Be well, Hadrack, and come back with the prize. The future of the kingdom depends on you."

We locked forearms. "I'll find it, Malo. You can count on that."

We broke apart just as the sound of a shrill horn summoning the Pilgrims to the mountain cut through the morning stillness. I headed for the exit. The sky was brightening, I saw as I stepped outside, and the rain had lessened, though it still fell at a steady pace. My men were standing in a circle where I had left them, conversing in low tones. Sabina stood ten paces away, talking to an unhappy-looking Son-In-Waiting. Pilgrims were hurrying from their tents, speaking in hushed, excited voices as they flowed past me, heading north toward the imposing cliff face of Mount Halas.

"There he is now," Sabina said, smiling beneath her hood as I approached.

"My name is Topar," the Son-In-Waiting said, introducing himself to me in a clipped tone. He was tall and thin, with a weak cleft chin, and dark, heavy eyebrows that stood out starkly against his pale flesh. He shifted uncomfortably in his wet apprentice robe. It was apparent to me that he was far from pleased to be out in the rain. "I have been assigned to accompany you on the journey to Second Step."

I looked at the apprentice in surprise. Second Step, I knew, was a campsite halfway up the mountain where we would be stopping to rest and eat. "Is that normal?" I asked. "Does a Son-In-Waiting accompany all Pilgrim pairs?"

Topar shook his head, looking wet and miserable. "No, it is quite unusual," he admitted.

I glanced at Sabina, and we both frowned in puzzlement. "Why us, then?" I asked.

"How should I know?" Topar said with a sniff. He rubbed his nose, then sneezed loudly before pinching the bridge of his nose with thumb and forefinger and blowing out briskly onto the ground. "I was shaken from my bed and told to seek out Rorian and Thera of Afrenia and take them ahead to the First Rank, and so, here I am."

"Told by who?" I asked.

"Son Michan."

I frowned at the unfamiliar name as Malo came out of the tent to join us. "Did you speak with a Son Michan last night?" I asked the House Agent.

Malo shook his head. "No. Just a Son-In-Waiting and then Son Partal. No one else."

I gestured to Topar. "Son Michan sent this apprentice to watch over us," I said. "The question is, why?"

"What does it matter?" Topar said in exasperation. "You should feel grateful. Few commoners are afforded the honor of joining the

First Rank." The rain had weakened even more now and the apprentice turned, sweeping his hand toward the mountain. "Please, we must go. We are already late. You need to put aside your questions and follow me."

The tall apprentice headed away, his chin pressed tightly to his narrow chest as he focused on the ground, trying unsuccessfully to avoid the ankle-deep puddles.

"What do you make of it?" I asked Malo uneasily. "Should we be worried?"

"I'm not sure," the House Agent said. His hard eyes studied the Son-In-Waiting's receding back thoughtfully. "This must have something to do with the Cardians. Maybe it's their way of protecting Rorian. Either way, be careful and don't trust anyone."

I didn't bother responding as I turned away. I had no intention of trusting anyone in this place except for Sabina. The garrison was alive with motion now, with more and more Pilgrims exiting their tents as the horn continued to summon them. Sons-In-Waiting lined the route as we walked, guiding us onward through the rain with forced smiles, hard biscuits, and mugs of hot ale. I wolfed down my biscuit, then drained my ale in one gulp. I could feel the heat warming my belly pleasantly as Topar led us through a vine-covered stone archway into a high-walled courtyard.

Pilgrims dressed in their heavy cloaks were streaming up an incline to the north ahead of us, but Topar surprised me by turning right toward a narrow, wrought-iron gate. He opened it and gestured us inside, then closed the gate firmly behind us. We found ourselves standing in a well-maintained orchard of pear and plum trees ripe with rain-washed fruit hanging from drooping branches. Topar brushed past me, urging us to hurry as he scurried down an overgrown cobblestone pathway lined with neatly-trimmed, waist-high hedges.

I looked through the bars of the gate at the Pilgrims passing by. "Why are we the only ones going this way?" I called out.

Topar stopped and turned, looking back at me impatiently. "Because you are now in the First Rank, just as I told you earlier. This is the quickest route to get there from the courtyard." He raised his bushy eyebrows. "Unless you would rather push your way through hundreds of unwashed Pilgrims instead?"

I nodded, not satisfied with the answer, but motioning him to lead on just the same. The Son-In-Waiting—despite his obvious displeasure at being out in the rain—appeared guileless as far as I could tell. If something were amiss here, I knew it would present itself soon enough. I'd deal with it then.

We walked for another few minutes, alone but for the sounds of birds chirping and our breathing. The rain suddenly stopped, and the sun came out as hundreds of orange and black butterflies appeared from the trees' protection, flitting around us in a dazzling display.

"They're so beautiful!" Sabina cried in wonder. She put out her hand and one of the butterflies landed almost immediately on her finger. Sabina giggled as the butterfly fanned its wings several times before darting away over our heads. "Did you see that?" she breathed, her eyes shining. "It tickled my skin."

I grunted, unmoved. A feeling of imminent danger had begun to settle over me and I scanned the path ahead. Nothing looked out of the ordinary to me, yet I knew instinctively that something was wrong. I considered reaching for the sword hanging down my back, but then I changed my mind. Patience, I told myself. It could be nothing. If I revealed that I was armed now and I was wrong, I would lose my only weapon before the trip up the mountain had even started.

We finally reached a fountain overflowing with rainwater and Topar headed around it purposefully. The pathway on the other side of the fountain branched off three ways. One to the north. One straight ahead of us to the east. And one south. The Son-In-Waiting turned left, heading north as we followed several paces behind him. The hedges grew taller as we progressed, and before long, I could no longer see over them. The path took a sharp turn ahead and I knew if something were to happen, this would be a perfect spot. I put my hand on Sabina's arm, stopping her just as Topar disappeared from our view.

"What?" Sabina asked.

I put a finger to my lips, listening. Had I just heard a muffled yelp of pain?

"I'm not sure," I whispered, straining my ears. No other sounds came from around the bend, but I noticed the butterflies were gone and the birds had stopped chirping, which added to my unease. I took off my cloak and let it fall to the ground. "I'm going to take a look. Stay right here."

I unsheathed Malo's short sword and inched forward until I reached the bend. I peered cautiously around the hedges to see Topar lying sprawled out on the cobblestones, his bald head smeared wetly with blood. The path was empty except for the apprentice's prone body. I took two steps forward and paused just as a form burst out from the foliage, knocking me to the ground. I twisted away instinctively, narrowly avoiding having my skull split in two as my attacker's blade rang off the stones with a metallic clang.

I rolled, coming up on the balls of my feet with my sword leveled as I whirled to face my assailant. The man was of medium height, but built wide. His beard and hair were tangled and dirty like a peasant's, but he wore fine armor that belied that impression. He waved his sword back and forth in front of him, his face set in determination as he advanced on me. I could see a second man running down the path toward us out of the corner of my eye. I didn't know if he was coming to help my attacker or me, but the way my luck had been going lately, I had to assume it wasn't me.

"What do you want?" I demanded.

"Tell us where the codex is and we'll let you live."

I frowned. "Who are you?"

My assailant grinned. "Someone who holds the lives of you and your wife in his hands."

I glanced at the longsword the other man held and shifted my grip on Malo's short sword. If only I had Wolf's Head with me. I flicked my eyes toward the second man, who was approaching quickly. I would have to make a move before he arrived.

"We know who you are, Rorian," my attacker added. "So, don't try to pretend you don't know what I'm talking about."

I tried not to show my surprise at being mistaken for the scholar. Whoever these men were, they knew about the codex, but not that someone had taken Rorian's place.

"Who sent you?"

"The True King, of course."

I had only a moment to digest that news before my assailant leaped at me, taking a vicious, two-handed slash at my midriff. I jumped back, then twisted, dropping to one knee as I spun around with my sword. The blade caught my attacker high on the thigh, lower than I had intended, yet effective, nonetheless. The wounded man retreated, bellowing in pain just as his companion arrived to take his place.

This man was taller than the first, with long black hair and broken teeth. I ducked beneath his impatient swing, then powered hard into him with my shoulder, using the strength in my legs to propel him back into the hedges. The man fell with a cry amid the sounds of snapping branches and an outraged bird that squawked at us as it flapped away. The fallen man cursed at me as he struggled to gain his feet, and I kicked him hard in the stomach. The man sagged, his face reddening as he fought for air. I kicked him again for good measure, then slashed open his neck with a quick, efficient cross-stroke.

I bent and dragged the dead man's longsword out of the hedge, then waited for his wounded companion, who continued to limp stubbornly toward me along the path. That's when I heard a scream from behind me. I cursed. I had forgotten about Sabina. I ran back the way that I had come and hurtled around the bend. Two men with drawn swords held Sabina as she struggled in their grasp. I roared and charged forward, lashing out with a foot at the closest man's knee, feeling it snap with a satisfying crack. The man screamed, releasing Sabina as his companion swung his sword one-handed at me. I easily parried it with the longsword in my right hand, then lashed upward with the butt of the short sword in my left, smashing the metal savagely into his face. The man fell back, clawing at his shattered nose as I dropped the short sword to the ground. I swung the longsword two-handed, severing one of his hands and his head as blood splattered the greenery around us.

"Behind you!" Sabina screamed in warning.

I ducked, feeling the whoosh of air over my head even as I reversed my sword and stabbed blindly over my shoulder. The tip somehow found the vulnerable flesh of the limping man and I felt it sink in deeply. He groaned and dropped his sword, then fell in a clatter of armor. I barely glanced at the body as I stalked toward the lone survivor lying on the ground. He was moaning loudly as he clutched at his shattered knee. The man's weapon lay nearby, ignored for the moment. I kicked it away.

I rested the point of my sword against the man's injured leg. "How did you learn about us and the codex?" I demanded. The wounded man licked his lips, staring in fascination at the blade pressing against his flesh. "I asked you a question," I growled. I prodded with the sword, eliciting a howl of pain from the fallen man.

"I...I don't know anything!"

"Undoubtedly true regarding most things," I said with a grimace. "But you do know something about this. Why did you try to kill us?"

The fallen man shook his head vigorously as he glanced at Sabina. "We weren't trying to kill you."

"You're lying."

"I swear it's the truth. Our orders were to capture you alive." He lowered his eyes. "It was supposed to be an easy job. Just a simple scholar and his wife."

"Nothing is ever what it seems," I grunted. "Who hired you?"

"The Advisor," the man replied immediately.

I frowned at the unfamiliar title. "Who?"

The man looked surprised. "Everyone knows who Hervi Desh is."

My head snapped back at the name as though I had just been slapped. Desh! That filthy rat-bastard! I fought to control my breathing as the fallen man began to tremble at the look on my face.

Sabina shook my arm. "Hadrack? What's going on? Who are these people?"

"Nothing but pond scum," I said tightly. I lifted my sword to the man's throat. "What is your name?"

"Bagen," came back the shaky reply.

"Well, Bagen," I growled, dropping to my knees so that we were almost eye level. "You are going to do something for me. Do you understand?" Bagen nodded eagerly, staring at me with bulging eyes that were beginning to shine with hope. "You are going to go back to that foul place known as Gandertown, and you are going to give Hervi Desh a message. Do I make myself clear?"

Bagen swallowed loudly. "Very clear."

"Good," I said as I stood. "Tell the bastard that the Wolf is coming for him."

Bagen blinked up at me in confusion. "That's all?"

"That's all," I grunted. I turned and threw the longsword in my hands over the hedges, then bent and picked up Malo's short sword. I sheathed it and put my cloak back on before taking Sabina by the elbow. "Let's go see if that apprentice is still alive."

Topar was indeed still alive when we reached him, sitting up and groaning as he rubbed his bloody head. I helped him to his feet and quickly explained what had happened, blaming thieves who had mistaken us for someone else. It wasn't much, I knew, but I hoped the apprentice would be so shaken by the attack that he wouldn't focus too much on my explanation. The Son-In-Waiting had just been an unknowing pawn in all this, I realized, sent by Son Michan to draw Sabina and me to this spot, far away from prying eyes. I doubt our attackers had meant for him to live.

"But it makes no sense at all," Topar said weakly as I steadied him. "I have never heard of such a thing happening in First Step."

"There's a first time for everything," I said grimly.

The apprentice wobbled in my grip and Sabina hurried to support his other arm. A stone bench sat further down the pathway, embedded neatly into a section of trimmed hedge. I gestured toward it and we led Topar there, lowering him gently onto the weathered stone. The Son-In-Waiting hissed in pain as he sat, his eyes half-closed as he swayed back and forth.

"Are you going to be all right?" Sabina asked in a concerned voice.

Topar nodded, his face white. "I think so. Everything is just a little foggy at the moment." He gestured weakly down the path. "You two go on ahead. I'll catch up to you once my head clears." I patted the apprentice on the shoulder in agreement, relieved to be rid of him. "You better hurry," Topar called after us. "If you're late, you will lose your place in the First Rank."

I waved a hand over my shoulder in acknowledgment. The Son-In-Waiting didn't need to know that I had no intention of joining that First Rank, if indeed, we were ever actually meant to be there. Forces were in play against us, and it seemed a certainty that they would continue to look for us. Those forces would probably start searching with the lords, ladies, and other highborn of the First Rank. But behind those privileged few would be hundreds of regular Pilgrims all massed together in a confusing array of identical cloaks. A perfect place for Sabina and me to lose ourselves.

Sometimes the best way to hide is to hide in plain sight.

16: Second Step

    The ascent to Second Step turned out to be more difficult than I think any of us had anticipated. The route we traveled proved to be narrow, steep, and treacherous, boxed in on both sides by towering walls of formidable rock. Despite the rapidly strengthening sun overhead, the rain that had fallen had left the ground slick with mud and covered in loose shale. More than one Pilgrim had already tumbled back down the sharp grade, only coming to a stop when soldiers bringing up the rear were able to slow them down.

    Sabina and I kept our hoods up and our eyes lowered, losing ourselves within the mass of sweating, cursing Pilgrims. I had seen no sign of searchers so far, but that didn't necessarily mean eyes weren't on us somewhere, watching. The morning sun grew warmer as we progressed, and some of the Pilgrims around us started to take off their cloaks. I was getting worried that if the trend continued, then eventually Sabina and I would begin to stand out. But, as midday fast approached, most began to put them back on again to ward off the frigid wind that had started to sweep down on us from higher up the mountain. I noticed small flakes of snow were being carried along on the breeze as well now, just as gruff voices rose ahead, calling for a halt. The First Rank had come to a towering ridge that blocked our path, rising at least fifty feet above their heads before flattening out. The Pilgrims milled about uncertainly near lines of heavy ropes dangling down from the ledge as soldiers barked at them to get moving.

    "You have got to be joking," Sabina said as she stared at the ridge in weary dismay.

    Pilgrims around us were muttering uneasily as some of the highborn reluctantly began the ascent.

"Maybe the climb isn't as bad as it looks from here," I suggested, trying to sound confident just as a woman's terrified scream rang out.

One of the Pilgrims had made it halfway up the rope before losing her balance and slipping down. She clung desperately with one hand while waving her other arm wildly about her, which only helped to make things worse. The woman's hood fell away from her face, revealing long blonde hair and pleasant features. She struggled to grab the rope again with her free hand, then cried out in dismay as she lost her grip entirely and plunged downward. Several soldiers had moved beneath her in case that happened, and one of them caught her awkwardly in his arms. He set her down, then gestured that she should try again.

"Soft are the ladies of the realm," someone sniggered from within the crowd.

"Aye," a man ahead of me called out in response. "With all the flesh concentrated in the bum, leaving little left for the arms."

"I'd not mind a moment or two with some of that noble bum," another man said wistfully to laughs and shouts of agreement.

I grinned, enjoying the camaraderie of the Pilgrims as we waited for our turn. We slowly began to move forward as the highborn eventually cleared the ropes and left them to the commoners, until finally, it was our turn to climb. I kept my face down as a grizzled soldier thrust the prickly rope into my hands.

"Once you start, don't stop," he advised me gruffly. "Whatever you do, don't look down and don't fall. You're one big bastard, and I'd not want to have to try catching you."

I started to climb, finding it surprisingly easy as I moved upward quickly and efficiently, going hand over hand with booted feet braced against the ridge face for balance. I paused at the halfway point, glancing down to where Sabina was ascending slowly but steadily below me. I studied her movements with a critical eye, then grunted in satisfaction, knowing that she was in little danger of falling. Eager faces appeared over the lip of the ledge as I neared the top, and I could hear their heartfelt shouts of encouragement. I wondered idly why no one offered me a helping hand, but assumed this was just one more silly test of the Pilgrimage.

I finally reached the lip of the ridge and pulled myself onto the smooth rock as Pilgrims clapped and shouted congratulations around me. Emand was one of them and I saw the relief on his face when he recognized me. His wife, Laurea, stood beside him with her thin arms crossed over her withered chest and her mouth turned down in perpetual disapproval.

"I thought you would be at the front with the other highborn," Emand said as he clapped me soundly on the back.

"Why would you think that?" I asked.

I saw a quick flash of caution in Emand's eyes that quickly disappeared as he smiled disarmingly. "Why, no reason at all, Rorian."

More Pilgrims were coming over the ledge behind me now and I moved aside for them, watching anxiously for Sabina. She finally appeared, looking winded as she hauled herself up and over the top. I leaned down and helped her to her feet, then drew her away from the lip.

"How goes the quest for the codex?" Emand asked in a conspiratorial whisper as he followed us. "Have you figured out where it is yet?"

I felt a coldness take over me at his words that had nothing to do with the temperature. I kept my features bland as I shrugged nonchalantly. "Not much has changed," I said.

"Except someone tried to kill us," Sabina added.

Emand's eyebrows rose in surprise. "Someone tried to kill you. Who?"

"It's a long story," I said gruffly. I looked at Sabina in irritation. "We're here and they aren't. That's all that matters."

The shoemaker must have read the look on my face, for he turned away, changing the subject as he gestured ahead. "Second Step is quite extraordinary, wouldn't you agree?"

The climb had brought us onto a surprisingly level plateau, where a smattering of stone buildings stood against the mountain's south-facing wall. The ground remained flat and straight for at least two hundred yards in front of me before falling off to the east into a deep gorge that cut through the land like a giant knife wound. Twisted trees and giant boulders lined the floor of the canyon, and as I looked down, I saw a brief flash of yellow as something large moved beneath the foliage. Emand had delighted in entertaining us with horrific tales of cat-like beasts that preyed upon unsuspecting Pilgrims up here. I wondered if I had just seen one. Thin, rounded rock formations shimmering under a light sheen of ice jutted out from the cliff face high above our heads, looking to me like gigantic, frozen fingers pointing off into the distance.

The wind had increased in strength and felt colder since we reached the ridge, with heavy wet snowflakes swirling in the air now like thousands of excited bees. The sun still remained visible through it all, however, turning each snowflake into a unique, glittering jewel. I shivered as the snow clung to my clothing and beard, and I drew my cloak tighter about me as the four of us began to move forward. As many as twenty iron cooking pots hissed and bubbled over roaring fires farther along the plateau, with bundled-up peasants working at stirring the contents inside. The land on the other side of the cooking fires remained flat for fifty more yards, then began to slope upward, narrowing slowly until the lip of the gorge and cliff face met. I could see a rectangular tunnel at the juncture of the two. That, clearly, would be our path out of Second Step once we had eaten.

The snow hitting the ground had initially melted on the rocks, but as it continued to fall, it started to accumulate quickly, turning our hard, rocky world into a soft-looking, white one within minutes. I sensed something moving above me and I looked up, protecting my eyes from the snowfall. A hawk with a massive wingspan glided serenely far above the camp, peering down at us with passive indifference despite the snow. I thought I could see several more birds just like it circling higher up.

"Red-shouldered hawks," Emand said, looking up as well. He grinned at me. "Nothing to fear from them." He winked. "The big cats are another story."

I grimaced, not relishing another of Emand's stories. "So, what happens now?" I asked to change his mind as we walked toward the cooking fires.

"We have an hour to rest and eat," the cordwainer responded. "After that, we climb again until we reach our final camp, Third Step. That will likely be well after dark, if I'm not mistaken."

"And then the Complex in the morning?" Sabina asked.

"Yes," Emand said with a cheery smile. "The Complex and Oasis."

Pilgrims were milling about the cooking pots ahead of us, with grinning peasants handing out steaming wooden bowls and mugs of warm cider. Emand and his wife pushed their way through the crowd, heading for an open cooking fire. I waited, and the moment the two were out of sight, I grabbed Sabina by the elbow and guided her in the opposite direction.

"What's wrong?" Sabina asked in confusion as I prodded her away. "I thought we were going to eat?"

"We are," I grunted. I looked over my shoulder, but the cordwainer and his wife were nowhere to be seen. "We're just going to do it away from them."

"Why?"

"I've gotten a little tired of Emand," I said, thinking of Malo's last words to me. Trust no one.

Sabina and I moved to an area far from the place where we had last seen the shoemaker. We gratefully accepted a generous bowl of steaming hunter's stew and a mug of cider each. We found a place to sit as the snow continued to fall, with Pilgrims hunched over and eating to either side of us and behind. No one spoke, conserving energy as they ate. The ground was cold and wet, and I could feel the chill slowly seeping through my cloak and clothing. Several soldiers were patrolling the perimeter of the massed Pilgrims as I ate and I studied them warily. They could just be there for our protection, I reasoned, but they could also be looking for Sabina and me.

"Maybe we should have stayed with Emand," Sabina said as she followed my gaze.

"Why?" I asked. I drained my mug and smacked my lips at the sweet and sour taste of the cider, wishing I had thought to grab another.

"Because they will be looking for two Pilgrims doing exactly what we are doing," Sabina answered.

"Which is?"

"Sitting alone, eating, and looking suspicious. At least with Emand and Laurea, we would have had someone to talk to."

I thought about that, then hesitated as a soldier focused on us. He blew on his hands to warm them, then slowly began to make his way forward. I cursed under my breath. Had he recognized us? I turned my face away and tapped the Pilgrim sitting behind me on the shoulder.

"Yes?" the man said. He had lowered his hood to eat and I could tell that he was around my age, though he was small of build with a sparse beard. His hair was tied back and covered in snow, and his nose and cheeks were bright red from the cold. A pretty girl with long brown hair twisted in braids down each side sat next to him, looking tired but glowing with an inner happiness.

"Where do you hale from, friend?" I asked in a pleasant voice.

"Blind Hills."

"I don't know it," I said with a shrug. "Where is that?"

"It's a small village near Fishingwood," the girl responded for him. She sniffed and wiped at her nose with her sleeve. "We both come from there. Lord Hathelway is our liege lord."

Sabina finally seemed to understand what I was doing and she turned to the girl. "I love the color of your hair." Sabina fingered the lengths of her own hair that hung from beneath her hood. "I hate mine."

"Oh, that's just silly!" the girl said. "It's a beautiful color." She and Sabina began to talk together enthusiastically.

"And you, friend?" my new companion asked. "Where do you call home?"

I thought of Emand. "Hillsfort. I'm a cordwainer there."

The Pilgrim looked impressed. "A noble trade, to be sure."

I casually glanced over my shoulder, then breathed a sigh of relief. The soldier had turned, meandering through the sitting Pilgrims now, his breath curling upward in a cloud as he headed away from us.

"What's your name?" the man asked.

I turned back to him and grinned. "The same as yours, of course. Just call me, Pilgrim."

The young man chuckled at that as he thrust out a hand. "It's a pleasure to meet you, Pilgrim."

"Likewise, Pilgrim," I said as we shook.

Sabina and I spoke with the couple from Blind Hills for some time, keeping a wary eye out for any suspicious-looking guards. The snow slowly tapered off as we talked and the sun regained its strength, taking some of the chill away. I could hear the melting snow beginning to drip off the rocks as a shrill horn sounded, signaling that it was time to move out. I stood and stretched as people rose to their feet, looking uncertain about what they should do next.

A few of the Pilgrim pairs who had been sitting farther down the plateau began sprinting northeast, clearly hoping to be one of the first through the tunnel. Other Pilgrims began to chase after them, and in no time, a solid mass of people started dashing through the slush toward the narrow path between the gorge and the cliff. I saw several fights break out within the pushing and cursing crowd as the space narrowed, and I could hear soldiers shouting for people to stop and turn back. If any Pilgrim heard, however, they ignored the commands in the sudden frenzy to be first.

A small group of twenty or so of the highborn had already gathered near the tunnel entrance. They stood and watched the approaching Pilgrims in amusement, apparently unaware of the danger approaching. One tall man seemed to understand and he strode forward purposefully. He lifted a hand, shouting a command that was lost to me on the wind. I winced as the first of the running Pilgrims reached him and he was brushed aside. The tall man fell, sliding along the slippery rock, until finally he rolled over the lip of the gorge with a cry and disappeared.

Soldiers started to wade into the crazed Pilgrims after that, swinging the flats of their swords wildly in all directions. I could hear more screams echoing from the gorge as several Pilgrims near the edge lost their balance and plunged downward. I thought of the flash of yellow I had seen earlier and I grimaced, trying not to imagine the fate waiting for any who might have survived the fall.

"We have to help them," Sabina said, starting to move forward.

I grabbed her wrist. "And draw attention to us?" Soldiers were finally beginning to gain control of the situation as they forced the Pilgrims back. I shook my head. "We can't risk being noticed."

A few of the highborn were pressed up against the cliff face, with a cordon of soldiers with drawn swords guarding them. The rest of the nobles had fled into the tunnel already. The Pilgrims' screams and cries began to taper off and a sudden, shocked silence filled the plateau as sanity slowly started to return. Many of the Pilgrims fell to their knees in the slush and began weeping uncontrollably.

"It's the height," I heard someone say. I turned to see Emand standing beside me. "The air is thinner up here, I'm told." He shook his head sadly. "Sometimes it can cause hallucinations, even hysteria like this. A shame, really, but not all that surprising."

I frowned. Emand's continued presence was beginning to annoy me. "You seem to know a lot," I grunted. I looked at him appraisingly. "For a cordwainer, that is."

Emand shrugged. "I like to stay informed."

"I'm sure you do," I muttered.

"What happened to you both back there, anyway?" Emand asked. "I thought we were going to eat together?"

"You thought wrong," I said. I turned to face the cordwainer. "Listen, Emand, we appreciate the help you have given us so far, but we need to be on our own from now on."

Emand fiddled with the sash of his cloak. "Did you know that I wasn't always a cordwainer, Rorian?"

"How could I?" I responded.

"True, quite true. How could you, indeed? The fact is, even though you might not guess it to look at me now, I was something of an adventurer as a younger man. I traveled much of the known world, selling my sword to the highest bidder." Emand looked at the ground. "I'm ashamed to admit this to you, but back then, I didn't worry much about the morals of what I was doing."

"And now?" I asked. "How are your morals now?"

"I have changed for the better," Emand pronounced modestly. "What I did in the past was wrong, but I've made amends for it since then."

"Something tells me that you haven't changed that much," I said sarcastically.

Emand laughed, looking unoffended as he waved a hand. "Don't be silly. I'm just a simple cordwainer now, on his way to meet The Mother and The Father with his beloved wife."

"You may be a cordwainer, Emand," I said as I drew Sabina away, "but I don't believe you are simple by any means." I paused three steps from him as a thought struck me, then I turned and went back until I towered over him. I held his eyes. "I'm only going to say this once," I growled low enough that only he could hear. "So, you had better pay attention. You keep showing up wherever we go, and I don't think that is a coincidence. If I see you anywhere near us again, I promise I will kill you."

Emand's eyes turned hard like glass. "Then I'd best not let you see me coming the next time, Hadrack of Corwick," he said softly.

I didn't see Emand or his unpleasant-looking wife for the remainder of that day, and Sabina and I reached Third Step without any further problems. Thirty-two climbers had been unable to make it to the third stage, turning back in exhaustion and defeat. Eight more Pilgrims had lost their lives in various accidents, including Lord Evensmire, who I had learned about from the drunk who approached me in First Step. I wondered idly if that drunken Pilgrim had managed to make it this far as Sabina and I settled into a small round tent that had been provided for us.

We had been given food and drink earlier and, with bellies full and feeling tired but content, we sat wrapped in furs against the cold, neither of us quite ready to go to sleep. I had initially worried that Sabina might try something like she had the previous night now that we were alone, but she gave no signs of being interested in anything of that sort.

"I still think Emand is harmless," Sabina said with a sniff. We had been given a stubby candle made of sheep wax and her features in the weak light were cast in deep shadows.

I stretched my legs and sighed. I hadn't told Sabina what the cordwainer had said to me earlier, not wishing to worry her. I'd wanted to keep her mind focused on the climb and not be forever looking back over her shoulder. Now seemed the appropriate time.

"He knows who I am," I said simply.

"What? Sabina gasped. "How?"

I shrugged. "I don't know. All I know is Emand isn't the man he claims to be."

Sabina sat in silence for a moment, digesting that. "Is he dangerous, do you think?" she finally asked. "He's so small and fat," she added doubtfully.

I snorted. "Rock snakes are small too, but they can kill you faster than you can blink." I shook my head. "I don't know what Emand's stake in all this is, but there is a lot more to the man than meets the eye. We would do well to avoid him from now on."

"Whatever you think is best, Hadrack," Sabina said, sounding tired now as she lay down. She shifted on the furs. "What is our plan for tomorrow, anyway?"

"We'll slip away the first chance we get once we reach the Complex," I said. "I'm sure with so many Pilgrims wandering around up there, that nobody is going to notice we are gone." I lay back and put my hands behind my head, staring up at the dancing shadows flickering across the tent's sloped ceiling. "Waldin said in his note that the cave is about four miles from the Complex. I just wish he'd been a little more specific about which direction. We might be out there a while before we find it."

"And when we do?" Sabina asked. "Then what? Getting up the mountain might seem easy compared to getting back down if they are watching for us."

I had been thinking much the same thing. "I know. One thing at a time. We'll find the codex first, then worry about how to get it to Malo after that."

I closed my eyes, feeling the day wearing on me as we lay in silence. I thought Sabina had finally fallen asleep until she surprised me by talking.

"Hadrack?"

"Hmmm?" I asked drowsily.

"Do you love her? I mean, really love her. Or is it just about her title and lands?"

I felt instant anger well up inside me, about to reply hotly, then I caught myself. The insinuation was maddening, yet I knew yelling at Sabina would accomplish nothing. It would probably only add to our problems. I swallowed my anger. "If you think that," I said instead, trying to keep my voice even, "then you don't know me at all."

"I'm sorry," Sabina responded. "I never should have said such a hurtful thing." I heard her move on the bedding, and I opened my eyes. She lay on her side, one hand propping up her head as she stared at me. "Sometimes, my mouth just blurts things out before my brain has had a chance to think about it."

I grinned back at her despite myself. "I have been doing that my entire life."

"So, you forgive me, then?" Sabina asked.

"Of course," I said. "It's been a long day." I paused, thinking about how Sabina's mood had shifted so dramatically this morning from the night before. "Can I ask you something?"

"Anything," Sabina replied instantly.

"Why were you so angry at me last night, and then so different this morning?" I asked. "What changed?"

Sabina lay back down and stared at the ceiling. I heard her breathe out slowly. "I was furious at you last night," she said. "I can't deny that. But then I realized something after a few hours and all my anger went away."

"What?"

"That Lady Shana is a long way from here," Sabina said in a soft voice. "She is in Calban and I am here with you." She rolled over and looked at me steadily. "A lot can change before you get back to her, Hadrack." She smiled confidently. "A lot."

17: The Complex

The next morning, we woke up to a bone-chilling cold, with snow falling heavily as a brisk wind whipped it about, reducing visibility down to mere feet. The harsh weather for this time of year was quite unusual, I was told, and the final climb to the Complex was now expected to take most of the day. There had been some debate initially about whether to wait until the following morning to set out, but that was quickly voted down by the highborn, who were anxious to end the journey. Besides, as they had quite rightly pointed out to the dissenters, the Pilgrimage rules were clear—no stoppage for any reason except during the designated times. Anyone had the right to turn back if they desired, but that meant The Walk was over for them. Those that chose to continue forward had only one task—keep going until the destination was reached.

We commoners had no say in the decision, of course, and though I was concerned about the storm, I was still relieved that we were leaving. I wasn't overly keen on the cold and I knew the going would be rough, but if the snow held until we reached the summit, I reasoned it might afford Sabina and me the perfect cover to slip away unnoticed.

Red banners snapped and crackled from tall poles that lined our route, guiding us upward as we plodded through drifting snow that was already reaching well past my ankles. Soldiers followed to either side of the struggling Pilgrims wearing heavy cloaks and burlap sacks wrapped around their faces that they had taken from the kitchens. I had managed to steal some rope and four of the burlap sacks for Sabina and myself the night before. But rather than use the bags on our faces, we filled them with provisions, then tied them together and hung them around our necks beneath our cloaks.

I had no idea how long it would take to find Waldin's cave, but I knew we wouldn't last long if the weather continued as it was without a ready source of food. The rough rope wore uncomfortably against the back of my neck with every step, but it was something that I knew I would have to learn to live with. I was sure the discomfort would prove to be the least of my problems that day. I tied the remaining rope around the thick glove on my left wrist, then secured the other end to Sabina's right wrist. There wasn't much more than five feet separating us this way, but I still preferred that to one of us wandering off in the confusion caused by the storm.

As the morning progressed and conditions worsened, we were forced to walk with our chins pressed to our chests and our hoods held closed as the pelting snow sought out our vulnerable eyes and faces. I lost track of how many Pilgrims fell in front and around me. Sabina fell four times herself during the first few hours of the climb, but she got up gamely and plodded onward each time. The fifth fall belonged to me as I lost my footing on the lip of a hidden rock. I tumbled to the ground as though pole-axed, cracking my shin hard on the edge of an exposed stone as I pulled Sabina down with me. I lay still for a moment, half-buried in snow and cursing at the pain in my leg. If it was broken, I knew I was a dead man.

"Are you all right, Hadrack?" Sabina shouted over the wind as she crawled through the snow to my side.

I slowly flexed my leg, wincing at the burning sensation that screamed down the length. It hurt something fierce, but I could tell that my leg wasn't broken. "Thank The Mother," I said to the blizzard-filled sky.

"What?" Sabina shouted at me.

"I'm fine," I said loudly. I struggled to my feet and put weight on the leg. There was pain, but not as bad as I had anticipated. I motioned upward. "Let's keep moving."

The snow continued to fall as we climbed, and eventually, we reached a narrow pass guarded by twin spires of ice-capped rock. Towering drifts had built up around the rock formations' bases and then joined in the center, creating a solid wall of white. The leading

Pilgrims were forced to push their way through the drifts with the snow reaching well past their waists. I chuckled to myself, wondering what the highborn thought of their vaunted privilege now as I followed the trail that they had conveniently left for the rest of us.

Another hour went by, with nothing but howling winds, blowing snow and deep cold to keep us company. I hadn't seen one of the red banners marking the route in a long time and wasn't entirely sure that we were heading in the right direction anymore. We were still going up, however, so I reasoned that meant we must be on the right course.

Hundreds of Pilgrims had started the journey with us that morning in a tightly-packed group. But now we were alone, with only the occasional fleeting glimpses of snowy forms stumbling around like half-frozen corpses. Were the others nearby, hidden by the snowfall? I wondered. Or had they just given up and turned back? I glanced behind me at Sabina, whose head and body were sheathed in a solid layer of white. She was wobbling like a drunkard through the drifts while the taut rope attaching us pulled her along like a hooked fish. I was so numb from the cold that I hadn't even noticed the resistance. I slowed, cursing myself for a fool as I let her catch up.

"Not much farther now!" I called out hoarsely, trying and failing to sound cheerful. If Sabina heard my words, she gave no sign.

Time lost all meaning after that, with no choice but to press onward or fall down and die where we were. I turned my mind inward as I put one foot into the deep snow ahead, then dragged the other out, then did it again, over, and over and over with mindless precision. Finally, I paused, sensing that something had changed around me. I wiped the ice from my eyes, blinking up at a formidable wall of rock that rose directly in my path two hundred feet away. Blowing snow swirled off the top of the cliff, twisting and spinning crazily with the wind. Several familiar red banners stood near the cliff's base, with a barely-seen soldier bracing himself on one of the poles as he urgently waved us in. I whooped for joy.

"We made it!" I cried out as I ran back and put my arm around Sabina. I half-pushed, half-dragged her forward as she stared at me in numb confusion.

"This way! Over here!" I heard the soldier shouting faintly as we drew closer. Snow had curled like frozen waves all along the cliff base, creating a hard, crusty wall that Sabina and I had to fight our way through before finally we reached the man. He clapped me on the back in congratulations. "Welcome, Pilgrims! I'm glad to see you. Are there any more out there?"

"I don't know," I said, barely able to make my frozen lips work. "Maybe."

The soldier nodded, his face covered with an ice-encrusted burlap sack. "I'll keep watch for a while longer, then." He motioned behind him to where the darkened entrance of a cavern awaited. "Get inside. A fire and a mug of hot ale is waiting for you. By the looks of you two, I'd wager you need it."

Sabina and I passed through the opening, then we both paused in surprise. The cavern wasn't really a cavern after all, I saw, but instead was just a convenient hole that led down into a narrow box canyon. Perhaps as many as sixty Pilgrims sat along the canyon's rocky floor, drinking ale and warming themselves near a crackling fire. Sabina and I made our way down several step-like shelves of flat rock toward the flames as silent, exhausted Pilgrims moved aside to make room for us. Sabina dropped gratefully to her knees in front of the fire, while I stood over her, enjoying the heat.

Someone thrust a mug at me and I accepted it gratefully. For the first time in hours, the biting wind that had torn at us was gone. It was a welcome relief after so long in its unforgiving grip. I drank and peered upward into the gloom, then grunted in amazement. Massive cornices of ice and wind-sculpted snow curled outward from the clifftops, as majestic as anything fashioned by man. The ice had expanded over time, thickening into beams that crisscrossed the canyon before becoming fused in the center, creating a supportive network that held up tons of crusted snow and ice. Small areas remained open to the skies and the elements here and there, but hardly any snow managed to make its way inside. I tried not to imagine what would happen if those beams suddenly gave way beneath all that weight.

The canyon wasn't large, but it was still big enough to hold at least twenty times the number of Pilgrims that were here. I wondered what had become of all the others. Surely more had made it than just these few. Soldiers stood at the far end of the canyon near a darkened opening, and one of them finally stepped toward the fire purposefully.

"All right, everyone," the man called out, his voice echoing loudly. "The others have already gone ahead. It looks like you are the last ones to make it this far." He pointed toward the opening behind him. "Each Pilgrim pair will go through here on their way to the Complex. This is the final leg of your journey, and the final test of your resolve. Keep your wits about you and work together, and you will make it." He turned away, then swung back and let his eyes roam over us. "I know you all have had a tough go of it out there. More so than any Walk that I have ever been a part of. The Black Way that leads to the Complex is intimidating in good weather, so I can only imagine what it will be like in this. Whatever you do, make sure you stay focused and don't look down. Good luck to you all."

The soldiers began to usher pairs through the passage one by one, leaving a gap of several minutes before sending the next.

"How are you holding up?" I asked Sabina as I squatted down beside her.

Sabina had taken her hood down and was drawing chunks of half-melted ice from her hair. I noticed someone had given her ale, but it sat untouched on the ground beside her.

"I have had better times," Sabina admitted. She flicked some ice into the fire as the flames hissed back angrily at her. She looked up at me and smiled wearily. "I'll be glad when this is finally over, Hadrack."

I nodded in agreement. I didn't think it prudent to mention our ordeal had only just begun. Sabina knew that as well as I did without having to be told.

"You two," a soldier called out, pointing our way. "You're next."

I helped Sabina to her feet, holding her hand as we passed through the torch-lit tunnel entrance. We walked for a hundred feet or so before we came to a rough opening leading outside. The wind we had become so familiar with began to buffet us again with renewed fury as we paused in dismay at what awaited us. A thin ridge lay ahead that had somehow been flattened out to create a pathway leading directly into an opening in a square-faced cliff three hundred feet away. The builders who had flattened the ridgetop had laid massive black stone slabs down, which must have been a spectacular sight to see in perfect weather. Today, however, the stones glinted treacherously as wind-whipped snow mixed with tiny ice pellets clattered against the slabs before being whisked away over the ridge.

I looked down. Thin pine trees grew far below me on either side of a steep slope, the swaying tips of their branches all but lost in the churning snow and ice. I turned my attention back to our destination, where a gigantic statue of a pair of open hands dominated the clifftop with the fingers curled toward the sky. Emand had described this place to me and I knew I was looking at Mother's Welcome, the gateway into the Complex. I took a cautious step forward onto the first slab, then drew my foot back quickly as my boot started to slide.

"Ice," I said to Sabina, though it clearly wasn't necessary.

Sabina leaned close to me. "Hadrack, where are the other Pilgrims who went ahead of us?"

I squinted at the ridge, lifting a hand to block the ice pellets that bounced painfully off my nose and cheeks. Finally, I pointed. "There they are!"

Two figures were moving cautiously on their hands and knees about halfway across the expanse, their dark cloaks all but lost against the stone as the wind and ice pounded them relentlessly. I watched in horror as one of the Pilgrims suddenly slipped and slid sideways, clawing desperately at the smooth stone slabs. The pair were tied together like Sabina and I were and I cried out in helpless anger as first one, and then the other was swept over the side without a sound. Sabina and I both glanced down at the rope binding us together, and I wordlessly untied it and threw it aside.

"We could turn around and wait until it's safer!" I called out over the wind.

"They will send us back if we do that!" Sabina shouted back.

I knew that she was right. The rules were clear. Stop or turn around and The Walk was done for you. I leaned forward and pressed my lips to her ear. "If you are sure you want to do this, then get my sword out for me."

Sabina looked at me quizzically, but she did as I asked anyway. I guided her behind me, then walked forward carefully as the wind rifled my clothing, threatening to flip me over the side into the gorge far below. I placed the tip of Malo's sword on the ridge's smooth stone as balls of ice bounced and slapped against it all around me. Then I pressed down and made several swooping cuts, scoring through the layer of ice and into the rock. I paused and knelt to survey my handiwork, pleased to see that shallow grey lines had been cut into the dark veneer of the stone. I made several more cuts in the opposite direction, then tentatively put one foot down. I grinned, feeling the tiny fragments of ice and rock that I'd cut out grind beneath my boot. I had traction. I took a second, more confident step, then scored the stone in front of me again.

I continued on that way, step by step for a good ten feet before pausing and looking back. Sabina was waiting for my signal and I motioned for her to come forward. I was surprised to see that other Pilgrims were standing alongside her now. They were cheering me on, I saw, though I could hear nothing over the howling wind. I turned back to my task.

I don't know how long it took us to cross that treacherous ridge. Sabina told me later that it had been hours, but I have always found that to be an exaggeration. I do know that when we finally got to the other side, I was shaking so hard with fatigue that Sabina and another burly Pilgrim had to drag me to safety through the high, rounded opening in the cliff face. Sabina had enough wits about her to take the short sword from my unfeeling hand and replace it just before a procession of chanting Sons appeared. The Sons were accompanied by Sons-In-Waiting, who scurried forward carrying heavy furs, which they hurried to wrap around us.

"Come, Pilgrim!" one of the apprentices said to me kindly. He was thin of face, with gentle eyes and a fur hat perched at an angle on his bald head. "Come inside. Your ordeal has come to an end. The salvation of The Mother and The Father awaits within."

Only one hundred and twenty-two Pilgrims of the four hundred that had set out on The Walk from Calban and Taskerbery Castle more than a week ago survived to see the Complex. Many who did make it were injured, with more than one, I learned, losing fingers, toes, and even noses to the extreme cold. The loss of life was staggering to comprehend, unheard of in the entire history of the Pilgrimage.

The Overseer of the Complex—a priest named Son Lawer—walked solemnly around the moaning, weeping Pilgrims, shaking his head, his face twisted in sorrow as he listened to the stories the survivors told of their ordeals. I believed the Son to be a pleasant man in most instances, going by the laugh lines around his mouth, but today there was no joy on his face, only sadness and reflection as he listened to each Pilgrim respectfully.

We were in a large amphitheater that sat deep within the mountain with rows of benches cut into the stone. Tight-lipped physicians, aided by apprentices, examined each of the sitting Pilgrims with precision and quiet authority. Sabina and I had been looked at already and deemed fit, though Sabina had a deep gash on her arm that she couldn't remember happening that required bandaging. My shin was already turning purple and black where I had struck it, but other than that and a gnawing fatigue pressing down on me, I felt surprisingly well. I was already planning a way for Sabina and me to slip away when Son Lawer stopped before us, looking down his prominent nose at me.

"I believe thanks are in order, Pilgrim," the Son said in a deep, somber voice. Several serious-faced Sons-In-Waiting flanked him.

"I'm not sure why, Son," I said. I felt uncomfortable craning my neck to look at him, so I stood.

Son Lawer's eyebrows rose as I towered over him. "My, but you are a big one, aren't you?" he muttered. He clasped his hands together over his bulging belly. "I have spoken with some of the other Pilgrims, and they inform me that it was you who had the ingenuity to scrape the ice off the walkway. An innovative and timely idea indeed. Had you not done so, I imagine there would be far fewer Pilgrims here than there are right now."

"Perhaps if help had been offered when it was needed most," I said reproachfully, "then I wouldn't have had to do it at all."

"How dare you!" one of the apprentices spat. He was squat and ugly, with broad shoulders and inflamed pimples covering his face and sloping forehead. "Do you know—"

Son Lawer held up a hand. I noticed absently that each of his fingers was encircled by a small ruby ring with a gold band. "That will be quite enough, Jamon." The apprentice closed his mouth with a snap as he glared at me darkly. "I appreciate how you must feel, Pilgrim," Son Lawer continued. "But as you know, the rules of The Walk are clear. And as much as it pains me to see needless lives lost, even I must not break those rules." I snorted, not bothering to respond as I helped Sabina to her feet. "While we are on the subject of rules," Son Lawer said, his face expressionless. "It has come to my attention that you may have a weapon with you. Is that true?"

I paused for a heartbeat before I shook my head. "Of course not, I'm a simple Pilgrim. What need would I have for a weapon?"

"A fine question," the priest said. I saw him glance away to one of the entrances, where soldiers had appeared. They began making their way toward us. "Yet the fact remains that several witnesses swear that you do possess just such an item, and it was this said weapon that you used to break the ice."

"They are mistaken," I said gruffly. "There is no great mystery about how I did it. I used a tree branch."

"A tree branch!" Jamon said in disbelief. "There are no trees anywhere near the Black Way."

Son Lawer took a deep breath and he turned to glare at the ugly apprentice. Jamon flushed and looked down as the priest turned back to me. "So, it was a tree branch, then?" he said thoughtfully. "Not a sword?"

"That's right, Son. The wind was blowing the snow in all directions, making it hard to see. The Pilgrims were exhausted. I imagine their minds told them that I held a sword, when in reality, it was only a branch."

Son Lawer rubbed his chin as he considered my words. Finally, he grunted in acceptance and waved off the approaching soldiers. "I believe you, Pilgrim." He put his hand on my forearm and squeezed. "My apologies for doubting you. You have our deepest thanks for what you did. I hope you both find the solace you seek on my mountain."

The priest nodded to Sabina and me, and then he moved off to speak to another pair with his grim-faced apprentices close on his heels. Jamon glowered at me with dislike as he followed after the Son.

I leaned close to Sabina once they were out of earshot. "We have to leave. Right now."

"You don't think the priest believed you?"

"I know he didn't," I said. I looked around, seeking a way out. "The question is, why didn't he press me on it?"

The amphitheater seating rose high above us, row upon row that seemed to go on forever. I could see several exits at the top, though none appeared to be guarded as far as I could tell. Serving girls dressed in flowing white robes had begun bringing food and water from the lower entrances, so I decided our best course was upward. I turned for the stairs, then froze as my eyes met those of Emand the cordwainer, who was standing at the other end of the room watching us. The shoemaker saw my gaze on him and he waved to us mockingly. His spindly wife sat on a bench beside him, clutching a bloody bandage to her forehead.

"Come on," I growled, taking Sabina's arm.

The rounded benches were separated into sections, with smooth, gleaming stairs running between them up to the top level. I guided Sabina to the closest steps, hurrying up them and expecting a cry to halt at any moment. No call came, however, and when we reached the top landing, I paused to look back down. No one appeared to have noticed us or seemed the least bit interested in what we were doing. I shifted my eyes toward where Emand stood. The cordwainer's wife still sat where she had been, pressing the cloth to her forehead, but the shoemaker was nowhere to be seen. Had he gone to get help?

I hustled Sabina out into a long corridor well lit by abundant torches. Several Sons-In-Waiting were walking down the hall and they nodded to us cordially as they passed, looking unsurprised by our sudden appearance.

"Which way?" Sabina whispered to me.

I looked to my right, following the direction the apprentices were heading, then left. The corridor was empty in that direction and stretched for twenty feet before curling out of sight. "This way," I said decisively, heading left.

Once we passed around the bend, we found ourselves in a much larger corridor with open archways along both walls every twenty feet. I peered through the first archway, where I could see half a dozen apprentices sitting in a circle on squat stone stools, listening to a Son as he spoke in a high, condescending voice. We kept moving. The corridor floor changed from rough stone to polished tile as we progressed, until finally, we entered a grand room with thirty-foot high ceilings supported by elegantly-sculpted white columns. Sons in black robes strode together in twos and threes, engaged in conversation, while around them, Sons-In-Waiting scurried urgently, many of them laden with leather-bound tomes and rolled parchments. Corridors led off the grand room in all directions, each one looking as indistinct as the next.

Sabina and I paused in indecision. "How do we get out of this place?" she muttered.

I lifted a hand to a short Son-In-Waiting as he hurried past, a stack of books balanced in his arms. "Excuse me, can you help us?" I asked.

The apprentice hesitated and he blinked up at me. His eyes were light blue and watery and shone with an inner dullness that offered little in the way of intelligence. "Help you, Pilgrim? How?"

"We're looking for the way out," I said.

The Son-In-Waiting blinked again, this time in confusion. "Out? Out of where?"

"This place," I said, trying not to let my frustration show as I gestured around me. "How do we get outside from here?"

"Outside? Why would you want to do that?"

"Because we do," I said, forcing a smile.

"But you are Pilgrims," the apprentice said, twitching his lips as he thought. "You were just outside. Why would you want to go back? It's a blizzard out there."

"We won't go far," Sabina said. "We're just not used to being underground. We need some air."

The apprentice stared at Sabina as though she had just grown a second head. "Air?" he mumbled. He looked around in confusion. "There is air right here."

I groaned to myself. Of all the Sons-In-Waiting in the entire Complex, I had to stop the only halfwit. "We need fresh air," I said patiently, stressing the word fresh. "We're not accustomed to breathing air as stale as this."

"Stale air," the apprentice repeated as he struggled with the concept. Finally, he shrugged. "I don't know much about the air either way, but you can't leave right now even if you wanted to. The Complex has been sealed."

"Why?" I growled, knowing it probably had something to do with Sabina and me.

"I don't know," the apprentice said, looking disinterested. "Maybe because of the storm?" He motioned with his head to one of the exits. "But if it's fresher air you want, that corridor there will take you down to Oasis."

"We can go there now?" Sabina asked, sounding surprised.

"Of course," the apprentice said. "Oasis is open to all. I find it smells nice down there, so hopefully it will fit your needs."

"What about the—" I began to say.

"Thank you," Sabina said, cutting me off. "That will do nicely."

The apprentice looked relieved. "I'm glad that I could help," he said as he hurried away.

"Well, now we're in trouble," I grunted. "They're looking for us."

"Come on," Sabina said. "I have an idea." She grabbed my hand and pulled me after her.

"Where are we going?" I protested.

"You have forgotten your lessons," Sabina admonished me as she dragged me toward the corridor for Oasis. I blinked at her in confusion. Now it was my turn to be the halfwit. Sabina grinned at me. "Oasis is open to the outside, Hadrack, remember?"

I rolled my eyes. "And it is also surrounded by cliffs," I said with a snort. "Very tall ones."

Oasis was located in a deep gorge torn through the heart of the mountain itself. The gorge was miles long, with walls rising more than thirteen hundred feet on all sides. "Do you expect us to climb out?" I asked sarcastically.

"Of course not, don't be silly. I'm talking about the Tapeau. If we can find them, then they can help us to get out."

I grunted, perking up with interest. The Tapeau were the natural custodians of Oasis. An ancient sect tasked with caring for the sacred place for the last thousand years. They lived on the mountain near the Complex and only entered the gorge through a tunnel from the outside. I grinned at Sabina in admiration. She was right, the tunnel could indeed be our way out.

The corridor we were traveling along ended abruptly, with narrow stairs heading downward. Torches lit the stairwell as we began the long descent, until finally we reached a short landing. That landing led to another set of stairs, with another long climb down to a second landing, then more stairs where an alcove finally awaited at the bottom. Two expressionless soldiers holding short pikes and wearing shields on their arms stood to either side of an arched opening facing the stairs.

The stairwell had reeked overwhelmingly of mildew and dust during the descent, but now the first faint smells of rich fauna coming from Oasis reached us. The gorge was warmed by hundreds of tiny hot springs that bubbled to the surface along the floor, releasing constant heat that enabled plants and trees to grow where they otherwise would have no business being. I could hear an underlying booming coming from the opening and I realized we were hearing The Purge, the famous waterfall near where The Father and Mother had consummated their love.

The bigger of the two guards nodded as we approached. "Welcome, Pilgrims," he rumbled in a flat voice.

I thought the soldiers might try to stop us and was prepared for it, but neither man said anything else, looking bored and disinterested. We walked past them unchallenged and stepped into a long corridor. I could feel a sudden rush of heat rolling down the corridor's length as sweat started to break out on my forehead. We approached an enormous chasm torn through the rock face and paused several paces inside its cavernous mouth. We had reached Oasis.

Despite what the halfwit apprentice had told us, the air coming from inside the gorge felt humid and oppressive as a light rain fell. Colorful birds flitted back and forth from the branches of hardy-looking trees, while below them, vines covered in supple purple flowers grew twisting and curling through a dense layer of leaves, grass, and small bushes. I noticed many of the trees were covered in a compact, web-like, grey growth.

"Strangler figs," Sabina explained. "The plant life on the floor gets very little sunlight, so the strangler figs use the tree trunks to climb above the branches."

A tiny red and yellow bird alighted on a vine near my feet and cocked its head, regarding me curiously before taking flight and disappearing. Something moved through the grasses in front of me and I stepped back just as a light green snake with white stripes slithered across my path before disappearing into the undergrowth.

"That was a Green Tree Boa," Sabina said. "You will probably see more of them hanging from the branches here and there." She saw the look on my face and chuckled. "Don't worry, Hadrack, they are harmless. They only eat birds and reptiles."

I kept one eye on the trail ahead and one on the trees we passed under as we moved into Oasis, expecting a snake to drop on me at any moment. The sound of rushing water and a strange hissing grew louder as we progressed, and three times we had to make our way around small hot springs with long tendrils of lazy steam rising from them. The fauna around each spring was lusher than anywhere else, I noticed, looking healthy and well-nourished as the leaves and grasses shone with wetness. At first, I thought the hissing sound came from the springs, but then I realized it was coming from farther to the north.

The rain that continued to fall was light and surprisingly warm as I stooped down and dipped my hand tentatively in and out of one of the springs. I had expected the water to be scalding hot and was surprised at the pleasant warmness. I stood and looked up. I could see far above that the snow was still falling, but the heat rising from the many springs guaranteed it would never reach the valley floor as anything but gentle rain. The rocks along the valley walls were dark and dripping rainwater above me, but after about two hundred feet, I could see the telltale glimmer of ice beginning to form here and there. Even if we wanted to try climbing out, I knew it would be impossible.

Sabina and I passed around a rocky outcrop, then stopped in surprise, staring upward at a giant plume of mist that rose fifty feet into the air. White, seething water poured out from a jagged crevice in the eastern cliff face, then fell at least four hundred yards into a deep basin of bubbling, steaming water. The cold water from the mountain was draining into the hot water pooling below, I realized, evaporating instantly into mist, which caused the strange hissing sound that I had been hearing.

We had reached The Purge.

Sabina started to move forward, her face struck with wonder just as I put my hand on her arm, holding her back. A man knelt on the rocky ledge overlooking the water with his forehead pressed to the stone. I ushered Sabina behind some bushes, motioning for her to stay silent as I studied the stranger. He was dressed entirely in animal skins and had a knife on his hip. His hair was brown, shorn on both sides and left long at the back and braided with string and colorful beads. He knelt barefoot, but I could see a hardy pair of fur-lined boots sitting nearby on the rocks. We had found one of the Tapeau.

I leaned toward Sabina. "We'll wait until he leaves, then follow him. Hopefully, he will lead us to the tunnel."

Sabina and I sat huddled in the bushes for many long minutes, and during that entire time, the Tapeau didn't move or utter a sound. Eventually, I couldn't take the burning in my thighs any longer and I shifted my legs carefully, wishing the Tapeau would just do something. Then I caught movement to my left. A man was approaching cautiously from the south, pushing his way through the undergrowth, but I could only see his boots and legs from my vantage point. The intruder might just be another Pilgrim come to worship, I reasoned, but something told me that he wasn't. I could see a second figure moving behind the first now, and finally, I got a good look at the leader's face. I had to force myself not to curse out loud. It was Emand, with his dour-looking wife coming stoically on behind him.

The cordwainer had a drawn sword in his hand as he focused warily on the motionless Tapeau. I knew the kneeling man couldn't hear anyone approaching with the sounds coming from the falls. I carefully drew Malo's sword as I debated what to do. Should I jump out now and deal with Emand once and for all, or wait to see what the shoemaker planned? There was always the chance that Emand might have more men with him, which made me hesitate as I weighed my options. Sabina and I were well hidden where we were, so the chances of discovery were slim. But leaving the Tapeau exposed the way that he was just didn't sit right with me. I had to do something to warn him.

I glanced down, searching the valley floor until I saw a small rock, then threw it high over the bushes in the direction of the Tapeau. I had hoped the rock would land on the overhang the Tapeau was kneeling on and alert him to danger, but my throw was more accurate than I had intended. Instead of the ledge, the stone cracked smartly against the bottom of the Tapeau's bare right foot.

The man reacted instantly, spinning sideways and snatching out his knife as he faced the surprised cordwainer. Emand clearly hadn't seen the small rock that I'd thrown as he lifted a hand to the Tapeau, looking as though he was trying to reassure him. I couldn't hear anything that was being said over the roar of the falls other than a few garbled words.

The Tapeau was lithe and muscular-looking, and now that he was aware of Emand, I felt better about the man's chances. I relaxed slightly, watching the trees for any sign of others. The Tapeau suddenly shook his head angrily and said something to Emand in sharp bursts. He motioned with his knife for emphasis, pointing back the way the two had come. Emand smiled disarmingly, letting his sword drop to his side, while Laurea moved out along the rocks, staring into the water. She stopped less than ten feet from the Tapeau and closed her eyes, breathing deeply with her hands clasped to her chest in reverence.

The Tapeau remained focused on Emand as the shoemaker took several steps closer. Again, the custodian shook his head as he gestured with his knife. Emand just laughed and shrugged. He said something as he pointed to his wife, who suddenly pounced, lashing out with her right hand as she raked it down the Tapeau's face. The attack was unexpected, yet Laurea was a slight woman and unarmed, so it seemed harmless enough to me. The Tapeau screamed in agony, however, and he fell back, spewing blood from his face. I was shocked to see skin hanging torn and bloody from his cheek. I felt a shimmer of superstitious awe roll along my back just as Laurea struck again, raking her fingers across the Tapeau's chest. The man screamed a second time, and he fell backward as Laurea leaped with blazing speed onto his chest. She raised her right hand in the air, then paused and looked behind her at Emand. The cordwainer was smiling as he strode forward. He casually kicked the Tapeau's knife into the bubbling water.

"What just happened?" Sabina whispered beside me. "How did she do that?"

I studied Laurea's raised right hand carefully. I saw what appeared to be a thin band of iron crossing her knuckles, with the points of four wicked claws dripping blood jutting out from her palm. I'd never seen anything like it before. Emand knelt beside the Tapeau as the man stared at him with dark blood welling from the gashes on his face. Emand said something, his body language suggesting amusement as he motioned around the valley with his sword. The Tapeau shook his head and Laurea put her clawed hand against his neck. Emand spoke again, and this time the Tapeau responded as he gestured northward. I assumed he was telling Emand where the tunnel was located. The cordwainer patted the Tapeau on the shoulder, and then he thrust his sword deep into the man's neck with a quick, efficient move. Sabina gasped in shock beside me as Emand casually wiped his blade clean on the Tapeau's clothing.

The shoemaker stood and glanced around, his face hard and cold-looking. Then he spoke to Laurea, gesturing for her to join him. The thin woman laughed, her face twisted ugly as she stood and slashed down with each hand, slicing deep into the dead man's neck. Laurea kicked savagely at the bloody head several times before finally dislodging it, and then she flicked the decapitated head into the water with her boot. Emand had waited patiently for her to finish, and now he pointed north as the two moved away, quickly disappearing through the undergrowth.

"What do we do?" Sabina whispered.

I was confident now that the two were alone as I stood up and helped Sabina to her feet. I had told Rorian that I didn't make war on women, but after what I had just seen, I was ready to revise my stance on that. At least for this woman, anyway.

"We follow them, and when the time is right, I'll kill them both," I growled.

18: Emand

    Jebido told me many times over the years that I should never underestimate my opponents. I realized that I had done just that with Emand. Because the man was so much older than me, small in stature, and seemed relatively harmless, I dismissed him as being any kind of serious threat. That had been a mistake. One that I made with his wife as well. Arrogance can be useful occasionally, but it can also be a trait that can get you killed, and I vowed not to underestimate either one of them again. I still wasn't positive who the pair were working for, but with the connection the couple had to Cardia, it seemed logical to believe that it was the Cardians. Emand had played a waiting game with me, hoping to win my friendship and trust and learn the codex's location in that way. He was sly and patient, I now knew, and his plan might have worked, had I really been the man he'd thought me to be.
    Thinking of that made me wonder how Emand had come to know my true identity in the first place. Then I shrugged the question off as pointless. I would be asking the bastard soon enough with the point of my sword at his throat. What was really puzzling, however, was that if Emand did work for Cardia like I believed, and the Cardians had hired Rorian to locate the codex, then why was Emand here at all?
    I watched Sabina as she knelt under the protection of a tree, studying the spoor left behind by our quarry. I was sweating in my heavy cloak and considered just taking it off, but quickly discarded the idea. I would need my hands free if Emand and his vicious wife doubled back on us. Besides, once we found the Tapeau tunnel, I knew we would be right back out in the harsh weather and I'd be very thankful for the warmth the cloak provided.

"They headed that way," Sabina said, pointing east to a half-moon shaped, bubbling spring surrounded in places by dense growths of prickly bushes.

I had a sudden vision of Patter's Bog and the bushes that I had hid behind as a child. I studied the spring warily. Were the shoemaker and his wife hiding in there right now, waiting for us to walk into their trap? Sabina knit her eyebrows together as she peered at the ground.

"What is it?" I asked.

"I'm not sure," Sabina muttered as she stood. She gestured ahead. "They were heading straight north, then suddenly veered off to the east toward that spring."

"They must have seen us," I said, confident that I was right. I knew the Tapeau had told Emand to go north, so changing course so suddenly could only mean one thing. They knew we were here.

Tall cypress trees grew in abundance on the far side of the spring, with the valley floor below them covered in the distinctive, feather-like leaves of the maidenhair, which was a type of fern that thrived in warm, moist temperatures. The imposing, rocky wall of the valley rose beyond the trees, hard and unyielding. I peered once again at the bushes, wondering if even now, Emand's eyes were on us as I flexed my hand on the leather grip of Malo's sword. Birds continued to sing and flit through the trees over our heads despite the steady rainfall. I could hear the deep, distinctive croak of a bullfrog lamenting somewhere behind us along with the drone of crickets and the occasional bee buzzing past. A woodpecker hammered away at a trunk far to the north as I stood in indecision.

"Stay here," I finally said to Sabina. "Find somewhere to hide and wait there until I call for you."

"I don't think splitting up is a good idea," Sabina said uneasily.

"Just do what you are told," I replied gruffly. I was in no mood to argue with Sabina right now. "If they are waiting for us on the other side of those bushes, I don't want to have to worry about you getting in my way."

Sabina looked as though she might protest again and I glared at her in warning, then I turned and stalked toward the spring. I hadn't known the Tapeau, but his death was gnawing at me like a rat on a corpse. He could have been a good man, a bad man, or somewhere in between, I had no way of knowing. But I did know that he hadn't deserved what had happened to him. What bothered me the most, I suppose, was that I knew I was ultimately responsible for his death. I'd led Emand and that bitch of a wife of his right to him. I couldn't bring the man back to life, but I could exact revenge for what they had done. And that was precisely what I planned on doing.

I was angry, but it wasn't a hot, reckless anger like in years past, but more like a cold, focused rage. I had initially trusted Emand, maybe even liked him a little, and I knew a great deal of my anger had to do with how wrong I had been about him. I took several steps, then paused to listen before moving forward, trying to avoid walking on any twigs or branches that might signal my approach. I could see through a wide gap in the bushes that the spring ahead was bubbling and seething, just like the larger one beneath The Purge. I had no idea why some of the springs were warm and some scalding hot like this one appeared to be. Perhaps the heat came from all the burning souls in the world of Father Below, I thought. It seemed as likely an answer as any other.

I had learned enough from Sabina over the last few weeks to follow Emand's trail quite easily as it led me toward the spring. The sounds coming from the bubbling water were louder now and would hide my approach, which was good, but it also hid any noise my adversaries might make as well. The gap in the thicket ahead was the width of a man, with the bushes to either side at least ten feet deep, with barbed thorns on them that gleamed from the rain. I knew there was little to no chance that anyone could be waiting to pounce at me from within them, which meant if I were to be attacked, it would happen on the other side.

I hesitated halfway, listening again as I carefully opened my cloak and drew the two sacks of provisions over my neck. I untied them, then twirled one several times before flinging it over the hedges six feet to my right, where it landed with a dull thud. I heard an exclamation of surprise and I jumped forward instantly, lifting the second bag as a shield. A shriek sounded at my appearance, then Laurea was on me, slashing wildly with her claws. The sack I held jumped twice on my arm as the food fell to the ground, but her claws hadn't reached me. I threw the bag in Laurea's face and whirled sideways, narrowly avoiding being skewered by Emand. I slapped his sword aside and took an off-balance swipe at the cordwainer, but the little man danced away nimbly. I retreated with my back to the bank of the spring.

Emand and his wife hesitated, one to either side of me. Laurea was growling deep in her slight chest as she clicked her claws together. I realized I had never actually heard the woman speak. She and Rorian's tongue-less wife would have gotten along famously if not for me, I thought, feeling my mouth twitch in amusement at the idea.

"You find the current situation funny, do you, Hadrack?" Emand asked.

"I was just thinking how much I'm going to enjoy killing you and this she-bitch, here."

Emand's eyes narrowed. "I'll not have you disparage my wife, Hadrack. It's unseemly."

I chuckled. "Unseemly, is it?" I shifted my stance, feeling the intense heat from the spring even through my cloak. "What is unseemly, you lying little bastard, is what this slut of yours did to that man back there."

Emand's faced darkened and his eyes glinted with anger. Good, I thought. I wanted him angry. An angry man can often make foolish mistakes, as I have learned all too well.

"Laurea can sometimes lose herself in the moment," Emand said as he smoothed his features, looking calmer now. "I'm sure you can understand how that might happen."

"All I understand is you murdered someone for no good reason," I spat back.

"Ah," Emand said with a rueful smile. "I agree, that was unfortunate. I made the assumption—a wrong one as it turned out—that you had already left Oasis using the tunnel. I didn't want to waste time trying to find out its location by…er…more gentler means." He shifted his gaze to his wife and smiled at her affectionately. "Besides, Laurea hadn't killed anyone in quite some time. She was starting to get anxious."

I glanced at Laurea, who was staring at me with a feral hunger in her eyes. "So, what's your plan now, Emand?" I asked. "If you kill me, you won't learn where the codex is."

"Not true," Emand said. He inched to his right, flanking me, while Laurea shifted left. "I'm sure Sabina will be most helpful with that, once we deal with you."

I snorted. "You are a fool, Emand. The girl is just some stupid whore I hired in Calban to get me into The Walk. She doesn't know anything."

Emand paused, regarding me thoughtfully. He glanced at his wife. "What do you think, my love?" Laurea shook her head slowly, never taking her eyes off of me. "Well, there you have it," Emand said. "Neither of us believe you."

I shrugged. "Then that leaves only one thing left, doesn't it?"

"Yes," Emand agreed. His face changed, turning cold and dangerous. "I do believe the time for talking has come to a close."

The shoemaker took several more steps to his right, casually flicking the full sack of food I had thrown to distract him into the spring. Then he glided toward the bank, while Laurea did the same on her side. I couldn't watch them both now, as I was forced to turn my head back and forth. By their practiced rhythm, I could tell that the cordwainer and his wife had been successful at this same maneuver before. I was determined to end that success right here and now. But of the two, who would be the one to strike first? My instinct was to watch for Emand to make the first move, but Laurea was quick like a cat and couldn't be discounted. Perhaps they would attack together on some mutual signal that they both knew?

My best chance, I decided, was to disrupt their rhythm and put them on the defensive. I checked on Laurea, then glanced down at Emand's feet. He was on his heels with one foot in front of the other, his sword ready. Judging by the way he held his body, I decided he wasn't the one who was going to attack first. It was Laurea. I bellowed and ran at the cordwainer, hoping he would step back and raise his sword in a defensive posture—which he did. I smashed Malo's short sword onto Emand's longer blade, staggering the little man, even as I heard movement from behind me.

I turned. Laurea was coming fast, howling like some crazed animal as I leaped sideways out of the way. I landed hard on the rock, feeling a burning sensation ripping down my thigh where the woman's claws had cut through my cloak and raked my skin. She was on me before I had a chance to rise, spitting and screaming as she pounced. I did the only thing that I could and I rolled left, evading her claws that cracked against the stone beneath me. Then I kicked out, catching the bitch hard in the knee, sending her tumbling away. Emand appeared over me with his sword raised and I rolled away from him, this time to my right. The cordwainer swung, cursing at me as his blade grazed my hair, taking a chunk off the top as it swished past. I swiped wildly at him, still off-balance, but coming close enough that the little man had to leap back. I'd gained a small amount of time, sufficient enough to allow me to get back to my feet as Emand advanced on me warily. Laurea was on her feet again as well, her face twisted with hatred as she came forward.

"You don't disappoint, Hadrack of Corwick," Emand said, his voice soft and deadly. "I am impressed."

"And shortly, you will be dead," I replied.

I took a glance over my shoulder. The spring was shaped in a half-moon, with the rounded back of it behind me. The fattest part of the spring was less than four feet from the bushes, and I retreated to that spot. If Emand and Laurea wanted to get to me, they would have to do it together in that narrow space, or even better, one at a time.

Emand smiled and lowered his sword. "I have enjoyed this, Hadrack. I really have. It's brought back memories of a more youthful time." Laurea stepped ahead of the cordwainer and she flipped her right wrist. The claws she wore on that hand came off with a snap and she dropped them to the ground. "But," Emand continued, "time catches up to us all." He gestured to Laurea, who was doing something with her hair. "My wife is a woman of unusual talents, as you will soon bear witness to. Observe."

Laurea withdrew her hand, and I saw she held a flat, metallic disc with knife-like spikes jutting out all around the exterior. She threw sideways without any warning and I cried out, my right leg giving way beneath me as the disc caught me just above the knee, burying deep into my flesh. I snarled in anger as I fought to rise while Emand moved to stand beside his wife. She withdrew another of the spiked weapons and grinned at me, showing long yellow fangs as she threw again. I tried to spin away, losing my balance as the steel points ripped along the meat of my left shoulder before the disc disappeared into the spring. I wobbled, then fell flat against the rock on my stomach as Malo's sword skittered away. Laurea stooped and picked up her claws, putting them on as she stalked toward me. I began to drag myself toward my sword, while behind me, I could hear Laurea's breathing rasping in her chest in excitement. I felt the cold metal of her claws on my boot, the touch almost a gentle caress.

"I've got you now," Laurea hissed, the first words that I had ever heard from her.

I looked at her over my shoulder. "Who's got who, you ugly bitch?"

Laurea's eyes widened as I grabbed her cloak by the collar. I yanked her toward me and smashed my forehead into her face, squashing her nose and breaking off several of her teeth. The woman squealed as I switched my grip to the back of her neck just as one of her claws caught me on the right cheek, tearing open the skin. I could feel the warm blood flowing, but I ignored it as I twisted and slammed Laurea's face into the rock floor. I heard bones snapping and I drew her back up, then smashed her down again, then a third time just to be sure. I tossed her limp body aside just as Emand reached me and put his sword to my throat. Tears were rolling unashamedly down Emand's cheeks as we stared at each other wordlessly. I could see my death in the little man's eyes.

"Is she dead, Hadrack?" Emand finally asked, his voice quivering.

"Oh, she's dead all right," I grunted. "I think she was still alive after the first two times, that's why I did it again." I glared up at him in challenge. "I found it very satisfying."

Emand glanced at Laurea's twisted body, and he nodded numbly. He slowly squatted in front of me so that we were eye to eye. The man might be grieving, but the sword he held to my throat never wavered an inch.

"I am going to kill you," he said flatly.

"Yes, I'm aware of that," I responded.

"Tell me where the codex is hidden and I will make it quick."

"No."

Emand sighed. Tears were still clinging to his cheeks, yet he ignored them. "My wife made these herself," he said sadly, gesturing to the steel half-buried in my leg. He wrenched the disc out in one quick motion as I screamed in surprise, then he casually tossed it aside. "I imagine that hurts," Emand said dispassionately. He pressed the blade of his sword tighter against my neck. "I recommend that you don't move, Hadrack." Emand reached into the gaping wound in my leg and began to poke around inside with his fingers. I screamed in agony, holding my body as rigid as I could as I felt the blade at my neck bite into my flesh. Finally, Emand grunted in satisfaction, and he withdrew his bloody fingers. I almost sobbed in relief. "Now, my friend, I will ask you again. Where is the codex hidden?"

"You were right, Emand," I managed to rasp out. "I did lie to you. Sabina isn't a whore at all."

"Is that so?" Emand said, looking unimpressed.

"Yes, she knows everything I do about the codex."

Emand chuckled. "Do you think telling me something that I already know will save you somehow?"

I shook my head. "No, I just feel bad about calling her a whore. I wanted you to know that before she bashes in your skull."

"What?" Emand grunted in surprise.

The cordwainer turned just as Sabina swung a thick branch, catching him squarely across the temple. The little man groaned and dropped to his hands and knees as Sabina struck him again, this time across the back, snapping the branch in two. I grabbed for the sword in Emand's hand, but he clutched at it possessively. Emand's face was covered in blood, but I could see the fire of determination burning in his eyes as we struggled over the weapon. He was surprisingly strong for such a small man. Sabina hovered over us with the remnants of her branch, waiting for another chance to strike.

"You bastard!" Emand hissed in my face.

Our noses were almost touching, and I grinned at him. "Tell your wife the Outlaw of Corwick says hello," I growled. I let go of the sword and grabbed Emand by the shoulders, then smashed my forehead into his face just like I'd done to his wife. The cordwainer gasped and he wobbled in my grip as his sword fell from nerveless fingers, landing with a splash into the bubbling spring behind us. I wrapped a hand around the little man's neck. "And while you are at it," I whispered. "Say hello to The Father as well."

Then I shoved Emand backward, knocking him down the spring bank and into the boiling water below.

My leg injury was severe, and progress through the undergrowth was slow and frustrating as we headed north along the western wall. We kept expecting to see the Tapeau tunnel at any moment, only to be continuously disappointed as the hours slowly went by. Sabina had bound my wounds and most of the bleeding had stopped, but even so, I still felt weak, lightheaded, and disorientated. I knew I wouldn't have been able to make it more than a few dozen steps if it wasn't for Sabina's help.

The gorge was cast in deep shadows when we finally reached the end of it, but the tunnel wasn't there either. I collapsed to the ground in exhaustion as I stared bitterly at the jumbled rock wall facing us. Oasis had originally been open to the north, but the cliffs to either side had collapsed long ago, boxing it in. Whether this had been the work of men or the gods themselves, I had no way of knowing. Nor did I care much at the moment.

"We must have missed it somehow," Sabina said in dismay.

"We didn't miss it," I said, knowing that I was right. "The Tapeau lied to Emand, Sabina. The tunnel must be along the eastern wall."

Sabina knelt beside me and inspected my bandages. "Well, wherever it is, we'll have to find it in the morning," she said. "You can't go on like this."

"No," I grunted stubbornly. "We have to keep moving. I just need a few more minutes to catch my breath."

Emand and his wife had been alone, but I knew sooner or later, others would come. If we stayed where we were, they would be sure to find us. My shoulder throbbed constantly, but the second disk Laurea threw at me had only torn off a chunk of skin in passing. I could still use the arm reasonably well. The leg was another matter. It flopped around like a headless chicken when I tried to walk and I had to drag it behind me like my father did when I was a boy. Even an experienced tracker would have little trouble following us with the trail that I had left behind.

Sabina made a face as she unwrapped the blood-soaked bandage around my leg. "This isn't good, Hadrack," she said. "The wound looks like it is getting infected."

I had to agree with her. My leg was already leaking a yellowish fluid, with the skin around the jagged gash red and angry-looking. I thought of Emand jamming his grimy fingers in there and I cursed softly. Maybe the bastard had killed me after all.

"Goldenseal," I muttered. Goldenseal was a plant that Malo had used to suck the infection from Baine and Jebido's wounds years ago. Maybe it would help. I closed my eyes as a wave of weakness settled over me. "Do you know of it?"

"Of course, I do," Sabina said, sounding relieved. "I should have thought of that. I'll go and try to find some."

I nodded, wishing her luck, but was too exhausted to bother opening my eyes. I lay where I was, dozing in and out of a fitful sleep, until a sudden memory from long ago appeared in my mind. My father was leaning on his axe, sweating in the morning sunlight as he took a break from chopping wood. I remembered the moment vividly from my childhood. I was sitting on the fence near the sty and marveling at my father's great muscles as curious pigs snuffled and snorted behind me. I was five years old.

"You must always be aware of your surroundings, Hadrack," my father said to me gravely. "Danger can appear from places where you least expect."

"What danger, Father?" I asked innocently as only a boy of five could. "We're safe here, aren't we?"

"People like us are never safe anywhere, Hadrack," my father replied. He swept his hand out. "When you look around, what do you see?"

I let my gaze slowly wander the farm and fields as my father waited patiently. My mother and sister were tending to the garden near the house, crouching down around the onions and beets. My mother stood stiffly as I watched, stretching her back as she peered east to where my brother, Lallo, worked digging rocks from the field. She waved and he waved back. I grinned and turned to my father, confident that I knew the answer. "I see my family," I said.

My father laughed. "Of course, that's obvious. But it is the things that are less obvious that require better attention."

"Why?" I asked.

"Because the world is a harsh place, lad, with even harsher men in it. That is why you must always be aware."

"I'm not afraid," I said proudly. "I'm going to be big and strong, just like you."

"And because of that, you think that I don't know fear?" my father rumbled, looking amused.

I could feel my eyes widening. The idea that my father could be afraid of anything seemed impossible. I shook my head. "Of course not."

"All men know fear, Hadrack," my father said. "At least the wise ones do," he added.

"Well, I won't be afraid of anything," I proclaimed. I stood up, balancing on the railing of the fence. I swung my arm as though it held a sword. "I'll be a great warrior and kill my enemies by the hundreds. The King will recognize my deeds and reward me with land and title. You will see, Father."

My father frowned, looking uncomfortable. "I fear you may be right about that." He wiped the sweat from his brow. "But not today, eh?" he said after a moment with a wry grin.

A dragonfly droned past me and I focused on it, mimicking the insect's flight in the air with my hand, my battle forgotten. I laughed as it swooped around me curiously before landing in my hair. "Look, Father!" I shouted gleefully. "Do you see? I'm the King of the dragonflies!"

My father chuckled, shaking his head as he took up his axe again. "Maybe you are. Maybe you are at that."

I snapped open my eyes, brought back to the present by the sounds of someone moving nearby. "Sabina?" I called out hoarsely.

"Not so loud!" came back the hushed response.

I waited, reaching for my sword as Sabina's shadowy form appeared through the brush.

"There are men with torches coming this way," Sabina whispered as she crouched down beside me.

I nodded wearily, not surprised. "Help me to my feet," I grunted.

Sabina held up several plants that she clutched in her hand. "First, the goldenseal."

I shook my head firmly. "There isn't time for that. We have to go now."

"Go where?" Sabina asked.

I pointed east. "That way. Maybe we can find the tunnel before they find us."

We started off, moving slowly as Sabina did her best to take as much of my weight as she could. The pain was excruciating, and after ten stumbling steps, I paused to pick up a small stick, which I planted firmly between my teeth to keep myself from crying out. The gorge was almost half a mile wide, but it felt ten times that width before we finally reached the eastern wall. We paused against the sloping, uneven rock as I fought to stay upright. I could see torches burning through the trees and hear the calls of the men as they searched for us. Soon, I knew, they would locate our tracks heading east.

"What now?" Sabina asked.

I closed my eyes, willing my mind to focus. "Can you go back and erase our trail?" I finally asked.

"All the way?" Sabina muttered doubtfully. "We don't have that much time."

I shook my head as I sucked in much-needed air. "No, just the last thirty feet or so."

"And then what?" Sabina asked.

"And then we go up," I said, slapping the rock face behind me. The ground along the cliff's base was made up of solid bedrock, scrubbed clean of soil from the wind. I knew we would leave no trace behind once we were above the floor of the gorge. The trick, of course, was going to be in the climb. Would I be able to manage it?

The look on Sabina's face told me all I needed to know about what she thought about my plan. She turned wordlessly and disappeared, returning in less than ten minutes.

I pointed upward when she joined me. "See that ledge there, about fifteen feet above us?"

Sabina peered up into the gloom. Finally, she nodded. "Yes, I see it."

"Can you climb up there?"

Sabina took a deep breath. "I think so. But it doesn't look like much to me."

"There's only one way to find out," I grunted.

Both the sacks of provisions that I had carried were lost—one shredded by Laurea's claws, the other when Emand kicked it into the spring. I'd gathered what scattered food I could, and Sabina had used the torn canvas for bandaging. I had almost thrown the rope away that held them around my neck but decided to hang onto it at the last moment. Now I was glad that I had as I offered it to Sabina. "When you get up there, tie the end of this to something, then empty your sacks of food and tie the rope to them. It should be long enough to reach me."

"You can't be serious," Sabina said, looking up again. "We don't even know how wide that ledge is."

I pushed Sabina forward. "We will just have to leave that part to the gods."

The valley wall sloped at an angle, steep, but not impossible. I grimaced. Not impossible for someone with two good legs, anyway. Sabina began to climb carefully, thrusting her hands and feet into crevices or whatever else she could find.

Small rocks clattered down around me and I looked up in alarm. "Sabina?" I hissed. "Are you all right?"

I heard a grunt come back, but that was all. The girl's dark cloak was lost to me now in the shadows of the wall. Finally, something whispered back and forth against the rock above my head. It was one of the canvas sacks dangling from a rope. I reached up, just able to grab onto it with my right hand. I gave an experimental tug, satisfied when it held firm.

"All right," I said under my breath. "This is going to hurt. A lot."

I reached as high as I could with my right hand, then, fighting the urge to cry out, I lifted my injured arm and wrapped the cloth around my hand. Then I pulled upward, fighting a wave of nausea as my wounded shoulder protested. I paused for a heartbeat, dangling off the ground and praying the rope would hold, then I propped the foot of my good leg on an outcrop of rock to support me. I counted to three, then pushed off with my foot and pulled myself upward at the same time. I could see Sabina's shadowy form leaning out above me with her hand outstretched. I pulled myself up with brute strength alone, trying to be quiet, until finally I reached the top.

Sabina helped me over the jagged lip and onto the surface of the ledge, which proved to be much wider than I could have hoped. I lay where I was, gasping for air as the excited calls from the searchers grew louder. I could see the reflection of their torches dancing on the rock face above me now as Sabina carefully drew up the rope. Then I felt her probing fingers on my body as she began to work in the darkness on my leg. I could hear her chewing the goldenseal leaves into a paste and smell the acrid stink of it before finally she pressed the result firmly into my wound.

I closed my eyes through it all and said nothing, listening to the pounding of my heart and trying not to concentrate on the pain wracking my body. When Sabina was done, she rewrapped my bandages and lay down beside me as the calls of our pursuers echoed out across the gorge. I felt her hand slide into mine as she nestled her body against me.

Sabina mumbled something into my shoulder—I don't know what—before exhaustion overcame us both and we slept.

19: Feverfew

When dawn broke the next day, I awoke to the distinctive songs of nightjars as they feasted on insects and fluttering moths in the growing light. Sabina was snoring softly beside me, her hair hanging fetchingly over half of her face. I sat up slowly as pain wracked my body and peered over the edge of the ridge. I was relieved to see that there were no signs of our pursuers from the night before. The valley floor was alive with other types of movement, however, as arrogant, shrill jays, odd-looking crossbills, and tiny yellow warblers, as well as reptiles and small mammals, moved through the trees and undergrowth. Sabina muttered something beside me and she clutched at me possessively before starting to snore again. I gently removed her hand and shook her shoulder.

"Sabina?" I whispered. "Wake up."

Sabina's eyes opened and she smiled when she saw me leaning over her. I shifted position on the stone without thinking and had to squash a scream as searing pain shot through my leg. Sabina saw the anguish on my face and she sat up quickly in concern, then carefully unwound the bandage on my leg. She made a face at the putrid smell. My leg looked swollen and angry from below the knee, almost to my thigh. The wound itself was packed with half-chewed goldenseal paste covered in pink and yellow slime. Sabina used her fingers to cautiously remove the paste, constantly dabbing with the filth-covered bandages as pinkish fluid oozed out over the lips of the cut. The skin all around the wound was puckered a strange yellow, with hints of black throughout. I also had a long gash on the outside of my thigh where Laurea's claws had raked me that was crusted over with blood. Sabina put her hand on my forehead, looking worried.

"How bad is it?" I finally asked when she didn't say anything.

"I've seen worse," Sabina answered, not meeting my eyes. "Let me have a look at the other one now." She helped me to take off my cloak, muttering to herself as she inspected my shoulder. "This one isn't as bad as I thought yesterday," she finally said, sitting back on her haunches. "The cut is deep enough, but it's straight and clean, and it doesn't look as though any of the muscles or tendons were severed."

I moved my arm experimentally, careful not to break open the wound again. "Feels pretty good," I said, surprised.

Sabina held up the soiled bandages. "These need to be cleaned. I'm going to find a spring and wash them."

"I'll come with you," I said, starting to get up.

Sabina put her hand on my chest, her eyes flashing with anger. "Are you really this stupid, Hadrack?" She gestured to my leg. "You can't walk on that, let alone climb down from here."

"Of course, I can," I grunted stubbornly, pushing her hand away. I started to rise, then fell backward on my rump, feeling dizzy and disorientated. My leg was screaming at me as though I had just doused it in pitch and then thrust it into a roaring fire.

"Satisfied?" Sabina asked, her hands on her hips. She threw the rope over the ledge and glared at me as she headed down. "Don't do anything foolish while I'm gone, Hadrack. Just stay here and rest. I will be back before you even know it."

I waved to her in defeat, too weak to speak as she disappeared over the edge. I lay back, gasping for air. My face felt on fire, but my body felt ice cold. I started to shake, and I reached for my cloak and drew it over me. I couldn't find a comfortable position lying prone on the rocks, and finally, I pulled myself to the wall, groaning at the pain as my heel dragged across the surface of the ledge.

Our refuge, I saw in the light of day, was no more than ten feet wide, scoured smooth by wind and rain. I looked south, realizing that the ledge ran along the rock face for as far as I could see. At times, the narrow shelf was no more than six or seven inches wide. If we needed to, I figured we could follow it along the gorge while we hunted for the Tapeau tunnel. I snorted in frustration at the idea. Who was I trying to fool? I was in no shape to move right now.

I lay my head back against the stone and closed my eyes. Our only hope was that Sabina could somehow stop the infection in my leg that I could feel burning inside me. I remembered what Baine had looked like after the Cardians had captured us after Gasterny fell. I shuddered. It had taken my friend weeks to recover, and only then because of Haverty the apothecary's skill. As much as Sabina had impressed me over the last few weeks, when it came to medicine, she paled in comparison to the strange apothecary.

Thinking of Baine had not helped my frame of mind any, and I could feel a deep depression taking over me. I had been through so many tight situations already in my life, but this time, I reflected bitterly, things may have gotten the better of me. I thought of Emand laughing happily at my predicament as The Father burned his soul. I angrily shook the vision of that traitorous bastard away as another image arose. It was my father again, but this time he appeared to me as an old man. Gone were his mighty muscles and long brown hair, replaced with a balding pate, a bent back, and stooped shoulders. This was what he would have looked like now, I realized, had he lived.

"So, you are giving up, then?" my father said, his face twisted in disapproval.

"I never said that I was giving up," I snapped, irritated that he, of all people, would think that.

"Yet, there you lie dying and doing nothing to prevent it."

"What would you have me do?" I demanded. "I'm hurt. Can't you see that?"

"All I see is a boy who says I can't, when what he should be saying is, I can."

I waved my hand in annoyance. "What do you know? You don't even exist."

My father leaned forward, and I studied his lined face, marveling at the changes that had taken place. The features that I remembered from my youth lay hidden somewhere within all those cracks and crevices, I knew, yet I couldn't help but feel that I was staring at a stranger. I found the idea oddly amusing. I giggled.

My father frowned in displeasure. "Hadrack," he said. He drew even closer, almost hovering over me. "Listen to me. I do exist."

I shook my head, trying to quell the oddly-pitched cackle coming from my lips. "No, Father. I saw you die. I buried your head, remember?" I wiped tears of mirth and pain from my eyes. "I was too small to bury all of you, so I dug a hole and put your head in it." I paused, blinking up at him in sudden confusion. "How come you still have a head, Father?"

"Hadrack," my father said again, speaking gently. "As long as you live to fulfill your vow, then I live along with you. If you give in to this, then you will not only lose your life, your sister and I will become nothing as well. We will be forgotten and never avenged. Is that what you want?"

My smile died on my lips at the mention of my long-ago vow. I sat up, ignoring the pain and the fever burning along my flesh as I thought furiously. My father was right. The war had made me complacent toward the remaining nine. I couldn't find any of them because of it and I had accepted that fact, allowing myself to get caught up in my oath to Daughter Gernet and the quest for the codex. If I died on this ledge now, then five men I had sworn to kill would live, while my family and I faded into nothingness. I couldn't let that happen. I reached up and grasped my father's hand, surprised at how cold and hard his flesh felt.

"I have lost my way," I said. "I am sorry. Please, forgive me."

My father stared gravely at me. "Swear to me that you will avenge us, Hadrack."

"I swear," I promised.

"No matter what?"

"No matter what," I agreed solemnly. "You have my word."

My father bowed his head, his features becoming blurry as he put his hand on my shoulder. "You truly are the king of the dragonflies and so much more, my son." He smiled sadly as he straightened his crooked back. "Remember, Hadrack, that you must never forget your surroundings. Not everything is obvious at first glance. Remember what I told you."

Then he was gone.

I lay back and closed my eyes again. I must have slept, for I didn't hear Sabina coming until the rope began to grind and twist against the jutting rock spire that she had tied it around. I thrust off my cloak with determination and stood, using the wall to support myself with my injured leg held off the ground several inches. I took a deep breath, then set my foot down and cautiously put weight on it. Crushing pain seared through me and I moaned, but I took the step anyway, absorbing it stubbornly. I took another unsteady step just as Sabina's head appeared over the rock ledge. She saw me standing there and her face registered surprise and alarm.

"Hadrack! What are you doing?"

I didn't answer, concentrating fiercely on staying upright as I leaned over and offered her my hand.

"Have you lost your mind?" Sabina snapped in anger. She ignored my outstretched hand.

"Maybe," I grunted as she pulled herself onto the ledge on her own. I grinned lopsidedly at her. "How would I know?"

Sabina snorted and she wrapped her arms around me. I could feel her entire body shaking with emotion. "You could have fallen to your death," she scolded me. "What were you thinking?"

I held her, grateful for the support as I swayed in her arms like a drunkard. "I was thinking that if I just lie on this ledge all day waiting for the gods to take me," I whispered in her ear. "Then, that is exactly what will happen. If I'm on my feet, they might decide I still have a fighting chance."

"Of course, you have a chance, silly," Sabina said, looking up at me in irritation. "I have more goldenseal and the bandages are clean. As long as we are careful, you will be fine in a few days. Now stop talking like that and let's get those wounds cleaned up and bound again."

I nodded, feeling light-headed as Sabina led me away from the lip. She helped me sit with my back against the wall again, and then she went to work cleaning my leg and adding more goldenseal. I sat through it grimly, determined not to cry out as I watched her delicate hands on me. I thought about mentioning that Malo had mixed the leaves with water and heated the concoction, then I decided to keep my mouth closed. We had no fire and nothing to carry the water in, so why mention it? I stared past her head instead, enjoying the view of the swaying trees and fluttering birds. The western wall of the gorge across lay mostly in darkness still, but the sun was rising rapidly. I watched as the light slowly crawled down the rock inch by inch, fascinated by the steady progression.

"There, all done," Sabina said in satisfaction. She cleaned and rebandaged my shoulder next and then covered me with my cloak when she was done. "How do you feel?"

"Really good," I said, lying.

Sabina tilted her head sideways and she studied me critically. "Are you telling me the truth?"

I smiled wearily and shook my head as I looked away, watching the sunlight glinting off the frozen rocks along the rim of Oasis. Sabina withdrew several long-stemmed white flowers from inside her cloak and began stripping them of leaves.

"Daisy's?" I asked in surprise.

Sabina shook her head. "No, these are called feverfew. They should help you relax and sleep better. Hopefully, it will take away some of the pain, too."

Sabina handed several of the leaves to me and I sniffed them suspiciously. They smelled unpleasantly bitter. I tentatively put one in my mouth and chewed reluctantly, trying not to gag on the taste. I swallowed, making a face as I shook my head. "I can't eat this! Are you trying to kill me?"

"You have to," Sabina insisted. "Your body needs it. Who cares what it tastes like?"

"Says the woman not eating any," I grumbled, picking flecks of the bitter leaf off of my tongue.

"Don't be a fool, Hadrack. This will help, and from the looks of you, you need all the help that you can get."

I knew she was right, of course, much as I hated to admit it to myself. The thought of eating any more of the bitter feverfew turned my stomach, but I needed a clear head more than a content stomach. If there was a chance the flower could help, then I had to try. I tore off another leaf and put it to my mouth, chewing automatically as I absently scanned the ground behind Sabina. A light grey, rocky protrusion caught my eye about fifty feet down from the rim of the gorge opposite us, gleaming as sunlight washed over it. The stone seemed oddly out of place, and I squinted, shading my eyes as I tried to understand what I was seeing. Then I felt a jolt of excitement flow through me.

"Help me up!" I snapped at Sabina, thrusting the cloak aside.

"What? Why?" Sabina asked, looking alarmed at my tone. She peered down into the valley, searching for any threat as I fought to rise.

"Help me up, damn you!" I hissed urgently. "I'll explain everything as soon as I know for sure." I clutched at Sabina as she reluctantly helped me to my feet. "Follow the ledge," I ordered, pointing south as I glanced again across the gorge. The rock was still there, I saw with relief, standing tall and proud, almost mocking me with its sheer perfection. I had been afraid with the fever taking over me that I might have imagined it.

"Hadrack, what is going on?" Sabina asked as I stumbled forward, dragging her with me.

The pain in my leg was gone now, whether taken away by the feverfew or the excitement, I wasn't sure. Either way, I was glad for the respite. We reached a narrow part of the ledge and I went first with my back pressed tightly against the wall. Sabina came close behind me, clutching at me like an over-protective mother.

"How long is Oasis?" I demanded as the ledge began to widen again.

Sabina wrinkled her brows in confusion. "What? Uh, four miles, I think."

"Ha!" I cried, putting the pieces together. "I knew it!"

My leg suddenly gave out beneath me and I stumbled and lost my balance. If not for Sabina, who steadied me, I probably would have fallen over the edge. I grinned at her in thanks. "We're almost there," I promised her.

"Almost where?" Sabina asked in exasperation. "What is going on?"

"My father told me something once," I said. I had no intention of telling her what I was about to say had come from a vision. I think Sabina thought my mind was addled enough as it was right now. I swept my arm out. "He told me to always be aware of my surroundings."

"I don't understand."

"Neither did I until just a few moments ago," I said. "Waldin wrote that his cave was four miles from the Complex, right?" Sabina nodded. "And what is the only other clue that we have?" I asked.

Sabina shrugged. "He could see giant mushrooms from the cave's mouth."

"Exactly," I said in triumph. I smiled and pointed across the gorge. "And what do you see there?"

Sabina turned, her eyes gliding over the trees and rocks. I waited, hoping she would see it on her own, but finally, she just shrugged, looking disappointed. "I see trees and bushes, rocks and hot springs, that's all. No mushrooms."

I laughed, enjoying myself. "I have a riddle for you. When is a mushroom not a mushroom?"

"What?"

"The answer is when it's a giant rock," I whispered. I sighted along my arm, leaning close to her as I pointed across the gorge. "Look there. That tall rock with the rounded head to the right of the crevice. What does that look like to you?"

Sabina knitted her eyebrows. "Well, I suppose it does sort of look like a mushroom," she said doubtfully.

"Of course, it does," I said, waving away her doubt. "It's worn and weathered now, but think what that stone must have looked like hundreds of years ago when Waldin stood here."

"But he specifically said mushrooms, not a single mushroom."

I was ready with an answer to that. I pointed. "Look there, and there, and over there. Those jumbled piles of rocks have to be the other mushrooms Waldin mentioned. They just collapsed over the years until only one was left."

I could see excitement starting to build in Sabina's eyes now as she worked it through. "And we are almost exactly four miles from the Complex," she said in wonder.

"It all makes sense," I said, grateful that she finally understood. "We just assumed when Waldin wrote four miles from the Complex, that he meant outside in the mountains."

The euphoria that I had felt at my discovery was beginning to wear off, and I suddenly felt weak and unwell. I could feel the pain returning with a vengeance in my leg as well, and I sagged against the rock wall, closing my eyes.

"Hadrack?"

I motioned ahead feebly, trying not to concentrate on the heat that I could feel burning across my cheeks and forehead. "Go on," I gasped, fighting for breath. "The cave has to be somewhere close. Find it and come back for me. I need a moment to rest."

Sabina studied me in concern, then she patted my arm and moved away, following the ledge southward. She was gone only a few minutes before she returned, her eyes shining with excitement.

"I've found it, Hadrack! I've found the cave!"

I smiled, trying to focus on her features, but her face was fading in and out strangely. "Don't do that," I mumbled in annoyance.

Then I collapsed as the darkness took me.

20: Waldin's Cave

Dreams. They have always been at the cusp of my awareness. Something barely remembered that quickly flees as consciousness returns and a new day begins. But now, there was no consciousness for me—at least, not the kind that I had been familiar with all my life. I was alternately freezing or raging hot, sometimes both at once, shivering and sweating in torturous tandem. I could hear a woman's voice periodically in the background, murmuring, but the words made no sense to me. I had no idea of my surroundings, or for that matter, if I was even alive.

Was I truly dead? I wondered, knowing that it was a fair question. Perhaps I was, I reflected, for many of the dead I had known in my life had come to see me recently. Some were as they had been, while others, like that bastard reeve, were quite different. The reeve was incredibly tall now, much taller than I remembered he'd been in life. He was still as ugly as a rat's ass, though. I guess some things just can't be fixed. The reeve carried a black cane in his right hand, and he had buttons running down the center of his face. Yes, actual buttons. Big, shiny ones like you would see on a rich man's cloak. It was odd, but far from the strangest thing that I would see in this new world of mine.

"You killed me," the reeve said reproachfully.

I noticed he floated in the air several inches from the ground, making him look even taller, but for some reason, I didn't find anything unusual about that. "You deserved it, you bastard!" I spat back at him. "I would be a farmer now, if not for you."

"Then you should thank me," the reeve said with a haughty sniff. "I rose you out of the filth and shit so that you could brush shoulders with lords and kings." He glared at me, his eyes bulging with indignation. "Where is my thanks, you ungrateful wolf pup?"

I grasped my sword. "Come here, you bastard, and I'll show you gratitude. I killed you once, and by The Mother, I'll gladly do it again."

"With that?" the reeve smirked.

I glanced at my hand in confusion. I held Angry's bridle, not a sword. I heard a whinny behind me and I turned, falling to the ground as Angry reared over me, iron-shod hooves aimed for my head, fire shooting from his nostrils. I cried out and lifted my arms to ward him off, and then he disappeared in a wall of smoke just as something warm and fluffy landed in my lap. It bleated loudly and I looked down in surprise. A lamb lay on me, staring up at me with dewy eyes. Its white ears stuck out to either side comically.

Shana appeared, cooing as she plucked the lamb away. "Ah, there you are, little one." She smiled at me serenely as she snuggled the lamb to her breasts. "Are you hungry, Hadrack?"

I nodded dumbly, unable to speak.

"I thought that you might be," Shana said knowingly. She hummed to herself as she stroked the lamb with love, then lifted a knife and slit its throat with a vicious slash. Blood squirted, drenching me as the reeve floated nearby, bobbing his head in approval.

"Why!?" I shouted in horror.

"Why what, Hadrack?"

Shana and the lamb were gone now, replaced by Betania, who had died in Gasterny.

"You're alive," I whispered, my voice cracking with emotion.

"Am I?" Betania said with a melancholy smile. Her features changed, looking at me now with reproof in her eyes. "You never kissed me, Hadrack. Why?"

"You were just a child and my friend," I protested.

"And that is all I'll ever be."

Betania turned away with tears on her cheeks, only to be replaced by Ania.

"Are you too tired to rut, Hadrack?" she asked coyly.

I could only stare in horror. Ania held her head in her hands, using her fingers to make the lips move. I screamed, closing my eyes as the reeve laughed.

More people came to visit me after that. An endless parade of the dead and the living. Einhard with his green eyes and dashing smile. My brother, Lallo, demanding that I return his Pair Stone. My sister, Jeanna, weeping and naked, her throat slit from ear to ear. Jebido with a missing nose and Baine, who sloshed past me angrily, his clothing dripping wet while dark seaweed writhed like snakes in his hair. Even my younger brother, who had died as a babe, appeared, riding a giant, grinning wolf. On and on it went as I thrashed and moaned, trying to escape the dungeon of my own mind.

Finally, I felt a hand on my forehead and heard the soft, soothing words of a woman. I calmed and opened my eyes to see Shana leaning over me. I recoiled, remembering the lamb, but Shana just shushed me, her expression filled with kindness. That's what the lamb had thought too, a part of my brain shouted at me in panic. I reluctantly thrust my unease aside, allowing my body to relax. Shana would never harm me. She loved me and I knew that I was safe with her. A fire crackled somewhere nearby. We were in her bedchambers in Calban. Shana stood, wearing a flowing dress of red made from Cardian capes. She slipped the dress off her milky-white shoulders and the wind took it, whisking it away as she stood naked before me.

I heard a lewd whistle of appreciation and I glared at the floating, leering reeve. "This isn't for your eyes, you bastard!" I shouted furiously.

The reeve had the grace to look embarrassed and he quickly undid the buttons on his face. His flesh drooped to either side obscenely, hiding his eyes, and I screamed in horror at the sight. Then he disappeared into nothingness.

"There, there," Shana whispered to me. "Everything is going to be all right."

Shana lifted the bedclothes and slid into bed beside me. I was naked, and she took my manhood in her hand, stroking it urgently.

"I love you," I said. "Marry me."

"I love you, too, Hadrack," Shana replied, smiling as she mounted me and guided me inside her. "And, of course, I will marry you."

I awoke to a pleasant feeling of warmth and contentment. I could hear birds chirping faintly somewhere and I sat up, wiping the crust from my eyes. I looked around. Stone walls surrounded me, rubbed smooth and sparkling with jagged purple and white veins embedded within them. I was in Waldin's cave, I knew. I looked down at myself. I was bare-chested, with a clean bandage wrapped tightly around my shoulder. I flexed my arm. The wound felt stiff, but there was little pain. Two cloaks had been used to cover me, I saw, and they were now bunched around my waist and legs. I shifted them aside. I was naked underneath. I gingerly ran my hand along my injured leg, stopping at the thick bandaging. There was pain, but not nearly as much as I had expected. The redness to either side of the bandage was gone as well, I noted, though the skin was still mottled and unhealthy looking.

I shifted my weight, realizing that I was sitting on a thick bed of leaves and grasses. A fire crackled in the center of the cave, burning feebly with a thin tendril of smoke rising to the ceiling. I peered upward. A circular hole in the rock directly over the fire conveniently allowed the smoke out. I twisted to look behind me and my arm hit a brown ceramic bowl sitting by the bedding. Pale liquid sloshed around inside and I sniffed the contents cautiously. I wrinkled my nose at the strong smell of piss. My clothing lay stacked neatly beside the bed, with the rips from the battle crudely repaired. I heard footsteps approaching from the east as Sabina appeared from a passage that I had overlooked, her arms laden with twigs and branches.

She paused in surprise when she saw me, and then her face lit up in delight. "Hadrack, you're awake!"

"And thirsty," I said, the words sounding odd and raspy.

"There's a bowl beside you," Sabina said over her shoulder as she dropped the wood by the fire.

I grimaced. "I'm not that thirsty."

"Not that one, darling," Sabina said with a short laugh. "This one."

She stooped and produced a second bowl half-filled with clear water and handed it to me. I was still trying to process the fact that she had called me darling as I drank greedily.

"How long have I been asleep?" I asked between gulps.

"Six days," Sabina said as she hunched down beside me. I gawked at her in surprise, barely noticing as she felt my forehead. "Your fever is gone. That's good news." Sabina sat back and absently stroked away a few strands of hair that had fallen into my eyes.

"Six days," I grunted in disbelief. I brushed Sabina's hand aside, irritated for some reason by her intimacy. "You brought me here all by yourself?"

"Of course," Sabina said with a shrug. "Who else is there? Are you hungry? There are still some biscuits left. I caught a nice fat rabbit this morning and was planning to cook it later. I can start now if you wish that as well."

I nodded, accepting the hard biscuits as I tore into them. I was starving. Sabina began skinning the rabbit with Malo's sword while I ate and took a closer look around. The cave was circular, with a smooth wall jutting out to the east where Sabina had come from, blocking my view of the entrance. What might have once been a bedframe lay in the northern corner of the cave, with a sagging table covered in spiderwebs and mold sitting against the back wall. More ceramic bowls, many of them broken, were piled near the remains of the bed. Waldin's bed, I thought. Waldin!

I turned back to Sabina. "The codex?" I asked anxiously.

Sabina glanced up from her work, her face serious. "You are not going to be happy, Hadrack."

I groaned. "Don't tell me it's ruined?"

Sabina shook her head. She wiped her greasy hands on her dress, then got up silently and went to the table. I hadn't noticed in the gloom that something was sitting on the tabletop. I felt my heart start to quicken. Sabina came back and she stood over me, not meeting my eyes as she handed me a cloth bundle. I took it, afraid to ask as I unwrapped the moldy cloth, revealing four thick scrolls inside. I looked up at her in surprise.

"I only took a glance at them," Sabina said with a shrug. "But they don't look like what we came here for."

I stared at the scrolls in disappointment. We had been through so much, lost so much, and now it looked like it had been all for nothing. "What is it, then, if not the codex?" I asked.

Sabina went back to work on the rabbit. "A journal as far as I could tell."

"A journal?" I frowned. "Whose?"

"Waldin's," Sabina answered. "I've looked everywhere in the cave, but those four scrolls are all there is."

I examined one of the scrolls bleakly. The fennels on the ends were made of heavily-tarnished silver, with the faded likeness of a lion's head on each side. Someone had stamped the number three into the head of one of the lions. I glanced at the other scrolls. Each of them had a number stamped into it as well. I picked up the first one and gently slid it open. The words inside were faded, but precise and neat, written on parchment sections weaved together with thread. The text ran horizontally rather than vertically.

I began to read.

Son Philap hates me! There can be no other explanation for his callousness toward me. I believe his hatred stems from jealousy, which, while understandable, does in no way change my estimation of him. He is a stupid, slovenly man whose only purpose in life, it seems—other than pointing out what he believes are my shortcomings—is to eat, defecate and belch, all in no particular order. Were I not possessed of a superior intellect and patient demeanor, I would long ago have gone over his head and made my feelings known to the First Son himself. I have not done so, however, because I believe Son Philap's ultimate purpose is to discredit me in the First Son's eyes. Leveling a claim of bias without proof would undoubtedly do just that. Oh, he is a crafty one, is Son Philap, but I am so much smarter than he, and I refuse to be baited. I am like the spider spinning its web, content to lay back as my enemies ensnare themselves ever deeper while I wait patiently in the shadows, preparing to pounce. Always the spider, never the prey, is the motto that I hold most dear.

I looked up, groaning with disappointment as Sabina skewered the skinned rabbit and placed it over the fire. She was right. This wasn't the codex, but instead appeared to be the rantings of a petty man embroiled in petty politics.

"Well?" Sabina asked.

I picked the other scrolls up one by one and quickly scanned a few words here and there, then I shook my head bitterly. "It doesn't look promising."

Sabina turned the rabbit, looking unconcerned. "Wait until you read it all, first. The codex might still be somewhere in all of that."

"We don't have time," I grunted. "We have to get moving. Malo and the others must be beside themselves with worry by now."

"Not on that leg," Sabina said firmly. "You are going to need at least another day or two before you can walk well enough." She pointed to the scrolls. "Time that will allow you to rest and read."

I took a deep breath and fingered the scrolls unenthusiastically. Judging by the little that I had read from Waldin already, I was confident that everything in front of me was simply an exercise in his own hubris. I turned back to the first scroll and skimmed over the writing, pausing at a passage that caught my eye.

How dare he! The smug, arrogant bastard! How dare he chastise me for a momentary slip, when I and everyone else in the Complex are acutely aware of his own infidelity. The sheer audacity of the man, to threaten me with expulsion. The woman was a common trollop, of no interest or concern to me. Can I help it if the fires below rage in me? Of course not. Am I not a man? Of course I am, born by the First Pair's grace with a man's needs and desires that sometimes leave me breathless, squeezing and squeezing until I yield and give in. To think that fat bastard just sat there, looking down his red-veined nose at me and demanded I beg forgiveness from the whore. Me! Beg someone like that! "Expulsion or talk to the girl," he'd said in that timid voice of his. How dare he! It's a wonder I can write these words at all, inflamed as I am. What will I do? It's a question that bears thought. I like neither option, yet I must choose one or the other. I must think about it. Yes, that is what I must do. I will consider carefully, and then I will act.

Always the spider, never the prey!

I rolled the scroll onward, interested despite myself, to know what Waldin had done. The next entry was a meaningless rant and contained nothing useful about the girl, so I moved to the following one.

So, the fat bastard thought he had me, did he? Ah, but what joy it was to see the look on his face when that bitch went to him, weeping and kissing his feet during public confession, begging for forgiveness. Son Philap had expected to see me on my knees at confession instead, but that didn't happen. Instead, I, Waldin of Brethelmire, stood in line with the other Sons-In-Waiting and watched as his carefully prepared trap for me, prostrated herself before him. How did I do it? It was surprisingly simple. I decided upon reflection that if the problem at hand could not be solved by conventional means, then it would be best to adapt and look at the issue unconventionally. One golden chalice removed from the monastery at night and placed in the girl's room was all it took. Not to mention a gentle nudge to the Complex guards on where to look. Fat Son Philap had little choice but to banish the girl, and with her any chance that he could use her to his advantage against me. The sheer brilliance of it has left me giddy with the need for release, but I know I must be cautious and control myself lest someone come by and see. If only I had somewhere to go. Somewhere private where I can do as I wish, with whomever I wish. I must dwell on it. There has to be a solution.

Always the spider, never the prey!

I glanced at the remains of the bed behind me with distaste. I had a good idea now what had gone on in this cave long ago. I skimmed through the rest of the scroll and reached for the second when Sabina told me the food was ready. I stood, resisting her offered help, pleased to find only mild pain when I put weight on my leg. I hobbled toward the fire, accepting Sabina's hand this time as I sat down stiffly.

"You had me worried," Sabina said, offering me a hunk of steaming meat on the point of Malo's sword. "You raved like a madman for days, screaming and smashing your fists on the floor for hours at a time."

I ate, ignoring the heat from the steaming meat as my stomach rumbled in appreciation. The meager biscuits had done little to appease my hunger. "I remember," I said, thinking of the floating reeve and Shana with her little lamb. I shook my head. "I still find it hard to believe that we have been here for six days already."

"I know," Sabina said. She glanced at the scrolls. "I was thinking that once you get those to Malo, we can go to my village. It's only a few days from here. I want to tell my brother about us. We can send word to my parents in Springlight and they can meet us there."

"Us?" I said, rabbit halfway to my lips. "What do you mean by us?"

"Don't be shy, Hadrack," Sabina said as she cut more meat. She chuckled and leaned forward, winking at me. "It's a little late for that now. We'll wait for my mother and father to return, then we will marry in the village square. The house is small, but with your help, I'm sure my father can add to it."

I stared at Sabina in astonishment, the food forgotten. "Married? What are you talking about?"

Sabina smiled at me happily. "We discussed all this, remember?" I looked at her blankly. "While we made love, silly," she prodded, rolling her eyes. "You asked me to marry you. You can't have forgotten that."

I just stared at her. I could feel a blackness coming over me and I had to force myself not to move or say anything. My dream about Shana had happened, only it hadn't been the woman I loved with me. It had been Sabina. She had taken advantage of me when I was at my weakest, I realized with growing fury. I had been out of my mind with fever and she had used me like a cheap whore. I felt my heart turn cold with anger and I knew the girl's very life was at stake as I tried to control myself. I could hear the reeve chuckling away in my head at the irony. Was there any difference between what he had done to my sister and what Sabina had done to me?

"Hadrack?" Sabina asked, looking unfazed. "Are you all right?"

I threw my food down. My appetite was suddenly gone. "What is wrong with you?" I growled.

Sabina drew her head back in surprise. "Wrong? What do you mean? Nothing is wrong with me. What's wrong with you?"

I stood carefully and looked down at her. "If you don't know," I said in disgust, "then there's no hope for you." I limped toward my bedding, my only thought to make it there without wrapping my hands around Sabina's pale throat.

"Hadrack, stop this silliness," Sabina chided from behind me. "Come back here and eat. We can talk about this. We don't have to get married as soon as we get home, if that's what is bothering you. We can wait a month or two."

I shut my ears to Sabina's words, sitting on the leaves and grass with my back to her. I was still sorely tempted to snap her neck, so I picked up the second scroll and unraveled it, preferring to be in Waldin's world right now, rather than my own. At least in his world, nobody died.

I killed them! I can't believe how easy it was. They thought they were smarter than me, those two. Try to extort me, will they? Ha! I showed them. They insisted we meet at the mountain's base at some beggarly inn near the new garrison being built. Bring the gold they had demanded, or we'll go to the First Son and tell him what you did. Oh, I brought them gold, all right. Just not the kind they were hoping to receive. A quick dash into the armory, then one of the ceremonial daggers with the golden hilt up my sleeve, and there you have it. Gold for two. Ha-ha! They were confident they had me when I walked into that stinking room, all smug and condescending. They should have realized who they were dealing with and known better. Unlucky for them, I guess. The day I'm bested by two commoners like those scum, is the day they put me in the ground. The big fellow didn't even see it coming—standing there with his muscular arms and bad teeth. He screamed like a girl when the knife first went in, writhing on the bed and begging for mercy. It was the most disgraceful display of cowardice that I've ever had the misfortune to witness. I had to stab the bastard at least five more times before he finally quit blubbering and had the good grace to die. The girl was another matter, though. I took my time with her. Luckily, the inn turned out to be a rotting cesspool filled with avarice and debauchery. The kind of place where screams are as commonplace as breaking wind and belching. The perfect harborage to conceal my deed. That was three days ago now, and I'm still reveling in the thrill of it all. I've been aflame with need both day and night ever since, so have taken to walking Oasis after dark each night, hidden from prying eyes so that I can relieve my disquiet in privacy. Plodding through bushes with all manner of creatures slithering and grunting around me is not what I would have wished for, but it's all there is for now, so it must suffice. I have set my mind to finding a solution to this inconvenient problem of mine, and I will not rest until I have.

Always the spider, never the prey!

I paused as I heard Sabina get up, already preparing an angry rebuke if she spoke of marriage again.

"I'm going for more water, Hadrack. I won't be gone long, darling."

I grunted without looking at her, relieved that she was leaving. What Sabina had done to me was unforgivable, yet at the same time, she had saved my life twice already on this cursed mountain. First, with Emand, then again, by bringing me back to health. That bore some weight that couldn't be discounted, helping to even the scales somewhat. But even if she saved me a thousand more times, I would never be able to get past how she knowingly corrupted me for her own selfish purpose. I heard her walk away and I relaxed as her footfalls diminished.

I turned back to the scroll, frowning with distaste. With every passage I read, my dislike for Waldin was growing, but even so, I was curious to see what the final result of all his scheming would be.

I have found love! There is no other way to describe what I feel inside my breast. Her name is Verica, a Daughter-In-Waiting newly arrived from the savage southern lands. She is young still, a child really, but already showing the promise of the curvaceous and bewitching woman that she will become. Her hair is golden blonde and shimmers like the brightest star, and her eyes are the strangest green. Captivating and intoxicating like lustrous jewels, with the shimmer of innocence and something more residing in their depths. I cannot take my gaze off her, and I feel my heart palpitating every time she is near. If she were to ever speak to me, I expect that the poor, over-worked organ would surge from my chest in a momentous eruption. But, if that is to be my fate, then it is one which I will gladly accept, if only to have a heartbeat's worth of her attention. I shiver with anticipation each day before prayers ever since she arrived on our mountain. Not for the chance to have pleasant discourse with The Mother and The Father anymore, but only to hear Verica sing. Her voice, ah, it is a marvel to listen to. The sweetness of it makes me weep for pure joy, while the strength and character of her timbre fills me with confidence and hope. She has not noticed me yet. I keep in the shadows, watching, listening, like the patient spider that I am. But one day, an opportunity will present itself, and I will be ready.
Always the spider, never the prey!

I paused in my reading and stood, stretching my stiff back. Sabina hadn't returned yet, and I was beginning to get an uneasy feeling that something was wrong. I limped along the cavern until I rounded the outcrop to find myself in a narrow, darkened corridor. I could see faint light ahead, more a crack than anything that might resemble a cave opening. I frowned, perplexed. Was something blocking the cave mouth? I used my hand to brace myself on the cold rock until I reached the end, then I shook my head in surprise. No wonder Waldin's cave had never been discovered. It had been in direct view from the gorge the entire time, but no one could tell. A solid rock wall protruded out from my right, with a second wall jutting out from my left about two feet further out, overlapping the first. I had to twist and turn to get around them, walking sideways until finally, I was outside. I paused on a short ledge overlooking the gorge as bright sunlight hit my face. It was well past midday, I realized. I'd never thought to ask Sabina when I awoke if it was day or night outside.

I heard sudden voices and I shrank back into the shadows, then cautiously peered around the stone shielding me. Men were moving in a line through the trees along the gorge's floor—men with dogs. I cursed, wondering what had happened to Sabina. Finally, I turned away and headed back. I was safe where I was, I knew, unless those men down there had captured the girl, that is. Would she tell? I shrugged. If she did, I would know soon enough.

Sabina had taken Malo's sword with her, which left me with few options to defend myself. I limped over to the remnants of Waldin's bed and rummaged through it, finally making do with a mostly-rotted plank that looked as though it would shatter at the slightest touch. It was better than nothing. I lay back down with the plank close to hand and began to read again.

Now he's gone too far. How dare he! First, I am overlooked once again to ascend to the position of Son. And now, I've been relegated to sifting through dusty tombs and maps in the monastery library. Sons-In-Waiting far my junior in chronology and acumen have been presented the black robe, while I wither away unnoticed over meaningless manuscripts like some eccentric, bygone relic. It's infuriating. How can I ever aspire to rise to First Son, if the one man standing in my way won't advance me my black robe? It's jealousy, I say, nothing but outrageous, bald-faced jealousy. I won't stand for it any longer. My honor and pride are at stake now. Either Son Philap goes, or I go. The Complex cannot contain the both of us. But how to do it? That is the question I must wrap my mind around. I must deliberate on this course I've charted very carefully, for killing the sniveling dimwit on my own—while a truly delicious idea—will have repercussions that may point back to me. I cannot allow that. I must find another way. But how?

    Always the spider, never the prey!

    Cardians! I had heard tales of these foul creatures but had given them little thought until now. They came on Pilgrimage last week, at least twenty or more, and some have decided to stay longer as they immerse themselves in the lore of the mountain. It is quite fortuitous for me that they did. I met one of these Cardians yesterday, a surly, unpleasant sort, who goes by the ridiculous name of Furt. He is a hulking brute, but appears just crafty enough to get the job done, though I find his churlish demeanor highly offensive. He has agreed—for a hefty price—to eliminate my foe, opening the door so that I might finally obtain the black robe that is my due. This Furt has demanded a princely sum for his services, which of course, I do not have, but he's too stupid to understand that. I gave him several gold coins that I found on the frozen body of some hapless Pilgrim, with the assurance that he'd be paid the balance after the deed has been done. Ha! We'll see about that.

    Always the spider, never the prey!

    I rolled the scroll to read more, but mold had spread along the parchment at the end of the text, leaving only a few lines here and there legible.

    I have found a safe haven, away from prying eyes. One which could only be—

    Verica is everything and more that I could have—

Oh, how I pine for the days of Son Philap, may his soul burn for all eternity. It has been a year since the loathsome Son left this world, and in that time, I've come to realize that his replacement, Son Jaynis, is, if it's possible, even blinder to my brilliance than—

That was all. Everything else was gone. I picked up the third scroll and unraveled it, my heart surging at the first words to greet my eyes.

I have made a momentous discovery! It is hard to comprehend just how prodigious this discovery is, even for someone of my advanced intelligence. The vastness of what I have learned takes my breath away, and I know I must guard this secret with my life until I decide what to do. I have found a codex within the monastery. A unique, wonderous codex that I am convinced was fated to end up in my hands all along. I don't know how it had come to fall behind the shelving in the library, lost from casual eyes these hundreds of years, but it's mine now. What I have gleaned from the words inside has the power to bring down all that we know. Should I burn it? It's a tempting thought, to be sure. Doing so, I know, would save both sides of the House profound embarrassment and protracted grief, should the connivance perpetrated on us all become known. But if I do that, then what? Toil within the monastery forever, waiting for my black robe that might never materialize, until finally my fingers cramp with arthritis and my back is twisted like a hook? No, that won't do at all. For now, I've hidden the codex inside another book in the library. Lately, I've had the uncomfortable sensation that I'm being watched, so I must be cautious. Perhaps it's just paranoia about Verica and has nothing to do with the codex? I'm not sure. We have been rendezvousing each night in the cave, glorying in each others' bodies, and doing all manner of unspeakable things. I have never been so happy in all my life, yet I am terrified of being found out. Not enough to stop, though. No, never that. I cannot stop, even if my life depended on it, which it just may. Verica's allure is too strong, and I am too weak. I will see her tonight and will tell her of the codex. Together, she and I will figure out what to do.

Always the spider, never the prey!

I realized I had been holding my breath the entire time that I'd been reading. I let it out slowly, noisily, trying to still the excitement inside me. Hours had gone by, but I gave it little thought. I wasn't even remotely tired. I had slept for six straight days, after all. I picked up the last scroll and read onward eagerly.

I have a particular gift, one that, I believe, should have propelled me long ago far above my current, lowly station. Others do not seem impressed by it, however, including Son Jaynis, which conclusively proves my theory that the man is an incompetent fool and a simpleton. I was born the fourth and, I daresay, most unwelcome child of a minor lord. Which in and of itself alone, could hardly be deemed worthy of comment. But I was different than other children. By the time I was five and had begun my lessons in earnest, it quickly became apparent that whatever I read could, upon request, be recited back perfectly, word for word. At first, it was simple nursery rhymes, but, as my reading skills increased, so did my abilities to recollect the written word. I became so adept at this remembrance that my father, who was usually a serious man with little time for children, would plant me on a stool to entertain his guests. I was eager for any attention from my father back then—I can't for the life of me imagine why now—so I indulged him and performed my so-called oddity like a well-trained monkey, to the obvious delight of everyone present. Which brings me to my point. I have begun the laborious task of copying the hidden codex word for word simply from memory. I believe that a storm is brewing on the horizon, and I must be prepared to seize the moment when it does. Twice now, I've come back to my room after prayers to find that it has been ransacked. Oh, not so that the casual observer might notice, of course. But I am so much more than that, and I know what has transpired. I was wise to hide the codex where I did, but sooner or later, it may fall into the wrong hands and disappear forever. Therefore, I will store the copy of the original codex here in my sanctuary, along with these priceless records of my struggles.

Someday, I believe, these eloquent words written by my hand will be studied widely, as the great minds of the day try and undoubtedly fail, to interpret my brilliance.

Always the spider, never the prey!

I snorted and rolled my eyes. Waldin was long dead, and I was glad of that fact, but his ego was alive and well in my hands. I didn't relish it, but I knew that I had to press on with his story on the off chance that he did mention the codex's location. Occasionally while I read, I'd wondered about Sabina, but I guessed if the men outside hadn't come for me by now, that meant they probably never would. Hopefully, the girl was all right and was waiting for an opportunity to return to the cave unseen. There was nothing for me to do but wait, so I stood and threw more wood on the fire, brightening the cave, then began to read the next passage.

Disaster! I am being transferred to that blight on the landscape, Gandertown. A place so foul and dirty, even the rats refuse to enter. What will I do? The codex copy is finally complete, bound and written on sheepskin just like the original so expertly that I doubt anyone other than myself could tell them apart. Yet, what good will it do me now? I have still not formulated a proper plan on how best to use the copy. But that must wait for the time being, as I must leave my hallowed sanctuary in two days, and, even worse, leave my sweet Verica behind. The indignities to my person continue, as I'm to travel—by foot no less—to the burgeoning library in Gandertown, where I've been instructed to organize its expansion. It's not enough that Son Jaynis wasted my talents all these years, having me move long-obsolete books and maps around, now I must do the same hundreds of miles away in a strange and barbaric city. The degradation that I've suffered at the hands of those who think themselves above me has become insufferable. I am tempted to refuse the assignment, but that will leave me open to banishment if I do. Something, I have no doubt, Son Jaynis would gleefully approve. I must plan how to use the codex to my advantage. But how? I must think about it.

Always the spider, never the prey.

This will be my last entry for some time. I journey to Gandertown in the morning and dare not bring the scrolls or either copy of the codex with me. Verica has stunned me by shunning her grey robe and shearing her hair. She will be free from the clutches of the Daughters in a week, once the First Daughter arrives in Halas and approves her resignation. I cannot say enough about how grateful I am to have met a woman such as she. I intend to ask for her hand in marriage, but only when I have obtained all the power and renown that I justly deserve. I will return to the Complex as soon as I possibly can, the gods willing. The library expansion in Gandertown is already well underway, and I pray that once I arrive, the organization of said institute will be mercifully quick and trouble-free. Let it be so, for already I feel a keening of loss for this place in my breast. Until my return, remember:
Always the spider, never the prey!

I muttered in disappointment as I got to the end of the scroll. That was it? There was no more? I paused. There was another inscription, I saw, written sideways that I had failed to notice pinched up against the roller. The writing was done in a different style than Waldin's. I carefully peeled the parchment paper back and began to read eagerly.

My dearest love, Waldin,

If you are reading this, then you have returned from Gandertown and are now aware that I have left the mountain. It has been over a year since you departed. A year in which I have labored under the strict eyes of Daughter Lucey. I have spent every day since you left thinking of you and wishing that I could feel your arms around me once more. The First Daughter, as you no doubt are aware, refused my resignation. She did not explain her reasoning for this, much as I pleaded with her. Instead, I was indoctrinated into what she referred to as my re-education. A term that I have grown to despise. Each night after lessons and chores, I was locked up in a cell alongside other malcontents like myself.

Yes, there are more of us. Seven others, to be precise—both men and women—who have lost their belief in the ways of The Mother and The Father. I have been careful, but I trust these people and have told them what we learned from the codex—though I made no mention of the tome itself. I hope you approve, my sweet Waldin, as I have been so lonely and needed to speak with other like-minded souls. I have waited impatiently for your return this past year, but I realized recently that I could not spend another moment bathing in the lies and hypocrisy that the House has become. And so, we eight have broken out tonight and plan momentarily to escape through the tunnel in Oasis. They will be hunting for us, and if they find us, I know they will kill us all.

I have risked much to come to your precious cave tonight and write these words, but I could not let you wonder what had become of me. The thought of the torment that not knowing my fate would cause you was just too horrible for me to contemplate. To go north is death, so we will be fleeing south, past the Kingdom of the Flins to the place where my mother was born. They will never find us there. I have drawn a map below of a special place where my mother's tribe worships. I will go there every day, waiting for your arrival. As for the codex itself, I have decided to take it with me. Please do not be angry with me about this, dear Waldin. I am fearful that—the True God forbid it—if you do not return to Oasis for some reason, the codex might be discovered and its secret destroyed. Rest assured, I will guard it with my life until it is in your hands once more. Be safe, my love, and come to me!

Yours in love and faith,

Verica

I sat back, reeling. Verica had taken the codex, which was surprising enough, but what had hit me like a punch in the stomach was that I recognized the drawing she had left behind. It was crudely done, true, yet good enough to make out a flat landscape surrounded by thick forests. Tall, shaft-like rocks stood at equal intervals around a stone square in the middle of the clearing. Smaller circles of stones lay on the ground some distance away from the base of the shafts. Ania had described this very place to me long ago. I lowered the scroll in wonder.

I was looking at the Ascension Grounds of the Piths.

21: The Markhor

I had only moments to reflect on what I had learned before I heard footsteps coming from the east. I stood, picking up the rotten plank, then relaxed as Sabina appeared, looking dirty and disheveled.

"What happened?" I asked, gruffer than I had intended. I was still angry with her and it showed in my voice.

"House Agents," Sabina answered with distaste. I noticed her sleeve was torn and stained crimson with dried blood. "I don't know how they know we are here, but they do."

"Let me see that," I said, concerned despite my anger at the amount of blood.

"It's nothing," Sabina responded, waving me away. "Just a scratch from some bushes that I had to hide in." She sat down by the fire as I brought her the remainder of the water. I watched as she tore a section of material off of her sleeve and dabbed it into the bowl, then began to clean the wound methodically. She paused and glanced up at me meaningfully. "The House Agents have set up camp about a half-mile from here. There must be at least thirty of them."

"Which means they haven't finished looking for us," I said grimly. Sabina nodded her head in agreement, then went back to her task. "Did you find the Tapeau tunnel while I raved with fever?" I asked.

Sabina snorted. "Of course I did, darling. It's about three hundred yards to the south of us." She looked up and smiled at me. "Just as obvious as our love."

I took a deep breath, deciding not to take the bait. Sabina and I needed each other right now, and I knew it would be best for both of us if I ignored any comments like the one she had just made and simply humored her. Once we were free of Oasis and the mountain, I would find a way to contact Malo and the others, then take Sabina to her village. Not to marry her, of course, but to deliver her to her brother safely and be free of her.

I started to pace, thinking about what Sabina had told me. The House Agents making camp meant that they were determined to locate us—which, being House Agents, also meant that they would find us eventually if we remained where we were. My leg wasn't where I'd like it to be, but it would have to do. We had to leave.

"We go now," I said decisively. "While most of them are asleep."

Sabina sighed. "I knew you were going to say that." She studied me critically. "Do you think you can make it?"

"There is only one way to find out," I said as I put on my cloak.

I stuffed Waldin's scrolls inside my clothing as Sabina gathered her things, then I followed her as we made our way outside. The sky was heavily overcast, with no hint of the moon or stars to be seen. Perfect, I thought as Sabina pressed her lips to my ear.

"The best way down is twenty feet to the south," she whispered. "Stay close to me and hug the wall until I tell you to stop. The ledge gets pretty narrow in places."

Lowering myself down by our sack rope would be quicker, I knew, but it also had the potential to be noisy if I slipped or dislodged small stones along the way. Sound echoes loudly in a gorge at night. Sabina and I decided we would do better to take the route that she had been using these last six days. The stones there, she told me, were laid out like giant jumbled steps, flat and stable, leading all the way down to the floor of the gorge. The key would be to make sure we took our time and were as quiet as possible. I was sure that the House Agents would have watchmen around their camp, and I didn't want them to be alerted to our movements. The descent down the mountain would be difficult enough in its own right, without having to elude House Agents the entire way as well.

We headed out with our backs pressed tightly to the stone wall as we carefully shuffled our feet along in the darkness. I could see very little and trusted in Sabina's familiarity with the ledge to lead while I held her arm blindly. My leg started to ache within moments, but it was a dull, steady throbbing that, while annoying, seemed manageable.

"This should be about right," Sabina finally whispered. She squatted and leaned forward, probing over the edge of the rock ledge. "Yes, this is the place." She worked my boots off and handed them to me. "The first drop is about four feet down. It gets easier after that. I'll position you in the right spot, then, when you are ready, you jump. All right?"

"Fair enough," I said softly, steeling myself for the pain that I knew was coming.

I moved forward with Sabina's guidance and sat down on the lip of the rock. I pictured the landing in my head as the light wind toyed with my hair. I needed to be quiet, land on the balls of my feet, and keep my balance all at the same time. A challenging task, considering my wound, but it had to be done. At best, I would make a muffled thud when I landed. At worst, well, I decided I didn't want to imagine that.

"Good luck, my love," Sabina whispered, rubbing my arm affectionately.

I growled low in my chest at her in irritation, then took a deep breath and pushed myself out into nothingness. I was airborne for a heartbeat, dropping through the still night before my heels slapped hard against the unseen, cold stone beneath them. I bent my knees at the impact, wobbling back and forth as pain fired along my leg. Somehow I managed to not only keep my balance, but remain silent doing so as well. I waited for a count of five, letting the pain wash over me, then I looked up, just able to discern Sabina's shadowy form against the darker rock behind her.

"I'm all right," I whispered.

"Move to your left about five feet," Sabina called out softly.

I did as she asked, then waited as I heard a faint rustling from above before she landed quietly on the stone nearby. The next drop was an easy two feet, then three more of varying heights, none more than three feet, before the final one to the gorge floor. We paused to rest on some rounded rocks while we donned our boots again. Other than the usual night cries of forest animals, and the ever-present drone of insects, all seemed peaceful. It appeared our descent had gone undetected.

Five minutes later, we were on our feet again, following the gorge's wall until we came to the Tapeau tunnel. We crouched in some bushes and I studied the entrance suspiciously. It seemed hard to imagine that the tunnel had been left unguarded. Finally, I saw a brief flash of movement in the shadows to one side. I peered at that spot without blinking, examining every inch. Movement again! This time I was able to discern the shape of a man leaning his back against the rock wall behind him. He was scratching at his neck where some insect had undoubtedly bitten him. A House Agent, judging by the outline of the man's square helmet. I turned my attention to the other side of the entrance. Sure enough, there was a second man there, hidden within the gloom of a tree.

I pressed my lips to Sabina's ear. "I think there are only two of them." Sabina nodded, her hair tickling my nose as I fought the urge to sneeze. "I want you to circle to the south, then get their attention and draw them to me. I'll handle it from there."

"I can help," Sabina protested.

I shook my head. "Not this time. It's dark and I might hit you by accident. Now go."

Sabina hesitated, her eyes searching mine, then finally she pecked me on the cheek and disappeared in a faint rustle of branches. I crouched even lower, grasping Malo's sword as I ran over in my head what I needed to do. Be quick, be strong, but above all else, I told myself, be quiet.

Long minutes went by, and I could feel my injured leg straining from remaining crouched where I was. Then I heard something, a soft mewling noise coming from the south, sounding much like an injured animal might, though I was sure it was no animal. I could hear the two House Agents muttering to one another, and I tensed as the cry came again, this time much closer to me. The men spoke at length, then a dark form detached from the shadows under the tree and moved cautiously forward. Perfect, I thought as the man drew closer. It would be much easier and safer to deal with one of them at a time.

The bushes moved near me and I sensed, rather than saw Sabina slithering like a snake along the valley floor until she was past me.

She made the injured cry again, this time pitched lower, but sounding more urgent, with a pitiful rattling at the end that made me shake my head in admiration. If I hadn't known it was Sabina, I would have been convinced I was listening to an animal in its death throes.

The House Agent came on, grunting as he hacked at the underbrush with his longsword. He stopped less than five feet from me, the sounds of his breathing loud in the sudden stillness. I could smell the stink of his unwashed body and even caught a whiff of the onions he'd eaten. Sabina had moved away from me by now, heading off to the House Agent's right. She made the noise again, then rustled the bushes as a further incentive. Her pursuer turned his back to me, searching the darkness with his eyes as I rose and ran silently toward him. My quarry must have heard me at the last moment, for he spun on his heels, bringing up his sword just a fraction too late. I stabbed Malo's blade deep into his kidneys and clamped my other hand over his mouth under his helmet, silencing his scream. The House Agent shuddered in my grip, then sagged as I lowered him carefully to the ground.

"Gastel?" the second House Agent called out, sounding bored.

I lowered my voice. "What?" I grunted.

"What was it?"

I headed through the bushes toward the Tapeau tunnel, marking the spot where I knew the second man stood hidden. I covered my mouth with my hand. "Just a filthy rat," I mumbled.

"What did you say?"

I was ten feet away and could see the House Agent's body against the rock behind him. I murmured something else, then pretended to stumble. The hidden man automatically stepped forward to steady me, and I grabbed him by the shoulder. "I found a rat," I growled as I stabbed upward, slicing through the man's windpipe, and piercing his brain. The House Agent squeaked, much like my make-believe rat, I thought, then his head lolled backward and he fell.

After that, Sabina and I dragged the dead men well inside the Tapeau tunnel and left them there as we headed out of Oasis. I was limping badly now, as the dull ache that I had been contending with all night had turned into a continuous pounding. I did my best to ignore the pain, concentrating on staying as close to Sabina as possible in the darkness. The tunnel was narrow, long, and sloped upward at an uncomfortable angle, which did little to help the discomfort in my leg. We walked for at least another half an hour before I started to feel a cold wind sweeping down on us from ahead. I drew my cloak tighter about me and raised my hood just as we broke out into the open.

We were free of Oasis, but the problem of how to make our way down the mountain still remained.

"So, now what?" Sabina asked, looking at me expectantly.

"Now we get away from this damn place," I grunted, taking the lead.

I had no idea where to go, but I figured the more distance we put between ourselves and the House Agents, the better. We came up the northern face of Mount Halas on The Walk, so I decided we would head south and hope for some luck. I guessed that First, Second, and Third Step would have been alerted by now and would be watching for us, so there was little choice but to find another way down. I knew the forces intent on capturing us believed we had the codex and that they wouldn't stop searching until they found us. I just prayed they wouldn't discover the dead House Agents until we were far away.

We headed off through the darkness, clutching our cloaks against the harsh wind that whistled along the rocks and peppered our eyes with tiny, knife-like shards of ice. The route that I had chosen proved to be a poor one, slippery in the dark, with swooping drifts of snow piled up against hundreds of small boulders that we had to skirt around continually. Twice we found a promising path that led downward, only to be disappointed when we ended up on windswept clifftops with nowhere to go, leaving us little choice but to turn back and start over.

The hours went by as we trudged onward, saying little to each other as we conserved our energy, until finally the sky began to brighten overhead. I'd had the feeling that we were being watched several times as we walked, but there were no signs of anyone on our backtrail and I finally shrugged it off as merely paranoia and fatigue. Morning came reluctantly to the mountain as a weak, unenthusiastic sun broke through the cloud cover in scattered beams. Sabina and I paused to rest on a craggy overhang that gave a spectacular view of the landscape far below. I could see dense woodlands and deep valleys, and even a small river meandering through a field, all appearing toy-like from our lofty height. It would take days at the rate we were moving to reach the bottom, I realized in dismay.

I started to say something to Sabina, then whirled as I sensed someone behind us. A man stood twenty feet away beneath the splayed branches of a gnarled pine tree with his arms crossed over his chest. His hair was silver and long, shorn on either side. He wore a light cloak that hung open to the wind, revealing an animal hide shirt and trousers. It was a Tapeau.

I took a step forward, motioning Sabina behind me as I showed the Tapeau my short sword. The man seemed unimpressed, and he stared at me expressionlessly. His eyes were dark, almost black, and they seemed alive with intelligence.

"What do you want?" I demanded.

"To take you where you wish to go," he said simply. His voice was low and deep, with little emotion in his words.

I stared in disbelief, hardly able to comprehend what the man had just said. "You mean down the mountain?" The Tapeau nodded, unmoving except for the occasional blink of his eyes. "Why?" I asked suspiciously.

"The Tapeau repay their debts."

"Debt? What debt?"

"You gave Tan-te-ak justice, and for this, the Tapeau feel gratitude. We have decided to help you."

I thought of the man Laurea had killed in Oasis. Tan-te-ak? I wondered. It could only be. "How could you know what happened?" I asked. "There was no one else there."

"Nothing happens on the mountain that we do not know about," the Tapeau said. "The square heads search for you and will not rest until they have captured you. But they are like children stumbling around in the dark and have finally asked for our help." I frowned. Square heads? He had to mean the House Agents. "We have agreed to help them," the Tapeau continued. The man's face cracked slightly in what might have been a smile. "Though our help will take the square heads west, where their swords and belligerent ways will be nullified." He bowed. "So it has been decided. So it shall be." He swept his arm behind him. "We must go."

"There are others with us," I said. "They're waiting in First Step. Can you get word to them?"

The Tapeau shook his head firmly. "They headed south four days ago."

"What?" I said in surprise.

"Son Partal told them that you and the girl died on The Walk," the Tapeau explained. "The one with the big nose did not believe him at first, but the Son can be compelling. The Rock soldiers made certain that the men left First Step after speaking with the Son, despite the angry one's protests."

Malo, I knew. I cursed under my breath, thinking of Jebido, and how devastated he must have been at the news we were dead. Now he believed he'd lost both his sons, all for a codex that had been gone for centuries. It was maddening.

"What about Waldin's cave?" I asked. "If you know so much, how come you didn't know it was there?"

"We have always known of it," the Tapeau said, surprising me.

"Yet, you did nothing, knowing what was inside?" I demanded.

The Tapeau shrugged. "We are the wardens of Oasis. Nothing more, nothing less. Everything beyond the task we have been given is merely clutter that ensnares the mind with doubts. The Tapeau have no doubts. So it has always been. So it shall always be. Now come, we must go."

We had little choice but to follow the Tapeau as he led us northward along a barely seen path. We walked for at least an hour, moving uphill the entire time. I began to protest at one point that we were going the wrong way, that we needed to go down, but the expression on the Tapeau's face changed my mind and I fell silent.

Our guide had said he would help us. I needed to have faith that he meant what he had said.

Finally, we reached a thicket of snow-covered trees and the Tapeau skirted them, pausing on a rocky bluff. Three odd-looking animals stood perilously close to the edge of the cliff, digging through the thinly-crusted snow there to find anything edible.

"Markhor," the Tapeau grunted to us. He moved toward the animals, speaking in a strange language and holding out his hand. The Markhor came forward eagerly, nibbling at the green shoots that he'd drawn from his cloak. The Tapeau smiled as he looked back at us. "They can be stubborn and temperamental at times, but nothing can climb these mountains like the Markhor."

"You expect us to ride those?" Sabina asked, looking horrified.

The Markhor were perhaps four feet tall at the shoulder, with long, grizzled coats of light brown and black. They had wispy, comical beards that hung to their chests, and their horns were curled and twisted strangely, reaching almost three feet in length back over their necks.

The Tapeau didn't respond as he gestured us closer, motioning that we should mount.

"I can't ride one of those," I protested. "I'm too big."

The Tapeau waved his hand dismissively, indicating the biggest of the Markhor, who I guessed must have topped out at several hundred pounds. "Tabent will bear your weight easily. You shall see. He is much stronger than his size might lead you to believe. Have no fear."

"I'm not getting on one of those things," Sabina said, shaking her head stubbornly.

Our guide's face hardened, the first sign I had seen of anger in him. "If you do not wish the help of the Tapeau, then I will go."

"Of course we want your help," I said before Sabina could respond. I held up a hand. "Just give us a moment." I took Sabina's arm and drew her several feet away. "We have to do this," I insisted. "There is no other way."

"But those creatures," Sabina said, looking back over her shoulder. "They're hideous."

"They probably think that about us, too," I said, forcing a smile. I put my hands on Sabina's shoulders. "It wouldn't have been my first choice either, but the Tapeau wouldn't be suggesting we ride these creatures if it weren't safe. We need to trust him."

"Are you sure it's the only way?" Sabina asked.

"The only way that makes any sense," I answered. I squeezed her shoulders, hating myself for what I was going to say next. "And once we are down the mountain, we'll go to your village, just like you asked."

Sabina's green eyes lit up with excitement. "Really? You mean it?"

"Of course," I said. "I can't wait to meet your brother."

Sabina grinned, her fears evaporating as she hurried toward the Tapeau. "Which one is mine?"

"Pasfey," the Tapeau said, indicating the smallest of the three animals. "She is fleet and sure of foot." He looked at Sabina appraisingly. "A fair match, I would say."

"What do I do?" Sabina asked as the Tapeau drew her to the female Markhor's side.

"Grab her horns like so," the Tapeau said, positioning Sabina's hands on each of the curled horns. Pasfey stamped her right hoof, but otherwise, seemed unperturbed. "Now, jump and pull yourself up, much like a horse."

Sabina jumped nimbly onto the Markhor's back, grinning at me. "It's not that bad at all, Hadrack."

"Now you," the Tapeau said, indicating me.

I put my hands on the horns of my Markhor. They were covered in moss just like tree bark after a rain and felt strangely soft and hard at the same time. I glanced at the Tapeau for reassurance, then flung my leg over the Markhor, stifling a gasp of pain as I settled on the animal's back. My feet were grazing the ground, but the beast seemed no worse for my weight.

"Very good," the Tapeau said, looking pleased. "There is just one last thing before we go." He rummaged in his clothing and withdrew two lengths of bright red cloth. He handed one to each of us.

"What are these for?" I asked, perplexed as I held up the thick cloth.

"For your eyes," the Tapeau said, motioning we should tie them around our heads.

I frowned. "You don't want us to see the path down, is that it? It's a secret?"

The Tapeau shook his head solemnly. "No. The Markhor go where no man can, so seeing the way down will matter little."

"Then, why do we need these?" I asked.

"Because if you see where the Markhor go," the Tapeau said, "then terror will take over your soul and you will fall." He leaped atop his Markhor and kicked his heels against the animal's flanks as he glanced back at us. "There will be things you do not wish to see on the descent. Put the blindfolds on. Never release your grip on your Markhor and trust it to do that which you cannot. Do this, and you will live to see the bottom."

Sabina and I hesitated for just a moment as our mounts began to follow the Tapeau, then we silently tied the cloths over our eyes.

22: Middleglen

I only lifted my blindfold once near the start of the journey, unable to resist the temptation. That was enough for me. The Tapeau had been right. The view was terrifying. All sky, pitiless rocks, and dizzying heights. I had quickly covered my eyes again and then spent the next few hours praying and holding on as the sturdy beast leaped and clattered down what to me felt like sheer cliff faces.

It turned out that the Tapeau was called He-mes-nak. Something that he grudgingly told us when we finally stopped to eat around midday. I found the name impossible to pronounce, so I began thinking of him simply as, Nak. In my estimation, he was perhaps as much as seventy years old, but was spry and agile like a man half his age. We had dismounted to eat in a narrow, windswept ravine where once I believed a stream had flowed. Now, there nothing was left but sparse bushes and polished, rounded stones to mark the water's route. I turned my face away from the cold northern wind that whistled along the rocks, grateful to finally be off Tabent, who had proven just as strong and durable as the Tapeau had promised. I rubbed the ache along my backside, which was competing throb for throb with the pain in my leg. My ride might be sturdy and sure of foot, but the beast's spine was unquestionably boney and rigid.

"How long until we reach the flatlands?" I asked Nak while we chewed on tasteless, shrunken dates.

"Two hours," Nak grunted as his long silver hair whipped around his head. He seemed unaffected by the cold. "There will be horses waiting for you."

The Markhor sniffed the date in Nak's hand curiously, then snorted in distaste, sending out twin plumes of frosty mist from its nostrils. The Tapeau said something in that strange tongue of his as he stroked the Markhor's beard affectionately. I was happy to hear about the horses, which meant we would reach Sabina's village that much quicker. Once I was finally free of her, I would ride to Witbridge Manor, confident that Jebido and the others would have headed there after learning of our deaths.

As for Malo, the House Agent undoubtedly went to Halhaven to report our failure to Daughter Gernet. I knew they would both be relieved to hear that I was alive, but also greatly disappointed to learn that the codex was gone. While Waldin's scrolls were informative at times, they contained little that would help end the stalemate between the Houses. Should I tell them that I knew where Verica had taken the codex? That was a question that had been bothering me since I had recognized her drawing. I wasn't sure what Daughter Gernet and the House Agent would do with that information, but I did know the thought of them turning their eyes on the Piths made me uncomfortable for some reason.

I glanced at Sabina, who had been quiet since we'd dismounted. Her face was deathly pale as she ate her dates unenthusiastically. Paler even than usual, I thought, despite the coldness of the wind. I guessed she had made the same mistake that I did and lifted her blindfold at some point that morning. My anger toward Sabina had diminished somewhat as the day progressed, though I could feel it hovering in the background every time I thought about what she'd done. I had a sudden thought of Shana, wondering what I would tell her of my time spent with Sabina. What had happened in Waldin's cave hadn't been my choice, but even so, it would be no easy thing to try to explain. Women see things differently than men do, and I was afraid of Shana's reaction when I told her the truth.

A part of my mind whispered, "Why tell her at all?"

"We go now," Nak said, cutting into my thoughts. He jumped nimbly onto his Markhor and clucked, urging the animal forward.

"How are you doing?" I asked Sabina as we mounted.

She paused, her blindfold halfway over her eyes. "I'm trying not to think about where these beasts are taking us. I'm focusing on pleasant thoughts instead."

"That's a good idea. That way, it will all be over before you know it."

Sabina smiled as she covered her eyes. "You will love Middleglen, Hadrack. I just know it!"

I sighed, tying my blindfold tightly as Tabent followed eagerly after Nak and Sabina.

Middleglen was Sabina's village, where—according to her—I was to spend the rest of my days toiling in the fields and fathering as many children as possible. I wasn't relishing telling her that wasn't going to happen, but until we reached the village, it was best to just go along with her delusions.

Tabent began to clamber downward as tiny rocks tumbled and clattered away beneath his hooves, forcing me to hold on to his horns tightly. Was not telling Sabina the truth right now wrong? I wondered as the sturdy beast moved sure-footed beneath me. I had done things in my past that I wasn't proud of, I reflected as I leaned forward, my nostrils filled with the musty odor of the Markhor. Things that could even be called wrong, depending upon your point of view. But not telling Sabina until we reached her village seemed more of a kindness to me than anything else. At least, that's what I told myself. Besides, if not telling her the truth was wrong, then what would the term be for what she'd done to me?

I spent the rest of the descent worrying about what I should or should not tell Shana. The cold wind that I'd become familiar with had vanished at some point, replaced by a warmer, gentler breeze. I took my hand off one of Tabent's horns to lower my hood, breathing in the heady scents of blooming flowers carried on the wind. Birds sang all around me and I heard the urgent thump of a rabbit signaling danger far off to my right. I cautiously lowered my blindfold to see that we were progressing down a gentle grade of flowing grasslands toward a thicket of pine that grew along the base of Mount Halas. I looked behind me at the mountain that towered impossibly high above me. It had taken almost two days to climb Mount Halas on foot, but on the Markhors, we had come down in less than a day.

Sabina rode three lengths ahead of me and I called out to her, "You can take off the blindfold now."

Nak circled back to us as Sabina drew her blindfold down. A crow flapped slowly overhead, chased by several pecking purple martins as Nak dismounted and put his forehead against the head of his Markhor. He whispered something, his eyes closed, then the Markhor turned and trotted back the way we'd come. Tabent and Sabina's Markhor began to stamp their hooves impatiently until we finally dismounted, then they followed after Nak's mount, disappearing over the grassy ridge.

"This is as good a place as any to part ways," Nak said. He pointed to the trees less than two hundred yards away. "The horses await you in there. Good luck to you." He turned and followed after the Markhors without another word.

I focused on the trees, eager to keep moving. "Come on," I said, motioning to Sabina. "There is still plenty of daylight left. The farther we get from here, the better I'll feel."

The horses were where Nak had said they would be. Two black mares with their reins attached to tree branches. One horse had a white patch on her forehead, the other four white strips on her ankles. There was no one in sight, but I was sure I could feel eyes on us and I scanned the forest warily. Hopefully, those eyes belonged to the Tapeau who had brought our mounts here. The horse with the white patch stamped her hooves nervously as we approached. I stroked her muzzle to calm her, then swung up into the saddle as Sabina mounted her horse. We trotted out from the trees and then paused in the open.

I looked at Sabina expectantly. "Which way to your village?" I asked.

"East," Sabina answered, taking the lead.

We rode for the rest of the day, staying off the main roads and avoiding anyone who came close. I doubted the House Agents were looking for us this far from the mountain, but even so, there was still a war on, so any strangers passing through would be automatically viewed with suspicion. We camped that night in a sprawling forest and chewed on shrunken dates and sweet figs that the Tapeau had left in our saddlebags. I didn't want to chance a fire, so we sat in the darkness eating, neither of us inclined to talk much.

Finally, I stood. "I'll take the first watch," I said, moving off.

"Do you really think that's necessary?" Sabina asked. "There's no one near for miles."

"Maybe," I grunted. "But I'd rather not take the chance."

Sabina might be right, I knew, but a forest of this size would be an ideal hideout for outlaws. After all we had been through to get this far, now was not the time to let our guard down. Besides, the suspicious part of me feared Sabina would try to use the opportunity to get close to me. Perhaps I was acting foolish and she had no such plans, but friendship is built on trust, and whatever faith I'd had in Sabina was now gone.

We were mounted and riding even as dawn broke the next morning. Sabina was in a gay mood, chatting and laughing while I rode stoically beside her, giving one or two-word responses. I studied her out of the corner of my eye as we passed under some giant elm trees. As always, I was surprised at her mood swings that could seemingly occur at a moments notice.

"They say my brother will be elected reeve soon," Sabina said. She'd been prattling on about her village and family for over an hour already. I had barely heard one word out of every ten, but if she realized that, she gave no indication.

"Reeve?" I grunted, brought to awareness by the title. I had a sudden picture of the floating reeve with buttons on his face and thrust it aside. "Why your brother and not your father? Surely he's earned the right?"

Sabina laughed. "Father has little interest in that kind of responsibility," she said.

"And your Lord will allow this?"

"He has no say in who we elect reeve."

I gaped at her. "No say?" I muttered. "How is that possible?"

Sabina laughed. "You are living in the past, Hadrack. Where I come from, the reeve is elected by the people, not the lord. It used to be that he would elevate one of his own, who cared nothing for us villagers. But now, we elect a man who we know and trust to represent us at the lord's court."

"Really?" I said in wonder. I shook my head, thinking how different my life would have turned out had that been the case in Corwick. "I'm still confused. If your village gets to choose the reeve, why would they not choose an older man like your father, rather than a youngster fresh from the war?"

Sabina giggled. "Youngster?" She rolled her eyes. "Hadrack, my brother is thirty-four years old."

I stared at Sabina in surprise. While five or even ten years differences in ages weren't that uncommon between siblings, I knew Sabina was sixteen, so having a brother more than twice her age seemed a little unusual. "I was a gift from the gods," Sabina explained, reading my look correctly. "Mother told me so herself. She was too old to become pregnant. Everyone knew that. Yet, by the grace of the First Pair, she did anyway, with me." Sabina smiled, looking off through the trees dreamily. "My mother told me I was special and would always be favored in my life because of it." She looked back at me and I was surprised to see tears in her eyes. "Now that we have found each other, I know this to be true."

I looked away so that she couldn't see the anger in my eyes and concentrated on where we were going. We reached a well-trodden road and Sabina cooed happily, pointing out a massive, gnarled tree sitting back in a field of wheat.

"That's the Hanging Tree," she said. "They hung Rander the Bold from those very branches three years ago. I remember I snuck away from the village with some friends and we came to see him late at night." Sabina made a face. "His tongue was hanging out, all swollen and purple, and his eyes had been plucked from his skull by ravens. It was ghastly, but oh so exciting."

"I'm sure it must have been," I mumbled as we turned a bend and left the Hanging Tree behind.

An old man leading an even older mule pulling a two-wheeled cart appeared on the road, heading our way. The man's head was down, his eyes focused on his worn boots as he plodded along wearily. Sabina's face lit up in recognition.

"A good day to you, Old Barl," Sabina cried, music in her voice.

The old man looked up, squinting before his bushy eyebrows rose in surprise. "Why, if it isn't Sabina of all people. Your father will be so relieved to see you safe, child."

Sabina's smile wavered, replaced by a look of sudden hope. "My father? He's here?"

The old man nodded as he absently tugged at one of his drooping ears. "Arrived two days ago." He paused to give me an appraising glance. "Brought your dear mother back to us, too, he did."

"Mother!" Sabina exclaimed, startling her horse. The girl fought to control the animal, hauling on the reins until it finally calmed. She peered down the road anxiously. "Please, tell me that she is well."

Old Barl grinned, showing us a single brown tooth surrounded by pink gums. "She is, child. She's still bedridden, but is improving every day. Your father and brother are organizing a search party for you as we speak. So, were I you, I'd stop wasting your time talking to me and go see them."

"Thank you!" Sabina said in excitement. She glanced at me, the look filled with joy, then she slapped her horse into motion, racing down the road in a cloud of dust.

Old Barl glared up at me after she had gone. One of his eyes was clouded and fixed, but the other held nothing but scorn. "You look like trouble," he grunted.

I urged my horse past him, not bothering to answer. What was there to say? The old man was right.

I followed the road at a more leisurely pace than Sabina had, in no hurry to meet her family. I passed through a small stand of trees onto a ridge overlooking a valley, and there I paused, staring down at the village of Middleglen. I counted as many as thirty houses, all lined up neatly on either side of the road. The houses were built from heavy straw bales and supported by wooden frames, with roofs of weathered thatch. I had seen dwellings made that way before and knew they were impressively warm in winter, an advantage that was offset by how easily they caught fire.

I could see a blacksmith shop at the near end of the village and hear the steady ring of the smith's hammer as he worked. A good-sized Holy House stood overlooking the town, and the lord's castle rose on the other side of the valley. Many people walked the street, with children playing and laughing as they chased one another. A peaceful looking, happy place, I thought as I guided my horse down the grade. Clearly, the war had not reached this town yet.

A man carrying a bundle on his back nodded to me politely as I held up a hand to him. "I'm looking for—" I paused, realizing after all this time that I didn't even know Sabina's father's name. "I'm a friend of Sabina," I said instead. "Can you direct me to the home of her father?"

The man turned, pointing to a house further down the street. I thanked him and moved on, approaching the building just as the front door crashed opened and Sabina came bustling out.

"There you are!" she exclaimed. I dismounted, leading my mount behind the house where I saw Sabina's mare was already tied. "I told them everything," Sabina breathed happily as she hurried after me.

I frowned at her in dismay. I'd briefly considered just riding away as fast as possible earlier, but that seemed like a cowardly thing to do. After everything we had been through together, I knew honor demanded that I tell Sabina face to face that I was leaving. Now that she had told her family about our supposed marriage, I knew things had just gotten a little more complicated. I hesitated with my horse's reins in my hand, wondering if I was making a mistake by staying. I decided to reason with the girl now, before things got worse, and I tied the mare to the hitching post.

"Sabina," I began uncomfortably. "You shouldn't have told them."

"Don't be silly," Sabina said, brushing me off. "They are dying to meet you."

Sabina grabbed my arm, not listening to my protests as she led me back along the house to the front porch. I grudgingly allowed her to guide me up the steps toward the door. I decided it would be rude not to meet the father and brother since I was here. Besides, I was somewhat curious about what they would be like, considering how much I'd been told about them these past few weeks. Perhaps some hot food and talk, then, when Sabina and I were alone again, I would inform her that I was leaving and that would be the end of it.

Sabina swung the door open and led me into a fair-sized room dominated by a table fashioned from rough planks. A big man with a thick grey and red beard stood by the table, his arms clasped behind his back. A second man stood crouched in front of a tiny wood stove, prodding at the weak flames inside with an iron poker. He only had one arm, with the sleeve of his missing arm rolled up and sewn to his shoulder.

"Father, Ragna," Sabina said proudly, wrapping her arm around my waist. "This is Hadrack of Corwick."

I stood in the doorway, unable to tear my eyes away from the older man's face. It was a face I knew—a face I had last seen as a boy. I reeled, feeling overwhelming emotion and anger explode inside me.

"Child!" Ragna the Elder whispered as he shifted his horrified gaze to his daughter. "What have you done?"

23: No Matter What

Jebido told me once that he believed The Mother had taken a vested interest in me and that there was no need for me to search for the surviving members of the nine. He claimed that She would deliver them to me when the time was right, and that I should stop worrying about it. I hadn't wanted to hear his words at the time, frustrated as I was with the lack of progress I'd had in locating them. It was true that Calen, Quant Ranes, and Searl Merk had all come to me in ways that might seem more than just mere coincidence, yet I had found Hape on my own, so there had been some remaining doubt in me.

But now, staring across the room at two of the men that I'd sworn to kill, I knew my friend had been right all along. My doubt was gone. The Mother had orchestrated this very moment from the beginning. Everything that had happened since Malo had summoned me to Springlight had been predetermined to bring Ragna the Elder, his son, and me together. Why The Mother had gone to such great lengths was a mystery to me—one which I had neither the time nor the desire to worry about. Now was the time for action and revenge in its most violent form, and nothing else. I glanced sideways at the girl standing frozen beside me, knowing that she would hate me forever for what I was about to do. The look of joy on Sabina's face had faltered, replaced now with one of confusion and unease as she shifted her eyes from me, to her father, then to her brother.

"Father?" Sabina finally asked in the awkward silence, her voice catching. "What's wrong?"

Ragna the Younger shifted away from the stove, the iron poker clutched in his only hand. Ragna the Elder put his fists on his hips as we locked eyes, until finally, the older man surprised me by dropping his gaze to the floor. I thought I saw a flush of shame creeping along his cheeks, but perhaps it was just a trick of the shadows combined with wishful thinking on my part. Ragna the Younger growled low in his chest behind his father, the poker lifted threateningly as he took two steps forward.

Ragna the Elder sighed in resignation, nodding his head wearily before raising a hand, stopping his son. "Wait," he said in a commanding tone.

"But, Father," Ragna the Younger protested.

The older man turned; his face angry now as he looked at his son. "You will abide me, boy! Are you in that much of a hurry to die?" Sabina's father turned back to me, the anger fading from his face. "I have been dreading this moment for so long now," he said to me with regret in his voice.

I couldn't respond, my mind filled with nothing but seething hatred and blind rage. Ragna the Elder had appeared big and formidable when I'd first entered, but now it seemed as though he had withered before my eyes, turning weak and broken. I didn't care in the least. He would die regardless. Malo's sword hung against my hip, tied there with rope. I put my hand on the hilt—a move none failed to notice. The older man facing me was unarmed, but I saw a longsword in a leather sheath propped up against the wall five feet away. I gestured to the weapon. "Pick it up," I spat, finding my tongue. "I'll not butcher unarmed men like you and your son did."

"Hadrack?" Sabina said, clutching at my arm. "What are you doing? What is going on?"

"Did you know!?" I snapped as I shook Sabina's hand off, feeling a coldness coming over me as I looked at her. The anger that I'd felt at what she had done in Waldin's cave was like nothing compared to the disgust that I now felt for her. She was the offspring of a heartless butcher of women and children. As far as I was concerned, she had ceased to exist in my eyes. "Stay out of the way, you conniving bitch," I growled. "Or you can suffer the same fate as the rest of your murderous family."

Sabina gasped, raising a hand to her mouth as she saw the promise of my words burning in my eyes. She shrunk away from me, pressing her back to the wall.

"The child knows nothing," Ragna said wearily. "She was barely able to walk then." He indicated his son. "Ragna and I left the employ of Lord Corwick not long after—" He paused, searching for the words. Finally, he shrugged. "Trust me, we never told her what happened. She is innocent in this."

"Told me what?" Sabina asked, finding her voice.

"I fear you will learn soon enough," the older man said sadly.

"Father," Ragna the Younger pleaded. The poker shook in his hand as he tried to restrain himself from rushing at me. I dearly wished he would.

"Let him loose," I urged the father.

"You will kill him," Ragna the Elder said.

"I'll kill him either way," I replied.

"Can we not talk about this? Will you stay your need for vengeance long enough to listen to me?"

I snorted. "Did you listen to anyone in Corwick when they pleaded for their lives?"

This time I saw Ragna the Elder flush deeply as he stole a glance toward his daughter. "That was a long time ago. I was a different man then."

"Maybe it was a long time ago for you!" I snapped. "But it feels like yesterday to me. Every time I close my eyes, I see my family and friends dying. I hear them crying out to you for mercy—mercy that never came. I see the women of my village stripped naked and violated in ways that sicken my stomach to this very day." I pointed at Ragna the Younger. "I see you doing that!" I hissed. "Rutting and laughing like a beast." I stabbed a finger at the older man. "And I see you as well, Ragna the Elder. I watched from the bog as Hape and Calen held Meanda down while you used her. I watched as you got off of her, your lust sated, then slit her throat and laughed as her life's blood poured into the mud." I heard Sabina gasp behind me, but I ignored her. I was shaking with fury as I pointed at her father. "So, don't you dare speak to me of being a changed man. I'll hear none of it. Whatever you think you have become since that day is meaningless to me. You will always be a murdering, raping bastard who has spent far too many days in the world of the living. Today, I swear by my father and sister that I will take care of that injustice, and when I am done, I'll spit on both of your filthy corpses."

"We were just following orders!" Ragna the Younger shouted. His face was twisted in rage. "We were soldiers. We did what we were told."

I could see the younger man was close to breaking, regardless of his father words. "You did it because you wanted to do it," I said, goading him on. "You can tell yourself whatever lies you want to make yourself feel better, but in the end, I know the true evil that lives inside of you."

"You bastard!" Ragna the Younger cried. "We should have killed you as a whelp when we had the chance."

I heard Ragna the Elder shout something and Sabina scream, but the one-armed man was beyond listening now as he ran at me, the poker raised. I waited, biding my time, then dodged out of the way as the iron point whistled past my head. I lifted a knee, catching Ragna the Younger in the stomach. He dropped to the reed-covered floor, retching, his grip lost on the poker as it fell. I grabbed the fallen man by his thick red hair and hauled him to his feet, glancing at his father. The older man stood watching, an expression of deep regret on his face. A look passed between us, and I knew that he would do nothing to interfere.

Ragnar the Younger was heavyset, with thick shoulders and sturdy legs. He would have been a formidable foe with two arms, but now he only had the one, which he was using to pound against my head and shoulders ineffectively. I wrapped my hand around his throat and pinned him to the wall, choking him. Then I struck with my fist. Once, twice, then a third time, I hit the man, reveling in the fear in his eyes and the blood spurting from his face. I felt a savagery taking over me as I continued to hit him over and over again, battering his features into an unrecognizable mess. I could hear wailing coming from behind me and I felt someone grab at my arm, trying to stop me. I knew it was Sabina and I shrugged her away as I continued to punch Ragna the Younger, having to hold him up now as I rained blows at will upon him. Finally, I released the lifeless body and stepped back, breathing heavily as the bloodied corpse sagged to the floor.

"Why, Hadrack? Why?" I heard between agonized sobs.

I turned to see Sabina on her knees behind me, blood rolling from a deep cut on her cheek. Another high-pitched howl of grief arose, coming from an old woman who had just dragged herself through a doorway at the back of the room. Sabina's ailing mother, I realized, recognizing her from Springlight. She was reaching out to her son, her mouth working before she collapsed and lay still. Sabina shrieked and ran to the woman as I faced her father.

"You could have helped him," I said, gesturing to his dead son.

Ragna the Elder shook his head slowly, his gaze falling on his wife and daughter sprawled on the floor. "His fate was sealed the moment you walked through that door, Hadrack," he said. He took a deep breath. "As was all of ours."

"She's dead!" Sabina wailed, rising to her knees. She stared at me with hatred in her eyes as she tore at her hair in grief. "You killed my mother, you bastard! You killed her!"

Ragna the Elder closed his eyes at the news. I felt a momentary pang of regret and started to move toward Sabina, but then I saw my father again in my mind that day on the ledge in Oasis.

"No matter what?" he'd said, referring to my vow.

"No matter what," I promised.

I felt my heart harden again as I looked away from Sabina's accusing eyes. I drew my sword, then motioned for Ragna to take up his.

The older man shook his head. "I won't fight you, Hadrack," he said. "I have done terrible things with a weapon in my hand. Now it's time to make amends for that."

"Do you think I won't cut you down where you stand, sword, or not?" I demanded.

Ragna shrugged. "The moment is yours to do with what you wish. Kill me or don't, it matters little to me." He gestured to his wife and son. "My actions from years past have brought ruin to my family, much like I have always feared they would. That day in your village has haunted my nights ever since, and not a moment goes by where I wish I hadn't just taken my son and ridden away from there." He sighed and wiped his eyes, looking old and frail now.

"My father was a good man," I said, fighting to keep my voice steady. "A good, decent man who had done nothing wrong." Ragna bowed his head. "My sister loved to work in the garden," I continued, more for me than for him. "She used to sing this song, I can't remember the words now, but it always made me smile." I gripped Malo's sword tighter and took several steps toward Ragna. "I found my father's head on a stake," I growled, the sword swishing back and forth in front of me. I knew tears were on my cheeks, but I felt no shame. I was a man now, far removed from that terrified, eight-year-old boy from long ago. Yet I knew he was still with me somewhere inside. I glared at the man before me. Young Hadrack and I would have our revenge together.

"I know," Ragna said, his voice thick with emotion. "I remember. Ranes placed it there."

"You murdered innocent people," I said, taking another step.

"I did," Ragna admitted.

"You raped innocent women." I took another step.

"Yes," Ragna said. He stared at me, no fear in his eyes, only acceptance.

"You murdered a Son and a Daughter and burned the Holy House," I rasped, now less than three feet from him. I could see Sabina crouched over her mother's body, listening to us in horror.

"The First Pair forgive me, I did," Ragna whispered. "All that you accuse me of, I am guilty of doing."

"There can be no forgiveness for you," I hissed. I put the blade to Ragna's throat. "None!" I shouted.

Ragna put his hands over mine on the sword hilt, moving slowly to show that he meant no aggression. I could see deep suffering and regret simmering within his eyes, but I cared nothing for it.

"Promise me you will take care of my daughter," he pleaded. "Marry her like you pledged to do before this all began."

I laughed, a harsh sound that came from deep within my belly. "Marry the spawn of a murdering bastard like you? Even if I had actually considered such a notion to begin with, there is no way I'd make good on it now."

Ragna's eyes widened at my words, and then he closed them in defeat. "For Corwick, then." He pressed his hands tighter over mine, then lunged forward, forcing the point of Malo's blade into his neck. Warm blood sprayed over my arm as Ragna gurgled and twitched, his eyes bugling before he went limp and slid to the ground.

I could hear Sabina's agonized sobs behind me as I reached under my clothing and drew out my brother's Pair Stone. "Thank you, Mother," I whispered. "I will never doubt you again." I turned and stalked toward the open door.

"Hadrack!"

I paused and glanced back. Sabina stood among the bodies of her family, staring at me with tears sliding down her cheeks. She spread her hands, red now with the blood of her brother and father on them. "Please, don't leave me like this," she pleaded.

I thought of a hundred things that I could say to Sabina at that moment, but in the end, I said none of them. There was nothing left to say between us. I stepped outside and headed for my horse, hesitating for only a heartbeat when I heard Sabina's forlorn cry echoing from inside.

"Come back for me, Hadrack! Come back!"

I have made many mistakes in my life, some through sheer stupidity and stubbornness, some from naivety or simple inexperience. But I have always believed that what happened in Ragna the Elder's house was not a mistake. That, despite how cruel my actions must have seemed to Sabina and those that heard of it, I was left with only one choice that made any sense. One which could not be denied. Were I a more forgiving man, perhaps I would have found an alternative, though even now in my old age and supposed wisdom, I cannot imagine what that alternative might have been.

What occurred in that house long ago was predestined, and we were just simple players in a much grander scheme. Or so I believed at the time. Now, as the pains grow worse daily and my memory fades, I occasionally wonder if it had actually happened the way that I think it did. The gods help me if it didn't.

After I slaughtered Sabina's family—for there is no other way to describe it—I mounted my horse, intending to head south. People were gathered outside Ragna the Elder's home when I rode around front again, whispering and muttering to each other. The talk quickly ceased when they saw me, all grim-faced and blood-splattered with a crimson sword still gripped in my hand. A woman clutching a small child to her legs shrunk from me as I trotted past her, while the toddler stared up at me with innocent fascination. I tried not to think what I must look like to that child, wondering if I had become no better than the nine themselves in some ways. It was a sobering thought, one that stayed with me for hours as I rode away from Middleglen.

I traveled for two days, moody and irritable, my thoughts always circling back to Sabina and the look of horror and revulsion on her face. My father tried to come me during the night while I slept, but I thrust him away, banishing him to a part of my mind where I wouldn't have to hear his words. I'd done what needed to be done, just as I had promised him, yet the nagging tug of guilt lay heavily upon me just the same. Killing Calen, Hape, Searl Merk, Quant Ranes, and even Ragna the Younger had been the best points of my life so far. I had no remorse for my actions. But Ragna the Elder, that was different. I had seen genuine regret in the older man's eyes before he'd died, though I hadn't wanted to acknowledge that fact. I had felt no happiness at his death, either—just a numb sense of doing what needed to be done.

Ragna had been as bad as any of the nine, perhaps worse, so why was I feeling this sudden apathy now that he was dead? It was a mystery, one which was beginning to annoy me as I crested a hill overlooking a small cluster of houses. I had no idea where I was, but I was tired and hungry and sick of being trapped within my own thoughts. I decided I needed company other than just my disinterested horse, and so I headed for the houses, my mood perking up slightly. It was a decision I would very quickly come to regret.

The village—if it could even be called that—was named Yellow Fields. Part of the fiefdom of Lord Graaf, who I'd heard of through Daughter Gernet. Lord Graaf was a powerful lord who had pledged his sword to Prince Tyrale and was warring somewhere to the south. His lands were vast and his coffers full, I'd heard—a prime target for the Outlaw of Corwick. I just hadn't gotten around to him yet.

Perhaps after I returned to Witbridge, I would rectify that, I thought as I dismounted beside the first house. Several scrawny chickens pecked at the narrow, dusty road, and a single hog stared at me with mean eyes through the twisted planks of a pen not far away. Seeing the pig made me think about Corwick and my farm from long ago, stealing away some of my improving mood. A bent, wizened-looking man sat outside the house, whittling on a stick as he watched me warily.

"Good day," I said, slapping the dust from my cloak. The old man bobbed his head in greeting. His skin was weathered and tough-looking, hanging down in wattles beneath his chin. "I could use something to eat."

"You'd be him, I expect."

Now it was my turn to stare warily. "Him, who?"

"Judging by that cloak of yours, the crazy Pilgrim, Rorian." The old man chuckled and shook his head, the flaps of skin beneath his chin wiggling. "Word travels fast around here, youngster." The old man pointed his whittling knife at me. "Were I you, I'd keep on riding. The Lord's men are close. I'd not want to be wearing your boots if they catch you."

I hesitated, my mind blank as I tried to understand. How? How could anyone know about me this far from Mount Halas? Then I grimaced, realizing what the answer was. Sabina. Sabina must have told someone. I turned, heading back for my horse.

"Youngster?" I glanced at the old man as I mounted. He was pointing with the knife again, this time to the north. Horsemen were streaming down a shallow hill there. "Head south two miles. You'll come to Ripper's Forest. You might lose them in there."

I nodded my gratitude, feeling my heart surging in my chest as I swung the black around, guiding her south at a gallop. I looked behind me, cursing. The riders had seen me and were giving chase. I hunched lower over the mare's saddle, urging her onward through weaving fields of golden wheat. I saw a valley of green lushness off to my left and I veered toward it, hoping to lose my pursuers there. But, before I'd reached even halfway, more riders appeared over the valley crest, racing toward me. I hauled back savagely on the black's reins, turning her south again as I looked desperately over my shoulder. The riders behind me were two hundred yards away. I could hear them whopping, confident that they had me. I wasn't sure that they were wrong.

The mare was fast—not as fast as Angry, of course—yet quick enough that even with my inexpert riding, we managed to keep the lead, though it was narrowing slowly. The second group of riders merged with the first, spreading out in a long line, clearly intent on ensnaring me. I looked ahead. The dark forest sprawled out five hundred yards in front of me, with my pursuers now less than a hundred yards behind. I could see individual faces amid brilliant flashes of green surcoats. A rider on a spotted brown and white horse surged forward from the pack, cutting the distance between us as he gave his mount its head. The man's metal helmet gleamed in the sunlight and he grinned, raising his sword as he swept toward me. I drew Malo's short sword and waited, hunched tightly over my horse's back, watching the quickly approaching rider beneath my armpit.

"I've got you now, you bastard!" the rider shouted, pulling even with me.

He swung his sword across his body, hard and vicious toward my head. I raised Malo's smaller sword, blocking the downward stroke, then twisted my wrist as metal screeched against metal, flinging the other man's weapon away. I was bouncing in my saddle, almost falling as I lunged outward, slashing across my assailant's chest. The rider wailed, throwing up his arms as the emblem of a giant yellow eagle on his green surcoat split open and blood gushed out. The man fell, somersaulting over his horse's rump as I pressed my face to the mare's ears, urging greater speed from her.

More riders were galloping on either side of me now, though none came within two sword lengths of me. I imagine after seeing their companion die so easily, the others had decided to take a more cautious approach. The forest lay less than a hundred yards away, but the outriders to either side were ahead of me now and were sweeping inward in a pincer-like movement. I had only moments before they closed off my escape route.

I took one final, regretful look at the forest, then yanked hard on the black's reins, intent on trying to swing around and ride through my pursuers. The mare screamed in protest at the suddenness of my move and she fought me, rising back on her hind legs as she kicked her forelegs. I felt myself sliding in the saddle and I released the reins and stabbed at the pommel with my free hand, but missed. I fell with a cry and hit the ground hard, then rolled in the dusty field as pawing, stamping hooves surrounded me. I twisted onto my back, looking up into the grinning face of a bearded man just as he struck downward with the hilt of his sword.

Then I knew nothing more.

24: Gandertown

Five days later, I arrived with an escort of ten men on the outskirts of Gandertown, where, I was told, I was to meet with the True King before my execution. I had slept little the past few days, but other than a headache and a constant, nagging fatigue, I found myself in reasonable shape. My captors were surprisingly decent men who had given me as much food and water as I wished, though they watched me night and day with a wary respect.

Their leader was a man named Wiflem, who, despite my original reluctance, I quickly came to like. He was an intelligent, powerful-looking man and had taken to riding beside me each day, talking about all manner of things. I rode the same black mare the Tapeau had given me, though now my ankles were lashed together by rope beneath the horse's belly, and my wrists were tied to my saddle.

"It's a shame, really," Wiflem was saying as we trotted down a busy road. He slicked sweat off his brow with his hand, then hocked and spat noisily into the swirling dust beneath us. "So many good men have died already in this stupid war. And for what?" He snorted. "So that one brother or the other becomes king? What does it matter?"

I looked at him in surprise. "You don't care who wins?"

Wiflem shrugged. "A king is a king. They shit just like you and I do, so why should I care? Will it make any difference to me which one sits on the throne?" He chuckled and shook his head, not waiting for me to answer. Wiflem did that a lot. "No, of course not. The king will make the laws and we will obey them, and that will be that. It's always been that way and it will always be that way. The actual man with his ass on the throne is meaningless."

"Yet, you can have a good and competent king, or a bad and inept one," I pointed out.

"So?" Wiflem said.

"So, one can make your life better," I answered, "while the other can only make it worse."

Wiflem laughed in amusement as he twirled his pointed mustache tips, which he seemed unabashedly proud of. "If only it were that simple, my friend. Even the best-intentioned of men can create problems for the likes of us." He raised an eyebrow at my look. "You don't believe me? Take my own Lord Graaf, for instance. A good man by all accounts." He winked at me. "The kind of man you are referring to, I would wager. He stops and kisses babies in the courtyard, of all things, and is known to be fair and reasonable when meting out justice at court."

"He sounds like a fine lord," I said, thankful now that the Outlaw of Corwick had not visited him.

"Yes," Wiflem said. "He is all that."

"Then I don't understand your point."

"Lord Graaf returned from the south three days ago," Wiflem went on. "We have had little rain since he left and some of the crops on his lands have begun to wither, ensuring a shortage this winter unless rain comes soon." I just blinked at the man, wondering where he was going with this. "My lord, in his wisdom, decided that rather than wait for a near-certain famine, he would purchase what we needed to see us through the winter now, so that none of his people would starve."

"A commendable act," I responded, impressed. Few if any lords I'd known would have done such a thing.

"Ah," Wiflem said, lifting a finger. "There is only one problem."

He stared at me expectantly and I accommodated him. "What?" I asked.

"Money. Lord Graaf has helped finance Prince Tyrale's war effort from the beginning, which has left his coffers decidedly weakened. He had enough money to pay his men through the winter, or enough to purchase supplies for the peasants, but not both."

"So, he paid for the supplies," I said, seeing his point now.

"Indeed, he did," Wiflem agreed. He glanced at me and I could see a hint of anger in his eyes. "Peasant farmers will sit by their fires this winter, their bellies full, while my family sits out in the cold because I will be unable to pay for their lodging."

"But surely a man like your lord will take that into account?" I protested. "From what you say about him, I doubt he would let such a thing happen."

"Your eyes are blind, my young friend," Wiflem grunted, "and your doubts wrong." He stared ahead moodily as the road wound around a deep bend. "We are warriors, men with a higher status than simple peasants. As such, we are expected to be prepared for anything. There will be no help coming from our lord. He would consider it an insult if we were to ask." Wiflem paused, wiping his face again with his hand. "So, as to my point. While Lord Graaf's act is a noble one, its very nobleness will affect me and mine directly, just as I told you. In comparison, a lesser lord might be inclined to let the peasants starve in favor of his men, who are the key to his power. Good does not always mean right."

"Unless you are one of the peasants," I said, looking down at my horse's twitching ears.

Wiflem glanced at me in irritation, then his lips slowly twisted into a smile. "A fair point."

We rode in silence for a time until Wiflem drew one of Waldin's scrolls from his saddlebags and began to read. I knew the soldier had looked at them already, though, up until now, he'd said little about them.

"This part here still has me confused," Wiflem said, turning the scroll toward me. I glanced at it but said nothing. "This imbecile claims to have made a copy of an important codex." Wiflem let the scroll drop to his lap as he studied me. "Does he mean the Halas Codex, do you think?"

Wiflem and his men had been told my true identity, but not what I'd been doing on Mount Halas. Their instructions were to simply bring me and everything on my person to Gandertown, nothing more. I nodded. "Yes, that's what he means."

Wiflem studied me thoughtfully. The man was no fool, I' had come to learn, and I knew he would be putting the pieces together.

"So, you went on The Walk disguised as this Rorian fellow, yes?" I grunted assent. "Who was he?"

"A scholar," I said.

"Did you kill him?"

"No."

Wiflem pursed his lips. "And this Rorian was looking for the second codex?"

"He was."

"But you took his place?"

"I did."

"Did you find it?"

I shook my head and gestured to the scroll. "Just those, nothing more." I realized Wiflem hadn't noticed the note left behind by Verica. If he had, he'd already know what had happened to the codex. I saw no reason to enlighten him.

Wiflem held up the scroll. "I imagine the prince will be disappointed with these."

"Undoubtedly," I agreed. "But, at least he will have my stretched neck to look forward to."

Wiflem chuckled. "True enough."

Riders appeared on the road and Wiflem signaled for us to move aside as soldiers wearing Prince Tyrale's prancing golden lion rode past in a long line. We returned to the road, riding onward in silence until we crested a sloping hill, looking down on a sprawling city, the likes of which I couldn't have even imagined. I'd thought Halhaven was big, but Gandertown dwarfed it in size. The city was built around the bases of two towering hills. A glittering palace of white stone dominated one, while on the second rose the largest Holy House that I had ever seen.

Wiflem grinned at the look on my face. "Impressive, is it not?"

"Indeed, it is," I said as we started downward.

I could see deep blue water stretching off behind the city walls to the north, with ships of every size and shape seemingly moving at random along the surface. The outer city walls rose twenty feet, with rectangular towers spaced every fifty feet along them. A second wall rose inside the first, twice as tall, with men holding long pikes pacing the battlements. The prince's lion pennant rose over every turret, with an oversized Rock of Life banner flapping proudly from the top of the Holy House. The double city gates stood open, each one three times the size of the gates at Halhaven.

Wiflem led us toward the gates as people moved aside to let us pass. I could hear hushed whispers as we rode until finally, somebody pointed at me.

"It's the Outlaw of Corwick!"

Wiflem cursed under his breath, grabbing my horse's reins and drawing the mare closer to him as shouts of anger began to rise. Something slapped wetly against my shoulder and slid off, landing on my thigh. A horse turd, I realized as I was struck again, this time in the chest. Wiflem drew his sword, shouting for people to make way as the furious crowd closed in on us, trying to drag me from my saddle. I don't think they noticed or maybe just didn't care that I was tied to my horse. Wiflem's men finally made a protective cordon around my jittery horse, slapping the flats of their swords across the backs and heads of the enraged mob as we used our mounts as battering rams to clear a path.

I heard a strident horn sound, then the clang of armor as men with pikes marched through the gates, prodding the crowd away from us. A half-eaten apple caromed painfully off the side of my nose and I turned to look back, blinking away tears. A girl of no more than ten raised her arm in triumph, pointing at me with hatred on her face, while her companion of a similar age threw another apple at me and missed. The second girl stuck her tongue out, disappointed at the miss before I passed through the gates and lost sight of her.

"My apologies for that," Wiflem said once we were safely through. "I should have anticipated that might happen."

I shrugged. "I doubt apples and shit will be the worst thing to happen to me today," I said soberly.

Wiflem regarded me thoughtfully, and I was surprised to see momentary regret in his eyes. "I fear you may be right about that," he responded.

Wiflem and his men led me toward the first hill where the palace lay. Soldiers with pikes marched behind and before us, discouraging a repeat of what had occurred outside the city walls. We climbed the hill slowly, with the cobblestone pathway lined with onlookers. Most raised their fists at me, shouting my name and insults, though no more projectiles came my way. Finally, we reached the palace courtyard, and my bonds were cut before our mounts were led away.

"Forgive me for this," Wiflem said, holding out a pair of iron manacles. I said nothing as he clamped them around my wrists. "You and you," Wiflem grunted to several of his men. "Come with me."

I was led into the palace, passing through a cavernous entrance that echoed loudly with every footfall we took on glittering, highly-polished golden tiles. A tall man approached us wearing a flowing black cape over a fine velvet jacket and rich trousers. His hair was thick and streaked with shoots of grey, and his beard was trimmed close to his jaw. I took a deep breath, working hard to control the rage that I felt inside. Wiflem frowned at me as I fidgeted, holding me tightly as the man approached us with long, easy strides. It was Hervi Desh, of course.

I was angry, but hardly surprised by Desh's appearance. In fact, I'd been expecting him to appear. Desh stopped in front of me and I felt calm take over me as I met his eyes. The Mother had planned this all along, I told myself. Just like She had with the two Ragnas. I just needed to be patient and bide my time until I understood what She had in store for the both of us.

"So, you caught him, then?" Desh said, glancing at Wiflem.

"We did, Advisor," Wiflem said, bowing slightly.

Hervi Desh leaned toward me, examining me from head to foot. "It has been a long time, Hadrack of Corwick. I can't tell you how much I have been looking forward to this."

I said nothing, turning my gaze upward to stare at the high ceiling above me. I pictured the look on Desh's face from years ago when I'd startled his horse, causing him to fall and strike his head. It wasn't much, considering my situation, but it gave me some solace knowing that I had hurt him back then.

Desh gestured to us with a carefully manicured hand. "Come."

He spun on his heel, then marched toward a set of double doors protected by two armed guards. The men opened the doors for Desh and we followed him inside, then made our way down a long aisle of sculpted stone that led into a grand room dominated by a raised dais at the opposite end. Two thrones stood side by side on the dais, with a man seated in each. We approached and halted ten feet away. The man sitting on the left throne was withered and shrunken almost to a corpse, the black robes he wore hanging on him like curtains. The First Son, I knew, feeling momentary awe sweep over me. The second man was young and blond, though he sat slumped as though exhausted or bored. His head was propped up by his balled fist, his elbow on his knee as he stared at me through hooded eyes. A crown of gold sat perched awkwardly on his head. I was looking at Prince Tyrale.

Hervi Desh moved to stand to the prince's left, a supportive hand on his shoulder. "Kneel in the presence of the True King," Desh said, motioning us down. Wiflem knelt, pulling me with him as his men dropped to one knee behind us. "You may rise," Desh said after a long pause, the ghost of a smile on his lips. He waved a hand. "You and your men may go," he said to Wiflem. He indicated the silent soldiers who stood around the room watching dispassionately. "My men can take care of the prisoner from here."

We rose and Wiflem paused to squeeze my arm in support before he and his men marched out of the room. I stood before the prince, the First Son, and Hervi Desh, smoldering with impotent anger.

The First Son cleared his throat weakly. "Come closer, boy," he said, crooking a spindly finger at me. I thought briefly about disobeying the order, but decided it would be better to pick my battles. The First Son wasn't my enemy—at least, not as far as I knew. I took a step closer to the dais, then at the priest's urging, a second. "You seem too young to have done all that has been laid at your feet," the First Son said gravely, regarding me with weary, watery blue eyes.

"I was even younger when that bastard destroyed my village and killed my family!" I spat, unable to contain myself any longer as I gestured toward Desh with my manacled hands.

The First Son's eyebrows rose and he swiveled his head on his scrawny neck to stare at Desh. "Advisor, what does he mean? Does he speak the truth?"

Desh smiled. "Yes, your Eminence. The worm is correct."

I stared at Desh in surprise, wondering what he was up to. Why would he openly admit to the killings? I felt the first stirrings of alarm, realizing that something wasn't right.

"You acknowledge his claim, then?" the First Son muttered, looking taken aback by the news.

"I do," Desh said. He grinned at me. "Though I can't take all the credit. There were others there as well."

"Well, this is most peculiar," the First Son said, blinking rapidly. "Most peculiar indeed." He stood, wobbling as he held the arms of the throne for support. "I must think about this." He started to walk unsteadily along the dais, heading for the back when Desh held up his hand.

"There is one other thing, Eminence," Desh said. He strode toward the First Son, offering his arm to the older man, who took it gratefully. Desh looked over his shoulder at me and smirked.

I felt a premonition of disaster, but was helpless to do anything.

"What is it, Advisor?" the First Son asked.

Desh leaned close, whispering just loud enough for me to hear. "I murdered the Son and Daughter in that filthy village too."

The First Son gasped and drew back just as a knife appeared in Desh's free hand. He grabbed the priest's sleeve and pulled him forward. "I enjoyed it immensely," the Advisor said as he plunged the knife into the old man's chest.

I shouted in protest, about to leap onto the dais, but two soldiers with drawn swords appeared by my side, holding me back as the First Son collapsed to the floor. Desh casually stooped and wiped his blade on the priest's robe, then returned to his original position beside the prince. I glanced at Prince Tyrale, but he remained as he'd been, unmoving, his head propped up by his fist as he stared at me.

"You seem surprised, Hadrack," Desh said as he tucked his knife away in his clothing.

"You bastard!" I whispered. "What have you done?"

Desh shrugged. "It's not so much what I have done," he said. He pointed at me. "It is more about what the heathen Outlaw of Corwick just did that matters most."

I glanced at the old priest's corpse, understanding now. "No one will believe you."

"Of course they will believe us," a voice said from behind me.

I turned, rocking back on my heels as Lord Corwick strode into the room. Behind him walked Son Oriel, his ugly features beaming with delight. I growled with hatred as the soldiers to either side of me tightened their grips on my arms. I spit on the floor in impotent rage.

"Tut, tut," Lord Corwick said reproachfully. "Is that any way to greet an old friend?"

"What are you doing here?" I managed to rasp out.

Lord Corwick stopped in front of me. "You have gotten bigger," he said, examining me. He lifted my chin, peering at my face. "Bigger and older." He clucked his tongue. "There is sorrow and death in your eyes, Hadrack. More so even than when we last met. Have you been having a bad time of it?"

"Let me loose, you bastard!" I hissed, struggling against the men holding me. "For once, be a man and fight me."

Lord Corwick slapped my cheek gently twice, shaking his head. "I think not. As enjoyable as killing you would be, I have better plans for you." He headed for the dais, pausing to pluck the crown from the unmoving prince's head before sitting in the second throne. Son Oriel moved to stand beside him, glancing down at the dead priest in triumph before focusing on me. Lord Corwick put the crown on and smiled at me regally.

"Do something!" I shouted at the prince. Prince Tyrale just stared blankly at me. I snorted in disgust and glared at Lord Corwick. "What's wrong with him?"

"Why, nothing," Lord Corwick said innocently. "My cousin tends to nod off sometimes. He really needs to get more sleep." Desh smirked as Lord Corwick continued, "But fear not, young Hadrack. The decision-making of the kingdom lies in the capable hands of the King's trusted advisor." Lord Corwick swept a hand toward Desh. "A man who I believe you remember with fondness from years gone by."

I shrugged off the soldiers to either side of me, glaring in warning at them. Lord Corwick stroked his beard, then motioned that they should back away. "I'm going to kill you both," I said, my voice low, steady and calm.

Lord Corwick tapped his chin several times. "That would be a most unfortunate error on your part," he said. "Assuming, of course, you could manage it somehow."

"The Mother will see to it," I promised.

Lord Corwick glanced up at Son Oriel in mock surprise. "Did you hear that, Son? The Mother will see to it."

The ugly priest sniffed, looking unimpressed. "The boy is talking out of his arse."

"Of course he is," Lord Corwick said. He leaned forward, his eyes narrowing as he focused on me. "Tell me about the codex."

"There is nothing to tell. It was gone."

Lord Corwick sat back, studying me. "You wouldn't lie to an old friend, now would you Hadrack?"

"What reason would I have?" I asked. "If I had found the codex, it would have been on me. It wasn't. That should be answer enough."

"True. True," Lord Corwick said thoughtfully. He accepted one of Waldin's scrolls from Son Oriel and tapped it against his leg. "Yet, you kept these worthless rants. Why?"

"I thought they might help people understand more about the times he lived in," I said, even though I knew it was a poor explanation.

Lord Corwick chuckled, handing the scroll back to the ugly priest. "Well, I think it would be more prudent to worry more about the here and now, don't you agree?" I said nothing, waiting, for I knew there was more. Lord Corwick stood and he began to pace, his hands behind his back. "I have a proposition for you, Hadrack. One which will prove beneficial to both of us."

"Whatever it is, forget it," I grunted.

Lord Corwick looked surprised. "Forget it? Don't you even want to hear what I propose?"

"No."

Lord Corwick raised his hands in the air and then slapped them against his sides in defeat. "So be it. I guess my forces outside of Witbridge Manor will just have to go ahead and raze the place to the ground, then." I tensed in alarm. "Oh, does that thought distress you?" Lord Corwick asked when he saw my expression. He shook his head. "I am sorry about this, Hadrack, but sometimes bold moves are necessary to bring about change for the better. I don't relish any of this, of course. I am by nature a squeamish man, but I also have a responsibility to the kingdom that I cannot shirk." He paused, his hands on his hips, his head hanging. "Sadly, I understand from my scouts that innocent women and children live in the village outside the manor walls. My men are usually well behaved, but with the pressure from the war and all, I simply cannot guarantee what they might do. I'm sure you can appreciate that."

"You bastard!" I hissed.

Lord Corwick pursed his lips. "Perhaps you might wish to reconsider helping us if this bothers you so much?"

"What do you want?" I growled.

"This war has dragged on long enough," Lord Corwick said. He paused beside Prince Tyrale's throne, clucking to himself with concern as he shifted the prince into a more comfortable position. "But my dear cousins are stubborn men, and I know neither one of them will give up until the other is dead."

"He looks most of the way there," I grunted, glancing at the prince.

"That he does," Lord Corwick agreed regretfully. "We do what we can for Tyrale, of course, but the situation is dire. Were he to die, the gods forbid, then his brother would become king by default. A situation that none of us in this room finds palatable, to say the least." Lord Corwick turned to me, his expression all business now. "Help us to rectify that, and you have my word no harm will befall Witbridge Manor."

"How?" I asked suspiciously.

Lord Corwick motioned for Desh to answer.

"We sent assassins to kill Prince Tyden four times already," Hervi Desh said. "All four attempts have failed. The prince is guarded day and night, with only those closest to him allowed to be anywhere near. His food is tasted first, even his ale and wine, so poison will not work."

"What has that got to do with me?" I demanded.

Lord Corwick smiled. "We need you to meet with Tyden. Use whatever excuse you can think of to get close to him, then kill him."

I gaped at Lord Corwick. "You're insane," I said. "I won't do it."

"Not even for Witbridge?" Lord Corwick asked.

I hesitated. Could I condemn all those people to death in favor of the life of one man? I closed my eyes, trying to come up with a solution, even though deep inside, I knew there wouldn't be one.

"There is one other thing that might sway your decision," Lord Corwick said. He snapped his fingers and Desh produced a cloth bundle. "I understand you and my sister have become close this past year," the lord added as he accepted the cloth.

I felt my heart lurch in my chest as Lord Corwick grabbed an end of the cloth with each hand, then snapped the bundle open in front of him with a dramatic flourish. Long, shiny black hair cascaded outward, falling in glistening strands across the dais.

"Shana," I whispered in dismay, knowing without a doubt that the hair belonged to her.

"Indeed," Lord Corwick responded gravely. "She is still alive, for the time being." He looked up as footfalls echoed within the grand room. Four House Agents were heading toward us down the corridor. "Ah, just in time," Lord Corwick said. He turned to me.

"The news of what you have done today is even now spreading throughout the city, Hadrack." He grinned smugly. "They will hunt you down from one end of the kingdom to the other for murdering the First Son. The only chance your people and my sister have to live is for you to do as I say and kill Tyden."

"How do I know you won't kill them all anyway even if I manage it?" I demanded.

Lord Corwick smiled condescendingly. "I'm a man of my word, Hadrack. Everyone knows this."

I glowered back at him. "If I do it and Tyrale becomes king, do you swear on The Mother and The Father that you will honor our agreement?"

Lord Corwick laughed condescendingly as he spread his arms. "What nonsense is that, now? I never said anything about my dear cousin gaining the throne." I blinked in confusion as Lord Corwick grinned mockingly at me. "With Tyden dead, I will have no further use for Tyrale. I'm afraid my cousin's fragile health will take a dramatic turn for the worse shortly after his brother's demise."

I closed my eyes and groaned, understanding it all now. "Which leaves you the next in line to the throne," I said, feeling sick to my stomach.

"Precisely right," Lord Corwick agreed. "But only if Tyden dies before Tyrale. That's imperative. So, the choice for you is quite simple, really."

"Do you promise to release Shana if I do what you want?" I asked bleakly.

"Come to Gandertown on the day of my coronation," Lord Corwick said. "The moment I am crowned king, you and she will be free to go wherever you wish, with a full pardon from the King himself."

The House Agents arrived in a clatter of armor, surrounding me, and I lowered my eyes to the floor. "I'll do it," I said, feeling demoralized and helpless.

"Of course, you will," Lord Corwick grunted. He motioned to one of the House Agents, who guided me up the dais toward a narrow archway that stood at the back. "Hadrack?" I turned to look over my shoulder. "They will be coming for you," Lord Corwick said. "So, you better not get caught, or my sister dies." He smiled. "Off you go now. Run, my little wolf, run."

25: Witbridge Manor

My escape from the palace was a well-planned affair. I was whisked along various abandoned passages to a small courtyard, where horses and a change of clothing were waiting for me. The House Agent in charge was a gruff man named Flidion, who had a no-nonsense way about him. I was disguised as a fellow House Agent, and with me riding in the middle, the five of us made our way through the streets. Bells of sorrow were ringing across the city, with the most prominent coming from the Holy House. People wept in the streets, pulling at their hair as they screamed for vengeance against the Outlaw of Corwick. Rioting had begun in places as well, as men, women, and even children encircled the palace, demanding my head on a pike. We turned down an ally, heading for one of the lesser gates as a knot of men fought each other in front of a burning building. I had no idea why the men were fighting, but soldiers arrived in a solid mass, only to have the two warring factions unite and turn on them.

"Madness," I heard one House Agent say through his closed helmet as we circled around the surging mob.

We reached a street lined on both sides with stone houses, where a woman beat an old man with a reed broom in front of one of the dwellings. The woman paused to stare at us suspiciously, saying nothing, then resumed the beating once we had passed.

"Be thankful they can't see you for what you are," Flidion said to me as we left the two behind. "If they will do this to each other, imagine what they would do to you."

I said nothing, staring straight ahead through my helmet. My hands were still manacled, but the House Agents had thrown a cheap blanket over them, hiding my bonds from prying eyes. I had to escape these men soon, I knew, but after seeing the lunacy that had taken hold in Gandertown, waiting until we were away from the city seemed the more prudent move.

We continued on through the narrow streets, twice having to detour around mobs of angry, chanting citizens. Finally, we reached the outer gates and passed unchallenged through them, leaving Gandertown behind us as plumes of black smoke rose from within her walls. We rode for three miles over sloping hills and across fields of long grass, until finally we reached a small inn standing alone beneath a giant aspen. Several men were waiting for us inside the inn, looking tense and anxious. I saw gold change hands, then bundles of clothing were produced. We changed into light tunics, cotton trousers, and heavy cloaks, then headed south at a gallop.

The House Agents were not men interested in idle chatter and we rode in silence, leaving me plenty of time to think about what had just occurred in Gandertown. Lord Corwick had assured me he would let Shana go, which, coming from that bastard, meant he had no intention of doing so. Shana was his half-sister and had royal blood in her veins, so there was no chance he would let her live. Lord Corwick had also said he would keep her safe until his coronation, and, on that, I believed him. Shana was his leverage over me to ensure I came back to Gandertown. I knew he intended to kill the both of us when I did. I needed to come up with a plan to make sure that didn't happen, but first, I needed to be free. The House Agents were alert right now, but hopefully, a chance would present itself once night set in.

Days went by, always with the hope that my escorts would make a mistake, but though I was watching for it, an opportunity never arose. The House Agents worked in tandem, with two of them close by me at all times. At night, I was tied propped up against the nearest tree, with my ankles lashed together for good measure. I was treated well enough, though with a certain amount of disdain that I knew was a familiar trait of House Agents. They might work for the Sons, but these men were no different from men like Malo and Odiman. Being a heartless bastard seemed to be a requirement to join their order, regardless of which side of the House they supported.

"Do you know Halhaven well?" Flidion asked me on the fourth day.

We were riding along a barely seen trail through browning scrub brush, skirting a forest of thick trees.

"Not well, no," I said grudgingly.

"Have you met Prince Tyden?"

I shook my head. "Never had the pleasure."

"How do you intend to gain an audience with him, then?"

I frowned. I hadn't thought that far ahead. "I'm not sure," I admitted.

Flidion glared at me. "Well, you had better be sure by the time we get there."

I looked away, staring down at the dusty path in front of my horse. The House Agents were intent on coming into Halhaven with me. How they expected to get in was a mystery that Flidion wasn't revealing. I wasn't sure how I would get in myself, let alone them. I wasn't sure about anything, actually. All I knew was I couldn't let Shana and my people at Witbridge die.

Dusk was settling in as we crested a rock-strewn hill and started down the other side. Thick bushes grew in bunches here, and suddenly a guttural bawling sound arose from one of them. We halted our horses, watching warily as the shadowy branches began to shake as something moved inside. The noise repeated, then a snout emerged from the bushes, followed by a mass of black fur. A bear cub, I realized.

The cub stared at us, wrinkling its nose and shifting back and forth on its paws uncertainly. I glanced around, tensing. Where was the mother? One of the House Agents muttered something and drew his sword as he trotted forward to dispatch the bear. The cub shrank back from him, huffing loudly and clacking its teeth just as something big and dark appeared from the forest line, hurtling toward us while grunting and groaning in distress. I have always found bears to be ungainly looking, but they are deceptively quick for such large animals. I remember as a boy seeing one run down a deer. My father had told me the bear would have to be starving to do that, as they rarely waste that much energy to obtain food. This bear wasn't starving, but instead was defending her cub from predators. Us.

The mother bear barrelled directly for the lead House Agent, while the rest of us fought to control our terrified horses. The cub ducked back into the bushes, wailing as the mother arrived and tore at the House Agent's screaming horse. Dust swirled in heavy clouds, making it hard for me to see what was happening. I could hear men shouting and horses shrieking as I swung the mare around, sending her at full gallop toward the trees. My opportunity had come.

I didn't look back as I rode, the sounds from behind slowly fading as the mare cut her way through the rapidly darkening forest. I had headed east initially, just happy to go in any direction, but after a mile or so, I turned north, hoping my pursuers would assume I would go south. I rode for another hour, always watching my backtrail, then I turned west, heading for the coast. I had no idea where I was—I just kept going—my ears attuned continuously to any sound that might be the House Agents.

I rode all night without seeing anyone, and the next morning, I reached a gentle valley where a flock of fat sheep were grazing peacefully on rich-looking grass. A boy lay on the grass near the valley crest, his hands behind his head, a battered straw hat covering his face. He didn't hear me approach until I was almost upon him, then he sat up, his face twisted in surprise as he squinted up at me.

"Good morning," I said amiably. The boy glanced around nervously, chewing on his bottom lip. "What is your name, lad?" I asked.

"Arel, lord."

"A fine name," I said. "What is the name of the closest town?"

"Wormwood, lord."

I pursed my lips. I'd never heard of the place. "What is the name of the closest town that matters," I asked, smiling to let the boy know that I meant no offense.

Arel blinked. "Uh, Hillsfort is twenty miles west of here, lord."

I grinned. I knew where I was. "Tell me, Arel," I said. "Have you any food?" The boy nodded reluctantly. "Good," I grunted. I glanced at the dull knife tucked away in his belt. "And I'll take your blade, too," I added, hoping the steel was sound enough to pry open my manacles. Arel handed me what little food he had, then the blade, his eyes widening when he saw my bonds. He glanced closer at my face beneath my hood and he gasped. "What?" I growled.

"It's you," the boy whispered. "The Outlaw of Corwick."

I frowned. "What nonsense is this?"

"I saw your face this morning on the posting tree," the boy said. I could see his body was trembling as he stared at me in awe. "The True King has offered a hundred Jorqs for you."

I groaned. Lord Corwick had certainly moved fast with his games. I turned the mare away just as the boy called out to me. I hesitated and looked back. "What?" I grunted.

Arel peered up at me, his face twisted in seriousness. "Why did you do it?"

"Here's some advice, boy," I said gravely. "Don't believe everything you hear."

I was tired but relieved when I finally crested the ridge that overlooked Witbridge Manor. I still wasn't sure what I was going to do about Prince Tyden, but at least I would have the sage advice of Jebido, Tyris, and the others to help me come up with a solution. It was well past midday with the sun glaring down on me as I paused on the ridge and stared down at Witbridge Manor. Whatever feelings I thought I would have at that moment fled as I stared with growing alarm at the faint tendrils of wispy smoke drifting up from where the village had once stood.

"The lying bastard!" I shouted in fury, slapping my horse into motion.

I rode haphazardly down the ridge face, my heart thudding with dread as I reached the valley floor and gave the mare her head. I could see more smoke coming from within the walls of the manor itself as the bell began to clang from the watchtower. Several riders appeared through the open gate, heading toward me. I recognized

Jebido, Tyris, and Sim, so I slowed to a more moderate pace. Whatever had happened here, I realized, had happened some time ago. Breaking my horse's legs would do nothing to change that.

Jebido was the first to reach me and he jumped to the ground as I dismounted, almost pulling me from my feet as he embraced me.

"Thank the gods!" he said, pushing me away to examine me. "You look terrible."

I grimaced, my eyes sliding past him to the ruins of the village. "What happened?" I growled.

"Outlaws, my lord," Tyris said. "They came two days ago."

"Outlaws?" I grunted, glaring at him. "You are certain of that? Not soldiers?"

"Not according to Finol, my lord. He insists it was outlaws."

"Finol? Weren't you here?"

Tyris shifted his gaze to Jebido, then looked away.

"No," Jebido said. "The outlaws must have been watching the manor and saw us leave."

"You left Witbridge undefended?"

"I did," Jebido said, his face coloring, though his eyes had a stubborn cast to them. "It seemed the right thing to do at the time."

"And how many people died because of that decision, Jebido?" I snapped. "How many?"

Jebido looked away and I could see the hurt in his eyes. "More than I care to think about," he whispered.

"Then why in the name of The Mother did you do it?"

Jebido sighed, looking old and worn suddenly. "Because we heard rumors that the Outlaw of Corwick had been seen to the east." He shrugged and stared at the ground. "I thought you were dead all this time, Hadrack, lost on that damn mountain. The information seemed credible, so I—" He hesitated and looked up at me, guilt heavy on his weathered face. "I had to know if you were alive. I'm sorry, I should have gone alone."

I closed my eyes as anger surged through me. The imposter again. I would deal with him once and for all, I promised myself. Finally, I nodded, accepting Jebido's explanation. Now was not the time to lay blame. Besides, I probably would have done the same thing, had I been in Jebido's position.

"There is something else you need to know," Jebido added.

I waited, steeling myself for more bad news.

"Flora is dead," Jebido said. "The babe too."

I groaned at the unfairness of it all and looked at the sky. Why Flora? Why the child? Wasn't taking Baine from me enough?

"Hadrack," Jebido said sorrowfully, putting a hand to my shoulder. "I had to let him go after the bastards. Nothing I said would keep him here. We only heard yesterday about what happened in Gandertown, and I knew you would be making your way back to us. I pleaded with him to wait for you, but he wouldn't hear of it. I'm sorry."

I blinked at Jebido in confusion. "Who? You begged who to wait?"

Now it was Jebido's turn to look confused. Realization finally struck him and his mouth sagged open. "Mother's tit, Hadrack, forgive me for being a stupid old fool. I just assumed you knew for some reason. Baine is alive."

26: On The Run

I stood by Flora's freshly dug grave, buffeted by so many emotions that I had trouble thinking. Somehow, miraculously, Baine had survived the storm, only to return to Witbridge after his ordeal to find that his wife and child had been brutally slain. I bowed my head wearily, thinking about how pitiless the gods can be to us mere mortals. The soil over the grave was still wet from the previous night's rain, and I could see deep depressions in the dirt where my friend had knelt, weeping. Shallow puddles filled the hollows, as if the grave itself had chosen to collect Baine's tears as a testament to his grief. I dropped to my knees where my friend had been, heedless of the muddy water, my own tears falling unchecked as I read the inscription Baine had cut into the marker over the grave.

Here lies Flora and baby Hadrack
Wife and son of Baine
I will not rest
I will not eat
I will not sleep
Until their killers pay

I felt a hand on my shoulder and I looked up at Jebido. "He should have waited for me," I whispered. "We could have dealt with this together."

"That's what I told him," Jebido said grimly. He squeezed my shoulder. "He told me to tell you that you, of all people, will understand that this is something he must do on his own."

I bowed my head in acknowledgment. I did understand. I understood all too well.

Jebido left me after that, and I knelt by Flora's grave for some time, thinking of the opinionated ex-whore and what she had meant to all of us. Flora had been beloved by everyone in the manor, as well as a favorite among the villagers, and I knew she would be sorely missed. I'd always felt guilty about how I had left Flora to die beneath Calban, bent only on saving Shana. I had even taken Shana to bed after the battle was won, more intent on my own selfish pleasure than the welfare of someone who had risked so much for me. I believe that was the lowest moment in my life, something that I have always deeply regretted. I'd meant to properly apologize to Flora at some point during the last year, but the time had never seemed right. Now it never would be.

"I'm sorry," I said as I stood and stared down at the grave. "You and your babe deserved better."

I turned and headed back to the manor house. I wondered where Baine was right now as I walked, a part of me thinking that I should just forget what he'd asked of me and go after him. Then I thought of Shana and Lord Corwick, knowing that I would have to sacrifice a friend in need for the woman I loved once again. I climbed the long slope up to Witbridge, feeling old beyond my years as I reached the summit and passed through the gate.

Finol was waiting for me in the courtyard, a squalling baby squirming in his arms. "Forgive the intrusion, my lord," Finol said, "but our supplies have dwindled and there is no money left. What would you have me do?"

I glanced at the child. His name was Walice, a recent orphan from the village who Margot, the ex-whore, had rescued from a burning hut. For reasons that escaped me, Finol, though older even than Jebido, had claimed the troublesome babe, vowing to raise him as his own.

"My lord?" Finol repeated.

I hesitated, my mind weary from the need to forever solve other peoples' problems. The imposter Outlaw of Corwick had somehow learned of our stash beneath the floor of Witbridge Manor. That's why the bastard had raided the holding, leaving us with nothing but a few silver coins. We were still trying to figure out who might have told him of the stash, but for now, I had neither the time nor the energy to conduct a raid to get us more money.

I shrugged. "Do what you can," I muttered, waving Finol off as I headed for the manor.

"But, my lord," Finol said in exasperation over the cries of the child.

The bell began to ring on the watchtower and I turned, shading my eyes as riders appeared over the crest of the hill.

"Close the gate," I commanded, my lethargy dissipating at the promise of action. Woe to any who tried to attack us now, I thought grimly.

"It's all right, my lord," Putt called down from the watchtower. He pointed over the wall. "It's Daughter Eleva, back from Halhaven."

I nodded, relieved and disappointed at the same time. Daughter Eleva was the village priestess and had been away from the Holy House when the attack occurred. Like me, I imagine she knew nothing of what had happened here. I walked to the gate and watched as she and her retinue hesitated on the ridge as I had, surveying the ruined village. Then they rode toward the manor house. The Daughter was in the lead, with two Daughters-In-Waiting following close behind, along with a grim-faced House Agent that I didn't recognize. One of the apprentices looked familiar and I squinted as they drew closer. I felt a sudden surge of pleasure and warmth come over me. It was Jin.

The Daughter reached the gate and I stepped aside as the horses entered.

"Hadrack!" Jin cried, leaping from her horse. She ran to me and threw her arms around me. "It's been so long!"

"This is not how proper Daughters-In-Waiting conduct themselves," Daughter Eleva said with a sniff. "Compose yourself, child."

Jin stepped back, lowering her eyes. "I have missed you so much, Hadrack," she whispered.

"What has happened here?" Daughter Eleva demanded. "Who is responsible for this atrocity?"

The baby chose that moment to scream again, startling all of us. Finol finally managed to quiet the child. "Outlaws seeking gold, I'm afraid," the steward said. "Many of the villagers died."

Daughter Eleva bowed her head and I saw her lips moving in prayer. Finally, she looked up. "Where are the survivors?"

"We tried to get them to come inside the walls," Finol explained, "but they refused. They set up a camp in the quarry for now."

"Then my place is there," Daughter Eleva said firmly. She turned her horse and trotted back through the gate, the House Agent silently following. "Come along, girls."

Jin held my hand, biting her lip in indecision as the other apprentice followed after the priestess dutifully.

"Now, Jin!" Daughter Eleva's voice sounded from outside the walls.

"You better go," I said. "We can talk later."

Jin reluctantly started to mount her horse, then she ran back and kissed me on the cheek. "You've changed, Hadrack. Something is different, but I'm glad you are well."

I watched Jin ride away. The girl had said I'd changed and I knew that she was right. Something had shifted in me on that mountain. Something that I could not put into words. I turned and headed for the manor house as Hanley limped toward me, his crooked arm held at an odd angle. The boy had fought well, I'd heard, taking down two outlaws on his own before being wounded in the leg.

"Gather everyone in the great hall," I ordered. "We need to talk."

Once we were settled, I told Margot and my men everything, only excluding what Sabina had done while I was out of my mind with fever. I still felt great shame about rutting with her, and I knew I wasn't ready to deal with the questions that would undoubtedly arise if I told them.

"I was right!" Jebido cried, smashing his fist on the great tabletop when I told them of Ragna the Elder and his son. "By The Mother, I knew She would send the bastards to you one way or another!"

"I should have known better than to doubt you, my friend," I said, standing at my familiar spot before the roaring fireplace.

"That's the truth," Jebido grunted.

"But Sabina's father and brother?" Tyris said, shaking his head in wonder. "They were two of the nine? It's hard to believe."

Jebido hooked a thumb at me. "The boy is being watched over by the gods. Nothing that happens to him surprises me anymore."

"This girl, Sabina," Margot said, her thin features looking thoughtful. "What became of her?"

"I neither know, nor care," I grunted a little too harshly, turning away.

I knew I appeared callous and cruel to everyone else in the room, but since I had no wish to explain further, that was the way it would have to be. I told them next of my capture by Lord Graaf's men and the journey to Gandertown, then about my meeting with the supposed, True King.

"You met the prince, my lord?" Niko asked. "What's he like?"

"Sleepy," I answered to the confused looks of my men.

I explained the elaborate scheme that Lord Corwick and Hervi Desh had spun, as gasps arose from the listeners. Finally, when I was done and the full significance of the problem had sunk in, the room filled with silence as my men digested the sobering news.

"So, that's why you thought soldiers had attacked Witbridge, my lord," Sim said.

"Yes," I nodded. "Lord Corwick said he had men nearby watching the holding."

Sim shook his head. "I have been scouting every day, my lord. I've seen no such force."

"A bluff, then?" Jebido asked.

"Perhaps," I said. "With Lord Corwick, it's hard to tell the truth from untruth." I put my hands on my hips and looked around. "Now, the question is, what are we going to do to stop him?"

Silence filled the room at that, and one by one, the eyes of my men dropped.

"We could try getting into the city like we did at Calban, my lord," Niko offered weakly.

I snorted. "Don't you think Lord Corwick is ready for that?"

Jebido sighed and ran his fingers through his silver hair. "I don't know, Hadrack. I don't see an easy way out of this one."

"You could just go ahead and kill Prince Tyden, my lord," Margot suggested. Everyone paused to look at her in surprise, and the ex-whore colored at the attention. "I mean, what is the life of one man compared to Lady Shana, anyway?"

"Because the moment Lord Corwick hears that Prince Tyden is dead," Putt said scornfully, "he will murder Prince Tyrale and claim the throne for himself. Then nothing will stop him from doing whatever he wants."

"Putt is right," I said. "The only way—" I paused in mid-sentence, my finger pointed at the red-haired outlaw as a thought suddenly struck me.

"What is it?" Jebido asked.

I turned, ignoring him as I began to pace before the roaring fire. Would it work? I wondered. I felt excitement starting to build. It just might, but I would need help—very specific help from someone that I could trust. "Niko," I snapped, spinning around. "Go to the quarry and get Jin right now."

"What does she have to do with any of this?" Jebido asked, looking confused.

I grinned at my old friend. "Jin is the key, Jebido. The key to everything."

I looked down from the hills overlooking Halhaven one week later, staring at the city from Angry's broad back as the morning sun brushed the town's walls with glittering light. Jebido and Sim sat their horses beside me, waiting together in mutual silence as I went over the plan in my head one more time. I fingered the knife in my belt beneath my soiled cloak, wondering if I had what it took to see this thing through. One mistake, one wrong turn, and Shana would die. It was a terrifying thought.

"There is still time to reconsider," Jebido said. "We can try to find another way."

I looked at my friend and shook my head. "There is no other way," I said. "We all agreed on that."

"If the House Agents catch you," Jebido warned, unable to hide the worry on his face, "they will kill you before you can explain."

"I'm aware of that," I grunted. I took a deep breath, peering at the sun as it rose majestically over the hills. "It's almost time," I said, dismounting. I handed Angry's reins to Sim and patted the big black affectionately, surprised when the horse grudgingly nuzzled me. I grinned, taking that as a good omen as I offered my hand to Sim.

"Good luck, my lord," the big outlaw said gravely.

I nodded, moving to Jebido's horse as I peered up at my friend. "If this goes badly for me," I began.

Jebido held up a hand, stopping me. "It won't. You just do what you have to do. We'll be ready afterward to get you out of there."

"You're becoming more of an optimist every day," I said with an admiring grin.

Jebido made a face as he thought about that, then he slowly smiled. "You know what, lad? I'm beginning to think you are right."

I patted Jebido's leg, then set my shoulders and turned away, heading down the narrow, beaten path toward the city. A butterfly danced gayly around me and I thought of Sabina, remembering that day in First Step and the butterflies that had delighted her so. I frowned at the thought of the girl, and instead turned my focus on where I put my feet along the steep path.

The morning sun was already getting hot, though it was still early. I was sweating as I walked, adding even more stains to the caked filth on my clothing as I reached level ground, heading for the open gates of the city. Merchants passed through the entrance with relative ease, with wary guards watching them silently from all sides. I was pleased, having been concerned that the gates might be sealed. Being this far south, Prince Tyden must have felt confident enough that his forces would detect any intrusion well before an enemy got close to Halhaven's walls.

I began to shuffle along, my back bent, my wild, grey-powdered hair dangling loosely in front of my eyes. I drew a bottle from my cloak and took a long pull on it, burping and wiping the back of my hand over my mouth.

"Hey, you!" a guard shouted, pointing at me as I used a merchant's cart to steady myself. "Where do you think you are going?" he demanded.

"To dine with the prince, of course," I slurred, waving the bottle in the air with a flourish. "Where else?"

The guards all laughed as I took another drink, barely tasting the weak wine as I anticipated one of them turning me away. My momentary notoriety fled just as quickly as it had appeared, however, as the guards promptly lost interest in me and turned their attention elsewhere. I stumbled through the gates, head down, mumbling to myself, until finally I slipped away unseen down a back alley.

I slowly made my way toward the Holy House, playing my beggarly drunkard role whenever someone came close. Finally, I reached the majestic building and headed for the walled courtyard at the back. The wrought iron gates there were usually locked firmly, I knew, but this time the chain had been left loose on purpose just enough that a man could slip through. I pushed my way inside with some effort, then quickly crossed the courtyard to the entrance and stepped cautiously through the doors. The familiar sounds of the fountain gushing in the cloister greeted me as I turned and followed the right-hand passage, praying that I wouldn't run into anyone. Jin had guaranteed the Daughters-In-Waiting would be at lessons, but there was always the chance that a House Agent or two could be around. I didn't know what I would do if one of them tried to stop me.

I reached the stairs that led to the Daughter's Tower undetected, then hurried up the winding steps until I reached the top floor. Two soldiers lay sprawled on the stone by the head of the stairs, a bottle lying between them. One of the men was snoring softly. I stepped over the still forms and crept along the passageway as voices echoed from the room ahead of me.

"I'm not sure I understand what brings you here at such an early hour, Your Highness," a woman was saying. I recognized Daughter Gernet's voice immediately.

"I was told that you wished to meet with me, Daughter," a deep voice replied. Prince Tyden, I knew. "A most delicate matter that required discretion above all else. One that you wished to keep away from the eyes and ears of the palace."

"Why, Your Highness, I asked for no such meeting! Who told you this fabrication?"

"Your girl did!" Prince Tyden said, sounding annoyed.

I nodded. So far, things were going to plan.

"Jin, explain yourself!" Daughter Gernet demanded, her voice rising with anger.

I crept toward the arched entrance, crouching low as I carefully peered inside the rounded room. Daughter Gernet sat on a bench at the table, her hands in her lap, her features twisted with displeasure. Prince Tyden stood by the fireplace, a look of irritation on his young face as he glared at Jin, who stood next to him, holding a scroll. I drew my knife, waiting for the agreed-upon moment as I hid in the shadows.

"A simple oversight," Jin said curtly, not looking at her grandmother. The girl turned her back and faced the fire, ignoring the priestess as the older woman sputtered in indignation. "If you would only look at this, Your Highness, it will explain everything," Jin said calmly, holding up the scroll and unraveling it.

Prince Tyden peered at the writing, then frowned. "I don't understand," he said, grabbing the scroll. He bent over, leaning closer to the fire to see the words better. "What does any of this even mean?"

Now was my chance, I knew. I launched myself forward, ignoring Daughter Gernet's horrified gasp as I swept past her, the knife raised. The prince straightened and turned, sensing his danger just as I reached him. He raised a hand to ward me off and I slapped it aside, then plunged the knife into his stomach. Blood spurted instantly as the prince fell back in shock, clutching at himself. He stumbled on the hearth, grasping for the mantle, but his hand slid off the smooth stone and he collapsed to the floor with blood pooling under him. Jin stood unmoving, her hands clasped to her mouth. I guess she hadn't expected so much blood. We shared a look, then I turned to go, stopping as my eyes met those of Daughter Gernet.

"Hadrack?" the Daughter asked uncertainly. Despite my powdered hair and disheveled look, I knew she had recognized me beneath my hood. Daughter Gernet stared at me in horrified disbelief. She glanced down at the dying prince. "What have you done?"

"I'm sorry," I said. "I had no other choice."

Then I started to run.

27: Coronation

    I made it to the courtyard outside the Holy House before the first sounds of alarm arose. I raced across the cobblestones, tearing off my filthy cloak as I ran. Beneath it, I was wearing the livery of a groom. The irony that I was posing as a caretaker of horses hadn't been lost on me, but we'd needed something that would allow me to move freely without being noticed. As a groom, I now fit that requirement perfectly, as there were so many on the streets of the sprawling city that they all seemed to blend together. I squeezed through the gap in the gates, then began to run north along a deserted back alley.

    Few, if any stable boy's had grey hair, I knew, so I paused at the first horse trough that I saw and dunked my head into the cold water, washing the powder away. I straightened and shook, sending water flying in all directions just as footsteps sounded from behind me.

"Hadrack?"

I turned, feeling a knot of dread in my stomach. Malo stood twenty feet from me; his usually placid face creased with torment.

"Why?" Malo growled as he took several paces forward. His hand fell to his sword hilt.

"Wait," I said, holding up a hand to him in warning." There's no time for this." I glanced around for a weapon, dearly wishing I had Wolf's Head, or any other sword for that matter. The knife I wore in my belt would be useless against a man like Malo.

"Do you know what you have done?" Malo hissed. I could see the fury burning in his eyes.

I glanced over my shoulder. The alley led onto a wider street, where I could see horses and people moving briskly along. I licked my lips and looked back at the House Agent. Could I make it to the street and lose myself in the traffic there before Malo caught me?

The man wasn't as big as I was, but I'd seen how fast he could move and I realized that I probably couldn't outrun him.

"Malo, you have to listen to me," I said. Malo drew his sword purposefully, the blade ringing off the silver-ringed locket at the head of his scabbard. "You don't know the full story," I added, taking a step back.

"All I know is you have brought ruin down on us all, you traitorous bastard," Malo said through clenched teeth. "Everything we've worked for is destroyed because of you." He stopped three feet from me, his sword tip at my throat. "Tell me why I shouldn't kill you right now."

"Because Shana will die and Lord Corwick will win," I said, knowing my only chance was to reason with the House Agent. I knew I couldn't tell him the entire truth. Not yet anyway, but hopefully I could give him enough that he'd let me go.

Malo grunted in surprise. "What does that mean?"

I told the House Agent about my capture and meeting with Lord Corwick and Hervi Desh. Then I described how they had schemed to win the throne, and how they had coerced me into helping them. Malo's sword began to waver, and then it dropped to his side as I continued to talk.

"So, by killing the prince, you save Lady Shana," Malo said when I was through. "But by doing so, you've effectively laid our kingdom at the feet of a madman." He sheathed his sword, a little too forcefully, I thought. I needed to be careful—I wasn't out of this yet. Malo frowned as he worked it out. "What makes you think Lord Corwick won't kill Lady Shana once he becomes king?"

I took a deep breath. I was ready for that question. I just had to tell Malo the lie without him becoming suspicious. "Because I have something that he wants in exchange for her."

"And what would that be?" Malo asked.

"The codex," I said, hoping the House Agent would be so surprised he wouldn't realize that once Lord Corwick was king, he'd have no use for it. He could side with the Sons no matter what the codex said.

Malo blinked several times in surprise. "You have it?"

I'd sent Niko to Halhaven the day after I had returned to Witbridge Manor, informing Daughter Gernet and Malo that the codex was long gone from Waldin's cave. I had debated mentioning that I knew where it was, but then decided to omit that. Only Sabina and I knew where it might be, and even she had only a vague notion. I saw no reason to divulge anything to Daughter Gernet until after I'd dealt with Lord Corwick. If, indeed, I decided to tell at all. I had also mentioned that I'd had nothing to do with the First Son's murder, though I liked to believe they knew that from the beginning.

I shook my head. "No, but I know where it is." I put my hand on Malo's shoulder. "You have to trust me, Malo. After all we have been through, you know I wouldn't betray you or Daughter Gernet. If my plan works, I will get Shana back alive, finally be rid of Lord Corwick, and the Daughters will have all the power over the House they desire." I squeezed. "But, all of that can only happen if I get away from Halhaven."

Malo studied me, his face and eyes clearly showing his indecision. Finally, he poked a finger into my chest. "You had better be right about this, Hadrack," he growled. "Because if you lied to me just now, then there won't be anywhere in this world where you can hide from me."

I returned with my men to Witbridge Manor and said my goodbyes all around. The Outlaw of Corwick was now wanted in the South, just as much as the North, and I couldn't risk the lives of anyone else, should someone think to come looking for me here. I didn't know what Malo would do with the information that I'd given him, but I couldn't chance Daughter Gernet's rage, should she decide to send House Agents down upon Witbridge. I knew there would be little threat to anyone else without me here, so I was leaving.

"How long do you think it will be, my lord?" Finol asked. He still held little Walice in his arms, tucked away in a swathe of blankets. I was just as impressed by his devotion as I was surprised by it.

I shrugged. "Who can say? We'll probably know more after Prince Tyden's funeral. I doubt Lord Corwick will wait long after that before making a move. I don't want to be seen before he does."

I mounted Angry and shifted Wolf's Head on my hip, glad to have the weapon back where it belonged. My father's axe was sheathed across my back, the familiar weight also a welcome return.

"Where will you go?" Jebido asked me.

I grinned. "My father took me on my first hunting trip in Bloomwood Forest when I was a boy," I said wistfully. "I think I'll go there."

Jebido frowned. "How will we find you?"

I tugged on Angry's reins, turning him toward the gate. "There is a small village to the east of the forest," I said. "When the coronation date has been set, leave a marker along the treeline facing the village. I'll return when I see it."

Then I started to ride, quelling the emotion threatening to rise in my chest as I left my friends behind. I paused on the crest overlooking the holding, staring back at the manor house. Would I ever return to this place that had sheltered me and helped me to grow? I turned away, motioning Angry onward until the buildings and walls were lost from view.

I spent two weeks in the sprawling forest of Bloomwood, resting, hunting, and fishing. It was, I would wager, two of the finest weeks of my life. Whatever was going on outside my sanctuary was beyond my control, and I used the time to reflect on all that had happened and what I hoped to achieve with the rest of my life—should it continue beyond the next few weeks. I didn't know if the gambit I had set into motion would work, but I did know I needed to be patient and see it through. My greatest concern was for Shana, which was what I fretted over in my furs at night. Would Lord Corwick keep her alive until his coronation? I had gambled that he would, knowing that his promise to do so would be the only thing that could draw me back into his clutches. But if I was wrong, then the woman I loved was already dead, and even if we won in the end, I knew that I would have lost everything. It was a heavy burden to bear.

At the beginning of the third week of my self-exile, I met a man hunting deer along the forest's southern edge. He was a strange little fellow, with a rounded back, grizzled face and bald pate covered in painful-looking sores. His bow was fashioned from a stout ash branch, which he threatened me with like a club when I appeared from the trees.

"I'm just passing through," the man said with a whine to his voice, his eyes searching the bushes furtively behind me. "I ain't doing nothing wrong."

I glanced down at the dead fawn lying at his feet, an arrow protruding from its shoulder. "Then lucky for you, this little fellow was kind enough to stick himself on that arrow of yours," I said, my lips twitching in amusement. The little man looked down at the fawn, his face falling as his mouth worked, trying to say something. I held up a hand. "Rest easy, friend. One fawn among hundreds won't be missed. Besides, this land is no longer a Royal Forest, so what is there to fear?"

"But it is a Royal Forest," the little man said. I could see the look of regret on his face the moment the words were spoken, as he knew he'd just admitted to a crime. "Er, I mean, it was," he added weakly.

"A Royal Forest by who's decree?" I asked, sensing that something might have changed in the halls of power.

"Advisor Desh," the little man whispered, looking over his shoulder as though he expected Desh to pop out from the bushes. "The new king will be coronated next week, and the Advisor has claimed many of the forests of the South in retaliation for its failed support of the heretic, Prince Tyden."

"Ah," I said, nodding my head. I'd checked for a marker three days ago, but there had been nothing. There probably was now. "So, it's begun then." The poacher looked at me in confusion. "Never mind," I said to him. I unhooked a string of fish that I had draped over my shoulder. "Here, I won't be needing these."

The little man took the fish, gaping at me as I turned and headed back to my camp. "Hey, where are you going?"

"To a coronation," I said over my shoulder.

The day of Lord Corwick's coronation turned out to be cold, rainy, and miserable. A fitting start to a rein that I was determined would not last nearly as long as some believed. I'd learned from Jebido that Prince Tyrale had mysteriously died three days after his brother's funeral, clearing the way for Lord Corwick to claim the throne. The death had been considered suspicious, but even so, there had been little dissent at the lord's claim. The kingdom had been torn in two this past year, and the people were weary from so much savagery and bloodshed. I imagine they would probably have accepted anyone on the throne, if only to move on.

I was relieved to hear that Shana had been seen every day since her imprisonment, walking the palace battlements alone. My gamble had paid off, at least so far. Son Oriel was now the First Son, which had caught me by surprise, though in hindsight, I should have seen it coming. As for Hervi Desh, the advisor was temporarily in charge of the kingdom, as Ganderland's rules were clear during a transition of power. No king could sit upon the throne until after his coronation. I could only shudder at the thought of what Lord Corwick must be planning for Ganderland once he became king.

Advisor Desh had moved quickly after Prince Tyrale's death, ruling in favor of the Sons over the Daughters, who had now been relegated to something resembling glorified servants as the Sons consolidated their hold on the House. Jebido told me that the First Daughter had collapsed at the news, and her health was so grievous that Daughter Gernet had been tasked with attending the coronation in her place. Learning of the First Daughter's ill-health was unwelcome, but even so, I was looking forward to seeing Daughter Gernet and, hopefully, Jin as well. I thought of my dear friend, knowing the apprentice and I would be the only two in the palace fully aware of what was happening. Would all our scheming work out, or had something gone wrong over the past weeks? There was no way for me to know for certain.

"We can still go with you," Jebido said as my men and I sat our horses outside the city. Gandertown was bedecked in celebration, with colorful streamers and pennants draped across the towers and walls in honor of the new king.

I shook my head regretfully. "No, you have to stay here and wait until the time is right."

Jebido sighed in resignation. "I know, but I've never been much good at waiting."

I glanced around at the grim faces of my men, then I smiled, letting them see a confidence in me that I wasn't sure I felt. "The hard part is over, lads," I said. "So, wipe those looks off your faces. We'll all be free men in an hour from now."

"Or swinging from a noose," Putt said gloomily.

I laughed and waved a hand dismissively at him as I guided Angry toward the city. Putt might be right, I knew, but I was damned if I would walk into Gandertown shaking in my boots. Whatever happened this day, the Outlaw of Corwick was done hiding.

I reached the city gates, where eager peasants had congregated along the road in the rain, watching as lords and ladies arrived for the coronation on fine horses, or riding in elegant carts. No one paid much attention to me, fixated as they were on grander sights. I was thankful for that fact, not wanting to cause a scene similar to the first time I'd entered Gandertown. Soldiers carefully checked the lords and ladies for royal invitations before letting them in, something which seemed to affront many of the highborn as they impatiently stood in line. I had no invitation, but I was certain I wouldn't need one. If I knew Lord Corwick like I thought I did, then my name alone should suffice to gain me entrance.

I waited as a fat, bald lord with a red face and sweaty brow produced his papers, all the while lamenting the fact that he was being given no respect. Finally, just as the rain stopped, the fat lord moved on, still grumbling as I halted in front of a squat soldier who held out his hand expectantly.

"Your invitation," the soldier said in a bored voice.

"I haven't one," I replied.

The soldier looked as though he wasn't sure he'd heard me correctly. Finally, he sighed and waved me away. "Then move on, you worthless dog, so that those that do may enter."

"I'm here to see the new king," I persisted in a growl.

The soldier scowled. "So are a thousand others, every one of them more important than you. So, either move along, or I'll break something on you. Whichever choice will suit me just fine."

"How about we do neither?" I said, controlling my temper. Now was not the time to put this obnoxious man in his place. "Please inform the new king that Hadrack, the Outlaw of Corwick, has come to see him as agreed upon." The soldier's eyes widened and he stared up at me in shock. "Hurry now," I said mockingly. "I don't have all day."

The soldier swallowed in indecision, and then he walked briskly over to a grey-haired man standing by the gates. They talked for a moment, then the grey-haired man strode toward me, his face hard, his hand on his sword.

He studied my features carefully, saying nothing, then finally nodded. "I had thought the order was some kind of jest, but I see that it is not. You really have come."

"I have," I said as trumpets flared from the walls. "Now, are you going to let me in, or am I to miss the coronation?"

"We'll need your weapons first."

"You can have them," I said softly, "but only when you pry them from my dead fingers."

The grey-haired man frowned, then he motioned that I should dismount. "Very well. My men will see to your horse." He pointed at me. "No tricks from you, understand? We have orders to bring you to the king unharmed, but try anything, and I promise you, orders or not, your blood will flow on the ground. Now follow me."

A thin youth looking awkward and wet in his over-sized armor took Angry's reins. "If any harm comes to him," I said, holding the boy's eyes. "I'll hold you responsible."

The youth just stared at me in awe, saying nothing as I was led away through the gates. I followed the grey-haired man down a wide street as a contingent of soldiers marched behind us, most of them fingering their swords nervously as they watched me. I shifted my father's axe on my back and several men tensed, one even moaning slightly. I grinned, taking a perverse pleasure from the effect I was having on them. My smile quickly disappeared, however, as we reached the palace ramp where Hervi Desh stood awaiting me.

"I didn't think you would come," Desh said as I climbed to meet him.

The soldiers moved to follow and Desh waved them off. I could tell by the look on his face that he considered me of little threat. He was right. I wasn't the threat at all, as he'd soon come to learn.

"I want Lady Shana," I growled. "Now."

Desh chuckled, taking me by the arm and whisking me into the palace. I had to resist the urge to hit him.

"I see you've brought your father's axe," Desh said, glancing at the weapon.

"Don't even think about trying to take it," I said low and threatening.

Desh raised his hands and he smiled. "I wouldn't even consider it."

I could hear singing now, sweet, beautiful voices that rang out with both hope and innocence.

"Ah," Desh said. "They have begun."

He led me down the corridor to the grand room packed with brightly garbed lords and ladies. The dais at the far end of the room was decked out in plush, bright purple carpeting. Son Oriel, dressed in the fine robes of the First Son, stood at the top of the dais, a glittering crown held in his hands. Lord Corwick knelt on the steps in front of him, dressed in a simple white tunic similar to the one I had worn as a Pilgrim.

Desh guided me forward, causing a stir as my name began to be whispered from one person to another. Son Oriel's eyes were closed as he mumbled words that I couldn't make out clearly, nor cared to hear. The ugly priest frowned as the singing stopped at our approach, opening his eyes in annoyance. He blinked when he saw me, then smiled a wolfish grin that laid bare the darkness in his soul. The Son bent and whispered something to Lord Corwick, who turned to look over his shoulder at me.

Lord Corwick stood smoothly, his face breaking out in a delighted grin. I glanced at him in disdain, then sifted through the packed lords and ladies standing to either side of the dais until my eyes met Shana's. My heart leaped and I had to force myself not to jump the distance between us and take her in my arms. I could see tears of dismay in her eyes and I looked away from them, afraid that I would weaken and do something that might give the moment away.

Shana didn't know what I knew.

"Well, I must say," Lord Corwick said loudly, moving to the top of the dais. "I had hoped you would put in an appearance, Hadrack, but I didn't think you'd actually be this stupid."

"I'm here to hold you to your vow," I said. "Release Lady Shana and let us go in peace."

"Well, I did promise that, didn't I?" Lord Corwick said, looking thoughtful. I saw Shana's face brighten in sudden hope out of the corner of my eye, only to be dashed a moment later. "But honestly, did you really think that I would honor a contract made with a common criminal?"

Desh chuckled in amusement, moving away as soldiers with drawn swords surrounded me, staying back a respectful distance. Several ladies screamed, and one rather plump one in the front row fainted, causing a stir when her dress rose up her legs in an unfortunate manner, revealing a goodly portion of her ample behind.

I glanced over my shoulder. Jebido was standing at the back of the corridor, waving to get my attention. He grinned when my eyes fell on him and motioned that all was ready. I hadn't realized how tense I'd been and I almost sagged to the floor in relief. The gamble had paid off. I turned to face Lord Corwick, setting my shoulders back as I felt a jolt of energy flow through me.

"So, you refuse to honor our agreement made in good faith, then?" I demanded.

Lord Corwick paused dramatically, then he grinned. "I do."

"That makes you a liar as well as a coward and murderer," I said with disgust. "I should have known."

Lord Corwick shrugged. "Yes, perhaps you should have." He waved a hand casually. "But I'm not an ungracious man, Hadrack. I have decided to allow you to watch as I am crowned king before I have my men kill you. I think it is the least that I can do since your actions, which I whole-heartedly denounce, have turned out to be so beneficial to me."

"You won't be crowned king this day, or any other, you bastard," I said. "There will only be one king crowned here today. The True King!"

I turned with a flourish, gesturing behind me as armed soldiers poured down the corridor to the cries and shouts of the lords and ladies recoiling away in fear. Lord Corwick's men moved to block their path and a vicious battle quickly began.

"What is the meaning of this!?" Lord Corwick roared over the din of weapons colliding as Son Oriel scurried along the dais to hide behind the First Son's throne.

"Behold!" I cried as a tall blond man marched into the room with his glittering blue eyes fixated firmly on Lord Corwick. Soldiers with shields and drawn weapons surrounded the blond man protectively as they forged a path through the battling factions. "King Tyden of Ganderland!" I shouted. "The one and only king!"

I have never felt such satisfaction as I did at that moment, watching the expressions of dismay and fear on Lord Corwick and Hervi Desh's faces. Jin had been the key to everything, just as I'd told Jebido. The Daughter-In-Waiting had met secretly with the prince after I had told her my plan of feigning his death. A pig's bladder filled with blood and a blunted knife, not to mention the murder witnessed by a respected Daughter, was all it had taken—that, and a lot of faith placed in me by a man that I had never met.

One of Lord Corwick's men rushed at me from the knot of fighting, cursing men nearby, cutting off my thoughts. I dodged sideways as he swung his sword, then took the weapon from the man and reversed it, gutting him. I let the soldier fall, unconsciously growling as I headed for the dais.

"In the name of the king, you will put down your weapons!" Tyden thundered.

I hesitated as the young prince strode past me, and I reluctantly lowered my sword. The fighting had all but stopped at Tyden's command, with the great room filled only with the sobbing of the women and the moaning of the wounded. Tyden paused at the dais's base and glared up at Lord Corwick, and then he slowly began to climb the stairs until they stood eye to eye.

"I am disappointed in you, cousin," Prince Tyden said reproachfully.

Son Oriel squealed and ran, his black robes billowing out behind him as he disappeared through the archway at the back of the dais. Hervi Desh watched him go, holding his ground for a moment longer, then he turned and dashed after him.

Prince Tyden snapped his fingers and pointed. "Bring those two to me."

Half a dozen soldiers ran to do his bidding as Tyden turned his focus back on Lord Corwick. "It was a good plan, Pernissy," he said grudgingly. The prince glanced at me. "But you made one mistake. You picked a man to do your bidding who has both honor and integrity." Tyden chuckled. "And I daresay, a man much smarter than you."

"Cousin," Lord Corwick said weakly. "This is all a simple misunderstanding."

"I think not," Prince Tyden said. He looked up as movement arose at the back of the dais. A soldier appeared through the doorway, leading Son Oriel by the arm. "Where is the other one?"

"He got away, Highness," the soldier replied.

"No matter," Prince Tyden said. "There is nowhere for him to go. We will catch him eventually." He gestured to Son Oriel. "You were about to perform a coronation, I believe, First Son?"

Son Oriel sniffed, pulling his arm away from the soldier's grasp. "Indeed," he said haughtily.

Prince Tyden inclined his head as soldiers dragged Lord Corwick off the dais. "Then, shall we continue?"

"Of course," Son Oriel said, his voice catching as someone returned the fallen crown to him.

The prince made his way down the steps, kneeling where Lord Corwick had been moments ago. Son Oriel held the crown over Tyden's blond locks, his hands shaking as he uttered the traditional words that elevated a man into a king. I paid little attention to the cumbersome ceremony, wishing it would just end as I sought out Shana again. Her hair was cut short, I realized, having somehow overlooked that fact earlier. I thought of the long, shimmering strands that had fallen on this same dais weeks ago and how close I'd come to losing her. Shana's hands were clasped over her chest, her blue eyes brimming with tears of joy as we stared at one another. I found her new look to be very fetching.

I mouthed the words, "I love you," then grinned with pleasure when she mouthed them back.

Son Oriel continued speaking for several more minutes, while the room waited in respectful silence, until finally, the priest pronounced Tyden to be king. I glanced at Lord Corwick, who looked ashen and sick as King Tyden stood, surveying his subjects as they cheered him. Finally, Tyden waved for silence, then gestured to his men to bring Lord Corwick closer. A Judgement Stool was brought forward and the lord pushed roughly onto it as the king took his place on the throne.

"You are accused of treason, cousin," Tyden said, getting directly to the point. "How do you plead?"

"This is preposterous!" Lord Corwick exploded. "He pointed a quivering finger at me. "This is all his doing! He's the one that forced me to do it!"

I snorted and shook my head. The man couldn't stop lying, even in the face of overwhelming evidence. I felt a nudge and turned to see Jebido beside me, his features twisted in a delighted grin. Tyris, Putt, Sim, and Niko were with him. I nodded to my men in greeting before turning back to the dais.

"Who murdered the First Son?" Tyden demanded in a booming voice.

Again, the quivering finger at me. "He did! The Outlaw of Corwick!"

Tyden sighed and sat back. He flicked his eyes to Son Oriel. "Who murdered the First Son?" he asked the ugly priest. Son Oriel's lips twitched and the king added, "I would advise you to answer carefully, First Son. Your current position is tenuous at best right now. Lie to me and you will find yourself back to being a lowly Son-In-Waiting before you can even blink."

Son Oriel shifted his calculating gaze to Lord Corwick. I wasn't sure if the new king had the power over the House to do as he had claimed, but I'd just seen a sly look appear briefly in the priest's eyes, so I knew it wouldn't matter. Son Oriel had just switched allegiances.

"Advisor Desh killed the First Son, Highness," Son Oriel stated firmly with a bow of his head. He gestured to Lord Corwick. "At this man's behest."

"You lying bastard!" Lord Corwick snarled, rising from his stool. A soldier stood to either side of the angry lord and they pushed him back down.

"Very well," Tyden said. "I will deal with Advisor Desh soon enough." He fixed his cold eyes on Lord Corwick. "My brother and I were close, once, Pernissy," he said. "As you well know, since we three played together as boys. It pained me greatly when Tyrale betrayed me, for he knew that I was the elder brother. Many of my subjects lost their lives because of his blind ambition." Tyden sighed and rubbed his eyes wearily. "That said, the man was still my brother, and what you did to him sickens my stomach."

"But Tyden—" Lord Corwick began.

"Silence!" the king shouted in sudden fury. "Not another word out of you, Pernissy, or your lying tongue will be cut off and thrown to the dogs." Lord Corwick looked down, his face flushed. "Now," Tyden continued, composing himself. "What is done is done and nothing I do can undo it. Our great kingdom has suffered this past year, but now the time has come for both sides to heal and learn forgiveness." The king glanced at me, then focused back on Lord Corwick. "For all your failings, Pernissy, you are still my cousin, and I am sick of all the death that I have seen this past year. I will not kill you for what you did." I saw Lord Corwick's face brighten with hope. "From this day forth, you are hereby stripped of all your lands and titles." Lord Corwick's face fell in dismay. "You will spend the rest of your days in the dungeons below the castle you once schemed to rule. That is my decision." Tyden waved his hand. "Take him away, and may the gods favor me by never having to look upon his face again."

After Lord Corwick had been dragged away, Tyden crooked a finger at me. "Come," he said, gesturing to the Judgment Stool.

I shared a worried look with Jebido, then climbed the stairs and sat down.

The king tapped his fingers on the throne while he studied me silently. "There have been many things said about you, Hadrack of Corwick," Tyden finally rumbled. "Many of them lies and half-truths, facilitated by those close to me." He indicated to his left, where I hadn't noticed Daughter Gernet, Malo, and Jin stood within the crowd. Jin and Daughter Gernet were smiling, while Malo had his ever-present frown on his face. "People of Ganderland," Tyden continued, looking around. "We owe this man a debt that can never be adequately repaid. This man who we thought an enemy, risked everything for our kingdom so that it could be made whole again. Nothing I can give him can express the gratitude we all feel, but even so, I will try.

"To begin with, all warrants for the capture of the Outlaw of Corwick have been rescinded. All crimes attributed to him, whether real or not, are absolved." The king leaned forward as a playful smile cracked his lips. "But now that he is free, what will we do with him?" Tyden rose and he came to stand over me. "Kneel before me," he commanded as he drew his sword. I lowered myself to the floor, taking one last confused glance at Shana before I bowed my head. "From this day forth, the man known as Hadrack of Corwick, will now be known as Lord Hadrack, the Lord of Corwick, with all the powers and lands of that holding at his disposal."

I sagged, unable to comprehend what had just happened as I felt the king's sword touch me gently on each shoulder.

"Rise, Lord Hadrack," Tyden said. He placed a hand on each of my shoulders and drew me to him in a hearty embrace. "Is there anything else you wish?" he asked as he held me.

I broke the embrace, wondering if I dare ask. Then I decided I had nothing to lose. "There is one other thing I would like, Highness."

"Name it and it is yours," Tyden said without hesitating.

So, I told him.

28: A Fitting End

Three weeks after the coronation, Shana and I stood above the graves of my father and sister. There were no mounds now, nothing to indicate that people had been buried here, but I knew without a doubt that I was in the right spot. I'd worried when we first set out that I might not be able to locate the graves after so long, but it was a concern I needn't have bothered myself with. This peaceful place where I used to fish and laugh with my sister and friends was forever burned into my memory. I could no more forget it than I could what had happened to the village of Corwick when I was a boy. The stream was wider in places now, and the trees taller, but the bank where I'd laid them to rest appeared relatively unchanged.

"You would have liked them," I told Shana. "You and my sister would have been great friends."

Shana squeezed my hand. "I have no doubt, my lord."

I still hadn't quite gotten used to Shana calling me lord. It seemed somehow wrong, yet she insisted, as did everyone else in Corwick. All except Jebido, of course. He had tried calling me lord once and I'd almost throttled him, making him swear never to repeat it again. My men and the vassals on my new lands were one thing, even Shana, since it pleased her so, but there was no way I would allow Jebido to call me that after all he had done for me. Our friendship went far beyond any title a faraway king might have given me.

"It must be close to midday," Shana said, trying not to sound worried and failing miserably.

I nodded, knowing that the others would be waiting for us at the old farm. Shana and I were to be married in two weeks, and I understood how upset she was that I'd refused to change my plans for this day. As much as I loved her and understood her concerns, there was nothing she or anyone else could say that would sway me from this final task.

"Is there nothing that will change your mind, my lord?" Shana asked as if reading my thoughts.

I shook my head, keeping my eyes on the graves. "This is how things must be. We have gone over this."

Shana breathed in deeply, then let it out in frustration. "You are a stubborn man, Lord Hadrack." She put her hands on either side of my head and turned me to face her. "Which is one of the reasons I love you so." We kissed, deeply and passionately, until finally she broke away, avoiding my eyes. "I'm heading back, my lord. I will wait for you at the castle."

I raised an eyebrow. "You're not going to watch?"

Shana smiled sadly. "Sometimes, men must do things that women have no wish to witness. This is one of them." She turned to go, then looked back at me. "I'll be waiting on the battlements for you, my lord. Promise me you won't be late."

"I won't," I said, giving her a reassuring smile. "You have my word."

Shana squeezed my hand one last time, and then she headed off through the trees. I listened to her footfalls receding, the smile on my face slowly fading. Her concern was valid, and I knew there was a chance that I might not survive the day, despite what I'd just told her. I thrust the future from my mind. What would be would be, but right now was not the time to think of it. This moment was strictly for me and my father and sister.

I knelt and put a hand on each of the graves. "I have missed you both so much these past years," I said. "Jeanna, I've missed your laugh and good-natured ways, and Father, your wisdom and strength. I have tried to be a good man and live up to the vow that I made to you so long ago. But I know at times that I have wavered in that task, putting my needs above yours. For that, I am sorry. I reaffirm that oath to you both once again. Six of the nine no longer walk this world, and soon the rest will follow. I will not stray again. You have my word."

I stood, pausing over the graves as I prayed, then I turned and headed back through the trees. I was only eight years old when I carried my sister's body and my father's head to the gravesite from the farm. It had taken me hours to make the trip back and forth twice, most of that time stumbling and falling from exhaustion and grief. Now, the journey took less than half an hour as I walked the fields where once our farm had been, my footsteps echoing those my father, brother, and I had taken so long ago as we sowed and reaped our crops.

The darkened trees that surrounded Patter's Bog rose in the distance, swaying as they watched me silently, looking just as hostile and sinister now as they had when I'd taken refuge there from the nine. I could see buildings rising far to the north where the village of Corwick had been rebuilt. It was larger now, with a stone Holy House and even an inn, I was told. Horses were gathered where my house had once stood, grazing happily on the long grasses as my men waited for me. For whatever reason, the swathe where the buildings had been was growing wild and unattended, free of crops. An aberration, or a sign of respect? I wasn't sure. A carriage drawn by two horses also waited nearby. I purposefully refused to look at it as I approached my men.

"We were beginning to wonder if you were coming," Jebido said, looking relieved.

"I wouldn't miss this for anything," I grunted. I gestured to the carriage, still refusing to look in that direction. "How does he appear?"

"Fit," Jebido grumbled unhappily. The king kept him healthy and well-fed, just as you asked. He frowned. "Are you sure about this?"

I unstrapped my sword and handed it to Hanley. "I have never been surer of anything." I glanced at Finol, who stood waiting by the carriage. The old man seemed nervous and jittery. "How is the babe doing, Steward?"

"The child does only three things, my lord," Finol said with distaste. "Shit, eat, and cry."

I laughed, enjoying the look on the old steward's face. "What were you expecting? Pleasant conversation?"

"Well, I thought he would have enough manners to settle down and be quiet once in a while," Finol said with a sniff.

"That won't happen for a few years yet," Jebido chuckled. "If at all, so you had better get used to it."

I took off my vest, then my tunic, feeling the brisk wind on my bare skin. I motioned toward the carriage, finally acknowledging its presence. "Let the bastard out. I want to get on with this."

Finol pursed his lips as he reluctantly opened the carriage door, which squeaked loudly like a wounded bird. A big man appeared and stepped out cautiously, blinking in the sunlight. His hair and beard were longer since I'd last seen him, and not nearly as well-groomed, yet there was no mistaking who he was. Hervi Desh.

"Ah," Desh said as he looked around. He smiled at me. "So, back to where it all started."

"You recognize the place, do you?" I asked.

Desh sniffed the air dramatically. "Of course. Even after so long, it still reeks of death." He stretched and yawned, looking disappointed that I hadn't reacted to his jibe. "I imagine you plan on adding to that stench with me," Desh added, looking unconcerned. I had to hand it to him, the man might be a lying, murderous bastard, but he was certainly no coward. "I'm surprised at you, Hadrack," Desh said. "I'd have thought you would come up with something a little more imaginative than just having your men slaughter me."

I said nothing as my men spread out warily around Desh, their weapons drawn. I could tell by the looks on their faces that none of them were happy about my instructions, but I knew they would follow through on them regardless of what happened next. I moved away, finally stopping in the spot that I'd chosen earlier, letting the tips of the tall grass tickle my fingers. Eventually, I turned and regarded Desh, feeling calm and relaxed. I had pictured this moment in my head for weeks now.

"This is where our house stood," I said.

"Is that so?" Desh replied, looking unimpressed. "It just looks like a field to me."

"Niko, Sim, please escort Advisor Desh closer," I grunted.

My men grabbed Desh roughly and guided him three feet from me. Then they backed respectfully away.

"The table was right here," I told Desh, stamping my foot. "Father built it from a huge butternut that had been struck by lightning in the forest. It took him a week to haul all the wood here." Desh said nothing, though I could tell that he was listening. I pointed. "Over there was the room we slept in, and here, my father's oak chest." I smiled, remembering. "It was an ungainly, awful-looking thing, but he never once let us see what was inside. I used to imagine all manner of things lay within it, but I never had the nerve to open it." I turned to face Desh. "Now, I'll never know."

Desh just shrugged and looked up at the sky as I studied him. The man's shoulders were thick and heavily padded with muscle, and I saw his knuckles were scarred and battered from a lifetime of scrapping. His nose had obviously been broken more than once, as well. I'd learned that Hervi Desh liked to kill men with his bare hands when he was younger and that he had been very good at it. He may have softened somewhat physically in the years spent in Gandertown, but he was still a fine specimen of a man even so. I was bigger and faster, and perhaps stronger, but he had a lot more experience than I did. All things considered, with his age and my relative inexperience, I thought everything added up to a fair match. Time would soon tell.

I could feel the hot sun on my chest and I closed my eyes, enjoying the warmth. Finally, I opened my eyes, nothing on my mind now but the task before me.

"Take your shirt off," I told Desh, my tone all business now.

"Why?" Desh asked. He glanced around warily at my men.

"Don't worry about them," I said. "This is just between you and me. No one will interfere."

Desh smirked. "Do you expect me to believe that?"

"Yes," I said, flexing the muscles in my arms to get the blood flowing. "My men have sworn that they won't lift a hand against you, no matter what happens here today. You have my word on that."

"So, just us, then?" Desh said doubtfully, though I could see hope in his eyes now. "To the death?"

"Just us," I agreed. "Right here, in this spot where my family once lived, with only one of us walking away."

Desh thought about that, and then he grunted his acceptance. He took off his tunic and threw it aside. The older man was hairy like a bear, with ropey, thickly-veined muscles bulging along his arms. A long, jagged scar cut through the greying hair on his chest from his left nipple, down to his stomach.

"I'm surprised that didn't kill you," I said, motioning to the scar.

"It was a near thing," Desh admitted. He cracked his knuckles and crouched, waiting for me to make the first move.

I began to circle warily with my hands held low in front of me. I would have rushed forward in a rage in years past, but now I took my time as my men ringed us, urging me on. I was almost twenty-one years old and stood four inches over six feet while weighing close to two hundred and sixty pounds. I was no longer a boy, but a fully grown man—one bent on vengeance. Desh was shorter than me, but just as wide and looked as strong as an ox. I knew the fight would be bloody and prolonged, which was exactly what I wanted.

"You're a fool for doing this," Desh said, looking confident. "And now you are going to pay the price for that foolishness."

Desh lunged forward without warning, lashing out with his right fist. The blow caught me on the cheek as I staggered backward in surprise, feeling blood start to flow. I wiped the blood away with the back of my hand, then came forward. Another blow landed, this time with Desh's left fist. I hadn't seen it coming at all and it caught me on the jaw, twisting my neck painfully around just as Desh's right fist slammed into my stomach. I grunted, wobbling as Desh hooked a foot out from under me. I fell, rolling over in the grass as Desh tried to cave in my skull with his boot. I grabbed his foot and twisted, tumbling him to the ground as I bounced to my feet.

Desh was already rising when I reached him and I struck him hard in the face with my right fist. Blood sprayed from Desh's nose, but the older man surprised me by ignoring it. He bellowed like a bull and grabbed me around the midsection, lifting me off the ground before throwing me over his head with a grunt of effort. I landed on my side awkwardly, stunned as my men screamed at me in warning. I rolled over onto my back, both feet poised above me as I kicked out blindly, catching Desh unprepared. The older man groaned as my heels sank into his belly. He fell back, gasping for air.

I rose, blood streaming into my left eye from a cut on my forehead. I blinked it away, closing on Desh and shrugging off the man's off-balance punch that still had enough force to numb my left shoulder for a moment. I struck at him with savage precision, pummeling his face with three powerful, rapid blows that sent him reeling in desperate retreat, his face a bloody, swollen mess. I could see panic in Desh's eyes as I stalked toward him and I screamed a challenge, certain that I had him now. The older man continued to back away from me, until finally he stumbled in the long grasses and fell. I growled in triumph, standing over him and reaching for his throat just as his knee caught me soundly between the legs. I howled in agony.

Now it was my turn to retreat on shaky legs as Desh rose and came for me with ferocious speed and power, punching and kicking anything he could reach. I protected myself from his blows as best I could, fighting to breathe and trying to block out the searing, biting pain from my groin.

"You are weak, boy!" Desh hissed at me as he struck. "Weak and slow."

The older man grabbed my hair, pinning my head between his arm and body as he squeezed relentlessly. I began to gag, fighting desperately for air. I only had moments, I knew, then it would be over. I reached desperately for Desh's legs and lifted him as high as I could, then I turned and slammed him into the ground. Desh's grip on me weakened and I spun away from him, retching as I hunched over on all fours.

I watched Desh rise ten feet from me, his face twisted with hatred as he came for me. I waited, knowing what he was going to do. The kick came, quick and vicious, heading for my stomach. I dropped beneath it, my back to the ground as I grabbed his boot and jerked upward. Desh cried out, landing on his ass, then I was up. I grabbed the older man by the hair and dragged him to his feet, slamming two lightning punches into his stomach. Then, as he sagged from the blows, I picked him up by the neck and legs, wobbling from his weight as I held him over my head.

"For Corwick!" I shouted at the sky.

I lowered myself to one knee in a smooth, fast motion, smashing Hervi Desh's struggling body heavily onto my upraised leg. Desh screamed in agony just as I heard a sharp crack ring out. I knew instinctively that his back had just broken as he went limp in my arms.

It was over.

I lowered Desh to the ground, where he lay sprawled on his crippled back, unable to move. I thought for a moment that he might be dead, but then he blinked, his mouth working as he fought to speak. I waited, kneeling as I stared at him with pitiless eyes.

"Kill me," Desh finally managed to say, his hand tugging weakly at my arm.

I shrugged him off contemptuously. That would be too easy. I slowly stood and looked up at the sky as several birds flew overhead, calling to each other as they headed north toward the new village of Corwick. The wind rose, sweeping my hair from my face, while the grass began to dance as though possessed by the souls of those long dead celebrating Desh's fall.

I closed my eyes. Everything seemed so peaceful now, so different from the last time that I had been here. I remembered the smoke and the smell of burning flesh, with bodies lying everywhere, torn and shattered. I'd had to walk through those bodies, looking for my father, while all manner of scavengers plucked and ripped at the corpses. It is a memory that I have never been able to shed from my mind, no matter how hard I have tried. I don't expect that I ever will.

Finally, I turned away, heading toward my horse while ignoring Desh's feeble pleas to end his life. I paused and looked back as Jebido motioned over my shoulder toward Patter's Bog. A lone wolf sat watching from in front of the stone wall that ringed the bog that

I'd helped build as a child. Overhead, the dark forms of several vultures were already circling.

"A fitting end to the bastard," I told Jebido.

I swung up into Angry's saddle, then paused as I saw a rider coming toward us. My first thought was that it was Shana, returning after having changed her mind. But then the rider drew closer and I understood who it was. I choked back a sea of emotions, waiting with my men as Baine approached, stopping his horse a pace from mine. We stared at each other, neither quite knowing what to say.

"So, I missed it, then?" Baine finally asked as he studied my bloodied and battered face.

My friend's voice seemed soft and unassuming, yet the words had an edge to them—an edge of hardness. When last I'd seen him, Baine had still been a boy on the cusp of manhood, but now he appeared different. There was an assuredness about him that hadn't been there before. A quiet confidence and perhaps even pride that he now wore easily.

"You did," I nodded. I looked back to where Desh lay dying, and I smiled grimly. "But it was a damn fine fight just the same." I focused again on Baine, one eyebrow raised. "And what about you? Is it done?"

Baine paused for a heartbeat, his eyes turning dark and violent, then they calmed and the Baine that I remembered returned. He grinned. "It's done, Hadrack."

"Good," I grunted in satisfaction. I looked around at the faces of my men. "Then let's go home. I promised Shana that I wouldn't be late."

Epilogue

I didn't perish beneath Casia's vengeful blade on the day of Haral's trial. Though I imagine that is somewhat obvious now, for, if I had, these words would never have been written. I almost wish the poor woman had succeeded and ended my life, but what we wish for and what we get are two very different things in this world.

I was just a boy when I killed the Reeve of Corwick. I didn't know what I was doing back then. I just reacted in a mindless act of rage that has haunted me my entire life. If not for a lowly rock and a lucky strike, I imagine things would have been quite different for a great many people. Would it have been better if I had missed stepping on that rock and instead died along with my family? That is a question that I have pondered many times, never coming up with a clear answer. Perhaps someday, people much wiser than me will decide on that, but for now, all I know is that taking a life—even one as foul as the reeve's—does not come without consequences.

Now, my grandson, Frankin, must live with the knowledge that he has taken a life, while I also must wear the guilt of his actions. The boy was just protecting me when he slid his knife into Casia's kidneys. I understand that more than most, yet I fear the gods might not see it that way. The girl's grievance with me was valid, and her entitlement to revenge unquestionable. I slaughtered her family much like the nine slaughtered mine, and Casia's retribution for that act should not have been denied, despite good intentions.

I shudder to imagine what the consequences will be for the boy's actions. For as sure as I'm sitting here writing this, there will be something. Were I a younger and more foolish man, I would spit into the face of those consequences, daring anything to try and hurt my family. But I am as old as time itself now, and I have seen and done too much to think that it will simply be forgotten. Somehow, someway, there will be a price to pay for what the boy did. There always is. The gods will make certain.

The Unified Kingdom of Ganderland quickly began to heal under the skilled guidance of King Tyden, who proved to be a wise and effective king. A man who, even today, long after his death, is still widely revered and respected. My reunion with Baine was one of the happiest moments of my life, and he, Jebido, and I spent the entire night of his return laughing, drinking, and talking. Baine's story of revenge against the imposter Outlaw of Corwick was a harrowing tale that kept Jebido and me riveted for hours. Someday, should the gods allow it, I will chronicle that tale. But for now, there is still more to tell of my own.

I chose to keep my knowledge of the location of the second codex secret, seeing no purpose in revealing what I knew. But doing so would soon prove to be a horrible mistake. The mystery of Emand and his murderous wife had bothered me for a time and I'd meant to look into it. Why had they been there at all? And who had hired them? But, as the days passed, I became preoccupied with my new duties as the Lord of Corwick, not to mention my new wife, and I simply forgot about the little cordwainer. With the last of the nine soon to be in my grasp, and Pernissy banished to the dungeons, it seemed I had no enemies left. I couldn't have been more wrong.

Soon, the winds of war would blow again for Ganderland. But this time, they would not be sweeping down from the north, but would come in a bloody wave of vengeance from the wildlands to the south. And I would come face to face with perhaps my greatest friend, who might also prove to be my greatest enemy as well.

THE END

Author's Note

Thank you, dear reader, for your continued support of this series. I began writing The Wolf On The Run at the beginning of the shutdown in Canada from the pandemic. I have my own business that I have been running since the late 1990s, and with the shutdown, that business came to a shuddering stop. I know I wasn't alone in this experience, and I fully understand the hardships other entrepreneurs worldwide have been going through during this crisis. I had just finished writing The Wolf At Large, and planned on focusing more of my attention on the business after the book was released, but, since I could not do that, I began writing The Wolf On The Run instead. The problem was, I had only a vague notion of where I wanted to go with it. As I mentioned before, I wrote The Nine for fun, and had no expectations anything would ever come of it—certainly not a third book. I left myself a lot of what I call 'traps' in The Nine, because I hadn't thought far enough ahead in the story arc. It has been a challenge at times to get around those traps, but also an interesting exercise in problem-solving as well.

Many authors write intricate plot outlines before they even sit down to start a book, but I don't do that. I work everything out in my head, usually chapter by chapter, while doing the most mundane things such as splitting wood or mowing the lawn. I imagine that would be considered a cardinal sin to most writing purists, but it seems to work for me for whatever reason. I would have to say the most challenging part of being an indie author is the editing process. They say you should never edit your own work— and there is a reason for that. I have lost track of how many times I went over this book and found errors that I couldn't believe. I used to shake my head when I'd see those same errors in other books and wonder—really, how could you have missed that? Now, I know. Thankfully, I have two wonderful women in my life who have helped me with the editing, and I can't say enough about how much that help has meant.

There will be a fourth book in this series, which is probably rather obvious, since two of the nine have yet to meet Hadrack's justice. Will there be more? That I'm not sure of. I don't want this series to become endless, and I do have other projects that I want to try, so time will tell on that. One of my favorite characters in the series is Baine, but I find he tends to get forgotten sometimes because Jebido and Hadrack are both such strong characters. I'm hoping at some point that I'll be able to give him his own book to tell about his revenge against the imposter Outlaw of Corwick.

The Kingdom of Ganderland and the people in it never existed, obviously, but the trees, plants, buildings, and animals that I write about in the books are real. Feverfew, goldenseal, green tree boas, and even the markhor that Hadrack and Sabina rode actually exist. If you get a chance, please take a moment to google the markhor, as they are one of the oddest-looking creatures on the planet. - Terry Cloutier October 2020

Books in The Wolf Of Corwick Castle Series

The Nine
The Wolf At Large
The Wolf On The Run

Books in The Zone War Series

The Demon Inside
The Balance of Power

Novella

Peter Pickler And The Cat That Talked Back